27 Days to Midnight

Kristine Kruppa

D1316126

Giant
Squid
Books

ISBN: 0692658955
ISBN 13: 9780692658956

A Project of Giant Squid Books
Founded by Readers to Support Writers
www.giantsquidbooks.com

For the other big and the lits.

Chapter One
An Encounter

✱

The sky was bright and clear on the day of Dahlia Walker's death.

Morning sun shone as she strode down the road, smiling and humming to herself. It was her eighteenth birthday. The paper bag tucked under her arm held a new dress for the occasion. Her steps clicked along the sidewalk in time to a quick, jaunty tune in her head. Her watch hung in its locked case around her neck.

People streamed in and out of shops arrayed in neat lines on either side of the cobblestone street. Clockwork horses drew carriages transporting chauffeurs, ladies in ruffled skirts, and straight-backed gentlemen. The occasional blue military airship patrolled overhead on a pleasant breeze. It was a bustling, wonderful day. A cake waited back at Dahlia's house, and she knew the mechanical servants would already be setting out the silver and chilling the birthday champagne for her party.

"Get your news! Get your daily news!" A young paperboy stood on the corner, brandishing copies of the *Sainsbury Herald*. "Anglian airships sighted over the Hattaran Mountains! Is Sainsbury their next target? Get your news, be ready!" A clockwork monkey crouched on his shoulder, its exposed gears whirring contentedly.

Dahlia paid them no heed; lately the papers reported on nothing but the war with Anglia, and she'd just about had enough of it. Under her breath, she sang along to the cheerful little tune in her head.

"Help, please!" A voice from a nearby alcove snapped the song away.

A hand snatched her sleeve and Dahlia spun.

"Let me go!" she shouted, jerking her arm back.

An old woman, wrinkled and gray, clung to Dahlia's carefully pressed blouse. Dirty hair curled in wisps around her head, and grime streaked her shapeless dress. Crooked yellow teeth peeked into view like rotting daisies. A pair of broken auto-focusing spectacles dangled uselessly around her neck. Dahlia coughed against the pungent smell: a combination of sewer water and unwashed skin.

"Please, you've got ta help me," the woman croaked, panic in her eyes. "Look…look at me watch!"

The misshapen crone thrust her watch in front of Dahlia's face. It took a moment for Dahlia to notice there were only three minutes left on it.

Surprise stunned Dahlia into silence.

The crone took full advantage of her shock: "What do I do? I ain't ready ta die yet! You've got ta do something!"

She shook the watch and something inside emitted an unhealthy rattling. A carriage in the street slowed as it passed.

"Pardon me, miss." A gentleman in a top hat leaned down from the control seat. "Do you need some help?"

"No, thank you," Dahlia tipped him a polite nod. "I can handle this."

She turned back to the old woman as the carriage sped off, bouncing along behind its mechanical horse.

"You know there's nothing anyone can do for you," Dahlia said after a moment. "You certainly seem to have led a long life."

"But I...I..." The woman's eyes welled up with tears.

Poor thing. But why did she have to bother me?

Dahlia surreptitiously reached down and began prying the crone's gnarled fingers from her silk blouse, trying not to imagine the last time those fingers had been washed. Or what they might have touched in the meantime.

"Your time's almost up. I'm sorry, but I can't help you."

The hand loosened. The crone fell silent, staring distantly at the cobblestone road.

"There. Go ahead, move along."

A few tears leaked from the crone's eyes. Dahlia waited to make sure the woman wasn't going to grab for her again, then she turned and continued on down the street.

She rejoined the river of busy shoppers on the sidewalk, trembling fingers tucking back a wayward strand of black hair.

How horrible. That poor woman...

A frown pulled at her mouth. But it was her birthday, her *eighteenth* birthday, and she wouldn't allow this to ruin it.

Click, click, click. Her steps once again synchronized with a cheerful marching tune. She hefted the shopping bag containing her new dress, tucking it more securely under one arm.

The dull thump of a body hitting the cobblestones echoed behind her. A lady gasped. Dahlia's heartbeat accelerated, but she refused to look back or change her pace—time had run out for that particular crone, and it was none of her concern. Back home, there was cake and champagne and a party to be had.

Chapter Two
Invasion

✳

"So exciting!" Dahlia whispered to herself, doing a brief mental dance in anticipation as she turned up the walkway of her house.

Finally, her eighteenth birthday: the day her father had promised to unlock her watch. Parents traditionally sealed their child's watch in a protective case until they were old enough to handle the truth. For most children, that day came when they turned ten.

I can't believe Papa made me wait eighteen years for this.

Her house was a fine two-story affair, whitewashed and gleaming, ringed by a sprawling patio arranged carefully around flowerbeds and gardens. Spotless brick pathways curved around perfect hedges. An immaculate lawn stretched to the property's edge, interspersed with ornamental plants.

A mechanical servant—Gardener, Model 2.5, wasn't it?—was completing a few final trims to the rosebushes near the door. Her father had invented the servants. They were less efficient than real ones, but he had too much fun tinkering to scrap them.

"Papa!" Dahlia twisted the knob and stepped into the foyer. "Papa, are you here?"

No response.

Downstairs working again, I'm sure.

"Good morning, Miss Walker." Archibald appeared beside her in a silver-striped suit that matched his hair. The butler was one of the few flesh-and-blood humans who worked on the estate. Dahlia smiled.

"Take this to my room," she said, and passed him the shopping bag containing her new dress. "Make sure it's pressed and ready for this evening."

"Yes, Miss Walker."

"Is my father in his workshop?"

"Yes, Miss Walker. Shall I fetch him for you?"

"No, thank you, Archibald."

The butler bowed slightly and strode off with her shopping.

Dahlia smoothed her black hair. The green dress matched her eyes, but she wished she could do something about her skin. It was a deep tan, like coffee with too much cream, and her pale countrymen loved commenting on it. They said she looked almost, but not quite, as if she had been born in the Southern Lands, where stories told how the sun baked color into the skin of the indigenous population.

Dahlia didn't appreciate the comparison.

Who would? She'd heard that the people talked strangely, that they were a backwards country of spice farmers and villagers. A proper lady would never want to be associated with that.

She pushed it out of her mind. Today was her birthday, after all, and there was no sense in worrying over what she couldn't change. Her feet carried her past the entranceway, through the sitting room, and into the library, stopping before a large oak bookcase. Her fingers traced a few of the well-read spines before coming to rest on: *Basic Processing Circuits for Mechanical Creatures: Volume III.*

She eased the upper corner of the book away from the case. A soft click.

The trapdoor in the floor dropped out. Then a swooping in her stomach and she fell, accelerating down a wide slide. She heaved a mental sigh.

Darkness prevented her from seeing the dirt smeared along the slide from unclean shoes, but she winced at the thought nonetheless. Yet the mechanic in Dahlia had to admire the ingenuity her father had required to craft such a contraption.

The end of the slide came an instant later, but Dahlia anticipated it. Her legs reached for the landing mat. They caught the edge and launched a dust cloud from the torn corners. She coughed, wobbled, and fell over into the mess.

This is a bad day for my clothes, she thought, thinking again of the crone's dirty fingers on her blouse.

"Not your smoothest landing, sweetie!" Her papa's laugh boomed out at her as she blinked away dust.

Tools and half-finished projects filled the workshop, shining under bright work lights. Bits of wire, steel plates, and a few failed experiments she knew all too well. Tiny, bright gears lay in heaps on shelves. A safe sat in the corner—protection for the most expensive watch parts, her father had told her.

It was how they could afford to live in such extravagance: by repairing watches people had damaged. Clients came knocking on their door in bandages or casts, proffering their watches to the best repairman in town.

People could not die by natural means before their time ran out. A serious injury could still kill, but a person couldn't receive such an injury until their watch ran dry. If they faced a runaway carriage, they would manage to leap aside. If they were trapped in a burning house, they would somehow struggle free. Survival was assured.

But watches and their owners were linked—if a person hurt their body, their watch suffered damage. If their watch was broken, injuries appeared on their body. And if a watch stopped working completely...so did its owner. Repairing watches while they still functioned was a delicate science, and her papa was a master of it.

He sat hunched over his workbench, a light bulb illuminating the tangle of wires in front of him. He pushed his chair back and strode over.

"Come on up!"

Strong fingers curled around her arm, lifting her to her feet.

Ansel Walker was not a large man, but his presence filled the cluttered workshop. Something about his laugh, his smile, the twinkle in his eyes. He wore an evening suit, no doubt put on in preparation for her birthday party and forgotten immediately. A pair of large-lensed auto-focusing spectacles sat atop his forehead, nudging his brown hair into messy spikes. Dahlia suppressed a giggle.

Typical.

"I wish you'd replace that mat." Dahlia forced sternness into her voice through the smile creeping up her lips.

"I keep forgetting." He winked. "Maybe for your next birthday? But, speaking of birthdays..." He turned toward the workbench. "You're just in time to help me put the finishing touches on your present."

"*Please* tell me it's not another flying backpack. I don't think I can handle that kind of humiliation again."

Ansel's laugh echoed from the walls. "No, sweetie. That one's not ready yet. A few more months, maybe. Anyway: hold this wire while I solder it."

Dahlia obediently gripped the wire as Ansel lowered his goggles and began applying solder. Smoke curled from the end of the iron.

"What is it?" she asked.

It's too small to be dangerous. But you can never tell with Papa...

Ansel leaned back from the project and blew away the lingering solder smoke.

"This," he said, laying the iron in its tray with a flourish, "is a wonderful little device made to play these."

He reached across the bench, knocked a stack of drawings to the floor, and snatched up what looked like a roll of camera film.

"They're like photographs, but of sound," he said proudly, ignoring the drawings littering the ground. "Want to see?" Excitement shone in his eyes.

"Of course."

The device appeared to be a repurposed music box, carved from sweet-smelling cedar. Ansel eased a cover over the finished wiring. He snapped the sound tape into place on a spindle.

"I already recorded it with this switch——," he pointed, "——then you install the tape, close the lid, turn this pin to wind the spring...like that...and press the other switch to listen to it."

A crackling emanated from the box. Dahlia raised her eyebrows.

"Sound playback device, test one." The tinny voice issuing from the speaker was unmistakably Ansel's.

"Huh? Huh?" Ansel grinned and nudged her shoulder. "Look at that! It works!"

"Are you surprised?"

"Not at all. You?"

"A little."

Ansel crossed his arms in mock indignation. Dahlia couldn't stop herself from laughing.

"It's neat. Very pretty." She picked up the box and turned it over in her hands, admiring it. "But what am I supposed to *use* it for?"

"Recording things? But, really, this is just how you listen to your real present."

Ansel bent and yanked a brown burlap bag from a shelf under the workbench; metal clinked inside. He hesitated, eyes unexpectedly serious.

"I don't know how many times you've asked me about your mother, and I haven't told you. You deserve...you deserve to know." He paused and took a deep breath, looking down as if suddenly fascinated by the backs of his hands. "These are sound tapes I've pre-recorded." Ansel offered the bag to her. "They explain everything."

"Papa..." She took it, stomach tight with excitement. "Why don't you just *tell* me?"

"Trust me, sweetie."

He winked at her and smiled widely, dissipating the brief moment of awkwardness.

"Fine," she said.

She waited, holding the simple sack full of the truth she'd wanted for so many years. But there was another present; there was another truth she needed.

"You forgot something," she said.

"Probably."

Dahlia inhaled, steeled herself, and released the words all in one breath.

"You promised to unlock my watch when I turned eighteen."

Her stomach churned. Ansel stared down at his hands again, silent. His lips twitched as he tried to speak.

"Y...Yes. I guess I did." He smiled, but there was no sparkle in his brown eyes. "I almost forgot."

He extended a hand and she slid the chain of the watch

necklace over her head, offering it to him. Removing it felt odd, like taking off a fragment of herself. A watch was as much a part of its owner's body as bones or flesh. Someone could be separated from their watch by a few yards, but significant distances were impossible, and deadly.

Ansel spun the combination and pried open the case. Her watch lay inside.

The burnished gold surface glittered under the exposed bulb above the workbench. Subtle letters etched into the metal spelled her name: *Dahlia Walker*. Her breath quickened in anticipation. She wanted desperately to touch it, to hold it, to feel the foreign metal against her skin.

Finally.

"Open it," she demanded. "Show me my time."

Ansel set the case aside, cradling her watch in both hands.

"Tell me what you know about time, Dahlia. About the time this will show you."

"What I know about...fine." She crossed her arms and recited the lessons her papa had burned into her mind over the years. Her voice brimmed with indignation:

"Watches show the time—years, days, hours, minutes, seconds—that their owners have left to live. It doesn't matter how the person dies: age, disease, violence...the watch is always right. But if someone's watch is destroyed, they die whether they have time left or not."

Ansel gazed at her, his expression inscrutable. "Very good."

"Can I..." Dahlia's hands twitched toward the object in his hands.

Ansel gave an immense sigh. For a moment Dahlia thought he would refuse to give it over, but then he leaned forward and offered her the final birthday present.

She reached...

"Mister Walker!" Archibald's panicked voice burst from the communication tube in the wall. The other end led upstairs to the sitting room.

Ansel spun toward it, fingers closing around the watch.

"Archibald, what's wrong?"

"Airships, Mister Walker! Anglian airships over the city!"

"We're coming up," said Ansel. "Get to the shelter."

"Yes, sir."

Ansel yanked Dahlia along by the arm, almost before she could stuff the music box into the burlap sack with its sound tapes. A lever opened a panel in the concrete wall. They raced up the dank staircase behind it, slipping and sliding on moisture that had leaked through cracks in the walls.

Dahlia barely noticed the dirt caking her blouse as she brushed the tunnel—she'd become filthier in a single day than she normally managed in an entire week. The airships didn't worry her. Sainsbury wasn't the capital of Delmar, but it was one of the country's most populous cities. Anglian attack would have come sooner or later. What bothered her was that she'd been *so close* to finally seeing her watch! How many decades did she have left? Five? Six? *Seven?*

Papa has more than forty years left. He doesn't understand what not knowing is like.

Her feet skidded and she jerked back to reality in time to catch herself. Ansel paused on the top stair, fiddling with the latch on the door. She watched him for an instant before speaking.

"Papa, where's my watch?"

Ansel was absorbed in yanking on a lever. "In my pocket. Don't worry—you'll get it later."

Dahlia began to protest when the door swung open and her father stepped out into the sitting room. She followed, slamming it behind her.

"Come on, Dahlia." He took a few steps, glancing around as if the enemy airships might be lurking underneath a coffee table. "The shelter—"

A violent crash split the silence.

Chapter Three
Death in the Sitting Room

✶

"What was that? Was that a bomb?" Dahlia felt a twinge of shame at the panic in her words.

"Shhh!" Ansel held up a hand.

"There's someone here!" a strange male voice yelled from the front door. Heavy, booted footsteps immediately followed his exclamation. There were people—there were *intruders* running through her house.

Ansel twisted on his heel and hissed: "Dahlia, the door. Go back to the workshop."

"I closed it. It's locked—we'll have to go through the trapdoor in the library."

Her papa swore under his breath, something she couldn't remember him ever doing. The footsteps were almost upon them.

"Get behind something, Dahlia. Hide…"

"Well, well, well."

The voice cut like icy steel.

Dahlia stiffened as the invaders stepped through the sitting room doorway. Her intake of breath was loud in her ears.

There were four of them. Three wore the dark camouflage of Anglian soldiers and clutched complicated tesla rifles leveled at her and Ansel. The fourth—he could only be the leader—was dressed in a crisp obsidian uniform. He held no weapons, but the way he stood drew Dahlia's gaze immediately to the pistol and sword strapped to his thin waist. His slow, deliberate words dripped with malice.

"Ansel Walker. How many years has it been?"

"Not enough, Sebastian, not enough."

What's happening? Who is he?

Ansel subtly shifted his weight so he stood between her and the men.

"Dahlia, sweetie, this gentleman is Sebastian Macall. He's a...an old friend."

Her mind was processing everything in slow motion; it took her a few heartbeats to remember her manners and deliver the proper reply.

"It's a pleasure to meet you, Mr. Macall." Her body attempted a curtsy, but it came out a stumble. Every nerve rang with alarm.

"Likewise, young lady."

Silence reigned for a moment, and then Sebastian spoke again: "Your father must tell you often, but you...you look just like your mother."

"Quiet, Sebastian!" Ansel snapped. "You have no right!"

"I have every right," Sebastian said coolly.

Any semblance of awkward politeness evaporated with his words. The Anglian soldiers shifted their weapons, readying themselves as the tension in the room ratcheted up a notch.

"You know why I'm here, Ansel."

"To reminisce? I'm sorry I didn't prepare a welcome for you, Sebastian. If I'd known you were coming, I'd have done the place up. And here I thought Delmar's borders were secure."

"Shut your mouth, idiot," Sebastian said, his lips a thin line. "Where's your research? Your time research?"

What time research?

"I left it behind somewhere," said Ansel. "We've moved so many times—avoiding you—that I must've lost track of it. I thought we could finally settle down in Sainsbury, what with the air force patrols here."

"Don't lie to me." Sebastian Macall nodded to the soldiers. One man leapt forward like a released spring, tesla rifle in hand.

Dahlia barely registered what was happening before the expressionless soldier seized her shoulder in an iron grip. The barrel of the rifle pressed into her throat. Her fingers fluttered open and the burlap sack hit the floor, contents clinking.

Oh God, oh God, oh God...

She shook like a leaf in a storm, her mind racing yet utterly blank. She had never been so afraid. Heat coursed through her veins.

"Stop, Sebastian, stop! Get him away from her!" Her papa's voice cracked and he reached for her, then thought better of it.

"Tell me where your research is," growled Sebastian. "All those brilliant theories. The science division had volumes of them."

"In the workshop! The workshop downstairs. Through the library, you pull out the book on processing circuits and it activates a trapdoor. The safe combination is twenty-four, thirty-four, two."

Another nod from Sebastian and the soldier released Dahlia. He retreated a few steps before stopping to await further orders.

"You'll take me there, of course." Sebastian picked at a fingernail with mock nonchalance. "To prove that your trapdoor is not, in reality, a trap."

"And you'll let my daughter and me go?"

"You, Ansel, will come back to Port Argun with us. I'll need you in case your theories are incomplete."

"And me?" Dahlia was surprised to hear herself speak. Her voice squeaked, high with fear.

"You, my dear...will be motivation for your father."

He's going to let me live.

She sent up a mental prayer of thanks to whatever god was looking out for her. Sebastian laughed at her relieved expression, the sound chillingly hollow.

"But you'll only be a useful catalyst for his resurrection work if you need to be resurrected." He nodded once more at the sinister soldiers. "Kill her."

The bottom dropped out of her stomach.

"WAIT!" Ansel shrieked. He threw himself in front of her. The soldiers froze, black-gloved fingers tight against the triggers.

"You're outnumbered, Ansel."

"Just...just let me say goodbye," he choked.

"I don't see why I should, seeing as you never gave *me* that luxury. She must be scheduled to die today anyway, with the way you're panicking. Shoot her."

Dahlia heard the rifles crack once, twice, deafening in such a confined space. Bright pain blazed in her chest and shoulder. She couldn't breathe, couldn't think...

It was all jumbled up. There was a ringing in her ears, then a silence, then Ansel yelling, yelling, yelling, screaming her name.

Stop being so loud.

He should know that behavior was meant for the outdoors, not for when they sat inside chatting. The floor pressed against her back, but she couldn't remember falling.

How silly of me. I think I've had a bit too much of this birthday champagne. It's starting to go to my head!

But she hadn't had any champagne at all...

She giggled childishly and tried sitting up, but the dizzy fuzziness in her head tipped her over again. She laughed out loud at the ridiculousness of it all. When the noise reached her ears it sounded like a scream.

Why do I hurt...?

Dahlia snapped back into the moment, sprawled on the sitting room carpet. She gasped for air. Wetness coated her chest, her throat prickled, thick with what had to be blood.

"Dahlia, Dahlia, oh God, Dahlia..."

Water dripped from Ansel's eyes onto her upturned face. Somehow her head had ended up in his lap. His left hand fumbled in the breast pocket of his suit, the right stroking her tousled hair.

"Pa...pa...?"

What happened? Those men, Sebastian's men, they shot me!

"Look, Dahlia. See it?" Ansel's voice shook as he held up her watch.

He flicked it open with a fingernail so she could finally gaze upon the object she had wanted for so long. Dahlia tried to be excited for it. But she was so tired and everything was so confusing...

The ivory watch face shone a little too bright for her eyes, yet the black markings were easily distinguished. Stark and unmistakable, every hand pointed at zero...save one.

Twenty seconds. I have twenty seconds to live.

Pure terror. She tried to scream again and recoiled at how it gurgled the blood pooling in her lungs. Nausea twisted her stomach.

"Shhh...shhh." She could feel her papa's cheek trembling as he leaned down to whisper in her ear. The faint stubble scratched her face. "Look carefully, sweetie, don't forget this."

Ansel held a strange copper object above her eyes next to the watch. He said something else, but the words blurred together, twisted in the darkness growing at the edges of her vision. It was becoming difficult to keep her eyes open.

"I love you, Dahlia." Ansel bent forward and kissed her forehead. "Goodbye, sweetie."

No, don't say that!

The seconds on her watch ticked down: six, five, four...it was all moving too fast!

No, no, no! I can't, I'm not ready to die yet! What should my last thought be? What should I say? What...

Ansel moved suddenly, quickly, scrambling with the copper object in one hand and her watch in the other. He did something, but she couldn't see...all the colors were running together.

Three, two, one... The seconds tolled like a muffled bell.

I love you, Papa.

Everything went black.

Chapter Four
Sebastian Macall

✶

General Sebastian Macall was livid. He had meant to kill just the daughter, the one who looked so uncannily like Sita, but now both she and her despicable father lay crumpled on the floor. Ansel slumped over her body in a bright scarlet pool. The shattered remains of his watch glittered beside him where he had smashed it. Everything was quiet, but for the muted creak of floorboards under Sebastian's feet.

He killed himself, the coward.

With one jet-black leather boot, Sebastian kicked the elder Walker's corpse onto the carpet in disgust. Ansel's body thudded dully onto its side, eyes staring, messy brown hair still matted with sweat. How Sebastian loathed him.

"Why didn't you stop him?" he snapped at the soldiers without turning. His voice shook with fury. "Why didn't you shoot his hand before he smashed the watch?"

"Sir?" The three men shifted with unease, gripping their tesla rifles.

"I said, *why didn't you stop him?*"

But before they could formulate a response, before they could even blink, Sebastian had drawn his sword and was upon them.

He spun in a steel whirlwind, cool, and precise, and

merciless. One man died almost instantly, the watch around his neck slashed through. Sebastian slit his throat just to watch it spit blood into the air. The second man scarcely attempted to lift his weapon before the blade found him too.

Much to Sebastian's surprise, the last soldier managed a wild shot into the ceiling. Then the sword flashed and he fell in two pieces—one on each side of the doorway.

It was quiet again. Sebastian sighed heavily and wiped his sword on one soldier's dark fatigues. He would clean it properly later, once he returned to the fleet above the city. For now he focused only on the research downstairs. The pages holding the secrets of time...and one secret in particular.

It took Sebastian barely fifteen minutes to activate the trapdoor, pile the pages onto a mechanical walking platform, and find his way back out of the workshop. He paused one last time above Ansel's corpse. How many years had that man evaded him?

"Bastard." The word would have been too soft for Ansel to hear, even if he had been alive.

A glint of copper on the floor drew his gaze.

Is that...?

It was. He picked up the device, noting the damage where Ansel had tried to destroy it as well.

The science division can fix that.

He tucked it into his pocket with the utmost care.

Then he turned toward the door and his eyes found Sita's face.

"Dahlia's face. It's *Dahlia's* face," he said to no one. He ran one hand over his chin, wiping away a splatter of wayward blood that wasn't his.

"But look at the black hair, the tan skin, the fine features. You know, she could've been... Shut up!"

Furious, Sebastian ripped open a pouch at his waist and drew out a dented metal sphere. A few movements folded the tangled gears and wires into a mechanical pigeon. He jabbed a button and spoke his message:

"Airship *Imperial Might*, this is General Macall. I've completed the objective and am requesting a flier for pickup. Location marked by a red smoke flare."

He thought for a moment.

"And signal the fleet to prepare for bombardment; we'll destroy the city before departure. End message. Deliver to the bridge of the airship *Imperial Might*."

At the phrase 'end message,' the mechanical pigeon flexed its wings, testing the gears and wheels. Then, satisfied, it emitted a tinny chirp and took flight. Sebastian watched it flap jerkily toward the largest one of a dozen black Anglian airships hovering above Sainsbury like bulbous angels of death.

He picked his way over the soldiers' bodies and through the splintered front door, the mechanical walking platform stumbling along behind him on spindly legs. Blood made his boots sticky.

He looked forward to the bombing.

Chapter Five
The Airman

✳

Farren Reed loved war; it suited him, and he it. War was simple: you either won or lost, killed or were killed, lived or died. Not that he considered himself a simple-minded man; he just found it easier to deal in absolutes than in the complex variations of other occupations.

The *Imperial Might* rolled slightly in the wind and Farren wedged his feet under the access rungs for stability. He was alone atop the airship, and for good reason. More than a few daring aviators had fallen to their deaths from here. Watches were reduced to smithereens upon meeting the ground from such a height.

That won't be me.

He didn't mind the risk. The outer envelope was the only place he could be alone on a ship bursting with crewmen.

Farren twisted the chain of his watch absently around his fingers. *Twenty-seven days and*—he glanced at it—*thirty eight minutes.*

He tucked it back into his jacket pocket with sweaty hands, exchanging it for his flask of vodka. It only took a few burning sips for the time to slip out of his mind again.

A smile stretched across his mouth as he stared at the world spread out beneath him. Warm sunshine peeked through low, scudding clouds to illuminate the city below in isolated patches of brightness. Sainsbury had devolved into chaos at the sight of the waiting airships. Their only protection—the slipshod Delmarean air force—already lay smoldering at the edge of the city. Anglia's superior fleet hadn't just beaten them, they'd destroyed them…

But the panic in the city became little more than white noise so far above. It seemed almost calm, the buildings standing stolidly as they had for decades, looking much like any city Farren had seen back in Anglia.

The breeze ruffled his straw-blond hair as he scratched at the stubble on his chin. *This is the life. A clear sky, a following wind, and a good drink. All I really need is a woman beside me and I'm set.*

The fantasy melted away as he spied a mechanical pigeon making a beeline for the main gondola. It had to be the message from General Macall: the orders the *Imperial Might* and the rest of the fleet had been awaiting.

"Time to go? Already?"

A sigh escaped him. These moments of peace never lasted long enough. Then he screwed the top onto the flask, stretched, yawned, and began climbing down to the main gondola.

* * *

Farren stepped onto the bridge and into a hive of activity. Airmen skittered past on the way to their stations, mechanical men hauled tools and pushed carts of supplies. Multicolored lights blinked on instrument panels lining the walls among a sea of levers and dials. Somewhere, a forgotten ballast alarm beeped insistently.

"Hey Reed, you headed off to crash a flier?" Harper appeared at his shoulder and darted in for a headlock.

Farren anticipated the attack and dodged with ease; headlocks were David Harper's signature greeting. "You been hitting the booze again?"

"Shut it," Farren said, leaning in conspiratorially. "Or do you want them to refuse to let me fly the damn thing?"

"Might be better than you flying drunk…" Harper grinned.

"Airman Reed! You certainly took your time."

Farren snapped his right hand to his forehead in a salute at the Captain's voice. "Apologies, Cap'n."

"We've been calling you through the tubes for the past four minutes. I was about ready to send out a different pilot." Captain Raleigh stood beside the airship's wheel, cradling a mechanical pigeon in one hand. His salt-and-pepper mustache quivered with irritation.

"Sorry, Cap'n."

"You're to pick up General Macall, three soldiers, and a prisoner underneath a red smoke flare. Be quick about it—we have orders to prepare for bombing."

"Bombing?" Farren blinked, taken aback. His thoughts seemed sluggish. Slow.

Of course we're bombing, you idiot, why else would we bring two dozen ships for an easy operation?

"Just make the pickup, airman." Captain Raleigh turned away, already barking orders to a man sitting behind the instrument panel.

"Yes, Cap'n." Farren saluted again, then set off for the docking bay.

* * *

Shrike fliers were small vessels, standard fare for pickups, drop-offs, and reconnaissance. Squashing six people into the tiny, open compartment would be awfully cozy.

Farren sauntered into the aft docking bay and found a group of mechanics scampering around a Shrike. They worked with more enthusiasm than he hoped he would ever have to muster up. Running flight checks, greasing bearings, stretching out the folding plate wings...it looked exhausting.

"That's good enough." He waved off a mechanic immersed in wiping down the windshield. His fingers itched for the controls; he hadn't flown in *days*. And who had time for clean windshields when the General was waiting below? "Go take care of the bay door."

A few short minutes later, the wings were out and the engine was purring. He hopped into the pilot's seat, kicked the machine into gear, and leapt out into the sky.

For one wild moment Farren plummeted out of control.

Caught in a downdraft, he thought pensively. *Turbulence from the wind flow around the airship.*

Then the engine revved, wings bit into the air, and he soared.

Flying never ceased to amaze him. The wind blowing in his face, the wings stretching on both sides, and the joystick in his grasp acknowledging his every whim. Glorious. The swooping sensation in his gut when the craft descended reminded him how precarious it all was. One wayward motion and everything would be gone.

He laughed out loud and unearthed the flask from his jacket.

To freedom! To life! To however the hell many days I've got left!

Farren took a deep drink and the flier wavered.

Maybe Harper was right. Maybe he *was* drunk, but he didn't care. He was invincible until the accursed watch in his pocket decided otherwise, and he intended to enjoy every waking moment he had left.

The flare went up two hundred yards away at fifteen degrees to starboard. He adjusted course, mentally marking the spot in case the smoke dissipated before he reached it.

Wouldn't wanna miss picking up the General.

Farren hadn't met General Macall in person, but everyone heard the stories told in the mess hall when there were no officers about. The deadly swordsman. The war hero who had served on the border twenty years ago, when Anglia had first invaded Delmar. Some soldiers even whispered that he *enjoyed* killing. That people had been known to disappear around him.

Not the type of man who would tolerate lateness.

Farren set the Shrike down under the flare on a lawn of immaculate grass, chuckling as the landing gear ripped divots into it. The craft creaked as it rolled to a stop.

"You took your time." General Macall stomped across the lawn, his face a mask of dissatisfaction.

That's the second time I've heard that today.

"Apologies, sir."

Farren attempted to leap out of the flier with a flourish and salute. His boot smacked the edge of the cockpit. Momentum threw him face-first into the grass, the metal flask of vodka jabbing his ribs accusingly.

"Apologies again, sir."

He got to his feet and brushed the dirt from his jacket as if nothing had happened.

Macall frowned, walking toward the flier without speaking. He was tall and thin, but Farren could see defined lines of muscle beneath his sleeves. Jet black hair brushed the tops of his ears. A sword and pistol swung from the belt around his waist.

"Get ready for takeoff while I load these." The General

gestured at a walking platform behind him. Walking platforms were just that: flat metal plates with legs. This one groaned and shuddered under stacks of papers. It tried to step toward Farren, quivered, and collapsed into a mess of gears.

"Yes, sir."

Farren had just struggled back into the flier when he realized something was out of place.

"Sir?"

Macall grabbed an armful of documents from the twitching machine and thrust them wordlessly into a sack.

"Sir, I thought there'd be five passengers. Where are the rest?"

The General busied himself with another stack of papers, Farren noticed the brief hesitation before he replied.

"They're...dead. Walker killed all three of my soldiers and then committed suicide."

Alarm bells blared in Farren's mind. They'd been told the target was an untrained civilian. Easy. Since when did a civilian have the skills to do away with an Anglian infiltration team?

He pretended to adjust something on the control panel. The Shrike was prepped for flight, but he didn't want to rush Macall—the man might be insulted.

"Did you have the chance to fight him, sir? I don't wanna pry, but I've heard you're good with a blade."

The General placed a hand on the edge of the flier and pulled himself up, hoisting the bulging sack after him.

"No, I didn't fight—I arrived just in time to see Walker destroy his own watch."

"Ah."

"Ah, *sir*." Macall plucked out a hair that had dangled into his eye. "Are you ready to fly?"

"Yes, sir. Ready as we'll ever be."

We're not even bringing back the bodies of our own soldiers? Something's wrong…

Farren's hands danced over the controls. The flier rumbled to life and taxied over the formerly flawless grass.

Gears clicked and whirred. The flier creaked, and there was a rush of movement as he accelerated. Then they were off. Buildings and streets receded on both sides, quiet and nervous.

Everyone's in shelters—they know we're going to bomb them.

The Shrike rose, ascending on an updraft like a vulture circling above the city. Farren kept both hands on the joystick. Updrafts could be squirrelly, unpredictable; he never knew where they might…

He stared at the sword strapped to General Macall's waist, updraft forgotten. Beads of fresh blood shimmered and dried on the hilt, a few rusty flaked peeled away in the wind.

"Sir, you said you didn't fight."

Macall looked over his shoulder, lips thinned in irritation. "I didn't. What does it matter?"

Farren pointed to the sword with one shaking finger, his other hand clenched white on the joystick. He wanted Macall to say something, to tell him he was mistaken, that it was ridiculous to even *consider* that a General would kill his own men.

Macall hesitated. The look in his eyes as they flicked toward Farren told him all he needed to know.

"That's old," said the General, wiping the blood away with the corner of his uniform. "I don't clean my weapons as often as I should."

He's lying. He killed those soldiers.

Farren's stomach lurched. He hadn't known the three soldiers personally, but he'd seen them in the corridors, eaten with them in the same mess hall, even sat through the same sleepy military history lectures in training. Good men, all of them.

What kind of general kills his own people?

Maybe if he'd had a bit less to drink, he might not have said it. But the fuzziness dulling his thoughts and the knowledge that he still had twenty-seven days and…a little more…threw out the words before he could swallow them.

"Killing your own soldiers is a crime, sir. Punishable by hanging."

General Macall turned languidly in his seat, his expression unreadable. For a moment he didn't respond. The tight dread squeezing Farren's chest eased. Perhaps he hadn't heard…

"An interesting fact, airman. Here's another: more members of our air force are killed before their time is up than in any other branch of the military. Do you know why?"

"Bad luck, sir?"

"Their watches are destroyed——," Macall's face was an inch from his own, but Farren had no time to react, "——by falls."

The General seized his collar and heaved him headfirst over the side.

Shit shit shit shit shit…

Farren flailed through the air, heart in his throat, gasping for breath like a beached fish. The wind ripped tears from his eyes. He couldn't be sure there weren't real ones mixed in.

That murdering bastard!

How could his life end this way? How…? It wasn't right! It wasn't fair! It wasn't——

Impact.

Farren smacked water, but it felt like falling on stone.

An excruciating pain jolted through his left leg. All the breath whooshed from his lungs.

Don't scream, don't scream.

If he screamed, he would inhale water and drown. It took an immense effort to clamp his mouth shut.

Farren sank rapidly, the bulky jacket and boots weighing him down. He dragged himself to the surface. The shoreline lay only a few yards away; it was a concrete bank jutting just above the water, the edge of an artificial canal.

Farren heaved himself halfway up onto the bank and sprawled there, shaking. He panted from exertion and pain. His leg was on fire.

What have you gotten yourself into now, idiot?

There he was: half-drowned, leg probably broken, helpless in an enemy city and mere minutes from being annihilated by his own airships.

How am I gonna get out of this one?

He blacked out.

Chapter Six
Resolve

✴

Dahlia opened her eyes.

She breathed. Confusion twinged and echoed in her mind—hadn't she been hurt?

Her hands flew to her chest and came away slick with blood, but there was no pain, no wound. A glance down the front of her ruined blouse revealed two pinched scars hollowed out in her skin. She'd been shot. Yet she was healed.

How?

An image flashed into her mind: Ansel leaning over her, clutching a strange copper object and her watch. What had he done? She'd seen her time run out! She'd *seen* it! By all rights she should be dead.

Her father had done something to save her.

It was the only explanation.

"Papa? Papa, where are you?" Dahlia's voice creaked and her body ached like she'd been beaten. She pushed herself upright. "Papa?"

She saw him.

Her heart stuttered and she clenched her eyes shut. *No no no no. It's not real.*

If she couldn't see it, it had never happened. And maybe Ansel was sitting up. And maybe he was smiling and maybe it was all a trick—yes, a cruel trick—but he'd always been such a prankster, her papa, such a comedian...

She opened her eyes again.

Ansel Walker, her precious papa, her world and her family and her whole heart and her...he was lying there. Just lying there. The shattered remains of his watch sparkled beside him.

Dahlia couldn't breathe. Seconds stretched into years.

Then her fingers reached out to gently close his eyes, and smooth his disheveled hair into a more acceptable shape. There. Now he could be sleeping. Dahlia curled up next to him; his body was still warm, it felt like being hugged. She didn't know what else to do.

She still lay there when bombs began shaking Sainsbury.

They fell like apocalyptic rain from the hand of an avenging god, chewing ragged craters through the quaint cobblestone streets. People fled. Metal screeched and melted. Fire devoured buildings. Dust from the explosions poisoned the air, trapping the hellish glow of the fires until even the sky seemed streaked with ghastly flame. The black Anglian airships floated serenely over it all as they made their way through the city. Everywhere, watches ticked down into death.

Dahlia was numb. Shock blurred her thoughts, made them sluggish. She knew she should do something...wasn't there a shelter? But the idea slipped away like water through her fingers.

"It'll be all right." Dahlia stroked her papa's hair. "It'll be all right."

Acrid smoke tickled her nostrils. She closed her eyes and surrendered to the sound of the bombs.

* * *

Dahlia sat up after the last explosion had echoed itself out among the ruined streets. She blinked away a thin layer of dust. It lay over everything in the room like volcanic ash.

I'm still alive.

She looked down at her papa's lifeless face. Dust coated his skin; she wiped it clean with the edge of her blouse. A raw emptiness stung her heart, a void like someone had hacked out the place in her soul where Ansel had been.

"I can't stay here," Dahlia murmured.

Then, with a herculean effort, she struggled to her feet and set off in search of supplies.

What do I need? Food, water, books, money, birthday presents, watch repair tools... Her thoughts seemed ethereal and dreamlike. She stuffed anything even remotely useful into a large backpack from the servants' quarters. At first she wasn't sure why she was packing, but then it dawned on her:

I'm going to find Sebastian Macall.

Her hand trembled so hard that she dropped a loaf of walnut bread.

Macall wanted something from Papa...

Scraps of conversation filtered through her mind: Sebastian Macall demanding Ansel's time research.

His *resurrection* research.

She didn't understand how such a thing was possible, or how her papa and Macall were involved in it. But none of that mattered.

Her heart swelled in her chest, sudden hope making her dizzy. What if she could use the research to resurrect Ansel Walker? What if she could have him back?

She covered her mouth with a hand.

A few hours ago, she would have dismissed it as

impossible. That was before an Anglian fleet had come after her papa's research. Before she had seen the bullet scars in her chest heal, despite the time on her watch.

Calm down. The longer I spend here, the farther away Macall gets.

A notepad sat on a table in the library. Dahlia tore a sheet from the top and scribbled down a quick explanation for Archibald. He could look after her papa's...body...while she was away. She wouldn't be gone more than a few days—how difficult could it be to track down all those airships? In a week, she'd have her papa back, and they'd laugh about how strange and ridiculous this had all been.

Dahlia trembled with excitement as she set down the pen and returned to the sitting room. It stank like blood. Like death.

She looked for the strange copper object Ansel Walker had held beside her watch as she lay dying, but it was nowhere to be found. A glint of metal in her papa's hand caught her eye. Her watch. After pining for it for so long, Dahlia couldn't care less what time it displayed anymore. The watch went into her leather handbag without a second thought. She scooped the scattered bits of Ansel's watch into the bag too.

"Goodbye, Papa. I'll see you in a little while."

She folded his hands pensively on his chest, then flattened his wayward hair. Her lips brushed his forehead.

On the way out she plucked a tesla rifle from a dead Anglian soldier in the doorway.

"I hope you don't mind if I borrow this."

Dahlia looked back only once, as she stood on the front lawn. Smoke spiraled and curled from a bomb-struck house beside hers. Somewhere, unseen flames crackled. But she hardly noticed. Her thoughts were inside the house, with the man lying on the carpet.

I'll fix you, she thought. *I'll fix everything.*

Dahlia turned away. She hoisted the backpack onto her shoulders and the rifle into her arms, then set off down the silent, cratered street.

* * *

There had been a multitude of low bridges over the canal running through town, but most succumbed to the bombing. Dahlia detoured through the streets along the canal for several blocks, searching for a crossing. She tried not to look at the remains of the little boutique that had sold her favorite scarves, the ruined façade of the tea shop she had loved, or the bookstore whose owner always recommended the best new novels. Her throat tightened as she picked her way along the edges of craters in the street.

The rifle felt awkward in her hands. Heavy and uncouth. She had never held a weapon in her life—in a city so far from the war, it had never seemed important for her to learn. Yes, there were stories of battles along the eastern border, but Sainsbury had remained peaceful. The largest inconvenice had been the time the men installing their bomb shelter had torn up her favorite patch of flowers. It had been a simple thing to ignore the newspaper stories.

Not anymore.

Her city was ruined, her father was…gone, and she had suddenly become part of the war that had never mattered to her.

She felt very alone.

The streets were empty. A few harmless mechanical men wandered dazedly, their artificial thought processors unable to adjust to the new situation.

What would happen when people began emerging

from their shelters and saw her toting an Anglian-made tesla rifle through the ruins of Sainsbury?   She didn't fancy explaining it.

She turned down a stairway to walk down by the canal instead. It might smell less pleasant but at least—

She stopped. A man lay facedown on the concrete bank.

"Hello?" Dahlia tried. He didn't move, his waist and legs dangled limply in the murky canal.

She reached for the poor man with one hand, intending to pull him farther onto the concrete bank.

Her eyes caught sight of his clothing: an airman's dark brown jacket and black pants. A stylized silver falcon was embroidered on the back of the jacket.

"An Anglian!" Dahlia stopped.

An Anglian, like the soldier who had killed her papa. An Anglian, like the men who had destroyed her city. Icy hate narrowed her eyes, sapping whatever pity she'd had for him. She would have shot him then, if she'd known how. But she'd never held a gun before in her life.

Tesla rifles could fire either bullets or electric bolts. Bullets could kill, but only if their target's time was up. Electric bolts were used to incapacitate targets who might have time left, allowing the attacker to destroy the enemy's watch at his leisure.

An instant of fumbling with the foreign components ended with the realization that she was more likely to injure herself than anything. Dahlia gave up and turned to leave the villain to his fate, then froze.

A thought popped into her head.

This was no chance meeting; this was an opportunity.

He was an Anglian soldier. An Anglian soldier could lead her to Macall.

Dahlia took a deep breath, swallowed against her

jittering apprehension, and extended the barrel of the tesla rifle. It nudged the man's shoulder.

"Wake up." Fear made her voice too high-pitched, so she tried again: "Wake up!" and punctuated the exclamation with an aggressive rifle prod.

He groaned and shifted. Dahlia hopped back with a startled squeak, instantly mortified at herself.

I have the weapon—I'm in control here!

The man lay still once more. Dahlia, exasperated and thoroughly embarrassed, jabbed him one last time.

"I said, wake up!"

"I heard you the first time, goddammit! Quit it!"

The man propped himself up on his elbows and glared at her through a curtain of blond bangs plastered to his forehead. Dahlia swallowed and stared right back. He was young; perhaps twenty or so, with vivid blue eyes and several days' worth of stubble gracing his chin.

"What's your name, Anglian?" Dahlia kept the rifle aimed at him. She had no idea how to use it, but he didn't know that.

"Reed. Farren Reed, Aviator First Class in His Majesty King Bespalov's air force."

"What are you doing here, Mr. Reed?" She kept her tone hostile, intimidating.

"Fell...out of a goddamn flier." He held her gaze for another second, then groaned and lowered his head onto his hands as muddy water lapped against his legs. He mumbled something vaguely profane that made Dahlia's ears burn.

"Keep your language to yourself," she sniffed. "Listen, I'm looking for an Anglian soldier named Sebastian Macall. Do you know him?"

Farren gave a rough laugh and rolled onto his back, his brown leather jacket squelched on the concrete. He attempted an amused smile. It was executed as more of a grimace.

"Sebastian Macall? Maybe I know him, maybe I don't. Who's asking, sweetheart?"

"Don't call me that. My name's Dahlia. Macall stole something from me, and I need to take it back."

"Well, whaaat do ya know?" Farren raised his eyebrows as he drew out the word. "I have a bone to pick with Macall myself. Sounds like we're going the same way. Although I only have—"

He reached one dirty hand into his jacket pocket (Dahlia tightened her grip on the tesla rifle), drew out a battered watch, and pried it open.

"—twenty-six days, twenty-two hours, and thirty-one minutes to get there. And, *dammit*, it looks like my watch dented when I hit."

True to his words, a dent glimmered in the metal case on the side of his watch.

"Your language, Mr. Reed. Do you know where I can find Macall?"

"'Course I do. He'll be headed back to the capital. Port Argun." Farren sat up warily and deposited his watch back into his jacket pocket. "Tell you what, sweetheart. You help me get out of this city—my left leg's broken and I don't think I can walk—and I'll show you the way to Port Argun.

He shook his arms in an effort to dry them, flinging droplets of muddy water onto her skirt. Dahlia quickly shuffled backward.

Disgusting, filthy Anglian, she thought, *but I need him.*

"Fine, Mr. Reed. Do we have a deal, then?"

Farren's gaze regarded her curiously as he extended one grubby hand. "Deal."

They shook on it.

Chapter Seven
Flight from Sainsbury

✳

Dahlia found an abandoned clockwork horse and cart a block away. After a few mishaps and minor collisions, she maneuvered it to the top of the canal stairway. It was a simple delivery cart, open to the elements, but it would fit their needs perfectly.

It began to dawn on her that she had never done much with her life. Never held a gun, never driven a cart, never been so vulnerable or alone...

She climbed down from the driver's seat, careful not to damage her clothing. In the spirit of practicality, she wore a brown jacket over her favorite everyday burgundy blouse and skirt. The skirt was creamy white, ending below her knees in a few subdued ruffles. Trousers might have been more suitable, but Dahlia couldn't bring herself to commit such a serious fashion transgression.

"You'd better not expect me to get up those stairs by myself," Farren said from the concrete bank below.

"I think you can do it."

He snorted in amusement. "Broken leg, sweetheart."

She glanced over the low wall that separated the road and the ten-foot drop to the canal. Farren was sitting where she had found him, his feet dangling in the water.

I hoped I wouldn't have to touch him. That water isn't

exactly sanitary...

With a 'why me?' sigh, Dahlia descended the stairs.

"What should I do?"

"Just help me walk—let me lean on you to take the weight off my leg."

"Fine." She extended a hand to help him up, conscious of how clean it looked beside his grime-streaked fingers. *So much for that.*

Farren took it and nearly yanked her over; she tilted back to stay on her feet. He curled his right leg gingerly underneath himself and stood, breathing hard. The color drained from his face.

Then came the leaning part. Farren smelled like the canal water looked, plus a hefty dose of alcohol. His arm snaked around her shoulders.

"You're kinda short, aren't you?"

"I'm actually average."

"Whatever you say, sweetheart."

"Don't call me that."

They climbed to the street one stair at a time, pausing every few steps for Farren to rest. He was panting by the time they reached the cart. Dahlia couldn't remember ever being more disgusted in her life. There she was, daughter of...she mentally skirted the name... There she was, an upper-class lady, being manhandled by a reeking enemy soldier.

Getting Farren into the cart proved even more challenging. It took strategy, physical support from Dahlia, and getting her fingers crushed between the cart and Farren's boot before he collapsed inside.

I hate him.

She had barely settled into the driver's seat when a voice yelled across the street.

"Hey!" A man emerged from a shop where he had been

sheltering. "Hey, that's mine!"

Dahlia imagined she would have happily bought the cart from him under normal circumstances; perhaps she would have even offered him a paid position as her driver. But she had an Anglian aviator sprawled in the back of the cart. One glance and they were both doomed. He would be imprisoned, and they would accuse her of aiding the enemy.

We have to get out of here.

Dahlia fiddled with the levers and the clockwork horse shuffled backwards.

"Wrong lever," she muttered, flicking it off. The man advanced, skirting a twisted pile of rubble.

Dahlia yanked another lever as he started to run. The clockwork horse jerked forward, stalled, and exploded into a gallop that nearly knocked her from her perch.

"Hey!" the man cried again.

But they were long gone.

Dahlia careened through the city, narrowly missing buildings, craters, and citizens braving the outdoors. It was impossible to guess which lever would slow the cart, and she refused to take her eyes off the road long enough to find out. The cart bucked along over rubble. Farren swore mightily from behind her. It would have been exhilarating if not for the dull emptiness throbbing in her heart.

Hours—at least it felt like hours—later they found themselves at the edge of Sainsbury. Dahlia yanked one control after another until the clockwork horse skidded to a stop. It had started to wobble during the last few minutes.

"Devil's blood, woman!" Farren said through gritted teeth. "Are you cracked? What the hell was that stampeding for?"

She ignored him and relaxed in the driver's seat. That poor man who owned the cart must have had a steel backside to sit for so long on bare wood. Her entire rear felt like one enormous bruise. She resisted the urge to rub it; doing so in front of a man would be the gravest of unladylike behaviors.

Instead she lifted her arms over her head and stretched, fingers reaching for the evening sky. The city fanned out behind them. They had survived—for now. But the sun was drooping toward the horizon, and she didn't fancy trying to nagivate the road at night.

"Mr. Reed." Dahlia turned to look at him.

He curled up amidst the stray screws and gears rolling about the back of the cart. If he had been pitiable before, he looked positively wretched now. The dirty water had dried onto his clothes. His pale face shone with sweat. A wave of sympathy washed over Dahlia before she remembered that his people had killed her papa.

He deserves it, foul Anglian.

"Mr. Reed, there should be a town a few miles ahead. We can make it before dark."

"'Before dark' with or without the galloping?"

"Without."

"Thank god. I know we're on a schedule, but come on, sweetheart."

"Don't call me that."

Her hands learned the controls and they continued along the dirt road. Old, overgrown farm fields stretched toward the horizon. Trash, wires, and broken mechanical creatures lay strewn beside the road. Sainsbury receded gradually behind them. Somewhere among its cratered streets, hidden among rubble and coals, lay the body of the only person she'd ever loved.

* * *

Dahlia had heard stories of small-town inns.

Repugnant, nasty places frequented by highway bandits and drunks. She raised her eyebrows in surprise when they pulled up under the warm lights and swept porch of *The Rack and Pinion*. Two stories tall, it featured open windows and a mechanical receptionist built into the alcove. The automaton whirred to life when Dahlia approached the doorway.

"Welcome to *The Rack and Pinion*," it said. "How may I help you?"

"I'd like two rooms for the night."

"One moment, please." Components whirred beneath its thinly-plated skull. "Yes, there are two rooms available. Please pay the man at the bar inside."

It reached out one hand and turned a crank connected to a large wheel. A rapid clicking issued from behind the wooden walls, the door slid aside on a rack and pinion gearing system.

Ah, hence the name.

Dahlia glanced back at the cart. Surely Farren could handle himself while she sorted out their rooms? She gave a mental shrug, thanked the automaton, and entered.

The interior of the inn complemented the outside: homey and inoffensive. Cozy. She stood in a common area amidst wooden tables and chairs and a few mismatched couches. Fire crackled in a hearth. A bar stretched along one wall, bottles of various liquors glittering on the shelves behind it. Several patrons sat there, drinking. The rest talked and ate over tables.

This isn't bad.

Dahlia wove her way between the tables toward the elderly bartender, who was immersed in pouring bubbling liquid into a glass.

"I'd like two rooms for the night, please."

The man finished pouring and shuffled several steps to

present the glass to a customer, then shuffled back to her. Lamplight gleamed on his bald head.

"A hundred twenty gilvers."

"Just a moment." Dahlia dug into her handbag, emerging with a heaping handful of coins. A few slipped through her fingers and clinked on the floorboards. She bent to pick them up.

Silence spread throughout the room—every tap of the gilvers seemed abnormally loud. The bartender gazed at the coins, his eyes growing like cream-filled saucers. Dahlia swallowed back her alarm as she counted the money out onto the bar top.

"...one hundred...one hundred twenty gilvers." She pushed the stack toward him.

"A hundred twenty gilvers *each*."

"Each? I thought...oh, never mind." Dahlia dispensed another set of coins, then dropped the remainder out of sight into her bag. She worried the man's eyes might pop out of his skull if he stared any longer.

"Rooms eight and nine, up the stairs and to the right." The bartender swept away the gilvers and handed her two keys from beneath the counter.

"Oh, one more thing." Dahlia lowered her voice. "My...friend's a bit under the weather. Is there another entrance he can use? I don't want him disturbing your customers."

"There's a door 'round back to the rear stairs."

"Thank you." Dahlia scurried back outside, conscious of the heavy handbag dragging at her shoulder. Several stares followed her.

The stolen cart was, mercifully, still in one piece. She clambered up, glanced back to confirm that Farren was still sleeping in the back, and drove it around behind *The Rack and Pinion*.

"Mr. Reed." She rapped his shoulder. "Wake up."

He was still sprawled unconscious in the back of the cart, broken leg twisted at an unnatural angle. He didn't react. She smacked him harder, with the same effect.

At least he's quiet this way.

Dahlia noticed a walking platform leaning against the back wall of the inn. She had never liked them; their shambling motion evoked images of spiders. But that was no reason to discount their usefulness.

She hauled Farren from the cart, dropping him and bumping his head in the process. *Oops.* Her boot accidentally came down on his fingers while she rolled him onto the platform. *Sorry!*

Still, Dahlia felt slightly proud when she led the walking platform up the rear stairs. She dumped him onto the bed in room eight, unloaded her things in the adjacent room, and returned.

"Now, where's your watch?"

Farren's leg would not heal until his watch was repaired, and Dahlia didn't fancy lugging him halfway across the continent. She found the watch in the first place she checked: folded into the still-damp pocket of his Anglian leather jacket. It felt odd, almost taboo, to hold another person's watch. She had helped her…her papa repair hundreds of watches for clients, but that had been different. Farren was an enemy. His country destroyed everything she had, and now she held his life in her hands.

I could kill him if I wanted to.

Dahlia shot him a surreptitious peek to be certain he was asleep, then pried open the cover. The dent warped the case and made the halves difficult to get apart. When it finally popped open, the time matched what Farren had said.

Twenty-six days, eleven hours, thirty-three minutes. She

glanced from the watch to his incapacitated form and back again. *Why isn't he afraid?*

"It's none of my business."

She snapped it shut with a metallic click.

Back in her room, Dahlia laid out the watch repair tools. The repair kit had been a gift from her papa when she first expressed her dream to follow in his footsteps. Women didn't typically repair watches, particularly well-to-do ladies such as herself, but she didn't care. The repair kit was the size of a hardcover book; made from leather and lined with fabric to cushion the delicate instruments. Frayed edges spoke of frequent use.

It'll be a difficult fix, she thought, tucking a strand of black hair behind her ear as she bent over the watch. But she had watched her papa repair plenty like it before. Her hands hesitated for a moment, then selected the first tool and began.

* * *

Dahlia folded the repair kit closed and ran a finger over the watch's freshly mended surface. It wasn't flawless—perhaps the airman would walk with a limp—but it would do. And with the watch repaired, his body could finally begin healing.

She grabbed a book from her backpack and deflated onto the worn bed. The wool blanket was warm but itchy, and mattress springs dug into Dahlia's back. The spine crackled as she opened the book, a brand new copy of her favorite adventure novel, but her eyes couldn't seem to focus on the text. Instead, they drifted to the stars speckling the night sky outside the window.

A memory floated into her mind: she was six, seated next to Ansel Walker in a carriage. They were moving to a new house in a new city during the night. Dahlia couldn't sleep; she was too excited.

"Look, sweetie." Ansel pointed out the window. *"Do you see that star out there? The really bright one?"*

"I see it, Papa."

"That's the Pathfinder Star. It shows you which way is north—that's how the early airship pilots sailed over the seas."

He leaned back and let her press her nose to the glass.

"If you're ever lost, just follow that star."

"I think I'm lost now, Papa." In the silence, she heard the breath catch in her throat, but her eyes stayed dry. Her heart ached so badly it hurt.

Chapter Eight
An Unfortunate Bit of Banditry

✳

Farren awoke to a headache and a knock at the door. He lay fully clothed on a strange bed in a strange room; it looked like an inn, but he couldn't be sure. The first rays of sunlight wafting through the glass window warmed the walls. A quick glance confirmed he was alone. *Too bad. I could sure use some female company.*

"Mr. Reed?" A woman called from outside the door. "Mr. Reed, are you decent?"

"No, I'm not 'decent.'" He flinched at the haggard quality of his own voice. "I have no idea where the hell I am, I don't remember the last time I ate anything, and I feel like *shit*."

He swung his legs over the side of the mattress and stood. An excruciating pain shot through his left leg. He crumpled to the floor, clutching the leg but only succeeding in twisting it further.

"Devil's blood!"

Forgot I broke that...

The pain slammed him back to the present as memories of the last twenty-four hours flooded his sleep-addled brain. He let loose a long stream of curses.

"Mr. Reed? I'm coming in. You'd better be decent."

A key scratched in the lock and Dahlia stepped inside.

"Why are you on the floor? What have you done to yourself? And stop with that language."

"Tried to...stand up..."

"Why would you do that?"

Farren didn't think her tone warranted an answer and remained silent, doing his best to subdue both the pain in his leg and his labored breathing. Dahlia tossed her hair in irritation.

"I repaired your watch," she tossed it onto his chest, "and I made you an appointment with a physician today."

He snatched up the watch for inspection, noting that the metal case was in better condition than it had been even before his fall. It disappeared into the pocket of his flight jacket.

"Looks great, sweetheart. Wanna help me up?"

Dahlia did, frowning with distaste during the entire process. He hadn't bathed in days and enterprising stubble covered his cheeks. Farren thought it made him look dashing, but he suspected Dahlia disagreed. What was *with* that woman? She acted so high and mighty, but he could tell from the way she carried herself that she didn't know what she was doing. At least she smelled nice—like lavender, or maybe lilac? He'd never been good with flowers.

"Got any food?" he asked when he was sitting safely back on the bed.

"They had biscuits downstairs." She held a fist-sized pastry wrapped in napkins. It didn't look particularly filling.

"Is that all? No muffins or anything?"

Dahlia ignored him.

"Tell me your clothing measurements and I'll see if I can buy you something...cleaner to wear. And a new jacket—that falcon on yours is obviously Anglian. You'll have to leave it here."

"Leave it? ...but this is my *flight jacket*. I can't just..."

"Would you rather be sent to a prison camp? In Delmar, we don't show your people any mercy." She stood up straighter. "Your blond hair and blue eyes are suspicious enough, but if you go parading around wearing Anglia's national symbol you're almost sure to be arrested."

"I'm not giving up the jacket, sweetheart."

Dahlia stared at him like he was deranged.

"Here's your biscuit." She deposited the pastry and a sheet of paper on the blankets beside him. "There's a walking platform outside the door you can ride. The physician's address is on the paper. You won't need any money; I already paid him."

After Dahlia left with his clothing measurements, Farren took the walking platform to the bar downstairs and bought a bottle of liquor with the last few coins in his pockets. If he was going to have some doctor rip up his leg, he wanted to be good and drunk for the experience.

* * *

The physician looked reputable enough, and the alcohol dulling Farren's brain kept the pain in check while the man set his leg. Dahlia had even paid for an expensive walking brace.

She's probably sick of carting me around everywhere. Ha...carting.

"Where did you get that jacket?" the doctor asked while he tightened the brace around Farren's leg. He was middle-aged, sporting a neat mustache and pudgy physique. His eyes narrowed as he contemplated the Anglian falcon.

"Oh, this? Yeah, it's my flight jacket."

"*Your* flight jacket? Those are Anglian symbols, you know. Are you an aviator?"

"I'm not just *any* aviator. I'm one of the best pilots in

the air force."

"Is that so? It's odd to see a man of your caliber wearing enemy symbols."

Farren twitched as the brace clicked into place, but it wasn't from the discomfort. He was an idiot. In his desperation to get his hands on a drink and his subsequent inebriation, he'd forgotten Dahlia's advice.

Stupid. Stupid. Stupid. Think fast or you're dead.

"Enemy symbols? I don't see how it's odd." Farren drew himself up and assumed his best offended expression. "I took this off the first Anglian I ever killed. Shot him down over the Hattaran Mountains in the middle of winter. He survived, so I made another pass in my flier to finish him. But I'd run out of ammo. So I landed on the mountain and beat him to death with my bare hands."

He looked right into the man's eyes. "I've killed a lot more since then, but he was my first."

The physician didn't respond. Farren couldn't tell if he'd bought the lie or not. Rather than acknowledging Farren's anecdote, he addressed the mechanism affixed to his leg.

"This is the most advanced brace I use. When you're wearing it, you'll be able to do any activity you normally could: walk, run, beat men to death on mountaintops... It's hardwired into your leg muscles and receives electrical signals directly from your body when you want it to move. If you're careful, your bones should heal in four months. Come back then and I'll remove the brace for a small fee."

Farren slid off the operating table and stood warily, testing. *It seems sturdy enough.* The brace clicked on the tile floor as he took a lap around the room.

"Has your watch been repaired yet? I'd be happy to refer you—"

"No thanks. I've already seen a repairman."

"Well, if that's all, then you're good to go. Best of luck to you, *aviator*."

A chill ran down Farren's neck as he exited the office. The physician's gaze felt like a tesla rifle pressed between his shoulder blades.

He knows.

* * *

Farren found Dahlia walking along the road on his way back to the inn. He joined her, eyeing the stack of wrapped parcels in her arms.

"What're those?" he asked.

"Your new clothes." She thrust the pile at him. He took it, struggling to contain the loose parcels.

"How many did you get, woman?" The top package slid off into the road. "This is enough to wear a new outfit every day for the rest of my life!"

"Every other day, actually. I didn't think even you could manage to scrap one *every* day."

Farren flung back his head and laughed at the unreservedly serious expression on her face. She frowned, which only made him laugh all the harder.

"You're *funny*, sweetheart!" he snorted.

"Don't call me that." She spun on her heel and stomped off toward the inn.

"Huh?" Farren ruffled his blond hair with one hand. "Geez, woman!"

"And you can quit calling me that too!"

Goddammit, she's coming back. Farren arranged his features into what he hoped was a look of neutral concern.

"Quit calling you what, 'woman'? But you *are*."

"It isn't the word I object to, it's the tone!" Dahlia halted in front of him and poked a finger into his chest, knocking off more packages. "Like you're insulting me! And I. Am. *Tired* of it!" She punctuated each word with a jab of increasing force.

"I'm sorry, sweet—I mean, Dahlia."

"No you're not! You're just trying to get me to leave you alone!"

"And you're just trying to pick a fight." Farren couldn't hold back any longer. "I don't know what the problem is!"

"The problem is...is...arrgh!" She flung up her hands and set off for the inn again, black hair billowing behind her.

What in the world was that *all about?* He gathered up the fallen parcels one at a time.

"Get in the cart, Mr. Reed," Dahlia yelled without turning. "We're leaving—we've lost enough time here already."

Farren started to ask why they were still using the cart instead of hiring an airship. Then he stopped.

Best not to talk to her right now. It's not my *problem if she makes it to Port Argun. I promised to point her in the right direction, not babysit her.*

"On my way," he yelled back.

* * *

The cart bumped over potholes along the dirt road. Dahlia sat up front in the driver's seat again, consigning Farren to the cargo area. He didn't mind: it offered the perfect opportunity for a quick nap. A verdant forest canopy rippled overhead, dappling the light so it flickered across his face. Overall, he mused, it could be a lot worse. Farren's eyes drifted shut.

A hidden bird whistled from somewhere in the trees

and another answered it. The clockwork horse clicked and whirred.

"Stop right there."

The cart jerked to a halt and Farren sat bolt upright, snapping awake. Four men stood in the road, black tesla rifles waiting in their hands.

"Dahlia, do you know these fine gentlemen?" he said calmly, arms neutral at his sides.

"They're…they were in the inn when I went to pay." She was trembling.

Good, that means they probably weren't sent by Doctor Suspicious.

"Quit talking." The largest man stepped forward. He was muscular but ill-kempt; greasy bronze hair hung past a pair of overlarge ears. The rifle clenched in his pudgy hands looked out of place.

"Now," he continued, "we don't want anybody to get hurt. Hand over the money and we'll let you live."

Farren glanced into the bottom of the cart. The Anglian tesla rifle Dahlia had been carrying the previous day lay next to her backpack. The question was: was it charged?

He spoke, keeping his voice steady and his hands in plain view, "We don't want any trouble either, sir. The lady would be happy to hand over her bag—just let her take her watch out first."

"Fine."

Dahlia reached one shaking arm toward the leather handbag hanging from her shoulders. It took two tries for her to undo the clasp, rummage around inside, and remove her watch. The clasp clicked as she re-fastened it.

The lead bandit extended a hand.

"Give it."

Dahlia fought to get the strap over her head, but her movements were jerky.

"Here, let me get that for ya." Farren moved forward and eased the strap off her. He addressed the man before them, "I'll toss you this and then we'll all go our separate ways."

The lead bandit nodded.

Farren swung his right hand back as if winding up for a throw. In the instant his body shielded the bag from view, he flipped the clasp back open and flung the bag high into the air.

Coins poured out. They spiraled, sparkling in the sun like escaping butterflies.

"What the..." All four thieves stared at the whirling money.

Now!

Farren grabbed Dahlia with his outstretched arm and toppled her into the back of the cart. The rifle was in his hand before she hit. *Please let it be charged!* He sighted and pressed the trigger.

The leader's head disappeared in an explosion of blood.

"Bill!" shrieked another bandit as gore splattered his face.

Whoops. Someone left this set on bullet instead of electricity. Guess his time ran out today.

That was the last round in the gun. He glanced at the battery indicator—not enough power for a bolt. Instead, he whipped the rifle back and flung it javelin-style. It whacked a bandit's jaw with a stomach-churning crack. The man collapsed, folding limply into the dust like a broken mannequin.

Silence permeated the air as the two remaining thieves contemplated the bodies of their companions.

"Get out of here!" Farren yelled.

The men fled through the forest, squealing in a

decidedly un-masculine fashion. One ran headlong into a tree. He grunted, scrambled up, and continued sprinting.

Farren stood, watching as their cries receded. Once they were out of earshot he started laughing. It began as a nervous reaction, but soon devolved into genuine mirth.

"Did you see that one hit the tree?" He slapped his good leg and turned toward Dahlia. "Hilarious!"

She certainly didn't seem to think so: her face was pallid, eyes huge. She sat trembling with her knees hugged tight to her chest. Did she have *any* sense of humor at all?

"Come on, sweet—Dahlia. It's okay!" He patted her shoulder apprehensively. "Look, they didn't even take any of the money; we just have to pick it all up."

"Don't touch me!" She flinched and jerked back as if burned, pushing herself into the corner of the cart. "Don't you dare touch me!"

What the hell?

"Okay, okay." He held up his hands. "Listen, I'm just gonna go pick up your stuff and we can leave. Don't go nuts or anything."

Farren lowered himself to the ground and gathered the fallen coins. Blood coated a handful of them. These he wiped on the dead man's shirt, leaving angry crimson streaks on the cloth. The other bandit had survived, but Farren guessed he wouldn't be holding up any carts in the near future.

A fleeting look into the cart confirmed that Dahlia still huddled in the back corner. Farren shrugged and climbed into the driver's seat, leg brace humming as the electronic actuators worked. He could hardly feel the thing apart from the additional weight.

His fingers flickered over the instrument panel and they eased into motion. The clockwork horse acted as if nothing had happened—it had no senses of its own, reliant only on inputs from the levers and the shape of the ground under its hooves. It was a simple, purposeful creation. Farren almost envied it.

In two short days, his entire world had changed. He wanted nothing more than to live out his remaining time aboard the *Imperial Might*. In his imagination, he'd always envisioned himself going out in a fireball during some wild aerial battle. He'd pictured it a thousand times: his flier shattering onto the earth, scattering his bones into the endless sky. It wouldn't have been a bad way to die.

But now...now it looked as if he would enjoy his last breath in front of some money-crazed highway bandit. Or perhaps he and Dahlia would make it to Port Argun after all, and he'd take a blade in the gut from his own General. Depressing.

But he'd made a deal with Dahlia, and his word came before his nation. Without her, he would have been fated for an appalling death in one of Delmar's prison camps. So, if she had made it her goal to find Sebastian Macall or bust, well, then it was his duty to make sure she succeeded. Besides, he wasn't too keen on the General anyway.

Chapter Nine
Opening the Watch

✳

They were still deep in the woods when twilight made it difficult to see the road ahead. Trees pressed in on all sides. Farren scrutinized the horizon, searching for the telltale glow of a town. He saw nothing but interminable, monotonous forest.

"We should make camp," he said when a small clearing disrupted the trees.

Dahlia voiced no objections. He took that as agreement and maneuvered the cart off the road. The clockwork horse had been growing increasingly jerky throughout the day. But it still ran, and that was good enough.

Farren hopped down from the cart, clenching his teeth as the impact ricocheted through his broken leg. He ignored the pain.

"Come on down, sweetheart," he shouted. Dahlia hadn't moved from where she sat, curled, in the bottom of the cart. He could only imagine how sore she must be. "Come on—I'll make a fire. How about you clear a sleeping area?"

She didn't move. He hadn't expected her to.

Some previous traveler had abandoned a stack of wood nearby. A blackened stain next to it implied a crude fire pit.

Must be pretty far from town, if other people have stopped here. But he was grateful nonetheless. It took military survival skills, patience, and a little luck to coax a flame from the branches. Sparks scorched his fingertips.

"Ow! Dammit!"

Dahlia approached when the branches kindled. Farren looked up in surprise as she seated herself delicately on the grass nearby, his lapse in attention almost caused the infant fire to go out. She cradled a semi-crushed loaf of bread and a book.

Farren sat back once a few larger logs had caught. His burned fingers throbbed. Dahlia didn't speak; the only sounds issued from droning crickets and the snickering fire. His stomach gurgled.

"Mind sharing some of that?" he ventured. Dahlia wordlessly ripped the bread in half, tossed him a piece, and nibbled at her own. Farren caught it before it hit the grass and took a bite. Stale crust crunched unappetizingly.

Hell with this. Farren gave up, felt around in his jacket pocket for a moment, and emerged with a handful of in-shell sunflower seeds left over from who-knows-when. He popped a few into his mouth. Dahlia opened the book on her knees, but her eyes were on him. Disapproving.

"So what was that earlier?" he asked, more for the sake of conversation than anything. "Why'd you go crazy?"

She leaned toward the flames: in the flickering light she seemed pasty and waifish. Fragile. Shadows filled the dark circles under her eyes, deepening them, carving weary lines on her face.

"If you must know, Mr. Reed, it's because you scared me today."

"Scared you? Because I saved us from those bandits?"

"Well, yes." Dahlia pulled at her hair, running it through her fingers as she thought. "You shot that man."

"I saved our lives! And your cash."

"You killed him."

"His watch must have run out anyway. How is that my fault? Next time, maybe I'll just stand there and let 'em kill *you*."

Her mouth opened and closed mutely.

"What?" Farren bit down on a sunflower seed.

"You're terrible, Mr. Reed." Her voice was too high pitched.

Oh, God, she's gonna cry.

Indeed she was. Tears leaked down her face and she sniffed, choked, and buried her head in her hands.

"Shit." Nothing made Farren feel more helpless than a crying woman—particularly when he had caused her distress. What should he do? Pat her on the shoulder?

"Sorry, sweetheart. I didn't mean it, I…"

"Have you ever been shot before?" She raised her head, watching him from beneath dewy eyelashes.

"Can't say that I have. I've been gunned down in fliers, but I've never taken a bullet."

"This is what happens when you shoot people."

Dahlia suddenly yanked down her red blouse so he could see the top of her chest. For one wild, beautiful moment Farren thought she was going to take it off and forgot all about the crying. Then he recoiled.

A terrible scar defaced the center of her chest, directly over her heart. Sunken, crumpled like someone had gouged out a chunk of flesh. Farren had seen bullet scars before, but they had never looked quite so *clean*. And he had never known one nestled atop a vital organ. Dahlia pulled at her shirt to reveal a second, matching scar on her shoulder.

Farren prided himself on the fact that he didn't frighten easily. He could stare down the business end of a gun with utter calm, could charge an enemy ship without so much as a shiver. But he was afraid now.

"How…how are you…alive?"

"I don't know. My watch ran out two days ago. They shot me and I was bleeding and I thought it was all over, but then I woke up and…"

She stopped and readjusted her blouse. Farren was somewhat disappointed when it shrouded her chest again.

"I don't know," she finished.

"What does your watch say?"

"I haven't looked at it yet."

"Well, look at it now!" Farren said, appalled. *How can she not know her time?*

"I'm…I'm not sure I want to know what it says."

"Here." He held out a hand. "Give it to me and I'll check it for you."

Dahlia opened the clasp on her handbag and proffered the watch, her face anxious. The tiny object felt cool in Farren's grasp. He flipped it over and read the name inscribed on the case: *Dahlia Walker*.

"Walker? Walker is your last name?"

"That's what the watch says, isn't it?"

"Any relation to Ansel Walker?" His stomach clenched. Ansel Walker had been the target of the Anglian operation in Sainsbury. The man the *Imperial Might* and the rest of the fleet had been hunting. The man the Captain had told Farren to pick up with Macall.

"He was my father."

The key word was 'was.'

"You know him, don't you? When your air force came from Anglia, you wanted to steal his time research and kill him."

Farren was caught. He refused to look at her, but he could feel her accusing gaze boring into him. *No wonder she hates me. I'd hate me too.* Rather than formulate a response, he tightened his grip on the watch and opened it.

It slithered through his numb fingers into the grass. He jerked, staring at Dahlia. She hadn't moved. He snatched it up and looked from it to her and back again. *Devil's blood! What is this woman?*

The watch had run out.

Every hand—from the whisper-thin decade, year, month, and day indicators to the heavy hour and minute lines—hovered over the zero mark. They stayed frozen when he tapped at the glass with his fingernail as if trying to knock them into motion.

Farren had seen watches like it before, but none with owners who still breathed.

"What does it say?"

He raised it in one shaking fist so she could see the time clearly in the firelight. She took it from him and examined it: rapped the case, jiggled it, held it upside down and observed it from below. She sighed and held the watch above her face, studying it against the backdrop of stars. Farren cleared his throat.

"So, what do you reckon is the matter with it? Are you sure that's your watch?"

"It's got my name on it, doesn't it? My father gave it to me; it ended when I thought I'd died. But he...he did something to it, I think."

Farren didn't reply. Slowly, he unearthed his own watch from his pocket and checked it. Dahlia's malfunction made him wary; *Dahlia* made him wary.

"Twenty-five days, eight hours, four minutes." It wasn't until he spoke that he realized he'd said it aloud.

"Say what?"

"That's how long I have to get you to Sebastian Macall."

When Dahlia didn't speak again, he lay down a few

feet from the burning coals. It was late. He was sure she would be raring to take off early the next morning.

The forest murmured: crickets, the occasional owl, a chorus of spring peepers. Farren mentally rehashed their conversation as he drifted toward sleep. He couldn't forget the obscene bullet scars splattered on Dahlia's chest, the frightened tears in her eyes.

My people shot her, murdered her father, devastated her city… I can't imagine how much she must hate me.

I owe her.

Chapter Ten
Answers from the Sound Tape

✳

Dahlia awoke covered in morning dew and aching from sleeping on the bare ground. She sat up, groaning and blinking in abright sunrise. Birds twittered in the trees nearby.

Never again. It's inns from now on.

She found a canteen of water in her backpack and sipped it slowly, the clean liquid washing sleep from her mouth.

Dahlia glared at Farren's snoring form. Blond hair dangled into his eyes and a thin streak of drool clung to his lips. He'd been the one to suggest stopping and sleeping by the road like a pair of homeless vagabonds.

But now that she finally had a few minutes to herself... Dahlia opened the backpack again and extracted the burlap sack: her father's last birthday present to her. Shiny metal canisters the size of her thumb spilled out, clinking, when she removed the repurposed music box.

She picked one up and inspected it. The number 4 was scratched onto the screw-on top.

If there's a four, there must be a one. Dahlia rifled through the pile until she found it, then carefully snapped the sound tape into place. A sip of water, and she pressed the playback switch.

"Hello, Dahlia." It was her papa's voice. Her finger jerked the switch off. Icy hands squeezed her chest—for a moment she thought she would cry.

Stop it. Stop it, Dahlia. All you need to do is listen. She pinched the bridge of her nose and focused on the physical pain.

She flicked the switch again.

"This is the first sound tape," said Ansel. "I probably told you on your birthday that these tapes will answer what you wanted to know about your mother, but there's more to them. I've also included things about my past—and yours—that you need to know.

"But first: if you're listening to these at all, then..." Ansel paused and gave a subdued cough, "then I'm dead. I'd have told you face-to-face if I'd survived. But here we are."

Dahlia stole a furtive glance at Farren, who was still snoring away.

"Anyway," Ansel went on, "here's what you need to know: When you were born, I realized from your watch that you were destined to die on your eighteenth birthday. Maybe I should have told you, but I wanted you to be happy with what you had. And I wanted...I wanted to save you. I've done some work in the past in resurrection theories, but there are...issues...with that. So I settled on time transfer.

"In other words, you survived because I gave you some of my time. I don't know how much time you have now. I don't think watches can change their time, so your display might not look right anymore. You might have ended up with days, or years...or more. Playing with time is fickle. For all we know, you might have *centuries* left."

"Well, aren't you lucky?" Farren opened one eye. Dahlia threw the switch so violently that she feared she'd broken it.

"Mr. Reed! How long have you been awake?"

"Only long enough for that last part." He sat up and stretched. "You've got *centuries*? Damn."

"Or days. Or maybe minutes, idiot." Dahlia stuffed the box and canisters back into the sack, imagining she was flinging them at Farren's head. "And I don't feel lucky at all. I've gone my whole life without seeing my time, and now I'll never know."

Her resentment didn't faze Farren; he was gradually becoming immune to it.

"Well, at least that's better than certain death in——," he yanked out his watch and checked the time, "——twenty-five days and eleven minutes."

I wish he'd quit doing that. Did he think she *cared* how many days he had left, as long as he guided her to Port Argun first?

Dahlia got to her feet, slipping a little on the dew-wet grass.

"I just hope I live long enough to catch Macall," she spat.

"Catch him for what?" asked Farren, standing with her.

Dahlia didn't need to explain herself, but she did anyway.

"Macall stole my father's time research. I need it back."

"He murdered your father, didn't he?"

Dahlia turned toward the cart without replying and began loading their supplies. It was only after they had started off again, Farren driving, that she said:

"Yes, Mr. Reed. Yes, he did."

* * *

Blackton was not quite a city, but neither could it be

called a town. There were proper cobblestone streets instead of dirt, a busy press of citizens, and shops with bells tied above the doors. Yet the entire affair housed perhaps only a quarter of Sainsbury's population. Clockwork horses drew carts heaped with vegetables instead of carriages filled with the wealthy. Several passersby clutched farm implements.

All Dahlia cared about was that there was more than one inn to choose from. Naturally, she selected the best and most expensive. They could have traveled many miles before dark, but she needed to address a few things while they had an urban area on hand. The first being a shower.

An hour later, Dahlia stood in the doorway of Farren's room, combing her wet hair and explaining her plans.

"I've decided to book us passage on an airship. In case I can't find one, you need to search for someone who can take a look at our clockwork horse."

The machine had developed a troubling rattle. Dahlia suspected a bearing issue, but bringing it to a repairman would be simpler than fixing the problem herself. Besides, she mended watches, not mechanical creatures.

She offered Farren a stack of gilvers from her handbag.

"See if you can't buy some food too. And for heaven's sake *take off that jacket*. People were staring when we arrived. This isn't a small town like the first one—they'll have police here, maybe even soldiers."

Farren dropped the coins into his jacket pocket.

"How many times do I gotta tell you? I'm not giving up the jacket, sweetheart."

"Suit yourself," Dahlia sniffed. "But I don't want you arrested before we're even out of Delmar. We made a deal, remember? I did my part, you still have to do yours."

She nodded at the brace on his broken leg for emphasis, then turned and set off down the hall. Her walk purposefully advertised more confidence than she felt. *If he's captured, I'll never be able to infiltrate the military base in Port Argun. It's not just his own neck he's risking.*

Dahlia asked a reputable-looking passerby where to find the port and followed his directions through Blackton. The city reminded her of a working man's version of Sainsbury: more subdued, fewer pleasant little luxuries. Practical. Vegetable stands and blacksmiths replaced cafés and theaters.

She started when she saw the first soldier. He was a young man dressed in gray army fatigues, sporting a tesla rifle on a shoulder strap. The crown of Delmar was embroidered over his chest pocket and he leaned nonchalantly against a wall, but Dahlia only noticed the weapon. She held her breath as she walked by.

Don't think about him. You're making yourself look suspicious!

Then she was past. The sloping street revealed the port several blocks ahead. There were half a dozen docks: lofty steel platforms with concrete foundations below for anchoring airships. Every one stood empty.

Unperturbed, Dahlia approached a bored man seated in the docking fee booth.

"Wanna reserve a space?" He perked up as he saw her and gestured toward a price list painted onto a board. Dahlia's eyes widened. The man's left arm was a mess of clicking, humming machinery. Steel plates and wire stretched from his fingertips to the bottom of his grease-stained sleeve in the approximate shape of a human arm.

A cyborg.

She had seen cyborgs before, of course, mainly amputees who replaced their lost limbs with mechanical equivalents. One man who worked at a shoe shop in Sainsbury even had a mechanical eye.

Dahlia couldn't tear her gaze away from the man's arm. *Incredible technology. How do the electrical signals travel from—*

"Full-size berths only fifty gilvers a day if you reserve this week," the man chirped.

"No, thank you," she said.

"Half-size for thirty gilvers a day!"

"No, thank you again. I need to book passage on an airship. Are there any arriving soon?"

The man visibly deflated at her disinterest. He wiped his nose on a sleeve, leaning against the back of the chair.

"Hard to say, ma'am. A whole Anglian fleet sailed past a couple days ago—like big black demons they was. Thought they was gonna start an air raid! They gone and spooked all the traders."

"But why are the traders frightened?"

"They shoot 'em outta the sky. Or board 'em and steal the cargo."

"No mercy for enemy commerce, I suppose," Dahlia sighed. She and Farren had no choice but to carry on in the detestable cart.

"But if it's passage you're after, you'll be wanting to try Lawson's Ridge. Big merchant port. A lot of 'em trade in Anglia too, so they don't touch those ships."

She stood up straighter and smoothed the crinkles from her skirt. Now they were getting somewhere!

"How do I reach Lawson's Ridge?"

* * *

Farren meandered through Blackton, whistling, hands stuffed in the pockets of his flight jacket. Autumn sunshine warmed his face. The brace on his leg clicked with every step, heavy but not uncomfortable. A few soldiers stood on scattered street corners, relaxing or staring idly into space. Their eyes slid over him. Farren felt a tug of familiarity; guard duty was the same no matter which country's emblem was on the uniform.

He ducked into the first grocer he came across. It was a small store, packed with shelves groaning under the weight of vegetables, breads, cheeses, spices, and cooking ingredients. Flour dusted the floor.

I don't know why Dahlia wanted me *to get the food.* He'd never cooked anything more complicated than corn. And he'd burned that.

He stocked up on things that didn't require cooking and deposited the mess on the shopkeeper's counter. The lady, a sharp-nosed matron with flyaway hair, grumbled as she totaled it up. Farren waited. His eyes fell on a square packet of chocolate in a display behind her.

"Hey," he said. The shopkeeper looked up, her mathematic mumbling cut off. "How much for that?"

She glanced at the packet. "Thirty-four gilvers."

Farren resisted the urge to whistle. Of course it was expensive—it had to be imported from the Southern Lands. But Dahlia needed cheering up, and if there was one way he knew to make a woman happy, it was chocolate. At least, that's what the other airmen swore by. Farren usually preferred giving up and moving on when things weren't going well.

That's not really an option here.

He and Dahlia were stuck together until they reached Port Argun.

"I'll take it."

The shopkeeper added the chocolate to his pile and finished tallying the purchases.

"Seventy gilvers."

Farren reached into his pocket for Dahlia's coins,

hoping there would be enough. His watch fell out with the handful of gilvers. It *tinked* onto the wooden floor.

"Here." He slapped the coins onto the counter and snatched up his watch, wiping flour from the cover.

Damn thing.

Farren couldn't stop himself from opening it to check the time: twenty-four days. Not even a month.

What would happen to him in twenty-four days?

Don't think about it.

How could he *not* think about it?

"Wait," said Farren to the shopkeeper as she slid his change across the counter. "Do you sell vodka?"

She nodded, and Farren breathed a sigh of relief. He could forget again.

* * *

"The dockmaster said the journey is three days by clockwork horse cart." Dahlia unfolded a map she had purchased from the man in the booth. Farren peered over her shoulder as they stood at a desk in her room. "Lawson's Ridge is smack dab on the border with Anglia. It'll make things safer for you: you'll blend in with the crowd."

"You won't," Farren pointed out. "Dark skin, black hair...you'll never blend in."

"Yes, well..." Her finger traced out a route on the paper.

"What's your race? You know, I've heard about natives in the Southern Lands who have dark skin."

"Fascinating, I'm sure. Now, if we take this road..."

"The sun's supposed to be stronger there. People say it bakes the color in. But I don't think you look baked, more like lightly toasted. It's pretty."

Dahlia bristled. Comments on her skin color had

followed her ever since she could remember; she didn't need another reminder of how different she was, whether or not Farren thought it was pretty.

"Mr. Reed." Dahlia turned and was startled by how close he stood. She withdrew a step, leaning against the wooden desk. "Have you been drinking again? You smell like it."

"Just a little," Farren admitted, running a hand through his blond hair.

Dahlia sighed to convey her disappointment. *Why is he so difficult? Why am I stuck with an Anglian soldier who doubles as a raging alcoholic?*

"I got the supplies though," he gestured at a pile of bags next to her backpack. "Bread, cheese, sunflower seeds, even some chocolate for you."

"You used my money to buy *chocolate*? Don't you know how expensive that is?"

Farren remained silent, sensing her disapproval.

"Mr. Reed, we can't afford to be spending money on chocolate. We'll need to hire an airship to have any hope of making it to Port Argun before——" Farren stiffened, and she changed tack. "Maybe if you were sober once in a while, you'd think about these things. Why do you have to drink so much?"

It was a rhetorical question but Farren, in his inebriated state, interpreted it differently.

He gazed at her and reached one hand into the pocket of the jacket that so annoyed Dahlia. When the hand emerged, it held his watch. He opened it.

"I drink." He swayed and bumped into the desk. "I drink to forget I'll be dead soon."

Dahlia felt a prickle of guilt.

"And I hate it just as much as you do."

Farren made his way out, wobbling and still staring at

his watch. He stopped in the doorway and turned back long enough to say, "I thought some chocolate would cheer you up."

Then he was gone. The door to the next room opened and a resounding thump echoed through the hall as he collapsed onto the bed. Dahlia stood frozen.

"Mr. Reed?"

There was no response.

"Farren?"

Still nothing.

He's probably too drunk and tired to even hear me.

But that was the cynical part of her talking, and she knew it. Guilt jangled in her thoughts.

He didn't mean anything by it, he was just trying to help out.

Besides, Farren had decided to use the last of his time to help with her vendetta. She could at least spare him a little understanding.

The door to his room swung open at her touch. The lights were on, and Farren lay facedown where he had fallen atop the mattress. Presumably asleep. *Look at him; he didn't even take off his boots. How has he survived this long?*

But perhaps he hadn't always been this way, she mused. Maybe things had been better back when he had a year or two ahead of him. Dahlia had lived her entire life without knowing how much time she had left. Was it possible that knowing was a greater burden than ignorance?

A snore broke her reverie. *Definitely asleep.*

She shook her head to clear it. It didn't do much good to contemplate things she couldn't change.

Dahlia approached cautiously, as if he could snap awake at any moment. Her hands untied the dirt-encrusted boots dangling over the edge of the mattress and placed them by the headboard. The thick blanket bundled at

Farren's feet went over him. She told herself she did it to prevent him from catching cold. Not out of sympathy. Autumn in Delmar meant chilly nights, and if he fell ill their progress would slow.

Then she switched off the light, eased the door closed, and retreated to her own room.

Alone again.

The burlap sack in her backpack was easy to find. Dahlia settled into the desk chair, music box in front of her, and flicked the switch.

"So how does time transfer work?" Her papa's voice fizzled from the speakers. "Without going into the technical nitty-gritty, it involves energy and something to channel the energy. That something is a small copper device I invented. You connect two watches to it, then the person giving away time just winds it until they transfer however much they want."

So that's what Papa used to save me. Macall must have stolen it—that's what I need to take back from him.

"It took years to finish, but it still isn't perfect. While the time the receiver has to live increases, I don't think it affects what's displayed on their watch. And it's impossible to say how much time is actually given over—it could be more or less than you think, or even more than the giver's lifespan.

"But that's not the most serious problem." Ansel's voice took on the tone he used when deep in thought. "The real issue is finding an energy source able to affect the stream of time. Not only does it need an incredible amount of energy in a small volume, but it also needs the right *kind* of energy. You can't just hook it up to a generator."

Dahlia fiddled with her hair as she listened, her papa's words washing over her.

"It turns out the only viable energy source is a mineral

called 'promethium.' It's an incredibly rare crystal. Scientists have searched for it for centuries, but I only know one place to find it.

"Now, sweetie, this is very important. What I'm about to tell you is for your ears only. Don't let anyone listen."

Her papa paused for a few seconds. Dahlia checked the doors and windows, failing to discern any sign of eavesdroppers. She resumed her seat at the desk.

"Promethium is only found in one place on earth: Janmasthala. The country you know as the Southern Lands. There's a cave system at the eastern edge of the ruins of an ancient city called Vatana. Go inside and follow the carvings on the walls. They'll guide you to the promethium.

"Your...your mother and I discovered it. I took a few pieces for my research; I used the last one for you. I don't know if you'll need more, but you know where it is in case you do. Who knows, maybe you'll follow in my footsteps and perfect time transfer one day. You always wanted to carry on the family business!"

Her papa laughed. Dahlia's head reeled.

"I'll warn you against resurrection, though." He was suddenly serious. "There are some fundamental issues with it that can't be solved. We as humans can only do so much, when we're playing with God's intentions."

The sound tape stopped. She had reached the end of the roll.

Why warn me against resurrection?

Dahlia rewound the sound tape, plugged it back in, and listened to it again and again, until the words blurred in her head.

Chapter Eleven
Port Argun

✷

The Anglian fleet had returned to Port Argun. Air base workers rushed about securing lines, hydrogen hissed as ballast tanks adjusted, flags fluttered and snapped in the wind. Everywhere, men shouted orders. The *Imperial Might* descended through the chaos, settling into her berth like a great floating whale.

Sebastian Macall stood in the gangway and awaited the docking ramp. A series of mechanical men bearing stacks of Ansel Walker's research papers arrayed themselves behind him.

Soldiers and aviators stopped to salute whenever they rushed past, sometimes nearly knocking one another over as they scrambled to complete their tasks and refrain from disrespecting the General at the same time. Sebastian stared straight ahead, occasionally adjusting his coat.

He was the first across once the ramp had been secured. Heavy boots clanked on the metal platform. The airship docks were held high off the ground by steel frames and girders. Everything had been wooden until three years ago, when a hydrogen fire ripped through the main city docks. King Bespalov had ordered all port structures rebuilt from steel afterwards.

Workers along the platform scattered at his approach.

Those unfortunate enough to remain on the dock stood aside, saluting while he passed. No one cared to stand near the fifty foot drop, even with the railing present. But they chose that over displeasing Sebastian Macall.

Sebastian made his way out from the air base and boarded a waiting carriage. The mechanical men climbed inside with him, shuffling papers.

The driver slid aside a window into the carriage and spoke, "His Royal Highness King Bespalov has requested your presence at the palace, sir."

"Very well."

The vehicle wobbled as four armed guards jumped onto the foot rails. Through the small window, Sebastian could see one of the escort carriages waiting nearby to follow them.

They tightened security. Delmar must have been offended by the bombing.

* * *

Sebastian swept into the throne room and approached the King to deliver a deep bow.

"Your Highness."

King Alexander Bespalov had a propensity for flair. The throne room was a testament to that—adorned with thick tapestries, golden mechanical guards, and even a small fountain near the massive doorway. Sebastian's feet sank into a heavy carpet atop the marble tile. He had never understood the purpose of the splendor.

"You may rise, General Macall." The King's voice echoed through the room. Sebastian obeyed.

Alexander Bespalov was a large man, sturdy, with a softness around his middle. Purple robes draped over his shoulders and a glittering crown rested on his high forehead. A neatly-trimmed beard concealed his chin behind a screen of silver.

"Leave us." The King gestured at a row of human guards near the doorway.

The men hustled out, their tesla rifles clanking in the otherwise quiet room. Once they had gone, the mechanical guards along the walls were the only other beings in the room, and they were programmed to forget anything they heard.

Bespalov relaxed in his throne. The two men had known each other for decades—the King abandoned ceremony when Sebastian was the only one there to witness it.

"Tell me what you found. I know we discussed it over the radio, but I want to hear it again face-to-face."

Sebastian gestured at his mechanical men to bring the stacks of papers forward. Gears and motors whirred as they ascended the steps and laid their burdens at the King's feet.

"This is Ansel Walker's research: the data he stole and what he developed afterward. I already had it looked over by the science division on the *Imperial Might*. It's everything he had on time transfer and resurrection."

Alexander Bespalov leaned forward and picked up the top sheet.

"Did he actually succeed in either one?"

"Not to my knowledge."

"Pity. Well, we need that technology as soon as possible. Take these papers to the science division when you leave here. I want them to drop everything and focus on this."

"Yes, Your Highness. I'm confident this will give us the edge we need over Delmar. Imagine when we can resurrect our soldiers and steal time from prisoners of war...they won't stand a chance."

Bespalov returned the sheet to its place atop the teetering stack. He leaned back, regarding Sebastian with eyes the color of cold seawater.

"Don't think I'm blind to your other motives, Macall."

"Other motives? You know Anglian victory is my only goal." Sebastian's face displayed a façade of calm. Behind it he was reeling, his mind racing to cobble together an explanation.

How does he know...?

"I never said you couldn't use this technology for your own purposes, as long as they don't conflict with mine. Lead us to victory first. Then you can deal with your personal...aspirations."

"Anglia is always my first priority."

They both knew it was a lie. But as long as their goals lay along the same path, Bespalov did not seem eager to aggravate his only general.

There was a rap at the door. A voice murmured through the thick metal, "Lieutenant Warren to deliver a message for General Macall."

"Enter," said Bespalov.

The King reached down and threw a lever on the wall behind his throne. A moment passed, then a heavy clicking echoed from the walls as the enormous doors yawned open on hidden gears.

A soldier in a dress uniform marched through, snapping a salute to the General. He seemed unsure whether he should salute or bow to the King. He settled for something halfway between the two that ended up similar to a curtsy. Sebastian might have chuckled, if he had been a chuckling sort of man.

"Your message?" he asked.

"Sir!" The man jumped to attention, hands at his sides, and began: "Radio operators have received reports of an

Anglian aviator in a small town near Sainsbury. Our latest intel places him in Blackton."

"Likely a deserter." Sebastian said, waving a hand. "Why are you bothering me with this? Inform your commander to keep an eye out in case he tries to cross back into Anglia. I won't order retrieval of a man behind enemy lines for something this frivolous."

"My apologies, sir," Warren fumbled, "My superiors thought you'd be interested in his reported traveling companion."

"And his companion is…?"

"A young lady with dark skin and black hair. She paid for the deserter to be treated by a physician, gave her name as Dahlia Walker."

Sebastian's stomach lurched. *She's alive!* Her face— Sita's face?—floated accusingly in his mind. Their features were so alike that he could hardly differentiate the two.

Calm down. You're a General; you can't look weak.

"You're…" He cleared his throat to hide the crack in his voice. "You're a member of the radio division, yes?"

"Yes, sir."

"Tell your commanding officer to put out a bounty on both of them. Five-hundred gilvers for the deserter dead or alive. Thirty thousand for Dahlia Walker. Alive."

"And for Walker dead?"

"Nothing. Anything more to report?"

"No, sir."

"Dismissed."

The Lieutenant saluted, half-curtsied, and marched out. Another push of the actuating lever and the doors swung together.

How did she survive? Could it be time transfer?

Sebastian was surprised to hear his labored breathing plainly in the ensuing silence. He wrestled with himself, fighting to bring it under control. Jumping to conclusions would do no good, not until the science division had a chance to examine the research. He hadn't checked the girl's watch or her pulse; it was possible his soldiers had simply been careless when they'd shot her.

"Why did you offer up a bounty that large for a little girl?" Bespalov's irritation was unmistakable. "I thought we just discussed how Anglia is your first priority."

"It is, Your Highness. We need the girl if we have questions about her father's research. Who knows what Ansel Walker might have shared with her, or what she might have seen and heard from him? I'd be very surprised if he didn't share it with her. We need this technology. Anglia needs this technology. And if all it costs us is thirty thousand gilvers, then we've gotten quite a deal."

The King shrugged in agreement, adjusting his crown.

"Anything else, Your Majesty?"

"No, we're done here."

* * *

Once he had delivered Ansel Walker's research to the science division downstairs, Sebastian sought out a deserted basement hallway. He couldn't be seen like this. Hands clammy, breath loud in his ears, uniformed shoulders shivering...he looked nothing like the man leading Anglia's armed forces to war.

"Get a hold of yourself. She isn't Sita."

"But the face, the eyes, the hair..."

"She isn't Sita."

Sebastian leaned back against the cool concrete wall and slid to the floor. Head in his hands, he focused on the feeling of the rough wall, the dirt and dust accumulated along the edges of the hallway...anything to tear his mind away from the terrible feeling growing inside him.

"Dahlia is Sita's daughter. Half of her is…"

"Dahlia is Dahlia. Sita is *dead!*" Sebastian roared to the empty hallway, clenching his fists until fingernails sliced into his palms. "Ansel killed her, you killed him. It's over."

"It isn't over. Once they read the research…once they find out what he knew…"

Sebastian opened his fingers, staring at the thin half-moon cuts on his palms. His right hand itched for his sword. To use it might at least restrain this monster. If he could only lose himself in battle, or feel the wet splash of blood on his face, perhaps then he could forget. But there was nothing. Nothing except the emptiness, and the silence, and the memory of Sita.

Chapter Twelve
Bounty Hunters

✶

"You almost slept through breakfast."

Farren shook Dahlia awake. She was asleep in a rough wooden chair at the desk, her strange music box resting in front of her.

He shook her shoulder again.

"Wake up, sweetheart. They've got blueberry muffins in the kitchen downstairs."

He held one under her nose. If the smell of *that* didn't wake a person up, he didn't know what could.

Dahlia jerked, her eyes blinking open. Farren couldn't tell if the shaking or the promise of muffins had awakened her.

"What time is it?"

"Don't know. Early-ish."

She blinked at him and sat up, smoothing wayward hair back from her face. He offered her a hand but, as expected, she ignored it and stood on her own.

"Muffins?" He took a considerable bite of one and waved the remaining portion at her. "Beft breakfift you can git."

To his surprise, Dahlia consented to follow him downstairs for muffins. The shadows under her eyes implied a sleepless night.

"Why do you have more energy than I do?" she said as they sat at a table in the inn's common area, munching on pastries. A coffee mug the size of a pint glass steamed in front of her behind an open book. Her eyes regarded him over the top of the cover. "You passed out drunk last night."

"Already had my coffee," Farren said around the food in his mouth. "Three cups."

"*Three?*"

"I feel like running around the building a few times."

* * *

Despite the fact that they set off several hours later than intended, they made decent progress. The clockwork horse limped along winding roads through trees, over streams, and past meadows overflowing with dry grass.

Four or five more days until Lawson's Ridge. And an airship. Farren would be glad to fly again. After General Macall pushed him from the flier, he'd worried he might never have the chance.

Forest gave way to flat farmland. The warm sun beamed down unencumbered, without trees to obscure it. Miles fell away under their wheels. Ripe crops filled the fields on either side of the road: corn, wheat, and rows of low vegetables. Every farmer was preparing for harvest, if they hadn't already begun. Farren felt a pang of homesickness. Autumn looked the same in farm country, whether here in Delmar or back home in Anglia. Harvest had always been the most important time of the year. He remembered helping his parents pick vegetables and fruit as a child, blinking in the cool pre-dawn air while trying to hide the blueberry stains on his lips.

He smiled.

It was an easy day, made all the better when they

pulled into a town a few minutes after sunset. Farren smiled. Even the mangiest inn was better than sleeping beside the road.

They checked into an inn much like their first one: simple, spartan, and functional. Dahlia retreated into her room, and Farren relaxed in his.

He fell asleep as soon as his head touched the pillow.

* * *

Farren snapped awake. Darkness enveloped the world beyond the window; it felt as if he had only slept for a few hours. His soldier's senses rang with alarm.

Something's wrong.

A muffled thump outside the door. Farren's head swiveled toward it, his ears catching the whispered conversation in the hallway.

"Stop sniveling, Tom. You gonna pass up thirty-thousand gilvers cause yer too scared to take on a girl?"

"It's not just the girl. What if the aviator's with her?"

Farren slid from the mattress. He donned his flight jacket and boots with the barest whisper of fabric. In a few steps he was flattened to the wall beside the door.

"Don't worry 'bout the aviator—his bounty's dead or alive. Just shoot 'im and 'is watch."

Bounty hunters!

The doorknob rotated—Farren knew it wasn't locked. He entertained the thought of lunging for the latch. But cowering in his room would mean leaving Dahlia unprotected...

There was a soft creak as the door eased open, the hinges protesting. A shadowy head peeked into the room. *Were they both coming for him first, or was it one per room? Were there more than two?*

The intruder advanced, extending a pistol trained on Farren's abandoned bed. It was obvious there was no one in it—there hadn't been time to create a deceptive pile of blankets.

"Hey Clyde," the man said in a stage whisper, "I don't think there's anyone—"

A swift punch to the jaw cut him off. Tom staggered back as Farren spun out from behind the door. The pistol came his way—he ducked instinctively and felt the bullet nip his hair.

Too close!

He jabbed at the man's neck before he could get off another shot. Fist connected with flesh. The bounty hunter gurgled and doubled over, the weapon tumbling from his grasp.

Farren scooped up the gun. He squeezed the trigger without an instant's hesitation. The bullet bored into Tom's shoulder, spraying blood. An obscene splatter bloomed on the wall.

Farren didn't give him time to reach for another weapon. He brought the butt of the gun down, hard, on Tom's head. The man collapsed.

Should I look for his watch to kill him? "Farren!"

Dahlia's panicked shriek galvanized him into motion again. He took off, stumbling against the stained wall in his haste. His feet thudded on the wooden floorboards. Dahlia screamed again as he approached the open door to her room.

"Farren!"

"Shut up!" There was a muffled whack followed by a scrambled shuffle of blows. Anger blotted out Farren's thoughts.

If he hurts her...

Farren burst through the doorway without slowing,

the pistol held before him.

Moonlight glowing through the windowpane illuminated the scene. Clyde stood frozen in the center of the room, one arm twisted around Dahlia's neck. The other held a pistol to her temple.

Bastard's using her as a shield. A wave of rage made Farren dizzy.

"Don't move," said Clyde. "Unless you want 'er spending the rest of 'er time in a coma."

He shook the gun for emphasis. Dahlia was rigid yet calm. Farren had expected her to be trembling with fear, but his mind had no space for surprise just yet.

"Just set the gun down real slow and I won't hurt 'er. She still comes with me, though. This little lady's worth thirty-thousand gilvers."

Farren had been lucky with the other man—his watch must have been scheduled to run out when he was shot. Taking that risk here was too dangerous. Clyde wouldn't have dragged along his companion if he knew his own time would be up before he could bask in his reward.

"Gun on the floor," the man reiterated.

"Sure, whatever you say." Farren loosened his grip on the pistol. "Dahlia, how you doing, sweetheart?"

"I'm fine." Her voice sounded strong. "Are you letting him take me?"

"I've got no choice."

His weapon clattered on the floor. Fury and helplessness drummed in his veins. What should he do? He only needed to incapacitate the bounty hunter long enough to do away with his watch. But how?

"Real good. Now, step back against that wall there." Clyde gestured to the far side of the room with the end of the gun.

The instant the barrel left her temple, Dahlia sprang

into action. Her fingernails clawed at the man's eye. Clyde howled shrilly and released her to grip his face.

"Devil's blood! What'd ya do? What'd ya do to me eye ya little—" He dissolved into a stream of curses. The pistol waved maniacally through the air.

Farren didn't give him a chance to fire. He dove for the weapon.

His hand had barely curled around the grip when Dahlia brought one knee into the bounty hunter's crotch. Farren winced inwardly. Clyde's cursing ceased as he folded to the floor.

"Get his pistol, Dahlia," Farren ordered.

She had already leaned down to pry it from the squirming bounty hunter, who was no longer in any state to use it. The weapon looked out of place in her delicate hands.

Farren bent down next to her and pressed the business end of his gun to the man's forehead.

"See if you can find his watch."

Dahlia tilted her head; she must have known he didn't want to give it a nice polish. She hesitated and spoke.

"I don't think he'll be coming after us again."

"Damn right he won't. He'll be dead."

"No." She pulled uncomfortably at her hair. "I mean, he won't follow us even if we let him live."

"Dahlia, didn't you hear what he said? Someone's put out a bounty on you for thirty-thousand gilvers. These clowns are only the beginning. If we kill him today, that's one less to worry about tomorrow."

The object of their discussion shivered, clutching himself, one good eye darting back and forth between their faces. His clothing was ragged and his hair hung lank and disheveled. *Looks like a sad excuse for a bounty hunter.*

"No, Mr. Reed. This man is unarmed and injured, we

can't kill him." Dahlia stood and rested a hand on Farren's shoulder. "We should leave before someone comes."

"Oh for god's sake, woman." Farren reached his free hand into the chest pocket of their prisoner's shirt. No watch. He tried around the neck. "Ah ha!"

A sharp yank snapped the chain and the watch fell into his palm.

"No, please…" the bounty hunter gasped through what Farren knew was incredible pain. "Please, I've got a wife."

"Don't lie to me. No one would marry a scumbag like you."

Farren set the watch on the floor behind him and removed the pistol from the man's forehead. *Shooting it'll be easiest. Don't want glass in my hand.* But when he turned around, Dahlia's foot covered the watch.

"I told you we're not going to kill him," she said. "We need to leave."

"Stop being unreasonable."

"You're the one being unreasonable. Haven't you murdered enough people, Mr. Reed?"

The accusation in her tone was almost a physical blow. Farren was at a loss for words. He stubbornly refused to look at her, settling for gazing at her bare foot instead. A shaft of moonlight wafted the windowpane and illuminated the curve of her ankle. *She has nice feet, doesn't she?*

A whimper from the bounty hunter.

"Fine, sweetheart. We'll do it your way."

All his military training screamed at him to push her aside and kill the man. Why leave an enemy alive? He had killed so many. What was another corpse in the pantheon of those dead by his hand?

"What's going on up there?" someone shouted from past the doorway. Boots pounded in the hall.

Wordlessly, Dahlia raced to grab her backpack while

Farren snatched up both pistols. They left Clyde where he lay.

Farren stepped over him and fiddled with the window latch. Their first-floor rooms would make for an exceedingly easy exit.

He stuck his head into the nighttime air and glanced about for threats. The darkness carried a distinct chill. A commotion toward the front of the inn drew his attention, but he and Dahlia were out of sight on the side. A farm field teemed with tall corn in front of him.

Perfect.

An official sort of voice wafted around the corner. "…sent two men in to investigate. The owner said there were multiple gunshots."

"Dahlia, I think they've called guards," Farren whispered as she approached with the backpack on her shoulders.

She grinned wickedly. "I've never been a fugitive from the law before."

"I'm not sure you should be excited about this."

Dahlia ignored him and gestured at the window.

"Will you be going first then, Mr. Reed?"

What's gotten into her?

Without further urging, Farren climbed onto the windowsill and lowered himself to the ground. The brace on his leg whirred gently. He didn't offer to help Dahlia; she wouldn't have accepted it. She landed beside him a few seconds later.

"Go."

They disappeared into the corn field.

Chapter Thirteen
Captured

✴

"We left the money," wailed Dahlia. "I can't believe we left the money!"

"You said that already," Farren sighed as they walked. "Twice."

They had been hiking along the same country road for the past several hours with nothing to break the monotony of farm field after farm field. Dahlia, exhausted from lack of sleep the night before, had only just realized their mistake: her handbag was still hanging on a hook in her room at the inn. They'd forgotten it in their rush to leave ahead of the guards.

"But how could we leave the money?" she said again.

"That's five times."

Dahlia resisted the urge to hit him.

At least I put Papa's watch in the backpack, she thought. If they had lost the ruined remains of Ansel's watch, there would have been no choice but to go back.

They strode along the road in silence, past even more crops. The midday sun shone in a clear sky.

The straps on the heavy backpack were beginning to chafe Dahlia's shoulders. She would have asked Farren to carry it if his clothing hadn't been crusty with blood from the bounty hunter he had shot the previous night. They had stopped at an irrigation ditch earlier, but the muddy water only eliminated the worst of the gore.

She shifted the straps to an undamaged area. "Mr. Reed—"

"Do you know who Sebastian Macall is?" he interrupted.

Dahlia paused, taken aback by the sudden question.

"Some officer?" she ventured. "An officer in the Anglian air force."

"Wrong. He's King Bespalov's only general. He's in charge of all Anglia's armed forces." Farren glanced at her. "Don't you read the paper?"

Dahlia gaped.

"The general? Are you quite sure?" Her mind flashed back to the countless times she had snubbed the street corner paperboy in Sainsbury. "Why didn't you tell me before?"

"I thought you knew."

She tugged at her hair. *What am I going to do? He's sure to be well-guarded. I'll be killed!*

"This changes nothing," Dahlia declared, more for herself than for Farren.

"You know you don't stand a chance, right? Trying to steal back whatever it is you want?"

"I said it changes nothing."

Their footsteps crunched on the loose dirt. Something metallic clinked methodically in the backpack. Farren scratched at a bit of blood crusted onto his jacket.

"What's that?" He pointed out over a field of who-knows-what crop. "Is that an airship?"

Dahlia squinted; she'd always had a touch of nearsightedness, but she wasn't about to reveal that particular flaw.

"Where?"

"Right there." Farren leaned toward her and pointed again.

A smudged shape, a mere brown blob, hung low in the sky to the north. Dahlia inhaled sharply.

"It looks like an airship," she said.

"Called it."

Dahlia ignored him. She glanced about for a hiding spot, heart thudding in her chest. The crops were too low to provide any semblance of cover. She tried to remember the last tall cornfield they'd passed—how far back was it?

"There." She pointed at a nearby bush, a small, scraggly specimen whose twigs would doubtlessly ruin her already-messy hair. The word hadn't finished leaving her mouth when Farren yanked her toward it.

"Ladies first."

Dahlia crawled underneath, heedless of the sticks jabbing her skin and the dirt smudging her clothes. Farren dove under beside her an instant later. Their feet stuck out, but there was nothing to be done about that. Besides, no one had eyes good enough to see their two pairs of grimy shoes.

They lay side-by-side, squashed together on their stomachs, watching the airship approach. Farren's shoulder pressed against hers. She smelled the iron tang of blood, the faint aroma of leather that still clung to his battered flight jacket, and something else she couldn't place. A warm, rich smell halfway between muffins and summer rain. It was...oddly distracting.

Dahlia blinked to clear her thoughts.

"Is it Anglian?" she asked.

"Nope. See how the sun shimmers on it? It's reflecting off the bare metal. Every ship in our fleet is painted matte black so they're harder to see at night. They don't reflect that much sun."

"Bounty hunters, then?"

"Gotta be."

The airship drifted closer by the minute, but they could do nothing except wait. Farren checked the ammunition in his pistol. Dahlia followed his lead and pinched her finger in the slide. Farren chuckled.

"Remind me later to teach you how to use that."

The airship was a few hundred yards away and closing fast. It looked nothing like any ship Dahlia had ever seen. Small, perhaps half-size, with a hull cobbled together from various plates of scrap metal. Mismatched colors and sizes offended Dahlia's fashionable sensibilities. A single dented gondola swayed from the bottom like a child clinging weakly to its mother.

Dahlia jittered with nervousness. Farren checked his watch.

"Twenty-two days, eighteen hours, and forty-nine minutes."

"At least *you* know you're not scheduled to die today."

"I don't have to run out of time for them to break my watch."

A shadow floated over them. Dahlia flicked her eyes upward, picking out the many scratches adorning the ship. A speaker crackled to life from somewhere on the underside of the gondola.

"We can see your shoes, ya know." The voice was female.

Dahlia hardly dared to breathe. How could they distinguish something so small from that height? She glanced at Farren without moving her head.

Stay still, he mouthed.

"They're whispering now," a second voice, this one a deep booming male, echoed through the speaker. "The woman has dark skin. It's Walker."

Dahlia's heart stopped. She leapt to her feet, hardly noticing the twigs scratching her skin. The backpack slid from her shoulders.

"Run!"

She fled. The long skirt flapped at her ankles, threatening to catch on the lines of low crops. She didn't care. It was either run or be captured and sold to Anglia, into the clutches of the man who'd killed her papa...

"Dammit!" Farren's yell snapped through her adrenaline. Dahlia shot a glance over her shoulder without slowing.

The airman had only just managed to extricate himself from the bush. He jogged along, cursing the leg brace with every step, stumbling after her.

A panel slid open in the airship's gondola. Something leapt out, something huge and shadowy. The hulking shape dropped to the road, stirring dust and shaking pebbles. A pair of burning yellow eyes fixed on Dahlia.

It was a gargantuan mechanical man. Tall and hunched, covered in segmented armor plates that clicked as it started forward. It passed Farren in four massive strides.

Dahlia ran faster than she'd known she could. The mechanical thumped along behind her, heavy steps drawing closer. Panic gripped Dahlia. Her pulse pounded in her ears.

A pistol shot shattered the sound of the mechanical's metal plates. Dahlia risked a look back, just in time to watch Farren empty his clip into the thing's head. Four perfect shots.

It didn't even flinch. The bullets that should have torn through its processing circuits simply splattered against the back of its metal skullplate.

Then it was upon Dahlia. She shrieked with fear as a steel hand wrapped around her waist. The thumb jabbed into the small of her back, and the tips of the fingers pressed against her bellybutton. Her feet left the ground.

Dahlia struggled, beating vainly at arms the size of tree trunks. The mechanical turned her so they were face to face.

"Stop that," it ordered. The low voice rumbled up from deep within the creature. A slotted face grille shielded the place where its mouth should have been. It coughed, a grating scrape of metal on metal.

Dahlia pried at its fingers. She hadn't expected it to make a difference, so when the massive hand dropped her she hit the ground unprepared. Her knees buckled.

The mechanical coughed a second time. Then again and again, doubling over, steam issuing from vents hidden in its neck. Dahlia scrabbled backwards on hands and knees. What was wrong with it? Had she hurt it?

"Come on!" Farren was pulling her up. She found her footing and they fled, leaving the struggling mechanical behind.

"Hold it!" yelled a woman's voice.

No, thanks.

Dahlia didn't slow. The mechanical was out of commission now; they were home free…

"I said HOLD IT!"

A rifle shot cracked the air. Dahlia squeaked as she felt the bullet pass inches from her head, shredding the ends of her hair as it went.

"Stop or the next one goes in your leg."

Farren juddered to a halt. Dahlia stopped beside him. She was panting from the running and fear. Her back ached where the mechanical had held her. She glanced about for the source of the assault, but the only creature in view was the mechanical man, still bent over coughing.

"Tiberius, you okay?" shouted the woman. A flash of

pink on the underside of the airship caught Dahlia's attention. A woman lay just inside the hatch the mechanical had jumped through, her hair dyed a shocking combination of pink and blue. She clutched a long-barreled rifle more than half as tall as she was.

The mechanical man shuddered, trying to contain his coughs. It took a few dozen seconds. It felt much longer to Dahlia, who wasn't sure if she should be watching the woman pointing the rifle at her or the enormous mechanical a few yards away. Which one was more dangerous?

The question was answered for her when the mechanical recovered. It straightened, blinking yellow eyes as it drew in deep breaths through the face grille.

"You okay, darling?" the bright-haired woman shouted.

The mechanical nodded and stepped toward them. Dahlia couldn't move. If she fled, the rifle woman would shoot her, and she couldn't outrun the mechanical anyway. She could only stand there as the creature grabbed her waist, tucked her under its arm, and snatched up Farren with the same hand. It hung her fallen backpack from its forearm.

A small panel on the airship's gondola slid aside with a mechanical screech and a rope ladder poured out. The end struck the ground in front of them, spraying a few pebbles into Dahlia's exposed face.

"Ready?" asked the woman.

"Yes." The mechanical's voice was a low thunder. Dahlia, pressed against its side, felt the vibration in her teeth.

Then the creature grabbed the ladder, a motor whined above, and they rose toward the hatch.

Chapter Fourteen
Catching a Ride

✳

The mechanical clambered into the dark confines of the ship. Dahlia glimpsed a dimly-lit hallway built from steel plates, extending inboard toward a matching door at the far end.

Her mind whirled. If Farren still had his pistol, maybe they could stun the mechanical man long enough to make a break for it. But there was no pistol in Farren's hands, and they turned off down a side passageway before she could whisper to him.

Think! How do we get out of this?

The mechanical servants from her home in Sainsbury flashed through her thoughts. But those had been simple, innocent frivolities compared to this monster. She had never heard of thought processors advanced enough to manage the varied inputs this mechanical was handling with ease.

The creature opened a door. A handful of shabby cells, full of rust and mildew, were collected on the other side. Dahlia recoiled. She didn't want to know what would happen to her already-dirtied clothes if she was forced into there.

Can we make it cough again? We nearly got away before...

Then she realized: mechanical men didn't breathe—or

cough. And if it wasn't a mechanical, it had to be a human. A cyborg human, like the dockmaster back in Blackton, but with a watch damaged enough to cause severe, chronic respiratory problems.

I can repair watches.

The spark of an idea lit in her mind.

"Wait," said Dahlia as the creature jerked one cell open. The shriek of unoiled hinges drowned her out, so she repeated herself. "Wait. Stop! You're not a mechanical man, are you?"

The giant ignored her. It lifted Farren toward the first cell. He aimed a kick at the mechanical's head, missed, and ended up on the deck inside.

"You're a cyborg," Dahlia babbled in desperation. The cell door locked behind Farren before he could rise. "You're human!"

"Quiet," said the mechanical. It pried open another cell and set Dahlia inside, gently. She lunged for the open door. It slammed in her face, locking before she could try to pull it open. The mechanical turned to leave.

No!

"I can fix your watch!" Dahlia yelled.

The mechanical froze. Dahlia held her breath as the massive head rotated, pinning them in place with piercing yellow eyes.

"My father was the best watch repairman in Delmar," said Dahlia as she swallowed against her pounding heart. "He taught me everything he knew. If you let us go, I'll fix your watch."

The mechanical blinked, coughed a few times, and stomped out.

Farren turned to her.

"Well, you tried."

"You be quiet," she snapped. Hadn't she guessed right?

She'd been so sure…

"How'd you figure that stuff out anyway?" Farren asked.

"Easy," said Dahlia. She crossed her arms over her chest, leaning against the cleanest of the bars. Her disapproving gaze took in the rusting cell bars, the dirt coating the floor, and the cot sagging against the wall. "Mechanicals don't cough. That thing does. And he obviously has some sort of respiratory problem. I'm guessing he neglected his watch, or it has some damage that was never repaired."

"Huh."

"He'll be back, just you wait."

But, an hour later, the cyborg still hadn't returned.

Dahlia waited, standing until her feet grew sore before giving in and settling warily onto the threadbare cot. Her heart sank. She'd been so sure her plan would work.

Farren, already arranged comfortably against the back wall of his cell, glanced over.

"Think they'll feed us?"

"How can you think about food at a time like this?" Dahlia fumed.

"I'm hungry," Farren shrugged. "Besides, the cyborg is probably just talking it over with the rest of the bounty hunters."

Dahlia nodded, hoping against hope that he was right.

I have to get free to bring back Papa.

Her stomach twisted at the realization that she might never escape, that she might live out the rest of her life in prison and never see Ansel Walker again. The thought chased around her head as the hours wore on. It lingered in her dreams when she drifted into a fitful sleep.

* * *

Dahlia awoke to hulking steps of the cyborg as he stomped into the brig.

"Come with me."

He unlocked the cell doors—Dahlia thought briefly of running—and urged the two of them out into the corridor. The steel bulkheads hummed with engine noise from somewhere nearby, the sound a strange rumbling, like thunder that never stopped.

The cyborg walked behind them. Dahlia shifted uncomfortably, the rumble of his steps raising the hairs on the back of her neck. She had seen more than a few cyborgs, but he was the strangest. Usually they only had a few mechanical bits—perhaps an arm or leg that had been amputated, or even an eye (she remembered the unlucky bounty hunter whose eye she had mauled). But she had never imagined something of this caliber. Such a thorough integration of flesh and metal was unheard of…it was *wrong*.

The engines grew fainter as they made their way forward. They passed the now-closed entry hatch, rounded a bend, and the hallway opened into a control room that could only be the bridge. The cyborg ushered them inside. Banks of levers, buttons, lights, and gauges crammed the space, and a massive windshield stretched across the walls.

The view took Dahlia's breath away. Farm fields unfolded over flat land as far as the eye could see: green and gold lines of crops, interspersed with the occasional lonely tree. The shadows of the Hattaran Mountains loomed on the horizon.

She didn't immediately notice the woman sitting in the center of the room.

"Welcome aboard the *Wayfarer Elizabeth*. I'm Beatrice Hawkins." The woman stood and extended her hand. "Call me Keet."

"Dahlia Walker."

Keet's handshake was firm, confident, and just a wee bit overzealous. She wore a pair of moss-colored coveralls that somehow managed to flatter her figure despite the horrible fashion statement. The sleeves had been rolled up to her elbows, revealing black bracelets tattooed around her wrists. Her hair was cropped short, the left side dyed fluorescent pink and the right an electric blue. A pistol swung from a worn holster on her belt.

Farren introduced himself next. Dahlia frowned as they shook hands, hoping Farren failed to notice how remarkably attractive Keet looked in her coveralls.

"Dahlia," Keet flopped back into her torn pilot's chair, grinning. "Tiberius tells me you can fix watches."

Dahlia nodded. "My father taught me. Ansel Walker."

"The time researcher, of course."

How do they know about Papa's research?

Keet continued before Dahlia could open her mouth to ask about it. "Think you can fix Tiberius' watch? We've had trouble finding a repairman who will treat a cyborg."

Dahlia hadn't seen the watch yet, much less assessed the damage to see if it was within her skills to mend. But that wasn't what Keet wanted to hear.

"I can. *If* you let us go."

Keet snorted, raising a fist to her mouth as if Dahlia had said something ridiculous. Heat rose in Dahlia's cheeks. *What did she expect me to ask for?*

"Don't you know how much you're worth?" asked Keet. She didn't wait for Dahlia to guess at the amount. "Thirty-thousand gilvers. Thirty. Thousand." She said the last two words slowly, emphasizing the weight of them.

Dahlia didn't care. "Is that worth more than your friend's watch?"

Keet stood, arms crossed, dropping her teasing smile. "You're the prisoners here, you're not supposed to be bargaining for anything. How about you fix his watch, and be grateful we let you out of the brig long enough to do it?"

"Do you really want to trust me with his watch?" Dahlia crossed her arms to match Keet. Fear flickered in her pulse, but anger was stronger. She had been shot at, manhandled by a cyborg, hauled onto an airship, stuffed in a reeking cell, and now they wanted her to be grateful for the experience. *I don't think so.* "If I get my hands on that cyborg's watch right now, I'm going to smash it."

"I'd like to see you try."

"I'd like to see you stop me."

Keet's eyes narrowed. "You—"

A loud cough from Tiberius split their argument. Metal screeching on metal, human lungs protesting from somewhere deep within the cyborg's armor. All heads turned to him as he coughed again and again, the sound echoing from bulkheads and panels, filling the too-small room. Dahlia tried to ignore him (as much as anyone could ignore an eight-foot-tall cyborg). She was too busy putting together a few choice phrases to use in her argument once he quieted down.

Keet placed a hand on Tiberius' forearm, shouting to make herself heard. "You okay?"

He nodded. Then he shook his head as another wave of coughing rattled his panels. Keet waited, her fingers pale and tight on his arm. The aggression was slowly leaking out of her features as she watched him, and by the time he fell silent it had vanished.

No one spoke for a moment.

"That'll stop if I repair his watch," said Dahlia.

Keet and Tiberius exchanged a look. The cyborg's face revealed nothing to Dahlia, but Keet must have understood something in the yellow eyes. "Fine." Keet threw up her hands. "You know what? If you fix it, we'll let you go."

Dahlia blinked in surprise. Something was wrong; she hadn't expected the bounty hunters to give in that easily.

A hand touched Dahlia's back and Farren stepped up beside her, a scent of blood and leather. "Port Argun," he murmured.

"And," added Dahlia, "We want free passage to Port Argun."

Keet sighed deeply, running her hands over her face so they pulled at the bottoms of her eyelids. The effect was ridiculous. Mocking. "That's not how negotiation works. You can't just add things whenever you want."

Plans whirled through Dahlia's head, ideas flashing into being and then discarded. She half-wished Farren would say something.

No. This is my responsibility. It's my papa we're going to Port Argun for, and I'm the one who can get us out of this.

But what did she have to bargain with? Nothing, besides repairing Tiberius' watch.

Maybe that's all I need.

"I won't be able to fix it with the parts I have in my kit," said Dahlia. The lie burned hot across her lips. "Respiratory problems point to a broken balance wheel. That can throw off the harmonic oscillation that controls the resonant frequency of the watch."

She was met with blank stares.

"It's very bad," she explained. "I don't have any balance wheels, but I'm willing to examine it here and make some temporary repairs. Port Argun will have the parts I need. If you take us there, I can repair it completely."

"Deal." Keet stuck out her hand. "But if you're coming with us to Port Argun, then you're helping us nab the bounty we were going to pick up on the way."

Dahlia shook her hand before she could withdraw the offer. Keet grinned.

"Excellent," she said, "Tiberius, if you don't mind taking the wheel, I'll show these two to the guest room."

* * *

The airship was cramped and practical—barely large enough for Tiberius' wide shoulders. Everything was steel gray. Keet retrieved Dahlia's backpack from a closet nearby, then led them on a tour of the open area that served as a kitchen, dining room, and living room. There was a closet-sized medical bay and an office papered with wanted posters. A repair area overflowed with tools and scrap metal.

Keet had perked up considerably once the negotiations were over. "Engine room, hangar, and brig are aft—those are employees only—" she winked at them "—and down that hall is me and Tiberius' room. The gangway where you came in is back by the bridge. And right over here is our guest room."

She wrenched open a steel door leading from the living room.

"It sticks a bit, so you'll have to put some muscle into it. What do you think? The *Wayfarer Elizabeth* isn't much, but she's enough."

Dahlia peeked inside the room and saw more of the steel décor she had come to expect. She could deal with that. Her acceptance turned to dismay an instant later.

There's only one bed.

Her agitation must have shown on her face when she turned, because it set Keet laughing.

"Is there…" Dahlia felt her face redden. "Is there

another guest room? Another bed, perhaps?"

"Oh no!" Keet chuckled, rolling up a sleeve that had started to inch down toward her hand. "I assumed...you mean you two aren't together?"

"No," Dahlia snorted. "Absolutely not."

"It's okay," Farren said sullenly. "I'll sleep in the living room; there's a couch."

She mentally thanked him for nipping the situation in the bud. Run-of-the-mill embarrassment was one thing, but embarrassment on a strange airship in front of a giggling bounty hunter and Farren Reed was quite another.

"Well, I'll leave you two to unpack. I'll be on the bridge if you need me. Oh, and don't mind the spiders."

Keet bounded off. Farren stared after her.

"Well then."

Dahlia shrugged and took Keet's advice, dragging the backpack into the room. It was past time to clean it out; the thing had developed a smell that wrinkled her nose when she opened it.

Farren knocked on the open door.

"Mind if I use your bathroom to wash this off?" He gestured at the bloodstains on his clothing. They had faded to a sick, rusty brown since the previous night.

"Feel free."

He squeezed into the small restroom on the other side of her bed. Dahlia seated herself on the floor beside the backpack, her back to him. Water splashed from the bathroom faucet.

The zippered pockets opened smoothly. Books, bread, canteen, first aid kit, blanket, rope, the burlap sack of sound tape gear, watch repair kit, her clothes...they had forgotten the tesla rifle at the inn yesterday, but they had pistols. Farren's new wardrobe had been abandoned with the cart, apart from one outfit Dahlia had stashed.

"Mr. Reed, I found some fresh clothes for you." She tossed the creased packet backward in his general direction.

"Thanks, sweetheart."

"I don't know how many times I have to tell you not to call me that."

The packet rustled as he picked it up, then closed the bathroom door. Dahlia let out a sigh. It distressed her to have him undressing nearby, despite the fact that they were separated by ten feet of air and a half-inch of steel. She occupied herself with scooping some mysterious moldy thing from the backpack.

Dahlia pulled at her hair and began sorting through their meager supplies. She caught sight of the watch repair kit lying on the floor beside her.

"I would warn you against resurrection..."

Why would her papa say that? Perhaps he'd never had time to iron out all the kinks in his theories. She could finish what he'd started.

She unfolded the leather kit.

Once I have the plans for the resurrection device, I'll have to repair his watch. But how to do it? Her fingers danced over the gleaming instruments, selected one, returned it, and selected another.

If the glass is shattered, I'll need resin to mend that. The gears I might be able to unbend with a flat hammer. Case dents can be beaten out, the mainspring rewound...

Happiness swelled in her as the plan took shape in her head. It wouldn't be easy, that was assured, but any amount of work was worth having her papa back. In a few short weeks they could be back in Sainsbury, restarting their watch repair business and forgetting any of this had ever happened. Sebastian Macall would be only a fading memory.

And Farren...

"Whatcha doin?" Farren leaned over the edge of the bed. She hadn't heard him approach.

"Cleaning." Tools clattered as she snapped the case shut. What business was it of his?

"Ah. Well, I'm gonna go find a liquor cabinet—I've run dry." He slid off the bed, stretched, and ambled toward the living area.

A skittering sound under the bed drew Dahlia's attention. *What the...*

She lifted the edge of the sheet and, to her surprise, found two glowing eyes staring back. A tiny yip escaped her lips.

The mechanical spider was half the size of her palm, all thin legs, winking lights, and glittering lenses. *"Don't mind the spiders,"* Keet had warned. Cautiously, Dahlia lowered the blanket and scooted away to put the gutted backpack between her and the unwelcome arachnid.

"Mr. Reed?"

"Yeah?"

"What do you think of Keet and Tiberius? They could just turn us in once we get to Port Argun. Can we trust them?"

A clatter echoed from the kitchen as Farren began opening and closing cabinets.

"Do you think we have a choice?"

Chapter Fifteen
The Lorikeet and the Cyborg

✴

Dahlia's eyes bulged when she saw Tiberius' watch.

"What did you *do* to it?" she asked, accepting it from his massive hand as he offered it to her.

She sat at a rickety table in the living area, the cyborg seated across from her, and examined the horrible state of his watch.

It was black. The metal had been seared all over, discoloring the watch inside and out. Someone had tried to polish it at one point, but succeeded only in buffing it enough so the time was legible.

"Can you fix it?" asked Tiberius, his voice a low grating that Dahlia didn't think she could ever get used to. A series of hacking coughs followed the question.

"I think so," she said. "Like I said, I'll need a new balance wheel, but I can make temporary repairs now that will stop your coughing until we get to Port Argun."

It was a lie. Dahlia doubted whether she would need any new components to fix the watch, but Tiberius didn't need to know that. These particular repairs were all-or-nothing. She would fix it now, and as long as the bounty hunters *believed* the repair was temporary, they would deliver her safely to Port Argun.

Dahlia unfolded her repair kit under the scrutiny of

Tiberius' yellow eyes, flicked through a few tools, and set to work.

* * *

The *Wayfarer Elizabeth's* bridge was a mess, but Farren didn't care. He leaned against the instrument panel, a few stale crumbs crunching under his feet, and stared out at the rolling farm fields below. Shadows grew under trees beneath the late-afternoon sky. A few mechanical men roamed back and forth across a field of sunflowers, harvesting the seed-filled blossoms, their small forms barely visible from so far above.

This is how the world was meant to be seen.

"Whatcha think?" asked Keet.

Farren glanced at the aviatrix. She sat cross-legged in the pilot's chair, her hands draped languidly over the controls.

"Think of what?"

Keet nodded toward the vista below them, her pink-and-blue hair bobbing.

"I'm thinking this is the way to travel."

Keet laughed. "You and me both. How's Dahlia holding up? Some people get airsick; when Tiberius first started sailing he spent a week in bed barfing his guts out, then one day he got up and was fine."

Farren shrugged. The last time he'd seen Dahlia, she'd been ushering him out of the living area so she could focus on Tiberius' watch. She was feeling well, as far as he knew.

"So Tiberius is your...assistant?" he asked. "Your first mate?"

"I guess you could say that." Keet winked and waved her left hand. A simple silver band glittered on her ring finger. "But it's easier if you just call him my husband."

"Your *husband?* But he's a——"

"Watch it." A cloud passed over her face. "He hasn't always been...like that."

Farren held up his hands. "Sorry. He's just not like anything I've seen before."

* * *

"There. That's all I can do for now."

Dahlia slid Tiberius' watch across the kitchen table. The cyborg picked it up, winding the chain around his massive plated fingers. The formerly discolored metal shone clearly enough for Dahlia to see her tired eyes reflected in it. She'd buffed out the burns, wriggled it open to clean the components as they still functioned, and even applied a protective coating to the scratched face cover. The watch was as good as new.

"How do you feel?" asked Dahlia.

He inhaled experimentally, pulling air past the slotted grille covering the lower half of his face. His breaths were smooth.

Dahlia mentally congratulated herself; her work had bought their freedom.

"Good," Tiberius rumbled. He held up a hand and his palm unfolded, tiny motors whirring and pushing a set of screwdriver heads to the tips of his fingers. These he used to remove the screws securing the largest plate to his chest. It came off easily to reveal a mess of workings inside. Wires, gears, pistons, actuators. A second, smaller set of plates nestled behind the machinery, but these were arranged in a closer approximation of a human body, following the lines of a thin torso and shoulders. If there was any skin underneath, it remained hidden.

Dahlia gawked.

So he really does have a human body under all that.

Tiberius ignored her openmouthed stares, loosening a tiny compartment just above the place where his sternum should be. The watch fit inside. Satisfied, the cyborg replaced his panels and plates. The screwdrivers sank back into his palm in a flurry of deft movements and clicking.

Dahlia tore her eyes away from them.

"I have a few questions."

"No."

Tiberius pushed himself to his feet, the table creaking under his weight.

"How did you make all that?" asked Dahlia. The mechanic in her remembered the arrangements of his machinery, trying to puzzle out the power trains. "And why? I mean, I can understand the protection must be useful, but—"

"No. Help me cook dinner."

* * *

"You're gonna love Lawson's Ridge," Keet said, grinning. "It's an airship town, plenty of trade. People from all over the continent go there when they need to buy or sell…or disappear."

She leaned on the instrument panel, tracing shapes in the air with her hands for Farren's benefit.

"The docks are on the top level so the ships can access it. Then below that you have the restaurant area—there's a place there with the best bacon I've ever had. Then below *that*—"

Her forearm whacked a lever, sending a piercing alarm shrieking to the tune of a flashing light above the instrument panel. Farren nearly jumped out of his skin. The ship shuddered, a sudden vibration quaking its way through the deck plates.

Keet smacked it back into place with a sigh and the noise stopped as if it had never happened.

"Sorry, emergency buoyancy dump," she shook her head as Farren struggled to control the burst of adrenaline thumping in his head. "I did the same thing last week. Whoever thought to put that lever *there,* of all places…"

A few rust beetles, shaken down from the ceiling, clambered over Farren's shoulders. He brushed them off. Then, to calm himself, he downed what was left of his flask.

I went through that quick.

Alarm bells chimed in his brain; he never used to drink so much. But what was he supposed to do, with his watch ending in twenty-two days?

"Hey," Keet rotated her chair to face him. "You know, I think Dahlia likes you."

Farren's stomach lurched, nearly spewing his precious vodka all over the windshield. He clamped his mouth shut against it.

"L—*likes* me?" he choked.

"Yup, I can tell. Call it womanly intuition." Keet's smile grew as she watched his discomfort. "And you're clearly into her, so why don't you…you know? Make a move?"

"You don't understand," said Farren. "Dahlia isn't like that, she—she'd never want anything to do with me."

Saying it made him feel heavy, but he knew it was true. Keet wordlessly examined him for a few moments, thinking, sparing the occasional glance for the clear sky up ahead. Her gaze made his cheeks burn.

This is stupid.

His mouth opened to profess an excuse for him to leave: he was tired, he needed something to eat, or he wanted to go check up on the other two.

"Kinda easy to see why she doesn't want to be with you," Keet said, serious. "Women hate drunks."

Farren's stomach twisted.

He hated them too.

* * *

"I've never cooked anything before," Dahlia protested as Tiberius handed her a bowl and an armful of ingredients. He offered her an enormous yellow flower-print apron, which she declined.

"Make biscuits."

She stood beside a metal counter along one wall of the living area that doubled as a kitchen. Tiberius had already starting roasting a meticulously-prepared hunk of meat in the oven. The smell suffused through the ship: a delicious blend of spices overlaid with a gamey scent Dahlia couldn't place.

"In my house, we had servants to do the cooking," she said as she sullenly surveyed the bowl.

"Watch," Tiberius rumbled. His giant hands scooped up a paper bag from the counter and dumped flour into the bowl. "Carefully measured."

Dahlia couldn't tell if it was meant to be a joke or not.

"Salt."

She passed him a salt shaker and he tapped some out, then reached for a small box of baking soda.

"How do you know how much to add?" she asked, intrigued by the haphazard process.

"Just know. Stir that."

Stirring sounded simple enough. Dahlia found a large spoon in a drawer below the counter and attacked the mixture. A cloud of flour puffed into the air, settling over her arms and blouse in a fine coating of white.

Tiberius made a sound like scraping metal. Dahlia glared at him in irritation, spoon frozen lest she dirty herself further, wondering what in the world the scraping was supposed to signify. Then he passed her a hand towel and she realized.

"Are you...*laughing* at me?"

He nodded, expressionless yellow eyes unreadable, and patted her shoulder to send up another cloud of flour. Dahlia giggled.

This isn't so bad.

She brushed the rest of the flour off with the towel, flung it at him, and turned to the bowl.

"Alright," she smiled. "Show me how to do the rest."

Chapter Sixteen
Storytelling

✳

Farren sat atop the *Wayfarer Elizabeth's* peeling hull high above rolling farm fields. The ship pitched ever so slightly underneath him, almost like it was breathing. Half a bottle of purloined whiskey languished in his hand.

Up here, staring down at the world, it was easy to pretend he wasn't part of it. To pretend he knew nothing of weary roads, broken legs, or watches whose every tick meant one less beat of his heart. The sun set in the west, sinking lazily into rows of crops like a massive eye closing. He stared at it as long as he could before blinking the spots from his vision. That was calmness too. He thought of nothing, and felt nothing but a familiar bliss from the alcohol in his blood.

A light wind caressed his hair, the warmth a lover's touch. Whiskey sloshed back and forth lazily inside the glass bottle. He drank and lay back. A few bright stars winked at him, bravely speckling the firmament above.

How many more times would he watch the sun go down atop an airship? Would this be the last? What things had he already done for the last time?

He wouldn't miss the camaraderie of his fellow aviators, the frantic air battles, or the feasts on holidays. Wouldn't miss laughing over a prank with his best friend

Harper, or the feeling of drifting off to sleep after a long shift. Wouldn't even miss the worn leather flight jacket and the memories of the father he had barely known.

This is what he would truly miss. Farren's eyes prickled, but he didn't resist the tears. What did it matter, when he was the only one who would ever see them? There was no shame in tears at a farewell. And this, this moment of peace, was the only thing he had worth wishing farewell to.

This, and Dahlia.

Her dark face came into his mind unbidden, flitting among the receding sun spots. She was hiding under the bush beside him, their faces inches from one another. She was shielding the failed bounty hunter's watch from Farren's murderous intent. She was crying in front of their campfire in the forest, sadness glistening on her cheeks. Farren had the sudden urge to reach out and wipe away the tears. It was an advance he knew she would never accept, but he envisioned it all the same.

He stared into the darkening sky and thought of how her black hair swayed when she walked. Like waves in a nighttime sea. It framed her features in a delicate curtain that Farren longed to touch.

He sat up and rubbed his face. *What am I doing?* The bottle of whiskey felt accusingly light in his hand. Shameful. No wonder she didn't like him. He had drank more in the past week than he normally did in a month, and he hated it, drowning himself in alcohol because he couldn't face the time on his watch.

Coward.

Dahlia could never have feelings for him—why would she? He was slowly slipping away, drinking through his last days in a haze of sorrow and hope for things that could never be. That was no way to die.

Farren stared at the bottle, tilted it this way and that to catch the last rays of sun on the golden liquid inside. Then he hurtled it from the airship.

The glass didn't sparkle or shine as it fell. It arced, tumbling to earth silently, without fanfare.

I've had enough of that to last the rest of my life.

Farren shook as he stood, but from what he couldn't tell. Staring at the spot where the whiskey had landed, his thoughts tangled, he began the uneven climb back down to the gondola.

* * *

"Venison!" crowed Keet. "There's no finer meat, and no finer chef on the whole continent!"

She gestured at Tiberius, who stood stoically by the stove holding a pair of tongs and a spatula. A flower-print apron strung around his waist completed the spectacle. It would have been a gross understatement to say the cyborg looked out of place in a kitchen.

Dahlia stood beside him, grinning, a smattering of flour streaking her blouse. She wiped her face and some of the flour transferred itself to her cheek.

"Tiberius shot a deer a few days ago outside Blackton. Spectacular hunting over there, isn't it, darling? Whoops!"

Farren caught the plate as it slipped from a pile in Keet's arms. She had already sent one glass to the trash in splinters.

"Thanks!" The stack clattered when she set it down. "It's funny, I can snipe a target from a thousand yards, but I can't get the hang of these homey things."

"That *is* funny," Farren said, more for the sake of speaking than anything. He was coming to realize that Keet's conversations consisted mostly of, well, Keet talking.

I guess she has to make up for Tiberius' quietness somehow.

Dahlia sat down across from Farren at the rickety table, watching the two Hawkins finish preparing the meal. Farren resisted the urge to wipe the flour from her cheek.

There was no autopilot on the *Wayfarer Elizabeth*. The bounty hunters dealt with the unmanned bridge by tethering the ship to an oak tree below. Crude, but effective.

"What do you want to drink?" Keet asked. She stuck her head in the cool box. "We have water, chilled lemon tea, coffee, whiskey, beer… Take your pick."

"Water," Farren said hastily. Dahlia stared at him in disbelief.

Good. Let her be surprised.

"Lemon tea would be wonderful," said Dahlia.

Farren didn't allow himself to relax until the venison was steaming on the table. Tiberius was indeed an excellent cook, and the taste served as a welcome distraction from the swiftly-receding buzz in Farren's head.

"So, Keet." Dahlia turned to her and dabbed the corner of her mouth with a napkin. "You introduced yourself as Beatrice, but you call yourself something very different. I'm interested to learn where you got the nickname."

She was revealing the mannerisms of her high-class upbringing now that she was in a situation to which they could be applied. Farren would have felt awkward if their other companions hadn't been rough bounty hunters.

"I hated the name Beatrice. It's so…standoffish, you know?" Keet took a bite, continuing the story between chews. "So when I was a little girl, I found a picture of this bird in a book. It was the most colorful critter I'd ever seen. A lorikeet. After that I told everyone to call me Lorikeet, but that was too long, so I shortened it to Keet."

"A lorikeet? I've never heard of that," Farren said.

"It lives in the Southern Lands. In forests with trees that have leaves as big as this table."

The conversation died away and they returned to their food. Much to Farren's surprise, Tiberius ate with them. Every time the cyborg took a bite, he lifted his hinged face grille and the food disappeared inside. The metal creaked each time he did it. Farren found the process both fascinating and unnerving.

Close by, the scratching of a mechanical spider echoed in the silence. Dahlia had warned him about the arachnids, claiming there had been one in her room, but when she attempted to show him the creature was nowhere to be found.

He cleared his throat.

"So, how'd you two come by the *Wayfarer Elizabeth*? It must've cost a fortune."

"Ah, ah, ah." Keet leaned back in the chair, her plate clean. "I answered one of your questions. Now you have to answer one of mine."

"I wasn't aware this was a game."

"Everything is a game, Farren." Keet folded her hands behind her pink-and-blue hair. She still smiled, but something in her tone warned Farren that their frivolous conversation had taken a serious turn. "Tell me: How does a deserter from the Anglian air force—from the *Imperial Might* no less—come to be strolling along a country road in Delmar with the daughter of Ansel Walker, who was the most wanted man on the continent?"

She tipped her chair back on two legs and took a sip of beer. Her calculating eyes studied him over the edge of the glass.

"Now, I'm not sure I feel like telling you that." Farren set down his fork.

"It doesn't matter to me whether you feel like it or not. You're not in charge here. In fact...I'd say you're at a disadvantage."

Keet tilted her head toward Tiberius. The cyborg halted his meal operation to train his yellow gaze threateningly on Farren.

"I'll tell you." It was Dahlia who spoke. "But you have to answer something for me afterward."

"Fair enough."

Dahlia sighed deeply and began. Her story started before she met Farren, with Sebastian Macall murdering her father. She kept that part simple, glossy and unfocused, and it struck Farren how painful this had to be for her.

Her father died less than a week ago. Sure, she's going to resurrect him, but still...

"Then I found Farren lying on the side of the drainage canal. And...why *were* you lying on the side of the drainage canal?"

Farren blinked, caught off guard by the abrupt question.

"Why was I...?" He rubbed the stubble on his chin sheepishly. "Well, General Macall pushed me out of a flier."

"He *pushed* you?"

"I was drunk, okay? I was picking him up from, well, I suppose it was your house, and I said something stupid and...he pushed me."

"Oh."

There was a pause, and Dahlia continued her narration. She covered the important points, with Farren chipping in on occasion.

But not once did she mention what she had told Farren that night by the campfire. The perpetual zero on her watch, the soldiers shooting her, the bullet scars on her chest...those details she carefully skirted.

"And that's when we saw the *Wayfarer Elizabeth*," Dahlia finished. "I trust you can take it from there."

"Indeed." Keet deposited the last few drops of beer on her tongue. Farren's stomach squirmed. "What do you think, darling? Interesting yarn."

Tiberius nodded creakily.

"I don't disapprove of your feud with Macall. In fact, I'd like to see him taken down a peg. He rarely sends out bounties and his reputation among his soldiers is dirt poor."

Keet leaned over the table and folded her hands.

"But I think I should tell you: You'll never take back that research he stole. That man's an army unto himself. A girl with no combat experience and an aviator with a broken leg are no match for him. He'll carve you up. And he'll enjoy doing it."

I knew it. Macall's too much for her. I can get her inside the base, but there's nothing I can do when it comes to him.

"Thanks for the warning." Dahlia stared across the table into Keet's eyes. The challenge was palpable. "We know the risks."

"And you're still going after him?" The bounty hunter gave a whistle of feigned shock. "I can't decide if you're heroes or fools."

"Fools," Tiberius rumbled.

Farren started at the sound of the cyborg's voice. He managed to disguise the jerk of surprise as a violent cough. The echo of Tiberius' insult died away in the cramped room. For a few moments, no one moved. Then Keet pushed back her chair, gathered up her dishes, and dumped them in the wash basin. The clink of glass on metal broke the tension left after Tiberius' words.

"Now, Dahlia. You wanted to ask me something?" Keet rolled up the sleeves of her coveralls and began scrubbing at a plate, her back to them.

"Oh, yes," Dahlia cleared her throat. "You said my father is…was…the most wanted man on the continent. Are you sure it was him? I find it hard to believe he was wanted at all."

Farren recognized the careful tone. It was the same one she'd used when he'd wasted her money on chocolate.

Keet laughed, dropped a plate in the tub, and splashed soapy water on her clothes.

"Goddammit. I hate dishes." She rubbed at the soaking patch of fabric. It did no good, and she abandoned the effort.

"I'm quite sure. Ansel Walker—I never met him, but I'd recognize him in an instant. I've looked at his wanted poster so many times. He was worth ten times what you are."

"I don't believe it." Dahlia sat rigid in her chair. Farren glanced back and forth between the two women, feeling like he was intruding on something private.

"Believe it. His bounty wasn't widely circulated—I don't think Bespalov wanted to risk tipping him off. They only gave his information to bounty hunters who were skilled enough to handle it." Her chest puffed out with pride as she turned, finished with the cleaning. "The sheet's still hanging in our office. I can show it to you if you like. It needs to come down now anyway."

Farren thought that would be the last straw for Dahlia's restraint. The words themselves weren't offensive, but Keet's flippant tone made it clear Ansel Walker's death was nothing more than a mild inconvenience: tearing down a picture to redecorate.

"What was he wanted for?" Dahlia asked.

"Theft, of course. And treason. King Bespalov didn't share the particulars, but I do know this." Keet leaned back against the countertop, crossing her arms over the water stain on her coveralls. "Ansel stole some sort of research. He was one of Anglia's top time scientists. Worked in General Macall's department doing experiments for the military. When he ran away with your mother, he took all his work with him. I imagine the Anglians must have been rather keen to have it back."

A clatter ricocheted from the metal bulkheads. Dahlia stood ramrod-straight, quaking, chair toppled behind her.

"That's a lie! My papa would never do such a thing!"

Her tan skin flushed pink with fury, hair darting with every pronounced twitch. She looked like she might snap Keet in two given the slightest provocation.

"Go check his wanted sheet in the office," teased Keet. "Like I said, it's kinda vague, but there's enough to get the gist of it. Nothing to go breaking innocent chairs over. I'm surprised Ansel didn't tell you any of this."

"I don't need to see his wanted sheet."

Dahlia bent down and righted the chair, slamming the legs down with more force than was necessary. She glanced about as if looking for a way out. But in the confines of the airship, there was nowhere to escape to. Farren recognized the feeling. He felt the same way every time he looked at his watch.

"Dahlia." He eased to his feet, speaking as he would to a frightened animal. "Come on, let's go get some fresh air."

It was only when her eyes fixed on his extended hand that he realized he'd been offering it to her.

Put it down, you moron. She doesn't want your grubby hand.

"Fresh air would be wonderful," she said.

Farren led the way out of the living room with his hands tucked firmly into the pockets of his flight jacket. Dahlia stalked after him.

* * *

"See? It's safe." Farren dangled from a handhold on the *Wayfarer Elizabeth's* hull. A trail of disused ladder rungs ran to the top of the airship, starting outside the hatch where he and Dahlia had boarded. It was the only way up.

"It is most certainly *not* safe, Mr. Reed." Dahlia remained inside, sticking her head out to observe Farren's antics. "Get back in here before you fall and smash your watch. You were lucky once—better not push it."

Farren rolled his eyes and swung feet-first back through the hatch. He somersaulted on the landing, intending to spring up and impress Dahlia with his acrobatics. But the expensive brace caught on his right pant leg, locked his feet together, and catapulted him facedown onto the deck.

Why? Why me?

Embarrassment heated his aching cheeks against the cool metal. Dahlia giggled.

"Have you been drinking again?"

Farren flipped over and sat up, grinning and adopting an 'I did that on purpose' expression.

"Believe it or not, no, I haven't. I'm stone cold sober, sweetheart."

Dahlia tilted her head.

"Did you run out?"

"I've quit."

She sat down, back to the wall. A few stray black hairs caught on the uneven steel panels and stayed there, fluttering in the wind. Farren sat against the opposite wall, his outstretched feet a few inches from hers.

"Why would you quit? I thought…I thought you liked being drunk. I thought it helped you, you know…forget."

"It did. But…" *It was cowardly. It was making me hate myself. It was no way to live.* "It was stupid."

He wondered if she'd caught the pause, if she'd sensed the unsaid things clamoring behind it. She gave no indication that she had.

Dahlia cleared her throat.

"I'm not sure how to say this, but I guess I'm proud of you." It was her turn to blush. "That can't be easy."

A warm glow spread from the center of Farren's chest. The autumn breeze from the hatch was cool, but he hardly noticed. Dahlia Walker was proud of him. How could this be the same woman who had passionately hated him a few days ago?

"Thanks." He wanted to say more.

Dahlia didn't reply. Her head craned toward the banner of stars visible through the open hatch. She seemed deep in thought, likely about her confrontation with Keet.

Hearing her precious father derided like some common criminal must have been harsh at best. But however much Farren sympathized with Dahlia, Keet's story fit his limited knowledge of the situation. Ansel Walker's name wasn't well-known among the Anglian military. The man had been involved in some sort of scandal twenty-odd years ago. Farren had never been told much about it, and he hadn't cared to ask more. It was one of those things recent enough for the old-timers to remember, but too far in the past for anyone his age to bother with. He must have been only a few years old at the time.

"Do you know that star?" Dahlia pointed out into the night. Farren's eyes followed the curve of her arm.

"There are a lot of stars out there."

"The really bright one. See, look."

She skittered across the deck until she could point from beside him. Her hand hovered near his face, trying to show him precisely which pinprick of light she was indicating. Farren's heartbeat accelerated at her closeness.

"That one there. Do you know it?"

Farren looked.

"The Pathfinder Star? 'Course I know it. Navigation's one of the first things you learn in flight school, and the Pathfinder Star's one of the first things you learn in navigation."

Dahlia lowered her arm, sliding back to her spot on the wall across from him. Moonlight shimmered in her eyes.

"It shows you which way is north."

"That it does, sweetheart." Farren reached into the pocket of his jacket for the flask before remembering it was gone. His fingers brushed his watch.

I should check it again. It's been a few hours. But he left it alone. There was something special about this moment, something that would be extinguished if he did.

Dahlia sat there, elbows resting on knees, long skirt tickling her ankles. Black hair tumbled down her back. Her face was calm, neither frowning nor smiling, and she breathed gently. Farren wondered what she was thinking, whether it was painful or peaceful, light or dark. Perhaps he would never know. He clung to the idea of her, the image of her sitting there, the unspoken possibilities whispered away into the night.

Chapter Seventeen
Betrayal

✳

Suds and dirty dishwater tickled Keet's elbows as she stood over the sink, scrubbing food from the plates. She loathed housework. But water was hard on Tiberius' mechanical joints, and washing dishes was easier than scraping rust from his components.

"They didn't even finish their food. Rude, aren't they, darling?"

Keet talked simply to fill the air. She and Tiberius used to chatter together every hour of every day, until the *Wayfarer Elizabeth* brimmed over with their noise. But not since Tiberius transformed into a cyborg. Damaged vocal cords made talking difficult and painful. Worse still, his voice no longer sounded like that of Tiberius Hawkins.

Plates rattled as she placed them back into the cupboard. They didn't have many, and there was scant furniture to hold them, but they made do.

"What do you think of them? Of Dahlia and Farren?" Keet toppled onto the threadbare couch in the corner of the room. The cushions sank under her weight.

Tiberius rose from the table and clanked over to join her. A groan of complaint issued from the couch as he sat.

"They don't know what they're doing," he said.

"I agree. They seem kinda…unprepared. I think we're

making the right choice, turning them in at the bounty hunting office in Port Argun."

Keet took one of his massive segmented hands in both of hers and felt the cool metal. The artificiality of it. The myriad of mechanical vibrations thrumming through Tiberius' components, harmonizing with the steady beat of a human heart. It was sad. She was sad for it every waking moment, but it didn't make her love him any less.

"Dahlia will fix your watch the rest of the way. We walk away with another thirty-thousand gilvers in our pockets and they keep their lives, albeit in captivity. It's a better deal than they'd get if they fought the General head-on."

One heavy, plated arm reached out to pull her close. Keet pried her boots off and swung her feet onto the couch beside her so she could snuggle into his side. The heartbeat sounded stronger there, with her ear pressed against his chest armor.

"Dahlia is fixing my watch," Tiberius said.

"I know," said Keet. "And I'm grateful. But it only makes sense."

Tiberius was quiet, turning the idea over in his mind.

He's always been the nobler one.

"We'll have them help us catch Harold Grimes," she said. "He'll be a tough target. Then we'll take them to Port Argun and hand them over to the military. It's simple, sweet, and we come out ahead in every way."

Tiberius nodded. "Alright."

They sat together in silence for a while, listening to the sounds of the airship. A breeze puffing beyond the porthole glass, the rudder creaking, water dripping from a leaky sink. Tiny skittering claws heralded a mechanical spider making its rounds. The spiders were Keet's invention, designed to monitor the *Wayfarer Elizabeth's* engineering systems. They served a second, incidental, purpose as investigative devices. They could crawl into small spaces, search for targets, and report their findings. Such a capability was invaluable for bounty hunting operations.

Farren and Dahlia were nowhere to be seen. Keet guessed their guests had wandered to the gangway, or perhaps even outside the envelope. Farren seemed like the type who might be drawn to that.

Finally, she yawned and stretched.

"What say we head off? I'll take the first shift and set a course for Lawson's Ridge. The latest rumors say Harold Grimes is holed up there. A two-thousand gilver bounty for murder in Port Argun. Do you mind pulling up the anchor cable before heading to bed?"

"Of course not. Wake me when you get tired."

"I'll wake you halfway through the night, and not a minute sooner." Keet tapped his face grille with her nail. "You need your rest just as much as I do."

Tiberius embraced her tenderly, as if holding a baby bird. Every movement near her was careful: the actuators in his circuitry were built to break bones, not to cherish them.

"Good night, Keet."

"Night, darling."

Chapter Eighteen
A Dip into the Past

✳

Dahlia didn't open her bag until she could hear Farren snoring from the living room. There had been so much excitement lately—the attack at the inn, allying with Keet and Tiberius—that the sound tapes had dropped low on her list of priorities. But not now. Now she wanted answers.

The sound tape marked with a scratched number two consisted of Ansel detailing how promethium worked to fuel time transfer and resurrection. *I'm not interested in that right now.* She sealed it back in its canister and moved on to the third one.

"Hello, sweetie," said her papa. "I think it's about time I told you something about your mother, and about my past."

Dahlia lay atop the ragged blankets, head on her pillow, the music box resting on her chest. This was what she wanted.

"Understand that some of this—a lot of this—I'm not proud of. But these things are going to affect you, and you have the right to know."

Her papa cleared his throat as if preparing to deliver some unwelcome news. Dahlia steeled herself; whatever he said, she was determined not to think less of him. The memory of Ansel's smiling face burned behind her eyelids whenever she closed them.

"I haven't always been a watch repairman. I started my career as a time researcher working for Anglia's military. We worked on...special projects. Time transfer, resurrection theories, anything that could give our soldiers the advantage. Anglia's always been imperialistic, and they needed the best technology in order to expand. By the time I was in my early thirties I was one of the most respected scientists there.

"That's when I met your mother."

* * *

"Everyone, I'd like you to meet Sita Sen...Sen..."

"Senguptar," she said. "Sita Senguptar."

"Thank you," Jacob, the manager of the time research branch, nodded to her in appreciation. "Sita's the newest member of our team. She's come all the way from the Southern Lands to research time with us. I hope you'll all make her feel welcome."

Sita smiled, not bothering to correct Jacob on her country's name. Every Anglian she had met called Janmasthala 'the Southern Lands.'

She stood before a group of two-dozen scientists clustered near the entrance to what she assumed was their office. Clad in white lab coats and standing in a sterile white room, they looked dull compared to the plethora of color she was used to in the labs in Janmasthala.

"Ok, everyone," Jacob clapped his hands. "Back to work. The small crowd dispersed slowly, some introducing themselves to her as they passed. Jacob pulled one man aside.

"Ansel, are you busy today?" he asked. "Mind showing Sita around, finding her a lab coat, that sort of thing?"

"Sure," said the man, nodding a head messy with unkempt brown hair.

Jacob retreated into his office, leaving Sita alone with the man. She wondered how she must look, standing there fresh off a spice trader from Janmasthala, tan-skinned and black-haired, feeling stiff in a new suit instead of her favorite *sari*.

"Ansel Walker." The man extended his hand. His eyes were friendly, curious. "Nice to meet you, Sita."

"Likewise." They shook hands. It was an unfamiliar gesture, but Sita loved how warm his fingers felt in hers.

* * *

The following day, Sita stood in Ansel's lab while he explained their experimental processes.

"Right now I'm doing watch movement energy studies. I'm applying various energy sources to these watches here—" he gestured at a bare metal table, atop which lay dozens of labeled watches, "—and recording the effects."

Sita picked one up and pried it open with a fingernail. Her breath caught.

"This is a dead watch. Are they all like that?"

"Yes. It's easier to use watches from people once their time has run out. Of course, we can only study resurrection with these. For time transfer, where we need a living subject, we use criminals or prisoners of war."

The watch clicked as she returned it to the table. Experiments on living human beings? She'd heard Anglia had a strange approach to time studies, but this was something else.

It's not right.

She forced herself to swallow her disapproval before it

showed on her face. She'd come here to do research, and that's what she would do.

"So, Sita," Ansel began, busying himself with electrical cords behind a machine. "I've never met anyone from the Southern Lands before. What brings you to Anglia?"

Sita bit her lip, holding back from correcting him. She hadn't heard anyone in Anglia refer to her homeland as Janmasthala, and it bothered her. But she had to be polite.

Her eyes surveyed the room. Antiseptic white walls, white tiles, watch innards scattered on tables. For a moment, her heart ached for home. The comforting sound of a breeze ruffling banana leaves outside her laboratory window. The sharp, crisp scent of curry drifting from street stalls. The mechanical peacock calling out the time above her desk. And, most of all, the warm happiness of returning home to her mother and sisters at the end of each day.

"I wanted to research time," she said. "In my country, we study time in a different way than you do. I want to bridge the gap in our understandings."

She forced herself to smile. Ansel's cheeks turned red and he dropped the end of a cord. She laughed, her unhappiness gone in an instant.

I can do this. I can work here.

Ansel's face burned with embarrassment as he bent to pick up the cord.

"You're funny, Mr. Walker."

"Ansel. Just call me Ansel."

"Very well, Ansel."

* * *

A week later, Lieutenant Colonel Sebastian Macall visited the laboratories.

"He normally commands troops at the front," Jacob

explained as he and Sita walked through the low labyrinth of walls that formed their individual offices. "But he was wounded and had to come back here for a while to recover. Don't tell him I told you that...he's a proud man, the Lieutenant Colonel."

Sita nodded her understanding.

"He doesn't usually come to the labs," Jacob said. "But he said he wanted to meet you."

"Me? Why?"

Jacob shrugged and pushed open the door to his office. Macall was sitting on a chair inside. He rose when they entered, somehow managing to make the simple movement graceful. Fluid. He wore a crisp black uniform accented with bright medals, gold cuffs, and shoes that gleamed. The only thing out of place was the sling supporting his left arm.

Sita found him quite handsome.

"Lieutenant Colonel Macall," he said, extending a hand. "You must be Miss Senguptar."

"Yes," she said, then added. "Sir."

She took his hand, hoping he wouldn't notice the nervous sweat coating her fingers. His reassuring smile told her he had.

"It's an honor to finally meet you, Miss Senguptar. The science division has been buzzing about you for days. We've never had an employee from the Southern Lands."

"Janmasthala," she said, and instantly regretted it. Out of politeness, she'd tried to hold back from correcting Anglians since she arrived, but now she'd done it anyway.

"What?"

Sita reddened. Explaining it only called attention to her rudeness.

"We call it 'Janmasthala' where I'm from. In your language, it translates to 'birthplace.'"

Macall tilted his head. Something halfway between

interest and humor shone in his eyes.

"I've never heard that," he said. "You've certainly traveled a long way—why did you come to Anglia?"

"To research time. In Janmasthala we study it one way, but in Anglia you study it another. I wanted to combine our approaches. If we use the knowledge from both our countries, I think we can learn so much more about time. Perhaps even how to change it."

Sita found herself smiling. This was what she'd worked for; this was the ambition that had prompted her to cross seas and continents. Sebastian blinked, taken aback by her passion.

"What an admirable goal."

"It's my dream." Her eyes sparkled and she laughed.

The corners of Sebastian's mouth rose.

"I'd love to hear more, Miss Senguptar," he said. "Perhaps you'd care to join me for dinner tomorrow evening?"

Sita's heart skipped a beat.

"That sounds wonderful."

* * *

"What happened to your arm, Mr. Macall? If you don't mind me asking." Sita nodded at his sling.

She and the Lieutenant Colonel sat at an officer's restaurant on the military base, examining the menus. It was crowded for a weeknight. Still, they'd managed to secure a table on the outdoor patio. The evening was perfect: a warm summer breeze, the comforting wash of conversation, and the promise of a fantastic sunset. Tiny mechanical fireflies twirled above their heads, their incandescent bulbs winking on and off.

"Call me Sebastian, please. It's nothing. I was shot

during a skirmish near the border."

"You were shot!"

"Yes. It's not the first time, and I'm sure it won't be the last. But I'll be away from the front for a few months at least."

"That's terrible! Does it hurt?"

Her concern made Sebastian blush. The shoulder pained him, but he would never tell her that.

"Not at all."

"I'm glad," she said with genuine relief.

They ordered and made small talk over their food, remarking on the weather, the news, their work. Sebastian tried not to stare at her. Sita wore a cinnamon-colored wraparound dress, tinkling gold bracelets, and a necklace carved in the shape of a lotus flower. Her hair hung in a fresh braid to the small of her back. Sebastian wondered how long it had taken her to prepare for dinner, and marveled that she had devoted so much care to her appearance just to meet him. Was she as interested in him as he was in her?

"How does Anglia compare to the Southern L—to Janmasthala?" Sebastian asked, picking at the steak on his plate. "It must seem so strange."

"Have you been to Janmasthala?" Sita asked.

"No. And I don't know anyone who has. I've never even *heard* of someone traveling there, besides the odd spice merchant."

"No one I knew back home had ever been to Anglia, if that makes you feel any better." She winked. Sebastian's heart froze for a moment. "The biggest difference is the weather. It's so much colder here. But that's not what I notice most."

Sita glanced around conspiratorially, then waved him close. The two of them leaned over the table so she could whisper:

"What I notice most is…shoes!"

"Shoes?"

She giggled at his blank look. "Everyone goes barefoot in Janmasthala unless there's a reason not to. Here you have shoes for fighting, shoes for walking, shoes for warm days, shoes for cool days. You even have shoes to wear in your own houses before you go to sleep!"

She sat back in her chair again, then broke out in laughter. Sebastian grinned.

"Look!" Sita struggled to get the words out. "Look at your shirt!"

Sebastian glanced down and discovered his shirt (the best dress uniform he owned) had been pressed against his plate when he leaned forward. The steak had left an obvious impression, with mashed potatoes clinging to the edges.

It was too hilarious to be embarrassing. He joined her mirth, roaring with laughter as he scraped the potatoes off with a fork. That only made her laugh all the harder. Tears rolled down her cheeks. Customers at other tables watched curiously, but Sebastian couldn't have cared less.

* * *

They had dinner together again the following week, the one after that, and the one after that. Sebastian took Sita away from the base and showed her the city. Months passed. There were dances, lunches, museums, secret nights under the stars. They held hands at public functions, kissed at every socially acceptable opportunity. Sita was infatuated with him. His unwavering devotion was the envy of every couple they met.

But though Sebastian Macall was her lover, Ansel Walker was her confidant. They worked long days in the laboratory, testing and creating the most advanced time technology. Always searching for some way, some secret by which they could affect the passage of time. They talked between experiments. Sita discussed her feelings for Sebastian, but also her doubts.

"He's so sweet to me, but he's so protective," she said one evening as they worked late. "Yesterday he hit a man who whistled at me on the street. His nose was bleeding, maybe even broken. I don't think he'd ever hurt me, but sometimes he scares me."

Ansel carefully extracted a watch from an energy delivery machine. He reached into the unit with a pair of wooden tongs. They had built the machine by hand, which meant it didn't always provide the most reliable operation. The tongs protected Ansel in case the current arced.

"Well, he *is* a soldier," Ansel said. "Battle is ingrained in his personality. Not saying I approve—I don't—but that could be why."

The watch emerged singed black. It slipped from the tongs onto the metal table. Ansel opened it.

"What does it say?" Sita stepped beside him to look and felt her heart sink. Both hands pointed to zero: yet another failed experiment.

"The same thing as always." Ansel sat heavily in a chair and rubbed his face. "There's got to be a way. The theories are sound, I *know* they are. It's the energy source that isn't."

Sita took the watch from his hand and cradled it, staring at it in disappointment. The blackness stained her fingers.

"How about we take a break?" she suggested. "Want some dinner? I think I have some apples in my bag."

"Sure."

Sita stepped out into the dark office area to snatch her bag from beneath a desk. They had been working later and later over the past few weeks, and she'd quickly learned to either bring meals or go hungry.

Ansel had already pried the cover off the burned watch when Sita returned. Dismantling the watches was their standard experimental procedure. Maybe—just maybe—they would find something new inside.

Sita slung her bag onto the table beside the energy delivery machine. "Have something to eat," she started to say. But, just then, the needle on the energy dial twitched.

She blinked. The gauge, which should have pointed at zero, hovered just above twelve joules.

Please don't let it be broken. A faulty machine was the last thing they needed. She hefted her bag aside for a better look, setting it gingerly on the floor nearby so as not to damage the apples.

The gauge sank.

"Ansel!"

"What?"

"Watch this."

Sita brought her bag close to the machine and watched the dial rise again. Away, and it fell.

"Oh my God," breathed Ansel.

They tore apart the bag. The apples had no effect on the dial, neither did Sita's spare pen, her change purse, or her comb. Then she held up her lotus flower necklace and the gauge skyrocketed.

"What's that made out of?" asked Ansel.

"I don't know," Sita said, turning it over and over in her hands. The unassuming yellow-green flower stared back at her, the same as it always had. "My father gave it to me when I was a little girl. He bought it from a traveling merchant."

"Where?" demanded Ansel.

"In Champawat—," Sita said, and hurried to explain.

"The town where I grew up."

"Can we…is it alright if we test it?"

Sita tilted her head. "Why wouldn't we?"

"Well," Ansel rubbed the back of his neck nervously. "I mean, if it's important to you, and we ruin it…"

She laughed. "Believe me, I didn't come all this way to give up just so I could keep my necklace!"

But, inside, she was grateful that he cared enough to ask.

* * *

They spent an apple-fueled night testing, failing, and testing again. They scribbled theories onto the office blackboard. They rigged up a makeshift experimental apparatus to draw power from the stone in Sita's necklace. Then, just as the first rays of sun illuminated the dark circles under their eyes, they rushed down to the government prison for two test subjects.

The King had never been too picky about what was done with criminals. In Anglia, military superiority was the first, second, and third priority. If a few undesirable citizens were sacrificed for the sake of defense research, no one batted an eye.

Except Sita.

"It's not right," she insisted as a policeman escorted them through plain concrete hallways. "We can't ruin someone's life—even for this."

"They ruined their own lives already," said Ansel. He regretted the words the moment they left his mouth. When Sita didn't respond, he placed a comforting hand on her shoulder. "Listen, we'll just try to transfer five minutes. We don't need any more time than that to see if this works."

He hefted the device in his hand: an apparatus designed to hold two watches and Sita's necklace in place. Copper conduits would draw energy from the yellow mineral into the watches to—they hoped—fuel time transfer.

"Alright," said Sita as they passed through a heavy door flanked by two mechanical police dogs. It led to a windowless concrete room. Two men, greasy-haired and clothed in red jumpsuits, sat handcuffed to a table in the center. Their watches lay just out of reach in front of them.

"Don't get too close," warned the guard as he followed them in. The mechanical dogs were close on his heels, their metal claws clicking on the floor.

Sita picked up a watch from the table, her eyes not meeting those of the pale man who owned it. Ansel checked the other prisoner's watch.

"Four years, six months," said Sita.

"This one has twelve years. We'll take from him."

They worked quickly, attaching both watches to the device beside the yellow lotus flower.

"Ready?" asked Ansel, holding the completed contraption. Sita nodded. The prisoners looked on with wide eyes and shaking hands. .

Ansel wound the device, his heart pounding as he saw five minutes drain from the twelve-year watch. But what really mattered was the other one, the one that would prove whether all their hard work had been worth it...

The hand on the pale man's watch jumped by five minutes.

Ansel could hardly breathe. He looked up at Sita, who was grinning, her eyes shimmering with excitement.

"It works," she said. He laughed, the tension in the room suddenly broken.

The smile slid from Ansel's face when he felt the back of the device. He flipped it over, fingers searching for the yellow lotus flower carving that had been secured to it...but it was gone.

"Complete disintegration," Sita noted as she peered over his shoulder.

Ansel nodded.

"We need more."

* * *

Sita and Ansel met with the King soon after the success of their experiment.

"I want you to find more of this," his Highness said when they handed him a packet of data from the yellow lotus stone. "But next time you test it, test it for resurrection, not time transfer. Stealing time isn't enough; Anglia needs immortal soldiers. Men you can resurrect again and again, men who have no fear because death doesn't exist for them."

He passed the packet back to Sita.

"I'll order an expedition to the Southern Lands. Delmar is constructing a number of new airships that will be completed next year; we'll need our entire fleet to counter them. But I can spare you a ship for ten months." Sita felt her face light up.

I'm going home.

A few weeks later, they were aboard the airship *Cannonade* en route to Janmsathala.

Sebastian hadn't cared for the idea of Sita spending a year away from civilization, tumbling about in some dingy old airship. But the discoveries she dreamed of could lie at the end of the quest. There was no question that he would support her, even if he didn't wholly approve. He was being sent to the warfront again and would return in a year, just before the expedition was due back.

On the last night before Sita's departure, they sat together at the outdoor restaurant. Sebastian fidgeted all evening. Then just as they were preparing to order dessert, he knelt before her with a diamond ring.

"I don't know what to say," Sita admitted. "I think...I think I need more time."

"Take all the time you need." He rose and kissed her forehead, tucking the ring bitterly into his jacket. "Perhaps you'll be ready when you return."

There was no doubt in his tone. Once Sita took time to consider the proposal, he was certain she would accept.

* * *

It took thirty days in the old airship to reach Janmasthala. Then came the real work: tracking down the yellow stone. They docked in town after town, meeting with gem experts and digging through traveling merchants' wares. It wasn't until they pulled into a sweaty copper mining town that they found a lead.

"He knows it," said Sita, translating Janmasthalan for Ansel as they talked to a shopkeeper in a busy market. Brightly-dressed people streamed past, some leading mechanical tortoises loaded down with their purchases. A woman plucked music from the strings of a *sitar* while her daughter—a young girl with two artificial legs—danced for coins. They knocked into Sita as she struggled to hear what the little man behind the table full of jewelry was saying. The crowd didn't annoy her, it exhilarated her. She was home.

"We call it 'promethium,'" said the shopkeeper in Janmasthalan. "Very, very rare. I don't have any, but there is this emerald bracelet here—" he pointed at his table "—I can get you a very good price."

"*Shukriyaa*," said Sita. "Thank you, but no. We just need to know about the promethium."

The man nodded, an orange turban bobbling atop his head as he talked. The *sitar* player took a break to help her daughter oil the joints in her mechanical knees.

"A long time ago, many centuries, a great race lived in Janmasthala. They built beautiful cities filled with immortals who never died because they could transfer time—steal it from the common people. As long as there were enough peasants, the immortals could live forever."

Sita smiled pleasantly as he talked, despite the sinking in her chest. Stealing time? Was that all anyone could think to use time transfer for?

But the thrill of being somewhere familiar again soon washed away her doubts. Ansel stood beside her, sweating in his thick Anglian shirt and pants, watching the shopkeeper babble with a look of intense confusion. Sita had the sudden urge to hold his hand.

Instead, she asked, "How did the immortals steal time?"

"Promethium!" said the little man. "It was in the mines under their cities. They dug it and dug it and..." He waved his hands. "Poof. They disappeared."

Sita blinked, taken aback by the abrupt ending. "Why?"

"No one knows. Some people say the peasants revolted, others say the promethium ran out. Adventurers have searched for the promethium mines ever since. They have found empty mine shafts, ancient ruins, and sometimes—sometimes!—a tiny piece. But that is all."

Sita didn't know whether to be excited or worried. They finally had a lead, but if they couldn't find promethium...all their research would be useless. She turned to Ansel and related the story to him. He grinned, reached to hug her, and then seemed to think better of it.

"Sounds like we've got some more work to do."

Sita couldn't help smiling back.

He always knows how to cheer me up.

* * *

Ansel and Sita climbed back into the *Cannonade* and set off in search of an ancient city and its prized promethium mine. They followed lead after lead, dead-end after dead-end. They picked their way through countless ruins and explored every opening in the ground, searching. Finding nothing but miles of worthless stone.

During the long flights, they finalized plans for a resurrection device and constructed a prototype in the *Cannonade's* workshop. They talked as they worked, as they visited villages to ask about the legend, and as they walked through mazes of ruins. They talked in abandoned mines to allay the terror of being surrounded by the infinite dark.

"So," said Ansel one afternoon while Sita led the way out of another promethium-less mine shaft, picking her way gingerly over piles of loose stone, "where do you want to try next? That traveling merchant yesterday said something about old ruins east of Powalgarh—"

Sita's foot suddenly shot out from under her, sliding on a wet rock near the mine entrance. Ansel rushed to catch her. She fell just past his fingertips and hit the ground amid a pile of stones. Her firefly lantern smashed beside her.

"Sita!" he was at her side in an instant. "Are you alright?"

"I'm fine." She gave him a small smile, wiping scratched hands on her skirt. A few mechanical fireflies squeezed out of a crack in her fallen lantern and buzzed off merrily into the dark mine, like shooting stars in a black sky.

Ansel helped her up, but when she put her right foot down the breath hissed between her teeth.

"I think it's twisted," she said in response to his concern. "Don't worry—I can walk it off."

"I don't think so." Without asking, Ansel swept her off her feet and into his arms. Surprise flitted across her face. His stomach churned, sure that he'd crossed a line, but the uncertainty in her eyes was quickly replaced with happiness. A little spark, like something had clicked together.

"Are you sure you can carry me?" she asked. Typical Sita; even when she was hurt she was only worried about him.

"Of course."

He walked them back into the sunlight like that, with Sita's arms around his neck to help distribute her weight. Ansel hoped she couldn't feel his pounding heartbeat.

A disused path outside pointed the way back toward the village where the *Cannonade* drifted at anchor. As they traveled past large-leafed banana trees and groves of teak, Ansel cast about for something to say to break the silence. And to take his mind off the sweet vanilla scent of her hair.

"I'm curious, what got you interested in time research in the first place?" he asked.

It was a question he'd wondered about for a long time. No one packed up and moved to a strange continent on a whim, but he hadn't felt comfortable prying into her personal business...until now.

Sita didn't answer at first, her eyes downcast in thought. Ansel's arms began to burn.

Finally, she spoke, "My parents did."

Ansel nodded in understanding. His own parents had encouraged him to pursue time research from the moment he'd shown aptitude for math and science. It was a prestigious—and lucrative—career.

But Sita continued.

"In Janmasthala, it's traditional for young couples to show each other their watches before committing to…" she shrugged her shoulders, searching for the word "…romance, courting, love. That way, if their times are too different, they can break things off early. A person with fifty years would never marry a person with ten. What would they do for the last forty?"

Ansel spotted a boulder and perched her gently on it, taking the weight off his struggling muscles. Sita massaged her ankle as she went on, "But my mother and father fell in love too quickly, and they wouldn't stop courting even after seeing one another's time. My father said he had fifteen years left when they met. My mother had sixty-three.

"They married anyway. My mother always told me that fifteen years with him was worth spending the rest alone. But I wondered, what if they could have shared their time? If there had been a way for her to even out their years, she would have done it in a heartbeat."

She shrugged as if to brush it off, but Ansel heard the heaviness in her voice.

"My father died when I was twelve."

She fell silent. A few notes of muffled music drifted from the village just beyond the next banana grove. He didn't know what to say. His heart ached for her, but how could he put it into words?

Somehow, his hand found hers.

"I'm sorry," he offered as their fingers intertwined.

The music continued up ahead, loud enough to hear but soft enough so as not to interrupt. Sita stiffened at the tune.

"What?" he asked.

"Oh, just the music," she said. "It's…it's a

Janmasthalan wedding song."

Ansel dropped her hand like it was on fire. Suddenly, the few inches of space between them felt like a canyon.

What am I doing? She's going to accept Sebastian's proposal when we get back.

"Are you going to play it at your wedding?" asked Ansel. "I'm sure Sebastian wouldn't object, but I don't think Anglian orchestras know this song."

Even to his ears, his voice sounded bitter, like he was pushing her away with words.

"I haven't decided," she said.

"You might be able to find a player here who has the music written down."

"I mean, I haven't decided if I'm going to marry him."

"Oh."

Ansel could hardly breathe.

If she doesn't marry him, then...

A breeze ruffled the leaves above them as the music went on, carrying the lilting melody of a woman singing over instruments Ansel had no hope of recognizing. He focused on it in a vain attempt to bring his runaway thoughts under control.

Sita shifted, and Ansel knew she was about to ask if they could continue toward the ship. He opened his mouth to suggest it.

The question dissolved, unasked, when Sita's hand found his.

* * *

A few days later, Sita and Ansel sat in their office aboard the *Cannonade* on their way to the next ruin, poring over maps of Janmasthala and reminiscing about their lives in Anglia.

"Do you remember when the generator arced? And Jacob was so surprised he fell out of his chair?" Ansel chuckled, pantomiming the event.

"Yes!" Sita laughed, half at the memory and half at Ansel's antics. "What about when Dominik fell asleep and we painted his face green?"

"And then Sebastian came through to do an inspection. I've never seen Dom so embarrassed!"

Sita felt the grin slide off her face at the mention of Sebastian. Ansel shifted in his seat, noticing.

"Sita," Ansel said. "What you said about Sebastian the other day…did you…have you thought about it any more?" The night pressed in on the glass porthole pane above their desks.

"Yes." And she had. Exhaustively. Memories of Sebastian offering her the ring intermingled with the warm feeling that flooded her chest every time Ansel laughed. Every time he walked beside her through the old mines, his voice holding back the silence. Every time he watched her, a proud grin on the edges of his lips, while she talked in Janmasthalan.

She looked up into Ansel's face to see his beautiful, brown eyes full of concern. Her decision snapped into place.

"I…I don't think I love him anymore."And then she said it.

"I love *you*, Ansel."

"Sita…" He reached out, hesitated, and held a hand to her cheek. Her skin tingled where his fingers brushed it. "I've always loved you."

They fell into each other's arms.

* * *

Everything felt right from then on. The transition from best friends to lovers was seamless, as if they had known from the beginning they would end up that way. Time rolled by in blissful haze. Ansel found himself less and less concerned with the idea of discovering promethium, and more and more with thoughts of his future with Sita. It was perfect.

"How much time do you have left?" he asked her one day as they sat waiting for a pilot flier. They were resting on piles of stone ruins, sunning themselves after a long day underground.

It was a rude question, a taboo among the people of the continent. Such a fact was shared only with families and loved ones. Ansel hoped he qualified.

"Forty-seven years, the last time I checked. And you?"

"I've got you beat. Fifty, right on the dot."

"I don't know, I think I'm better off." Sita poked him impishly in the shoulder. "You won't die for three years after I do. I, however, will never have to live without you."

"Sounds like the makings of a proposition."

"Maybe." She giggled and kissed him. "We'll see. But I'm thinking yes."

* * *

Ten months into the expedition, the *Cannonade* anchored in Vatana. Ansel and Sita explored the sprawling ruins of the city, touring every inch of the mine shafts peppering the terrain. It was then, deep in a side tunnel at the edge of the city, that they found it.

A vein of crystals glowed in the light of their firefly lanterns. Shimmering, gleaming mysteriously, perhaps triumphantly.

"Do you think…" Sita brushed one with her fingertip

as if to confirm it was real.

"Only one way to find out."

Sita stayed with their discovery while Ansel fetched tools and the test subject from the airship. The subject was the corpse of a young boy—complete with zeroed watch—from their laboratory's morgue. By the time Ansel returned with it, Sita had already chipped away two small pieces of the potential promethium. She sealed one sample in a specimen bag.

"Here," Ansel reached for the second sample. "I'll do it."

"No."

He shot her a curious look and Sita averted her eyes, not wanting him to see her nervousness.

What if he did it and something went wrong?

"I'll just give up five minutes," Sita said. "That's nothing."

She held the resurrection device in one hand. It was small, barely larger than the watches clamped onto it. According to their theories, the resurrector had to sacrifice the time their subject would have to live once reanimated. Sita's watch was secured to the front of the device, and the corpse's to the back. The crystal went inside.

"Ready to take notes?" she asked. Ansel nodded, notepad in hand. "I'll begin in three, two, one."

Sita took a deep breath and wound the device, monitoring her watch to use precisely five minutes. She glanced up at boy's corpse, lying pale and still on a walking platform.

For a moment nothing happened. A sudden—but not unexpected—wave of disappointment washed over her.

Then the boy's eyes snapped open. He blinked

"Sita!" Ansel said, hushed with wonder. "That's it! Promethium."

The former corpse stared back at them without moving his head.

"What…am…" He sat bolt upright and the walking platform shuffled its legs to compensate for the weight shift.

Sita practically leapt with joy. This was it: the culmination of their research, the answer to her dream. Anglian technology had developed the resurrection device, but Janmasthala had yielded the final piece of the puzzle.

Then she looked down at the watches and all her happiness vanished.

"Ansel!"

The time wasn't stopping. Her watch, which had shown nearly five decades, was now at two and falling fast. Fear choked her.

"What's happening?" asked Ansel, leaning toward her and trying to see the watches.

Sita ignored him, scrabbling at the set screws holding her watch in place. She had one decade. Now five years.

Her fingers fumbled in panic.

Two years.

Finally, her watch fell free. It lay in her trembling palm, unreal, unbelievable, the hands settling at eight months.

Sita couldn't speak. This had to be a dream, no, a horrible nightmare… She barely heard Ansel's intake of breath as he saw her watch.

"It…hurts…" The boy, sitting forgotten on the walking platform, spoke again. Sita ignored him. Who cared about their experiment when she had eight months—*eight months*—to live?

"It hurts!" he screamed and snatched Sita's sleeve. She looked now.

Blood poured from the boy's mouth. His eyes bulged, red veins clearly visible against the stark white sclera. Sita shrieked. The child reached for her dress and she stumbled back over the uneven rock. His extended arm bent and twisted unnaturally. Lamplight shone off bare bone.

Ansel grabbed her arm, and they ran.

* * *

Sita counted her heartbeats as she and Ansel lay in bed that night aboard the *Cannonade*, listening to the thrum of the engines carrying them back toward Anglia. Seventy beats every minute. How many beats would there be in eight months? She started to calculate and then stopped herself.

I don't want to know.

She'd already cried, now she simply felt sick. Nausea rolled in her stomach and smothered her thoughts.

Their expedition was over. Failed. There was a flaw in their theories—where, she could not say—but it had drained her scientific spirit just as it had her life. Perhaps resurrection was impossible after all.

The corpse-boy's watch still lay deep in the tunnel where she'd dropped it. She'd seen the time before they ran. The child had been alive, but his watch had never shifted from zero. *Yet another flaw.*

She thought of the tiny promethium crystal still resting in its specimen bag in Ansel's coat pocket. It was all they had salvaged from the mine at Vatana.

Her stomach swirled again and she curled in on herself. Could fear really make people feel this awful? Maybe she'd eaten something bad, or caught a bug from a crowded market, or...

No. It can't be.

Sita rolled out of bed, threw on some decent clothes, and made for the medical bay. A short while later, she had her answer.

* * *

Ansel surfaced from sleep when Sita slipped back under the blankets. He started to ask if everything was all right, then stopped. Things had never been further from all right.

"Ansel?" she whispered.

"I'm awake." He turned to look at her, lying there, her black hair pooling on the pillow. A shaft of moonlight from the porthole lit her face. He felt a tug of affection for the beautiful, intelligent woman beside him.

Eight months.

It hurt to think about it. For a moment, he wished she would let him fall back asleep so he could forget about the world for a few more hours.

"Ansel…" Sita breathed in, held it, and let the rest of her sentence fall out with the exhale. "I'm pregnant."

* * *

The path ahead was clear. If—when—Sebastian learned what had transpired, he would doubtlessly kill Ansel. In the Lieutenant Colonel's mind he and Sita were as good as engaged. Her new relationship would be the ultimate betrayal.

The two of them fled the night the *Cannonade* returned to Port Argun. They commandeered a small airship—quarter-size—and stripped every page of research from the laboratory. If the other scientists ever discovered promethium, they would fall victim to the same terrible flaws in the resurrection theories. Neither Ansel nor Sita would allow that.

Ansel knew their experiments had been sound; the issue had to be with the act of resurrection itself, and if he had been a religious man he would have said it was punishment for meddling in the affairs of God. For delving too deeply into things humans were never meant to see.

* * *

"We escaped over the border to Delmar, but as soon as Sebastian returned from his tour of duty he hunted us." Ansel's voice sounded hoarse as it carried on dejectedly from the music box resting on Dahlia's chest.

"I don't know what he thought had happened—we never told anyone why we ran—but I can only assume he thought I'd kidnapped Sita. He'd never consider that she might abandon him. He chased us across the continent. His superiors approved the missions as military ventures because of the research we stole, the great investment they'd lost. We could never stay in one place for long."

Ansel sighed. Dahlia could picture him recording the tape, sitting at his workbench, head in his hands as he poured out his secrets.

"Sita died giving birth to you. I could have saved her, with time transfer, but she wouldn't allow it. She was afraid of what would happen to you if we tampered with her time. So she died in a forest where we had anchored, away from physicians or comfort...I buried her there with her watch."

The voice issuing from the speakers halted for a few seconds, and when it resumed it carried the high pitch of a man fighting back incredible sorrow.

"What I've pieced together, from rumors and newspapers and military communications, is that Sebastian found her grave not long after. He'd been devoted to her like no man I've ever seen. Obsessed.

"The grief drove him mad. But he was functionally insane, able to hide it. He rose through the ranks even as he became more and more fanatical about hunting me. He's a general now, sweetie. And I imagine he'll come after you.

"You see, he doesn't want the research back to further Anglia's imperial ambitions. He wants to use it to resurrect Sita. The insanity amplified Sebastian's violent tendencies. There have been numerous disappearances associated with him, but there's never been sufficient evidence to convict him of murder. He's a dangerous man, Dahlia."

There was another pause in the tape and Dahlia reached to switch it off. The story spun in her head. But her papa was not done.

"I went back to Vatana with you when you were an infant. I went back to the mine shaft at the edge of the ruined city because I had to know, I had to see for myself what was there.

"The boy was still alive. He was propped against the wall where we'd left him, barely conscious, his body a mess of old blood and rotting bones and bits of..." Ansel cleared his throat. "He couldn't die, but he couldn't live either. It's terrible, but all I could think of was how the immortals had finally returned to the ancient city."

He laughed desperately and Dahlia recoiled.

"I killed him, sweetie. I couldn't let the child live like that, it was... I smashed his watch."

Ansel began to cry. Dahlia couldn't see it, but she could hear it in his words. Her heart skittered.

"You can't let the same thing happen to Sita. Sebastian doesn't know we resurrected that child—we never wrote it down—and if he gets his hands on those research notes he'll try to bring your mother back to life. She'll come back like that boy did. I don't know why I didn't burn those papers. I guess it's because I didn't want to give up on all the work we did. I didn't want Sita to have died for nothing.

"The choice is yours to make now, sweetie. You can do whatever you want with the research as long as Sebastian doesn't get his hands on it. Because if he does, your mother will only be safe as long as he doesn't find the promethium. In fact, now that I'm presumably dead, you're the last person who knows where it is. I'm sorry to force this responsibility on you, but that's the way things have to be."

Chapter Nineteen
Changes

Dahlia lay awake as the first hints of sunrise filtered through the dirty porthole in the wall. She had hardly slept. Her mind wouldn't allow it, not with Ansel Walker's tale invading her every thought.

I had a mother.

Practically, she'd always known it; everyone had a mother. But hers had never seemed real until now.

Sita Senguptar.

It all made sense. Dahlia's dark skin, her constant moving between cities as a child, her papa's refusal to reveal his past. And Sebastian.

Dahlia's hands tightened into fists. How could Sita have ever loved him? It seemed impossible to reconcile the force of death and horror Dahlia knew with the lovesick man from the sound tapes. The man who had killed Ansel Walker.

A new realization hit her as she remembered the boy in the mine, and Ansel's earlier warnings about resurrection fell into place.

I can't bring Papa back.

The memory of Ansel clung to her. His hearty laugh, the way he called her 'sweetie,' the hours he had spent with her in the workshop teaching her the basics of watch repair.

The feeling of his arms around her when he scooped her into a warm hug.

Gone.

She curled in on herself under the blankets. A horrible aching echoed in her heart, louder and louder until she could hardly stand to be in her own skin. Before, it had felt as if her papa was merely sleeping, waiting for her to come home and set things right. Now...

Now he was dead. And her mother with him.

A crash from the living room split the silence. Dahlia jerked up, thankful for something, anything, to do. Her hands shoved away the blankets and yanked a jacket over the blouse she had slept in.

"Hello?" Dahlia cracked her door open.

It was Farren, standing in the kitchen area with his back to her, the doors to the liquor cabinet swinging wide next to him.

"God damn it, god *damn* it," he cursed without noticing her.

"Mr. Reed, are you all right?"

Farren whirled. The glittering remnants of a whiskey bottle defaced the floor, and his hand dripped deep scarlet blood. A piece of glass was embedded in his palm.

Dahlia sighed. "I thought you quit."

"Easier said than done."

Dahlia crept forward through the labyrinth of sharp pieces. A clean cutting board sat in the dish drying rack, and she snatched it up, using the edge to scrape the glass into a pile. She doubted that there was a broom aboard the *Wayfarer Elizabeth*, and it was the first alternative she could invent.

"Sit down, Mr. Reed, before you hurt yourself again." She gestured at the table. Farren slid into a chair and flashed an embarrassed grin that didn't reach his eyes. Dahlia tossed him a towel to hold against his hand.

"Sorry, sweetheart," he said. "I just..."

He waved a hand at the watch on the counter, lying there amid the shards of glass. It wasn't hard to guess why he'd been drawn to the liquor cabinet again.

"Stop looking at it, then," said Dahlia, regretting the irritation in her voice as soon as she spoke. Her thoughts were a mess that threatened to leap out with every word. It took everything she had to focus on the situation at hand, when her papa's face flashed in the darkness behind her eyelids whenever she blinked.

She straightened up. The floor was as clean as she could manage. Brushing dirt off her hands, she set about pouring Farren a glass of water.

"Thanks," he said, grabbing it and downing it in one gulp. He wiped his mouth on his sleeve. "Got anything to eat?"

Dahlia rummaged in the pantry cabinets, coming away with a bag of in-shell sunflower seeds that she deposited before Farren. He popped a few into his mouth and crunched them thoughtfully.

"If you really want to quit, you're going to have to try harder than this," said Dahlia as she sat down across from him.

Farren nodded, leaned back in the chair and closed his eyes, tipping his head back to rest on the dented wood. He tousled his hair absently with his intact hand. Dahlia knew they should tend to his injury, but the bleeding seemed to be slowing, and sitting down had given her thoughts space to turn back toward Ansel's story. If she moved, she was afraid she might shatter.

I just need a moment.

"What's wrong?" asked Farren.

"Nothing."

I don't want to talk to him. I'm not ready.

"Listen," Farren extracted a sunflower seed shell from his mouth and flicked it onto the floor. "I know when a woman says 'nothing,' what she really means is 'everything.'"

His smile wormed through her paltry defenses. Tears prickled at her eyes, sticking in her throat until she could hardly breathe.

Her parents were dead, and she would never have them back.

Dahlia was weeping almost before she understood what was happening, hot tears burning down her cheeks and onto the collar of her blouse. She turned away from Farren's confused face. She wanted to hide, to escape, to get away...

A warm hand patted her shoulder.

"Shhh. It's alright."

No, it's not.

She shook her head, hair clinging to the damp spots on her cheeks. The world was falling down around her, and the only person she had left would be dead in twenty-one days.

What do I do now? Finding Macall is useless.

The terrible ache in her chest coalesced into a bright, blinding core of hatred. He had done this to her.

She saw Ansel's body crumpled on the floor, hair askew, suit stained with her blood. The shattered pieces of her papa's watch glittered on the carpet like rain.

I'll make Macall pay for this.

But, how? She could steal back the research and the resurrection device, but that wouldn't be enough, not for what he'd done.

Kill him.

Dahlia's hands curled into fists on her lap. Could

she...?

Yes.

Suddenly, she could breathe again. Her sobs receded as her heartbeat slowed. The blurred grief leaked from her thoughts, leaving them cold and clear. Killing Sebastian Macall wasn't just vengeance, it was *justice*. It was *fair*. And it would stop him from subjecting Sita—the mother she had never known—to the terrors of resurrection.

If I can't have her back, I can at least protect her.

Dahlia wiped her eyes. In a halting voice, in words made wet by unshed tears, she told Farren what she had decided, and why. She explained the story from Ansel's sound tape. It didn't hurt as much, hearing it from her own lips rather than her papa's.

"Our bargain hasn't changed," she said at the end. "I helped you escape Sainsbury, and you'll still take me to Sebastian Macall."

"Dahlia, are you sure this is what you want?" he leaned forward and scanned her face, his expression full of concern. "I know you're upset, but—"

She cut him off with a nod. In all her life, she'd never been more certain of anything.

I have to kill Macall, no matter what it takes.

Perhaps, once he was dead, the horrible, yawning emptiness left by Ansel's death would finally be filled.

Farren reached for her and stopped, breath hissing through his teeth. The sound snapped Dahlia from her thoughts. He was holding his cut hand over the floor, watching it leak crimson onto the rust-flecked deck plates.

"Here," she waved him forward, feeling stupid for forgetting his injury. "Let me see it."

Farren extended his still-bleeding hand for Dahlia's inspection. She studied it carefully. A large shard of the whiskey bottle was embedded in the flesh, glistening with liquor and blood. It looked excruciating.

"Well, first thing to do is remove that," she observed, grateful for something to take her mind off…everything. "Let me just…"

"You have no idea what you're doing, do you?"

Dahlia fetched a clean towel and shielded her fingers with it while she grasped the glass. She gave it a halfhearted wiggle. Farren's sharp intake of breath was loud in the quiet.

"Devil's blood, sweetheart, just rip it out. It won't kill me."

"Whatever you say, Mr. Reed."

She tore the offending glass from his hand and tossed it into the trash bin. Blood trickled freely onto the tabletop. Farren rose dizzily and held it over the sink while Dahlia mopped up their makeshift surgical area, vowing never to eat at the tainted table again.

"You'll need stitches."

She yelped at Tiberius' voice. The stained towel slipped from her fingers. The cyborg's massive form filled the hall leading to his and Keet's bedroom; he must have awoken and come to investigate the commotion. Piercing yellow eyes burned behind his face grille.

He strode toward them, the deck flexing under his feet. Dahlia scrubbed at her eyes to rid them of the last vestiges of tears. Tiberius snatched Farren's arm in an iron grip, unseen gears buzzing. The cyborg bent and examined the wound. Farren looked sheepish amid the obvious shards of glass and the overpowering scent of whiskey.

"Yes, stitches. Both of you come with me."

He towed Farren by the arm to the medical bay, Dahlia following in their wake. A standard physician's operating table occupied most of the tiny space. The rest was filled with medical implements on shelves and a rusty service sink tucked in one corner. The cyborg stopped, lifting Farren onto the table with one arm.

"It's only a cut, I don't think this is really..." the aviator protested. But there was no reasoning with an eight-foot metal giant once he had put his mind to something.

"I used to be a surgeon. You'll need stitches."

Tiberius backed out of the medical bay long enough to propel Dahlia inside, then loomed in the doorway as if to block it.

"My hands cannot perform delicate work. Dahlia, I'll instruct you."

"You expect me to—"

"Wash your hands. Get the sterilizing fluid on the third shelf."

Dahlia began rummaging through the storage drawers. Glinting surgical implements, bandages, gauze, and other medical objects were arranged meticulously inside.

Tiberius guided her through the process of sterilizing Farren's hand and the suture needle. When the time came to stitch the cut closed, she was surprisingly unfazed. Actions that would have nauseated her a week ago seemed mere child's play now.

This is nothing compared to being shot.

Hate squeezed her thoughts as she remembered Sebastian ordering his soldiers to kill her.

"I don't think it's bad enough to have damaged your watch," said Dahlia as she worked. Her hand brushed the rough calluses at the bases of his fingers.

"Well, that's good news, isn't it?"

"It is. I don't feel like taking your watch apart again."

Farren's breathing twitched as Dahlia made another stitch through his skin. She could feel his eyes on her.

"Thanks for that, by the way."

"For sewing you up?"

"For fixing my watch back in that first town. 'Preciate it, sweetheart."

"Oh, you're welcome."

It felt awkward, being so close to him under Tiberius' watchful gaze. It felt awkward being close to him at all. Something about the warmth of his injured hand in hers, the unruly blonde hair falling over his eyes, and the way he looked at her when he thought she didn't see. She wondered—

Dahlia forced her thoughts away.

Stop. He's going to die in twenty-one days.

Why allow herself to get caught up in a childish fantasy when she knew how it would end? Farren was only a friend. Besides, she had more important things to worry about.

Like killing Sebastian Macall.

She licked her lips, tasting salt from dried tears.

"That's enough stitches," said Tiberius from the doorway.

"How can you see from that far?" Dahlia had to bend close over Farren's hand to work.

The cyborg tapped the plating near his eyes. "Auto-focusing."

"Ah."

She finished off the stitches, cut the suture thread, and prepared to tidy up the area as Farren flexed his fingers experimentally.

Suddenly, a voice rang from a funnel speaker on the ceiling.

"Darling!" Keet sang. "We're at Lawson's Ridge. Come on down to the war room so we can plan this gig. Two-thousand gilvers are walking around down there."

"The war room?" Dahlia asked.

"She means the bridge," rumbled the cyborg. "Clean up and follow."

He lumbered off, leaving Dahlia and Farren behind. Farren slid down from the table and took a few steps after the cyborg.

"Mr. Reed?" He turned. Dahlia glanced at his face, then at the deck, heart stuck in her throat. "Next time you feel like you need to forget, talk to me instead. You...you don't have to do this alone."

Farren didn't respond, but his eyes said more than words ever could.

Chapter Twenty
Lawson's Ridge

✳

Keet was poring over maps of Lawson's Ridge when Tiberius lumbered onto the bridge. The sheets spread before her on a foldout desk near the main control panel. She looked up.

"Hello, darling. Ready for some hunting?"

"Always." The cyborg crouched next to her, artificial eyes taking in the charts. "Our plan?"

"We'll have to find Harold Grimes first. He's definitely in the city, but I have no idea where. Once we figure that out we can draw up a capture plan. Where are our guests?"

"Coming."

"I'm thinking we'll exploit Dahlia's social skills for information collection. You know me; I'm not the best at…diplomacy."

Tiberius laughed his scratchy, mechanical laugh. Most people found it disturbing, but Keet didn't mind the sound.

"William Pikkin?"

"That wasn't my fault and you know it!" Keet grinned. "The scoundrel was asking for it. Besides, he didn't need all his teeth anyway."

"Nearly got arrested. Tavern brawling."

"But we didn't, did we?"

She tapped a fingernail on his metal shoulder plate, her expression one of mock seriousness.

"It's too bad they threw me out before I was done interrogating him. We could've nabbed his whole gang. They were worth five thousand all together, weren't they?"

"Five thousand two hundred."

Keet smiled, then stopped when she heard the clicking footsteps heralding Dahlia and Farren's entrance.

"Good morning," said Dahlia.

Farren was chewing, crunching on something that sounded like pebbles.

"What are you eating?" Keet asked.

Farren shrugged. "Sunflower seeds." He pulled a shell from his mouth in explanation before tucking it into the pocket of his flight jacket.

Keet sighed and turned toward the windshield. "As you can probably tell, we've arrived at Lawson's Ridge."

She swept one arm toward the panorama outside the windshield as if presenting a magic trick. Beyond it, enormous granite cliffs jutted above a sprawling forest. The sheer, craggy rock shone in the morning sun.

A city was built precariously onto the side of the cliffs, over a thousand yards in the air. All beams and towers and scaffolding, it clung to the rock by pure engineering brilliance. The buildings splashed over the cliffs in an artist's palette of color. It was as if the man-made structures were striving to compete with the natural grandeur...and failing miserably.

But Keet had to admit the attempt had yielded a beautiful city, and one impossible to access without an airship.

No wonder Harold Grimes is holed up here.

"We're docking at the port until we find our target and capture him. First order of business is gathering information; Dahlia, you'll be coming with me for that. You'll have to keep your face hidden, but you can still help negotiate. Tiberius is staying to guard the ship—he stands out too much. Bounty-hunting cyborgs aren't exactly common."

"And me?" said Farren.

Keet stared at him, considering.

"Can you fight with your leg in a brace? You can't be slowing us down if there's trouble."

"He can fight," Dahlia said. "Earlier this week he tore apart a gang of bandits, and two nights ago he did the same to some bounty hunters."

"Well then." The aviatrix was cool, calculating. "Seems they train them well in Anglia. Farren, you'll be with my team."

* * *

Keet presented Dahlia with a headscarf to conceal most of her face. Things would become complicated if she was recognized. Keet was loath to risk the thirty-thousand gilver reward on her head, but she needed Dahlia's social abilities. They had lost many a bounty over the years due to Keet's lack of subtlety. Tiberius had historically been the one taking on the softer side of the job: researching in taverns, following leads, slipping bribes into the right hands. But those tasks fell to Keet after he became a cyborg three years ago. She'd never adapted.

They marched through Lawson's Ridge in a tight group, the two fugitives trailing behind Keet's sure steps. A sniper tesla rifle strapped to her back banged against her hip. Wooden planks creaked under their feet.

Compact buildings rose on either side: bakers, butchers, watch repairmen, mechanical man builders. The city was hectic with people rushing about on their daily errands. Vehicles were oddly absent; the streets of the hanging city were too narrow to accommodate anything larger than a wheelbarrow or two.

They passed the occasional nonchalant policeman or soldier lounging beside the street. Keet heard Dahlia's intake of breath each time one came into view.

Come on, girl. You're only making it easier for them.

Farren and Dahlia each had a pistol tucked beneath their jackets. Dahlia had pinched her finger in the slide when Keet gave it to her, earning herself a quick lesson in weaponry.

"What are those?" Dahlia asked, pointing.

A pair of wanted posters was nailed to a nearby building. Dahlia approached one.

"Come on," said Keet. She had seen those sheets before; they hung in her office. Dahlia ignored her warning.

Dahlia stood there for a moment, staring at a sketch of her own face. WANTED: DAHLIA WALKER. 30,000 GILVER REWARD. The poster next to hers had no image, just a description of an Anglian deserter wearing a flight jacket matching the one Farren had on.

"Sweetheart..." The airman pulled at her sleeve. She turned to look at him and Keet, her expression hidden by the scarf. They resumed walking.

I swear these people are idiots, thought Keet.

"In here." The bounty hunter shoved open the door of a nondescript tavern tucked between two larger buildings. A messily painted sign proclaimed the establishment's name: *The Runaway Flywheel*.

It was dim inside, but clean. Neater than most taverns Keet patronized on the job. A handful of customers were sprinkled among wooden tables or hunched over the bar counter.

"Three beers," Keet said, settling onto a barstool.

"Two," amended Farren. "And a water."

A pleased smile tugged at Keet's lips.

The bartender, a middle-aged man with a scraggly beard, eyed them as he fetched the drinks. It was barely lunchtime, but Keet couldn't afford to wait until a socially acceptable drinking hour to hunt for information.

"Keet, isn't it?" The bartender said as the aviatrix sipped the froth off her beer.

"Indeed. Glad to see you remember me, Illyvitch."

"I thought I told you not to come back here. You knocked out four of Bill Pikkin's teeth, knocked 'em right onto my counter."

"I'm reformed now. Wouldn't hurt a fly." Keet grinned in a thoroughly unconvincing manner. "Me and my friends here are paying a visit to a certain Harold Grimes."

Keet reached into her pocket (Illyvitch flinched) and unfolded a wanted poster, flattening it out with the bottom of her glass.

"Grimes?" The bartender sniffed and glanced away. "Doesn't ring a bell."

"Come on. You know where every rat—rodent or human—makes its nest in this city. Grimes is a murderer, I'm bringing him to justice."

She deposited a small cloth bag onto the bar and rattled the coins inside for emphasis. Illyvitch turned to face them, his aloofness evaporating.

"What can I do for you, Mrs. Hawkins?" The bartender leaned close enough for Keet to see the individual hairs in his beard.

"Where's Grimes?"

"Living in an inn on the bottom level next to the water pump plant. Should be an easy grab."

Keet took a drink. Perhaps she wasn't so dismal at this

after all. She only needed to find the right people, grease the right palms…it was a snap.

Illyvitch swept away the bag of coins and tucked it under the bar without counting them. Judging by the weight, it contained at least fifty gilvers; more than enough for a little information.

"Who're your new friends, Keet?" said the bartender. His surliness returned once the money was his.

Keet looked down the bar at her two fugitives. Farren had finished his water and was crunching loudly on one of the ice cubes. Dahlia sat, concealed by the scarf, her drink untouched.

Oh, I forgot she can't drink with that on. There's four gilvers down the drain.

"They're my cousins," Keet lied. "Twice removed."

"Why all the—" The bartender waved his hand at Dahlia, indicating the scarf.

"Accident," said Keet. "Horrible scars. She's very self-conscious about them."

A warm proud glow spread through her. This was too easy.

"An accident?" Illyvitch scowled maliciously. "Was that one your fault too?"

Keet was over the counter and clenching his throat before any of them could blink. "You dirty bastard!" she roared. "I'll kill you!"

Illyvitch gurgled and scrabbled at her arm, eyes bulging. Keet flattened him to the wall and squeezed his windpipe viciously. Her face blazed.

"Keet!" Farren tried to leap the bar, caught his foot on a chair, and crashed to the floor behind the counter. A liquor bottle fell and shattered next to him.

"Where's your watch, Illyvitch? Tell me!"

Keet punched him in the face. *That felt good.* She struck

him again and again, knuckles scraping against teeth, aching under the force of the blows. She didn't care. She'd clobber him until her hand fell off, then she'd start on him with the other.

"That's enough."

Farren grabbed her fist before she could swing again. Keet struggled against him, muscles straining. But he was stronger.

"It's okay, Keet. Let him down," murmured a soft female voice.

Dahlia stood on her other side, voice soothing as she reached for the bloodied bartender. Panting, Keet felt the fight drain out of her. Her grip loosened. Illyvitch slumped into Dahlia's waiting arms.

Then, as Dahlia struggled with the plump man, her scarf caught on a hook in the wall. It tore away from her face.

Keet spun. Her heart sank: every patron in the tavern was staring, openmouthed, at the unfortunate trio. One spilled an entire beer down his front. Another dropped his and it burst in a spray of glass and liquor.

"Hey! That's Dahlia Walker!"

"She's worth a fortune!"

"Thirty-thousand gilvers!"

Keet shared a look of horror with her two expensive fugitives.

I'm not letting them take Dahlia!

"Run!"

Keet bolted. Dahlia and Farren didn't need to be told twice; they raced out onto the street after her. She shoved aside a random pedestrian in her path. He toppled onto his back like a helpless turtle.

Where to go? Where to go?

"Stop them!" yelled a voice. A crowd clattered from

the tavern doors. "They tried to kill the bartender!"

A street policeman noticed and shouted something. Keet ignored him.

Grimes is on the bottom level of the city. We've gotta go down.

"This way!"

She ran from the policeman, glancing back to check on Dahlia. The thirty-thousand gilver payday. But Keet could only collect it at the bounty hunting office in Port Argun.

A service ladder extended down from the edge of the street to the next level. Keet leapt onto the rungs. Lawson's Ridge was laid out in a series of nineteen switchback ramps stacked atop one other like a layer cake. Hairpin turns adorned the ends of each, and access ladders provided mid-layer shortcuts for service workers. Or fugitives.

She half-climbed, half-fell down. Dahlia followed closely. The airman trailed, struggling with his leg brace.

"Mr. Reed!" shouted Dahlia as she ran beside Keet across the lower street to a second ladder. "I got you the best brace money could buy, and you can't even climb down a ladder?"

"Shut it, sweetheart."

Farren swung his feet from the rungs, grabbed the side rail, and slid the rest of the way. Dahlia nodded in approval.

Keet started down the next ladder, glancing below to check their progress. Four levels to go.

I wonder if they're still following us.

"There they are!" A row of heads peeked over the edge.

Yup.

Keet's feet slapped the wooden street planks and she stood aside for Dahlia and Farren.

"Go to the next one. I'll deal with this."

She whipped the rifle from her back as the first pursuer grasped the rungs. It was designed for sniper work, but that didn't mean it couldn't stop a few would-be bounty hunters.

Keet hefted the gun, aimed, and fired. Blue electricity streaked from the barrel. It struck the man square between the shoulder blades, crackling over his skin. He screeched, muscles seizing, and tumbled down. She stepped out of the way so he could crash to the street unencumbered.

"Frank?" A man poked his head out and was greeted with another electric bolt. His limp body slumped over the edge.

That'll keep them cautious for a while.

Keet swung the tesla rifle strap over her shoulder and ran for the next ladder. It was time to meet Harold Grimes.

Chapter Twenty-one
The Mechanical Dog

✳

"I don't like it," said Farren. "Don't like it at all."

They crouched, exhausted and sweaty, in a narrow alley on the lowest level of Lawson's Ridge. One alley wall belonged to an old inn. The other supported the water pump plant. The cliff city drew water from wells in the forested ground far below, a feat requiring an impressive array of machinery and piping. The incessant humming of pumps concealed their words from infrequent passersby.

"It's easy," Keet said. "We waltz up to whoever's in charge, dump some money on his desk, and politely insist he tell Harold Grimes to come to the front desk."

"Would a man with a two-thousand gilver bounty really fall for that?" Farren pointed out. "He'd have to be stupid."

Keet shrugged.

"It never hurts to try. Besides, I have a few tricks up my sleeve if that doesn't work."

Farren shook his head. Ordinarily he would have advocated waiting until Grimes emerged from the inn. But who knew when their pursuers would search the lowest level? He doubted they'd given up; the price on Dahlia's head was a small fortune. Not the sort of thing people let slip through their fingers.

"How long has Grimes been on the run?" he asked.

"Three years. He killed a man over an argument in Port Argun. They tried to arrest him, he escaped to Delmar, the Anglian police put out a bounty."

Farren frowned. He was beginning to doubt the wisdom of helping Keet. Passage to Port Argun would be useless if they were lying in some dingy inn with their watches broken. But backing out now would leave them penniless, trapped in Lawson's Ridge at the mercy of their hunters.

"Okay," said Farren. "We'll try it your way. Just keep the beatings to our target this time."

The bounty hunter ignored the jab and walked toward the open end of the alley, patting her disheveled pink-and-blue hair into a more presentable arrangement. Dahlia fiddled with her torn headscarf. She tried tying the ripped ends behind her head to secure it over her face, but strands of hair tangled in the knot.

"Mr. Reed, could you help me?"

"Sure, sweetheart."

She turned around and passed off the ends of the fabric. Farren delicately untied the disastrous knot and set to work on a neater version, taking the opportunity to look at her while she couldn't see him.

Dahlia wore a long-sleeved blouse and skirt both for warmth and to conceal her dark skin. The clothing clung to the fine curve of her hips enough to admire, but remained loose enough to intrigue. She smelled of lavender.

She's a beautiful woman, mused Farren. *Cold, though. Distant.*

Would she ever spare him more than a passing thought? Did he even want her to, knowing he'd be dead soon? His fingers trembled as he finished off the knot.

"There ya go," Farren said, forcing himself to sound

neutral.

"Thank you, Mr. Reed."

*　*　*

Keet took the lead. They pushed open the door to the decrepit building, striding confidently up to the innkeeper's desk. A heavyset man lounged half-asleep on a groaning chair behind it. Apparently the business failed to turn enough profit to afford an automatic innkeeper. There was, however, a mechanical guard dog sitting poised beside the unfortunate chair. It growled as they approached. Hardened steel fangs poked from reinforced jaws.

The man's head jerked up when Keet tossed a bag of coins onto the desk. He wiped a trail of drool from his chin.

"How many rooms?" he mumbled. A wave of reeking morning breath flooded from his lips despite the fact that it was well into the afternoon.

"No rooms," said Keet, and held up the wanted poster. "We'd like to have a talk with this man. I understand he's staying here."

The innkeeper squinted blearily at the sheet, glanced down at the bag of gilvers and back at her. A second growl issued from the mechanical dog.

"Never seen him."

*　*　*

"He was lying," Dahlia declared once the door of the inn slammed shut behind them. "Grimes must have paid him off."

"Or he's afraid. Or he doesn't want a firefight in the common room of his...establishment." Keet wrinkled her nose.

"So what now?"

Keet leaned back against the wall of the alleyway, flashing a wicked grin.

"Spiders."

Spiders?

"I never go hunting without a few of these little guys," said Keet.

Farren started. Half a dozen mechanical spiders were picking their way up Keet's arms. They latched onto her shoulders and stayed there, glass eyes glittering disturbingly. Farren had a sudden urge, not for the first time that day, to be relaxing back atop the envelope of the *Wayfarer Elizabeth*.

Keet held up Grimes' poster and addressed the arachnids, "This is our target. I want you to search every room of this building here. Don't be seen or heard."

One by one, the creatures leapt off onto the wall of the inn and dug their needle legs into the soft wood. Then they paused, skittered around the corner, and were gone.

Farren gaped.

*Well, that was creepy. Wouldn't want to meet one of those in a dark...*Farren surveyed the dim alleyway where the three of them sat...*alley*. What he could see of Dahlia's expression told him she shared his sentiments. They waited in awkward silence. Farren checked his watch out of habit; he already knew how much time he had left.

"How long?" Dahlia asked, her eyes serious.

"Twenty-one days, thirteen hours, and nine minutes."

Keet clapped a hand over her mouth, a rare but sincere feminine gesture.

"Is that...how long you have left?" She lowered her hand, mouth parted in horror.

Farren nodded. Her reaction made him uncomfortable. He didn't want any pity from Keet; he already felt enough for himself. He wished he hadn't checked his watch. He wished he could forget about it. He wished—

Dahlia's hand came to rest on his shoulder, her touch feather-light but strong enough to hold back the fear. His muscles loosened. He unclenched his hands, trying to remember when they'd become fists.

"How long do *you* have left?" he asked Keet. He didn't care that it was a rude question. Anything to take the focus off himself and his time.

Keet unearthed a tarnished watch from a chain around her neck. She flashed him a mad grin. "No idea."

"What do you mean? How can you not know?"

The watch swung back and forth in Keet's grasp. "Easy. I don't look."

"But—"

"How can you enjoy life if you're too busy thinking about when it'll end? That's no fun at all."

The mechanical arachnids chose that moment to return, sparing Farren further incredulity. They lined up on the side of the inn and waited for Keet's orders. Rows of tiny dents and splinters marked their paths.

"Whatcha got for me?" Keet asked, tucking the watch back under her coveralls.

The spiders shuffled and one stepped forward. Keet listened to it closely, cupping her hand around it to direct whatever tiny noises it was making. Farren heard nothing but the odd click. Finally, she picked the creatures from the wall and tucked them away into her coveralls.

"He's on the second floor, the room right above us." Keet pointed to the window over their heads.

Farren frowned. *Let's hope he hasn't been listening to us.*

"How do we get up there?" Dahlia asked. "We can't go back past the innkeeper and his dog."

"I have some explosives." Keet patted a pack at her waist. "We could blow him up, but there's no guarantee that whatever's left will be identifiable enough to collect the bounty."

"Let's climb up inside the water pump plant," said Farren. "The roofs are close enough to cross over, then we'll just lower ourselves down to the window. You've got a rope?"

"Yup."

The plan was easier said than done, but several minutes later the three of them stood together on the inn's roof. Keet secured her rope to an exhaust stack nearby. The other end of it curled in the damp alleyway below.

"Farren, you go first," the bounty hunter said, "I'll follow, Dahlia will bring up the rear. Hit Grimes with an electric bolt as soon as you get in."

"My pistol doesn't have an electric setting. Neither of ours does." He gestured at Dahlia, who held up her own gun for proof.

Farren had no intention of spearheading the attack. He would be no more than cheap cannon fodder if Grimes was even remotely alert. The pistol made an excellent excuse.

Keet glanced from Farren to Dahlia and back, shifting the tesla rifle strap on her shoulder.

"If I go first, I'll have to use bullets," said Farren. "It'll be much trickier to take him down with those than with electricity." He nodded at her tesla rifle. "Why don't you go first?"

He had her, and she knew it. Keet licked her lips nervously.

"Fine," she said. "I'll stun him if I can. You two come in right behind me."

Farren nodded. The setting sun bathed their surroundings in splashes of pink and orange. The stark granite cliffs caught and reflected the colors until they almost seemed to glow. Night would come soon.

"Ready?" asked Keet. She balanced on the roof's edge, clinging to the rope with the tesla rifle poised in front of her.

"As we'll ever be," Dahlia replied, hefting her own smaller weapon.

Keet started down. Farren gripped the taut rope and positioned himself to follow but paused, waiting. Breaking glass tinkled. The rope went slack.

"She's in," said Dahlia. "You need to—"

A gunshot clipped her words.

"God damn it!" Keet's shriek was clearly audible through the shattered window. "Get back here, you slimy bastard!"

Farren dropped over the roof and through the window in an instant. He landed in the room just in time to glimpse Keet sprinting out of it. It was typical for inn accommodations: sink, dresser, rickety bed—all seasoned with a healthy dose of mold and squalor. A spray of blood on the floor slid under his boots.

"Keet!"

He raced after her, practically tumbling down the stairway into the common area. Dahlia's feet pounded the floorboards behind him. *She's fast.*

The innkeeper blinked awake and mumbled something incoherent. No threat. His mechanical guard dog, however, was on high alert.

The creature leapt for Farren as Grimes and Keet vanished out the front door. Its vicious snarl grated in his ears. Razor claws scarred the air beside his face. Farren ducked without slowing. A bolt of blue lightning crackled from its mouth and scorched the wooden wall.

Delmarean combat dogs were territorial. It would

leave them be if they could just get clear of the building. And the door was only a few feet away—he was nearly there...

Dahlia screamed.

Without thinking, Farren grabbed the doorjamb and spun around. His damaged hand twinged as the stitches tore. The dog was clamped onto Dahlia's arm, steel teeth tearing deep into skin. Dahlia battered it with her free hand. She shrieked.

The dog growled madly and went after her with the same claws Farren had dodged.

"Get off her!"

He raised his pistol and shot the mechanical dog in the head. Shot it again. Circuits fizzled and it snarled, but refused to let go. Blood dripped down its jaw. Dahlia yelled and struggled to pry it off.

Farren emptied the pistol clip into it. Rage and adrenaline lent him strength as he took hold of each jaw. The dog's red eyes flickered, sparks darting across the components. But the mouth remained locked shut.

"I said get OFF her!" Farren shouted. He wrenched it apart.

Teeth squelched sickeningly as the lower jaw ripped free and clattered to the floor. Dahlia slid her shaking arm from the upper jaw. A little gasp escaped her mouth.

Farren kicked the dog's broken body with all the pent-up wrath that killing it hadn't dissipated. It toppled over. Metal bits cracked off and scattered.

"Is it dead?" Dahlia shivered, staring at her mangled arm. Blood flowed from a neat line of miniature stab wounds, yet her eyes remained dry.

She's gotten stronger since I met her.

"Yeah, sweetheart, it's dead."

"Let's find Keet," Dahlia said. Her voice sounded high-pitched. "We need to get out of here."

The fat innkeeper watched, stunned, as they made their way out onto the street.

Chapter Twenty-two
Battle on the Docks

✴

"I got him!" Keet beamed triumphantly. She strode toward them along the deserted street, dragging the unconscious Harold Grimes by the foot. The man was tiny, one of the shortest Dahlia had ever seen. "The grimy—get it, *Grime*-y?—son of a bitch shot my trigger hand. But I got him."

The bounty hunter held up her right hand to reveal a makeshift bandage wrapped around the palm. It appeared to be a strip of fabric ripped from Grimes' shirt.

Dahlia was only half paying attention; it took so much concentration to hold back the waves of pain battering her arm. She gritted her teeth.

How can Keet be so chipper when she's shot?

Dahlia gripped Farren's upper arm as they walked. He didn't seem to mind, and it helped take her mind away from the injury.

"What happened to you?" asked Keet.

"Mechanical dog bite," said Farren.

"Ooh. Ouch." The bounty hunter paused to catch her breath, then continued towing Grimes along the wooden planks. His hair caught on every nail. He seemed to be in danger of premature balding if they continued much farther. "You should get a bandage on that. We'll see what my husband can do when we get back on the ship."

Dahlia was not in the mood to hear Keet's medical advice. She was hurt and tired, there were people hunting her, and night had just fallen. She wanted off the accursed cliff city this instant.

"Keet's right. Here," Farren said. Without asking permission, he slid Dahlia's scarf from her face and bound her wound with it. "Until we can get to the airship."

"So how do we get him——" Dahlia nodded at Grimes' prone form, "——and the rest of us up to the docks on the top level? I'm not carrying him up a ladder."

"No. There's got to be some sort of elevator," said Farren. Dahlia squeezed his arm. "A way for the rich to travel. Or at least to move cargo."

Keet snapped her fingers and dropped Grimes. His boot thudded on the wood; Dahlia would have found it amusing under better circumstances.

"Perfect! I'll bet there's one around here to service the water plant."

They found it after a brief search: a rusty elevator on the opposite side of the plant marked 'CARGO ONLY, NO PERSONNEL.'

"Well, we're not personnel," said Keet, tossing Grimes into the elevator cage. "We're more like guests."

The instrument panel inside featured a plethora of marked levers. Farren yanked the one labeled 'docks'. Metal screeched and the doors closed, leaving the trio trapped in the elevator cage. As the cramped box began rising, Dahlia breathed a sigh of relief at their luck. If they had been riding during daylight, the chain link walls would have left them helplessly visible to passersby. The swift darkness provided ideal concealment.

Dahlia stared out over the city, admiring the intermittent panorama she could glimpse through the buildings. It was quite a view. Perhaps she would come back one day. One day when Sebastian Macall was dead and her papa was avenged, when her mother was saved from a fate worse than death. The terrible ache of Ansel Walker's murder burned inside her like an empty pit—cruel, inescapable.

She had no other family, no real friends. It had always been her and Ansel against the world: hopping from city to city, hunching over his workbench contemplating a project, laughing at one of their jokes no one else could understand. Now she was alone.

The mechanical dog bite throbbed. Dahlia let her mind fade away in a haze of pain. The physical wounds were infinitely more manageable than the emotional ones.

The cargo elevator jerked and shuddered, but when it arrived at the top level they were unharmed. Or, at least, in the same state of harm they began in. It rattled as the doors opened.

"Docks are over there," Keet said.

She pointed with her damaged hand, grabbing Grimes' ankle with the other. Bright lights illuminating the upper level allowed Dahlia to properly examine their captive for the first time. He was neither young nor old, with severe features obscured by a messy beard. He exactly matched the sketch on the wanted poster—apart from an increase in the amount of facial hair. Jaw slack, head lolling, his miniature stunned body bumped along behind Keet.

* * *

Keet led the way toward the pier where the *Wayfarer Elizabeth* drifted in the air at the ends of its docking ropes like some chubby, mismatched creature. Light glowed from the bridge. The hatch shuddered open as they walked along the pier; Tiberius had seen their approach. A precarious steel plank gangway spanned the gap to the ship.

The docks were built at the edge of Lawson's Ridge where airships could easily maneuver in and out. No one had bothered with railing; piers ended in a thousand meter drop down the cliff face. It made for an invigorating walk.

They were passing the deserted fee booth, still fifty yards or more from the hatch, when the first shots rang out. A bullet whizzed past Farren's ear.

"There they are!"

"That's Dahlia Walker!"

Men streamed from the buildings beside the pier, brandishing pistols and tesla rifles. There were over a dozen—too many to fight.

They've been waiting for us, Farren realized. His heart sank. A streak of electricity blackened the ground near his feet.

"You two get Grimes on the ship," ordered Keet. "I'll cover you."

The bounty hunter heaved Grimes' small body at Farren and swung the tesla rifle from her back. Farren caught the unconscious man under the arms. Dahlia sprinted for the hatch without a backwards glance. *So much for a team effort.*

He hefted Grimes onto his back and ran. The leg brace was like a lead weight hampering his movements, dragging his foot down. A bolt of electricity struck the side of the airship in a shower of sparks. Smoke stung his nose. Grimes bumped up and down on his shoulders. *At least he makes a nice shield.*

Keet's tesla rifle crackled and a man screamed. Dull blue electricity flickered in the night. Bullets splintered the wooden dock near Farren's boots; the men with pistols were targeting their legs.

Tiberius stood on the ship's bridge, clearly illuminated by the interior lights. His massive hands danced across the control panels: igniting engines, directing power.

Dahlia scampered over the gangway. She ducked into the hatch, flattening herself against a bulkhead. Another electricity-induced scream issued from behind Farren. Keet shouted obscenities with every shot, her footsteps pounding the wooden planks.

"Come on!" Dahlia yelled as Farren reached the gangway.

It was a narrow metal plank, balanced unsteadily between the hatch and dock. Farren had traversed it slowly when they first arrived. The thought of another fall—this one from a thousand yards—held less appeal than the one he had experienced in Sainsbury. Now he sprinted across without a moment's hesitation.

He allowed Grimes to tumble onto the deck inside. Dahlia stood there, back against a wall, cradling her bandaged arm and watching the action unfolding on the dock. The pistol dangled from her hand.

"Are you alright?" Farren grabbed her chin, turning it roughly towards him. "Are you hit?"

"No," she said.

The disapproval in her eyes was plain. Farren dropped his hand and looked away. Caught up in the fear and excitement, he had momentarily forgotten himself. He felt like a fool.

"Good to hear, sweetheart."

Outside, Keet raced along the dock, shooting as she went. Men huddled behind barrels and boxes on the pier. Every few seconds one would lean out to fire. Two slumped, stunned, on the dock.

The woman's a brilliant shot.

Keet paused at the end of the gangway, crouched, and

fired the tesla rifle. A man hunkering next to a cargo crate was blasted from his hiding place.

Keet scrambled over the metal plank. Sweat streamed down her face, matting her bright hair. One sleeve of her coveralls was singed.

"Shove off the gangway," she ordered.

Farren and Dahlia obeyed, pushing the edge of the ramp off the airship. It toppled from the dock. Keet grabbed a funnel speaker on the wall.

"We're aboard. Let's go!"

Engines thrummed, gears whirred, and the *Wayfarer Elizabeth* began to rise. The men on the dock shouted, leaning out from their makeshift cover. Bullets and tesla bolts peppered the hull.

Keet stood at the hatch opening and watched their attacks light up the night. Her undamaged hand rested on the hatch door control lever. The airship hovered several feet above the docks, engines revving for flight. Loose anchor lines trailed like frayed hairs.

Harold Grimes groaned. Farren glanced at him, sprawled forgotten on the deck, as he twitched and rolled over.

Keet oughta stun him again before we take him to the brig. Farren was just opening his mouth to suggest it when everything happened at once.

Grimes yanked a pistol from beneath the folds of his jacket. Light from the docks shimmered and slid along the deadly barrel. Farren acted on instinct, shoving Dahlia aside, crushing her against the steel wall. Keet turned.

The bullet caught her square in the chest.

"Keet!" Dahlia pushed against Farren's back.

He stood frozen; it was unfolding in slow motion, but he had no time to react. Keet looked down at the blood spreading over her moss-colored coveralls. Surprise plastered itself across her features. She staggered, reached for the wall, missed. Fingernails scraped metal and she tumbled out the open hatch.

"Keet!"

Farren glanced outside and saw Keet lying facedown on the dock below. She had miraculously avoided the terrible drop down the cliff face. Tesla bolts flashed around her; a few found their mark. If she'd been conscious when she hit the dock, she wasn't now.

But Farren had a more pressing concern: the pistol aimed for him next. He was too quick for it. A surging tackle pinned Grimes to the floor. Farren batted away the pistol—it skittered along the hall—and punched Grimes viciously in the jaw.

Dahlia clutched the speaker funnel, yelling: "Tiberius, stop! Keet's been shot—she's back on the dock!"

The *Wayfarer Elizabeth* shuddered to a halt. Grimes struggled. Farren hit him again. This time the man lost consciousness and wilted, arms flopping to the ground.

Men on the dock scrambled toward Keet's prone form with weapons held at the ready. A dark stain spread underneath her.

How much time does she have? Is today her day?

Farren felt sick. He hadn't known Keet for long, but her feistiness and boundless energy had grown on him quickly. She didn't deserve this.

"They're going to capture her." Dahlia's eyes widened. "They'll arrest her for helping us, or for assaulting that barkeeper."

She looked at Farren, her expression inscrutable. Black hair shone in the inconsistent light.

"We need her, Farren."

He knew what she was going to do an instant before she did it.

"Dahlia, no!"

Dahlia leapt from the hatchway. She struck the wooden pier ten feet below and rolled. Momentum tried to throw her off the dock into the void of sky, but she caught herself on a loose plank and struggled up. Her pistol fired madly. It looked woefully inadequate next to the bulky tesla rifles toted by the approaching men.

Farren checked his belt for his own pistol. The airship drifted, the gap broadening. A running start would be his only hope of making the jump.

"Back off!" Dahlia screamed. Several of the assailants dropped to the dock to avoid her wild shots. How many bullets had she fired?

Farren retreated into the hall and sprinted forward. He prepared to leap, praying for enough momentum, when a massive hand snatched him back. Metal plates clamped his shoulder. Tiberius tossed him to the ground beside the unconscious Grimes.

"Fly the ship."

There was no mistaking the uncontrolled fury in the cyborg's tone, even filtered through his machine of a body. Raw power. Utter rage. He was an enormous shadow silhouetted between Farren and the hatch. Tiberius leaned toward the opening, throwing his armored head forward. An earsplitting roar shook the aviator to his bones. He couldn't see around Tiberius, but he imagined a terrified retreat was ensuing on the dock.

Steel scraped. The cyborg bent and launched into the air. He was an avenging demon, a half-seen shape barreling through the night. Wood buckled and cracked as he landed, crouched, next to Keet and Dahlia. Farren didn't envy whatever men were left.

The airman wanted to help, wanted to join the fray. Years of battle in the armed forces had taught him to aid any companion in need. But if he leapt, the *Wayfarer Elizabeth* would float away and leave them trapped. Fly the ship, Tiberius had said. So he would fly the ship.

Chapter Twenty-three
A Harsh Reality

✳

Tiberius' impact rattled the dock so violently Dahlia thought the entire structure would collapse. Splinters erupted beneath his feet.

Relief flooded her. She had jumped to defend Keet because the bounty hunter was their best chance of reaching Port Argun. It had taken only a second to leap from the airship, and another to regret it.

Before Ansel unlocked her watch, Dahlia always believed she had many years remaining. Risk didn't exist if she was sure to survive. But when the bullets began streaking past, she remembered the zero on her watch. *There's no telling how much time I have. It could be today.*

She felt terribly, undeniably mortal.

"Get behind me," Tiberius growled.

Dahlia snatched Keet's arm and tugged her away from the edge of the dock. They huddled behind the gargantuan cyborg.

Tiberius roared again and Dahlia felt the sound in her chest. Electricity arced from twin tesla rifles on his shoulders. Shrieks issued from somewhere near the pier—it sounded as if the men who hadn't scrambled for cover wouldn't have the chance to. The cyborg raised the built-in gun on his arm and fired bullets into the chaos. More shrieking.

The dock shuddered. Dahlia glanced around, hugging Keet's blood-soaked body tight to her chest. The *Wayfarer Elizabeth's* gondola had scraped the end of the dock. A chunk of wood was missing where it had struck. The airship shifted uncertainly.

Farren's piloting it; he's trying to bring it closer so we can board.

A storm of bullets and electricity flickered against the night. It was all from Tiberius' assault. Their attackers—the ones who could still move—were retreating en masse. Weapons littered the ground in their wake.

The airship drifted closer, bumped the dock again— Dahlia reeled her legs back from the impact zone—and steadied.

Go!

Dahlia grabbed Keet under the arms and hauled her through the open hatch. She yelled back out, "Tiberius! Let's move!"

The cyborg rotated his head. He caught sight of Keet safe inside and, without further consideration, lumbered after them. Not one person was brave enough to shoot as he retreated.

He stepped through the hatch, his steel form blocking the entryway. Yellow eyes glowed behind his slotted face grille.

"Take her to the medical bay." He took hold of the speaker funnel: "We're aboard. Fly, Mr. Reed."

Engines rumbled. The airship vibrated. Lawson's Ridge receded from Dahlia's limited view out the hatchway.

Harold Grimes stirred where he lay on the deck, blinking in confusion. Tiberius seized him. Two enormous armored hands clamped around Grimes' small torso. Dahlia knew what would happen next. She heaved Keet onto her shoulders and staggered toward the medical bay. Her mind screamed at her not to look, but she couldn't stop herself.

The cyborg held Grimes in the air and squeezed.

"No, no, stop!" The man was fully awake now. He struggled and beat against Tiberius' thick arms to no effect.

A shriek accompanied the sharp snaps of several ribs. It sounded like ice cracking on a frozen pond. Motors whirred. The cyborg squeezed harder.

"Please..." Grimes wheezed.

A sudden pop. Bile rose in Dahlia's throat. She'd played around with enough dead watches with her papa to recognize the noise one made when it was crushed. The man must have had it in his shirt pocket.

Grimes slumped, lifeless, in Tiberius' grip. Dahlia finally looked away and allowed her steps to carry her from the grisly scene. Her heart pounded. She didn't flee fast enough to avoid hearing the body thump onto the deck.

* * *

Keet lay motionless on the operating table. Sweaty, pale, and soaked in blood, she looked on the verge of death. Her face stood out starkly against the pink and blue hair. Tiberius hunched in the doorway, observing Dahlia as she cut away Keet's ruined coveralls. Dahlia's eyes darted to him, drawn to the massive hands. Those hands had cracked ribs and watches. Those hands had *killed*.

"She won't heal if I don't repair her watch first," Dahlia said.

"Then repair it. I'll do what I can for her."

Dahlia fumbled for Keet's watch, undoing the tarnished chain around her neck.

"Do you know how much time she has?" Dahlia asked

as she undid the chain. "If today's her day, trying to save her will be pointless. I know she *says* she doesn't look at her watch, but…"

Tiberius remained quiet while she examined the outside of the gleaming watch. There were no visible issues—the break had to be internal.

"I don't know," Tiberius rumbled faintly. "She didn't lie to you."

Dahlia flicked open Keet's watch, read the time, and clicked it shut.

"I'll repair it."

*   *   *

It was the escape wheel: the portion of the watch that regulated energy transfer between the pallet and the gear train. Keet's wound had bent the escape pinion and unbalanced the entire system. Dahlia examined the ticking device, her tools spread out on the kitchen table.

Seems to be a simple fix: I just need to tap the pinion back into position. Simple, yet stressful nonetheless. If she struck it too hard, or worked the metal back and forth too many times, the pinion could break and stop the watch.

She went to work. It was difficult, with the airship swaying and Tiberius' plates scraping distractingly in the background. Every time she heard them, the terrible image of Harold Grimes shrieking floated before her eyes. Her hands trembled.

Just focus. Keet will survive, but she'll only be in a condition to help if I fix her. That injury will have her unconscious as long as the watch is broken.

She rejoined Tiberius in the medical bay a few minutes later.

"It's repaired," Dahlia said, placing the watch next to

Keet on the operating table.

"I've stopped the bleeding." Tiberius backed away to give her space. "You do the rest. My hands…"

His armored face tilted down and he held up enormous, bloodied hands. They were far too clunky for delicate surgery.

Dahlia knew this had been coming. She didn't appreciate being selected for the role of physician-in-training, but there was no other way.

"Very well." She washed up in the service sink. "You should know Keet's watch has just over——"

"No!" boomed Tiberius. Dahlia flinched. "Don't tell me her time. I don't want to know."

Dahlia tilted her head.

How can he not want to know?

The cyborg was the oddest creature she'd ever met, and not only because he was half-machine.

I'm the only person who knows Keet's time.

She dried her hands on a towel, nodded to Tiberius, and began.

* * *

Dahlia finally sighed and leaned back from the table. Blood coated her front and hands. Keet looked the same, apart from a white bandage encircling her torso. Tiberius cradled her head, one metal finger stroking the pink half of her hair with exquisite tenderness. It seemed he was afraid any errant movement might damage his wife.

Exhaustion muddied Dahlia's thoughts. She sat at the foot of the operating table and looked down at herself, at the dried blood. Her mind had no room for disgust.

"She was like this when I met her."

Dahlia jerked at the low rumble of Tiberius' voice. He

had no human face, perhaps no vocal cords either, but somehow the emotion came through.

"Before I became a cyborg, I was a surgeon," he continued, unperturbed by Dahlia's silence. "She staggered into my clinic one night, shot by some criminal she was hunting. I patched her up. We talked. Most charming woman I'd ever met. Four months later she came back shot in the leg. I patched that too."

His sentences sounded strained, stubby. He stared into Keet's face as he held her head. Dahlia didn't know how to react to the awkward pile of words.

"She asked me to join up with her bounty hunting. I'd fallen in love. I said yes. We married a year later. Built an airship and named it the *Traveling Anne*. Had incredible adventures. Keet was the mechanic, the fighter. I collected information.

"The fire wasn't her fault, but she blames herself for it. Because she was our engineer. We were docked in Port Argun. She was out in the city—I don't remember why. There was an engine problem and the hydrogen ignited. The *Traveling Anne* exploded.

"I don't recall much. I was burned inside and out. Keet salvaged what she could, paid for a watch repairman and a physician. Physician said I would survive, barely. But I couldn't breathe without a machine. Couldn't stand, couldn't talk. I wanted to die…"

A grating noise issued from Tiberius. Dahlia couldn't tell if it was a sigh, a cry, a bitter laugh…

"Keet saved me. She made me into this so I could live again," he shrugged his huge shoulder plates to indicate himself. "We went back to bounty hunting two years ago. Things are different now. But the worst isn't this body. It's knowing Keet blames herself for it. The guilt eats her."

Artificial yellow eyes locked onto Dahlia's. She held

his gaze. Was this the same creature who had crushed a man to death earlier that evening? In some ways she still couldn't forgive him, but in others she understood his actions better than she wanted to admit.

There were no words, so she didn't speak any. They remained in silence, the woman and the cyborg. Keet's breaths gradually grew longer, deeper; the sounds of sleep rather than forced unconsciousness.

Dahlia didn't speak until exhaustion began drawing her eyelids down. She urged them open again.

"Tiberius, can I ask you a question?"

"Yes."

"That man, Harold Grimes. You killed him after he shot Keet. Why would you do that?"

Tiberius shifted.

"He hurt my wife."

Dahlia's hands clenched, knuckles white. She had already known the reason; it was the next part, the aftermath, that she cared about.

"And," Dahlia continued, tone laced with anticipation, "when you killed him, when you saw the life leave him, did you…did it make you…feel better?"

The cyborg laid Keet's head down on the operating table. His steel hands scratched the gleaming metal.

"No."

Chapter Twenty-four
The Bloodhound

✳

Sebastian Macall was the sword, and the sword was him. Polished steel sang through the air as he leapt and twisted, parried and slashed. Beads of sweat spun from his forehead. Booted feet swiveled and squeaked on coated concrete.

The practice room was empty apart from him, his sword, and the echo of his breathing. Assorted dummies and armor sat stacked in the corners. They were useful for training, or if he cared to compete against a fellow swordsman. But that was a rarity. There were few men whose skills held any interest for the General.

Today he simply wanted to feel the hilt in his grip, the blood pounding in his veins, and the heft of the sword. His thoughts had been muddled of late. Dahlia Walker's face blurred with Sita Senguptar's until he could no longer distinguish the two. The blade was the only thing that could grant any semblance of clarity.

"They'll find her," he said out loud between strikes. "No bounty hunter can resist such a reward."

"And what will you do when you have her?"

Light flickered along the sword as Sebastian conversed with himself.

"I can't kill her."

"No, you can't."

"I'm sure Ansel told her everything. She'll know where to find the promethium."

King Bespalov's science division had analyzed Ansel's research and shared their findings with Sebastian at his request. The last months of Ansel's writing were devoted to his expedition in Janmasthala. It had all been documented: the mines he and Sita had searched, the cities and villages they had visited... But then the story went blank. Were there pages missing? Sebastian doubted it. Ansel, that greedy criminal, never recorded it because he didn't want Sebastian to know what he had discovered. He had wanted to keep the promethium for himself.

"You lost, Ansel. Your daughter will tell me where it is."

"And the science division can fix the resurrection device."

"And we'll take the *Imperial Might* to Janmasthala to find promethium."

"To resurrect Sita."

The sword whistled. Sebastian dove, tumbled, and sprang up to impale the air with more vehemence than necessary. He imagined stabbing Ansel, imagined the screaming and the satisfying fountain of blood as the sword pierced his traitorous heart. It was disappointing that the son of a bitch had committed suicide. But then again, it only proved his cowardice.

"Why'd you kill yourself? Why'd you destroy your watch, Ansel?"

"I'd have been happy to do it for him."

"He probably didn't want you to see his time. You would have known he threw it all away to save Dahlia. You would've known she was alive."

"But did he use time transfer? Or resurrection?"

"I can't believe you didn't realize what he'd done until you left. He had *promethium* there, and a time device. You could've had it all."

Sebastian froze, poised at the end of a sweeping slash. Footsteps echoed in the hall outside. He lowered the sword and composed himself, wiping the worst of the sweat from his face with a sleeve.

A knock at the door resounded from the walls.

"General Macall, sir. Lieutenant Warren with a message."

"Come in."

The door opened and the young man from the radio division ducked inside. He stood stiffly at attention, hands stuck flat to his sides.

"Sir, Dahlia Walker's been sighted in Lawson's Ridge. The deserter is with her."

Sebastian felt a thrill of excitement. His heartbeat, already racing from the swordplay, accelerated further.

"Excellent, Lieutenant. Is she in custody?"

"No, sir. She's aboard an airship called *Wayfarer Elizabeth*. It's a bounty hunting vessel registered to Beatrice and Tiberius Hawkins."

"Have the thirty-thousand gilver reward ready when they arrive," Sebastian ordered, "and prepare an escort ship to meet them."

The Lieutenant's gaze darted to the floor and stayed there.

"Sir, they've...well, it doesn't look as if they're going to turn the fugitives in."

"What?"

"The criminals were working with the Hawkins' to capture another bounty target. They appear to have joined forces. Sir."

Sebastian struggled to conceal a wash of wrath. The

sword ached in his hand and he sheathed it hastily before he could kill the unfortunate messenger. Lieutenant Warren seemed to sense his peril. He broke attention and took a step back.

"Sir?"

"Tell your superiors to radio Colonel Puce at the Delmarean border. I want him to take one of his airships to intercept the *Wayfarer Elizabeth* immediately and retrieve Walker."

Lawson's Ridge was close to Anglia, and Sebastian was confident they could slip an airship in and out undetected. No sense in inciting an unplanned skirmish. He yearned to board the *Imperial Might* and pursue them himself, but they would be long gone by the time an operation could be organized.

"And what should we tell Colonel Puce do with the rest, sir? The deserter and Mr. and Mrs. Hawkins?"

"The deserter should be brought here with Walker to stand trial. Puce can do as he pleases with the bounty hunters, but I don't want to hear their names again."

Puce was well known for his merciless savagery. An open order of that sort would see the foolhardy Hawkinses dead without the General taking responsibility. People died all the time in war.

"Is that all, sir?"

"Yes. Dismissed."

After Lieutenant Warren had effectually fled the room, Sebastian drew his sword again, holding it in two hands to admire the deadly blade. His reflection stared back at him. Lank hair, skeletal cheekbones, droplets of sweat clinging to his temples. Sunken, haunted eyes.

"Colonel Puce will find her."

Chapter Twenty-five
The Pigeon Plot

✳

The Hattaran Mountains swept away under the hull of the *Wayfarer Elizabeth*. Peaks stretched in aimless succession: ivory, sharp, and deceptively small from where Dahlia perched far above. She stood on the bridge, her head tilted toward the glass windshield but not touching—such a pose would have been too childish in front of Farren.

The aviator himself languished in the pilot's seat, hands draped over the instrument panel. A bag of sunflower seeds slowly shrank beside him. The two of them were embroiled in rehashing the events of the previous day.

"All I'm saying, sweetheart, is that what you did was awful stupid," Farren said. "Jumping onto the dock when you've got no idea what your time is."

"But it worked, didn't it?" she replied. "I couldn't let Keet be captured. Tiberius would insist we rescue her, and who knows how long that would take?"

Dahlia glanced over her shoulder to check that they were still alone on the bridge. The cyborg was nowhere to be seen; he hadn't moved from Keet's bedside since her surgery.

Dahlia had already relayed Tiberius' story to Farren. As much as it felt like violating Tiberius' privacy, she'd thought the aviator needed to know.

"I still can't believe he crushed that guy," said Farren, popping a sunflower seed into his mouth.

"Do you blame him?" Dahlia frowned at the memory. "Grimes almost killed his wife."

"But still. I figured him for the silent, calm type."

She resisted the urge to snap at him. *What does he know about revenge?*

Dahlia placed one palm against the windshield and leaned back, staring at her own reflection. It was alarming how much the woman in the glass had changed. What had previously been an expensive blouse, skirt, and jacket were littered with dirt and rips. Her green eyes rested atop dark lines, souvenirs from a series of sleepless nights. Exhaustion clung to her. But she still had the same black hair, the same deep tan skin—'toasted,' Farren had called it. A bandage constricted her mechanical-dog-bitten arm.

She touched the reflection's cheek and imagined it was her papa touching hers.

Last night, before falling into bed, she had eased open the door to the bounty hunters' office. It was a mess: mechanical pigeons lying on the desk, wanted posters tacked to a giant corkboard, a map of the continent pin-cushioned with labeled needles: "Quill sighting, 21 August." "Ulbert rumored location, 16 September." "D. Walker escape, 3 October." But it wasn't her own name or the poster with her face that drew her attention. There, centered above a desk piled high with papers, was a photograph of Ansel Walker. Above him, the words: 'CONFIDENTIAL. WANTED: ANSEL WALKER. 300,000 GILVER REWARD'. She had believed the truth since listening to the sound tape. But seeing her papa's face there had brought it all into harsh, crushing reality.

He had caused all this. Without Ansel Walker, Sebastian Macall would have had no one to murder, and

Dahlia would have no one to avenge. His wanted poster—torn from the board—was tucked into her handbag.

Where did it all go wrong? she wondered, suddenly melancholy. It had been so easy, before, to blame the entire situation on Macall. Now she didn't know what to believe.

"You okay, sweetheart?"

Farren's voice jerked her from her musings.

"Yes. I was just thinking."

"Ah. Dangerous stuff."

"Dangerous, yes, but necessary. It's a pastime you might want to consider."

"Ouch," he grinned. They both knew it was banter. "Whatcha thinkin' 'bout?"

A thundering explosion drowned out Dahlia's witty reply. The deck tilted under her feet and she stumbled into the windshield. Mountains stretched like teeth below. Orange flames billowed in the sky to their left, close enough to heat her skin but too far to scorch the *Wayfarer Elizabeth*. She shoved herself back from the glass, mind whirling in confusion. An alarm blared nearby. *A malfunction?* Her skin crawled with the memory of Tiberius' story, the burning inside and out...

"Devil's blood! What was that?" Farren fought the controls to right the airship, easing the engines into idle. His face was white.

"A mechanical failure?" Dahlia said.

"I sure hope so."

His hands fluttered over the instrument panel, flicking switches and depressing buttons. The alarm stuttered into silence. Dahlia found herself grateful for his piloting experience.

A new light flashed among the multicolored collection, accompanied by an insistent beep.

"Radio alert," Farren responded when she pointed it

out. "We're being hailed. Shit."

A few more levers rotated the airship. Snowy peaks swirled beneath them as a smattering of ash from the explosion blew across the windshield. And there, directly behind their original heading, loomed an Anglian airship. It had no gondola; all operations took place inside the matte black hull. Tinted glass stretched across the bow. Weapons bristled from the sides. It was too close for the miss to have been anything but purposeful, a literal shot across the bow.

Dahlia gripped the back of Farren's pilot chair until her fingers ached. Her heartbeat pounded in her ears.

"What do we do?" she whispered.

Tiberius stormed onto the bridge before Farren could reply. The cyborg's yellow eyes roved over the Anglian vessel, the myriad of control lights. He grew still.

"Answer them," he ordered. One giant metal finger pointed at Dahlia, "You stay quiet."

Farren picked a sunflower seed shell from his mouth, let it fall to the deck, and flipped the radio switch.

"Military airship, this is *Wayfarer Elizabeth* responding to hail," he said.

"*Wayfarer Elizabeth*, this Colonel Puce of the warship *Debellatio*. I'm here to take custody of Dahlia Walker and the Anglian deserter on your vessel. I request that you secure your engines and prepare to be boarded."

"I'm sorry, Colonel, but I don't know who you're talking—"

"If you lie to me again I will target your hydrogen tanks. We have a dozen witnesses who saw Walker board your airship yesterday. Secure your engines immediately."

"Just…just a second, Colonel."

"You have five minutes. I should warn you that I have permission to destroy your ship if you don't give up Walker."

"Roger that."

Farren clicked the radio off and turned in his chair to look at Tiberius. His fingers curled around the grip of the pistol in his belt. Dahlia stepped back from both of them, pressing herself against the windshield.

Cornered.

"Mr. Reed——" she said. He held up a hand for her to be silent.

The cyborg and the aviator stared at one another as if challenging the other to blink first. Tiberius possessed no eyelids, yet Farren seemed unfazed.

"I promised this woman I'd see her to Port Argun," he growled as he stood, putting his face too close to Tiberius' grille. "And if you lay so much as one metal finger on her, I swear I'll blow your head off. I don't care if all I've got's a pistol... I'll find a way."

His pronouncement was met with silence. Dahlia braced herself for Tiberius' imminent attack. It felt like she was squeezing her eyes shut without closing them.

Then a scraping sound emanated from within the cyborg's armor. It was the one Dahlia had never been able to link to an emotion.

"No need for that," he rumbled. "Miss Walker risked herself to save my wife. It'd be criminal to repay her with betrayal."

Farren relaxed, but one hand lingered by his gun. Dahlia was surprised to discover she'd been holding her breath and let it out in a long sigh.

"But if I stay, they'll kill us all," she said. "The hydrogen——"

"That's just bluster," Farren replied. "They want you alive. They might try to shoot out our engines, but there's no way they'll go for the hydrogen. Tiberius—what sort of offensive capabilities do you have on this junk heap?"

"V50 tesla cannons. Two forward, one aft. Rotating manned gun turret under the gondola."

"V50s and bullets won't do any good against that ship. Got any explosives? Dynamite, TNT, nitrols?"

"Gelignite in the storeroom. But we don't have a launcher."

Farren paced as he thought. He paused and squinted at the black Anglian airship. His lips moved soundlessly, then he resumed pacing.

"Okay," he said at last, "I didn't sail on the *Debellatio*, but I was on another ship of the same class. They had issues with the outermost engine shaft bearings. Bad design; they couldn't hold up to impacts. If we can detonate some of that gelignite on one of those bearings, the ship'll lose the engine."

The aviator sat, messing his hair with an air of pride.

"Mechanical pigeons!" Dahlia blurted. The two men looked at her. "Oh, don't you see? We load a pigeon with explosives, send it to perch on the bearing, and detonate it!"

"That's it!" Farren jumped to his feet. The radio light on the instrument panel flashed again. "Tiberius, tell us where the storeroom is and we'll rig it up. Stall for time with Colonel Puce, would you?"

They left the cyborg standing on the bridge, flicking the radio switch despondently.

Chapter Twenty-six
Dogfight

✳

"Found it!" Dahlia knelt and yanked a box of explosives from the dust in a corner of the storeroom.

"Careful with that!"

"Oh, come on. It won't explode without a detonator, right?"

Farren shrugged. *Wish the air force had spent more time on explosives training.* He helped Dahlia lay the box on the floor next to the quartet of mechanical pigeons they had scrounged up. Four pigeons for four engines.

After a few fasteners and some quick-dry epoxy whose fumes made them both dizzy, the pigeon bombs were complete. Wrapped sticks of gelignite jutted out at odd angles from the backs of the birds. Radio detonators topped off the mess like bows on a present.

"Beautiful," said Farren as they each scooped up a pair of pigeons. "Just beautiful."

"I'm not quite sure I agree," Dahlia said.

They hurried out onto the gangway. Farren yanked the hatch control lever and flattened himself against the wall to avoid a blast of wind.

The *Debellatio* was close and moving closer with each passing moment. Ropes snapped and twisted against its black hull. The windshield was a giant glassy pupil.

"Okay, now." Farren lined up the four pigeons on the floor. "Usually you speak a message to these things and they deliver it. But we just want them to deliver, so," he depressed the button on the first mechanical creature, "end message. Deliver to the starboard forward engine of the airship *Debellatio*."

The pigeon flexed its wings in a quick system test, chirped, and disappeared through the open hatch. Dahlia squinted after it. Farren repeated the procedure with the remaining pigeon-turned-weapons.

"They all make it?" he asked.

"I'm not sure," said Dahlia, still scrunching her eyes. "I have trouble seeing long distances."

The aviator looked for her. From their position in front of the airship, he could only see the port and starboard forward engines. A tiny blotch of unpainted gray rested on each.

"They made it." He raised the first detonator, a metal radio device the size of his hand. He wanted to say something witty about Dahlia's nearsightedness, something she would giggle at. But fear of the Anglian airship stifled his humor.

"You want to do the honors, sweetheart?"

Dahlia plucked the detonator from his grasp, stared toward the *Debellatio*, and pressed it.

A crack split the cold air. Smoke trailed from the engine. Three more detonators, three more cracks, and the trail grew into a cloud.

"Got 'em all," Farren observed. "They're dead in the air—that was easy."

Bullets pinged against the *Wayfarer Elizabeth*. A pair of tesla cannons flashed blue electricity in their direction.

"Whoa!"

Dahlia had the presence of mind to close the hatch

door just before a hail of gunfire peppered it with dents.

* * *

Back on the bridge with Tiberius, they could see the great form of the Anglian warship hanging stagnant. Weapons flashed through the billowing smoke.

The *Wayfarer Elizabeth* fled the scene with all the power of its shabby single engine. A radio hail light blinked angrily on the instrument panel, but no one cared to hear what Colonel Puce had to say.

Probably a word or two about how he'll track us down and kill us.

Farren hadn't known the man personally, but he'd have to be a fearsome foe in order to command troops at the border. The section of Anglia near Delmar saw the most conflict of any region on the continent.

Dread nagged at the aviator. First he had angered General Macall, now he'd made an enemy of Colonel Puce. He was walking farther and farther down a treacherous path, and he didn't care to see what was at the end of it. Although it wasn't as if they could do him much harm. Not when he'd be dead in…

Farren reached into his pocket for his watch and almost dropped it when an explosion rattled the airship. Alarms burst to life around them.

"Devil's blood!" he swore. "What'd they hit?"

"Engine room," said Tiberius. "They've launched fliers."

True to his words, two dark shapes swooped in the *Wayfarer Elizabeth*'s wake. Farren recognized them as Ravenwings: a lethal combination of speed and weaponry. The *Debellatio* was too far to be a threat, but the fliers…

This is gonna be trouble.

"Tiberius, we'll need to use those tesla cannons!" he said. "You got any fliers in the hangar?"

"Two. We keep them ready to go."

Farren didn't wait for further information. He raced from the bridge, leaving Dahlia behind to watch the battle.

The metal-plated deck rattled beneath his feet as he clattered into the hangar. A pair of old Vireo 43-ARs lounged in the center of an otherwise empty room. It took him barely a minute to pick one, power up the systems, and tumble out the sliding hatch into the sky.

The pearly mountain snow blinded Farren for a few seconds. Wind scraped water from his eyes. Then his hands yanked the joystick and he soared. The *Debellatio* shrank in the distance, weapons quiet, but its two escorts were just getting started.

A line of bullets pricked the air. He pulled up, spun, and came out facing the Ravenwings. They were streamlined, cutting-edge, and could fly circles around him if they wanted. His stomach knotted. Being shot down at this height would obliterate his watch. He'd be as dead as if he'd waited twenty more days.

Farren found the weapon control stick and twisted it. The rotating gun on his Vireo's bow sparked to life. Flying past the Anglian aircraft while attacking was no mean feat. His vessel wobbled. The bullets missed by an embarrassingly wide margin.

Another explosion ripped at the *Wayfarer Elizabeth*. Farren caught sight of a cannon mounted to one of the Ravenwings. It wasn't much use against his small vessel, but the larger airship was an easy target.

He dodged a hail of bullets from the other Ravenwing and caught sight of the pilot's face through the windshield. It was no one he knew. He breathed a sigh of relief.

Farren ducked underneath both the Anglian fliers. He

focused on the one with the cannon: the obvious threat to the *Wayfarer Elizabeth*. His rotating gun spat bullets. Sparks scattered on the Ravenwing's hull, but it wasn't enough. The enemy flier pulled up and over the *Wayfarer Elizabeth's* envelope, barely missing the mismatched metal hull.

Damn! He's using the ship as cover!

The other Ravenwing was on his tail, but he had no time to address it. A cannon boomed. Smoke billowed from the airship.

If the hydrogen ignites, Dahlia's dead! And Keet and Tiberius, but they were incidental.

He jerked the controls and dove after the first Ravenwing. Bullets scored holes his Vireo's steel sides. Farren winced, waiting for the telltale burning scent or a vibration in the joystick. Nothing. By some miracle the internal machinery remained intact.

He laughed, half terrified, half ecstatic. It was flying at its best: the rush of excitement, the crazy contortions in his gut, the world spinning below. His Vireo skimmed a foot above the *Wayfarer Elizabeth*. Farren blasted the engine, spiraled, and rained bullets on the first Ravenwing.

This time he struck home. The enemy's fuselage erupted in flame that seared his cheeks as he whipped past. Its cannon died with it.

Gotcha.

But he had no time to watch his foe flail and break apart on the mountainside. The flier trailing him fired again. Farren ducked and wove away from the *Wayfarer Elizabeth*. Out in the open sky, far from Dahlia, he'd have one less thing to worry about.

He zigzagged, spiraled, and executed daring flips that seemed to crush his brain against his skull. The Ravenwing followed him through everything. It rained bullets between each maneuver that forced him to launch into yet another risky display.

The attacks drew closer and closer. Farren's hand sweated on the joystick. He abandoned the weapon control. What was the use in shooting when it took all he had to survive? His heart drummed in his chest.

Suddenly, the *Wayfarer Elizabeth* materialized in front of him. He reacted on instinct and streaked below it with inches to spare. When had he turned back? Somewhere in all the maneuvering he'd ended up where he'd started.

"Goddammit!"

The gondola loomed in his way, he had no choice but to slow down. It was that or plow straight through. The tone of the Vireo's engine deepened as it decelerated. He was utterly exposed. He hung there in the stillness for a split second that seemed to stretch into eternity.

Bullets snapped into the wings, gashed the engine block. The craft quavered beneath him. A flame crawled from the circuitry, accompanied by the thick smell of burning.

"No, no, no!"

The Vireo dipped towards the ground, the snow-capped peaks below looking more like a graveyard every moment. Farren wrenched the joystick so hard it nearly snapped. The open hangar door beckoned. If only he could get to it, if only that son of a bitch in the Ravenwing didn't—

More bullets assailed him. Farren screamed in frustration, clutching the controls for all he was worth. The nose pointed toward the hatch but it was drooping, arcing downward in slow motion. It wasn't fair—this wasn't his day. He couldn't die! No, he refused to die! Life was too bright, the wind too searing, his heartbeat too frantic...

Is this how Father—

Then he rocketed through the door and into the dim

hangar. He barely had time to screech to a halt before his aircraft could ram the opposite wall. Fire enveloped his entire engine. Orange flames licked at the metal plates, threatening to engulf the craft.

Fire on a hydrogen airship was every aviator's worst fear. Farren's instincts told him to leap out and escape the burning Vireo, but that would doom them all. He prayed and pulled the joystick again. Wheels squeaked as the dying vessel lurched forward, rotating to face the hangar door.

He thrust the controls, gathering speed. Then, when stopping became impossible, Farren threw himself from the Vireo. For once his foot didn't catch on the side.

The deck reached to meet him and he rolled to a halt inches from the open hatch. Miles of wicked sky lolled just out the doorway. Farren hung his head out and sucked at the air like a drowning man brought to the surface.

The flaming Vireo receded. Its fireball faded to a point of flickering light, then just smoke. Farren wiped his forehead with one trembling hand. A burnt taste lingered on his tongue, leaching the water from his mouth. Heat dissipated from his skin, but he was unharmed.

That was close.

He struggled to his feet, knees weak, when the second Ravenwing rose in front of him. It surged from beneath the airship and roared past, strafing the deck. Farren leaped back. Bullets rang, sparked, and scratched at the metal. Some came so close he could sense the wind of their passing.

"Shit!"

The Ravenwing pulled away in a wide arc that would take it past a second time. It banked in the distance, trailing a wave of sound.

Where was the lever to shut the hatch? Farren's eyes darted and—there! On the opposite side of the door. He sprinted for it. Running across the hangar, racing the Anglian aircraft for his life. The Ravenwing screamed by again when he was halfway there. The first bullets clawed at his steps. A thrill of terror echoed in his chest. He couldn't take a fatal hit, but what if he fell like Keet, or ended up in a coma, or was too injured to help Dahlia, or...

Blue lightning engulfed the Ravenwing. The *Wayfarer Elizabeth's* aft tesla cannon had awakened. It swatted the flier from the air like a pesky insect. The Ravenwing tumbled past, leaking electricity and bits of itself.

Farren watched it fizzle and bow downward, then plummet to the earth to join its comrade in the snow. A tiny tail of gray, almost too small to see, was all that remained.

He slumped against a wall. Every nerve felt stretched, his senses too alert, blood pumping loudly in his ears. Knees threatened to fold from the decrease in adrenaline; he had to cling to a metal pipe to stay upright.

Farren grinned—it had been a while since he'd felt this alive. It felt damn good.

Chapter Twenty-seven
Broken Bird

✳

Keet couldn't tell if she was having a nightmare or living one. A cacophony of alarms, the slinking aroma of smoke, the metallic taste of old blood in her mouth. She swung bare feet onto the metal deck and rose. Her chest throbbed against a bandage, but it wasn't the first time she'd been shot. She could take the pain.

"Darling?" she said, wincing. "Tiberius?"

Deck plates shook underneath her as she stumbled from the room, down the hallway, and toward the engines. Those alarms—she'd installed them herself—signaled damage to the main propulsion machinery. A miasma of fear smothered her thoughts. Confusion reigned. Was there a hydrogen leak? Smoke meant fire, and if fire found the volatile gas they would all die. And Tiberius…where was Tiberius?

Blackness billowed from the engine room as Keet lurched inside. Dizziness tried to trip her. Her heartbeat pummeled her ribs like an animal protesting against the bones of its cage. Orange-tinted lights filtered through the haze to reveal a scene of destruction.

A tattered hole gaped in the *Wayfarer Elizabeth's* side. The attack—were they under attack?—had struck near one of the two main boilers. Water spewed from its severed feedwater pipes and spread over the deck, carrying dirt and debris in a widening puddle.

"Dammit."

Keet scrambled to secure the boiler before the lack of incoming water could melt its steel components. No water meant no cooling, and no cooling would inevitably cause the boiler to explode.

Oil from the valve handles coated her fingers while she wrestled them closed. Heat, or fear, or both wrung sweat from her forehead. Smoke assailed her nose. She coughed, lungs burning, and the sudden pain in her chest forced her to pause.

Tiberius…his raw skin, what remained of it, was wet under her touch. Large patches had been seared completely away; bone gleamed in a few. Ash drifted through the air, sticking to him. She hugged his body to herself, somehow stood and carried him. Breath rattled in his lungs. Eyelids were gone. Nothing left underneath but horror and pain and the knowledge that her husband, her darling and her love, would be dead soon.

Keet fluttered between the past and present, the acrid smoke and the tang of panic swinging her memory. The boiler rattled, the engine room tilted.

He lay on the operating table, a mere shadow of the man she had adored. Keet longed to touch his hand. But the fresh skin was so fragile, like that of a newborn.

"He'll survive. Barely," the physician said. "Can't walk…needs a machine to breathe…never speak again…"

It was all her fault. She hadn't looked after the ship properly; she had forgotten to check the boilers for that one day in Port Argun.

"I'll fix him."

Steel, wires, motors, lenses. Months of sleepless nights hunched over the workbench or the medical table. He was still Tiberius, wasn't he? This mechanical man? Everything was different. His voice rumbled from artificial vocal cords, cold metal replaced a warm embrace, mechanisms sufficed for laughter. Keet knew blood still pulsed through his veins somewhere behind the armor. But somewhere behind it too, centered in his chest, was a watch blackened by fire.

The boiler hissed. She stepped back, checked to ensure it was off, and then allowed herself to sink to the deck. The air cleared languidly, gradually. Smoke sucked away through the hole in the hull. Keet sat cross-legged—she was too proud to lie down, even exhausted as she was—and curled dirty arms around her chest. Terror faded, allowing the full pain of the bullet wound to wash over her. Her fingers touched the bandage and came away crimson.

Keet didn't care. She'd survive; she'd survived everything life had thrown at her so far. The watch around her neck beckoned with the offer of certainty. It would take only a moment to know exactly how much time she had. Enticing…but not enticing enough.

Where's the danger if I know? Where's the fun?

The boiler ticked as it cooled. Keet eyes followed its edges, admiring the greasy metal cylinder, the menagerie of gauges and pipes growing like roots. She smiled.

I repaired it.

* * *

Tiberius found her there after leaving Farren to pilot the airship. The cyborg knew next to nothing about the engineering systems aboard the *Wayfarer Elizabeth*, but he admitted he was long past due to learn. Mechanics had always been Keet's prerogative.

"Are you alright?" he rumbled, concerned.

"The boiler's secure."

His wife's eyes sparkled, but blood stained her chest.

"We need to take care of that."

"Yeah," she sighed, "in a minute. Just come here and sit with me."

So Tiberius sat, and took her in his arms, and together they stared at the engine room where disaster had so recently been averted. The world flew by through the tear in the hull.

Chapter Twenty-eight
Fighting Lessons

✳

"What I wouldn't give for a couple muffins right now."

Farren flopped onto the threadbare sofa next to where Dahlia sat. Dust motes played through colored shafts of sunset trickling through a porthole.

"Make them yourself," Dahlia said. She scooted to the opposite side of the couch.

"I would," he grinned, "but I can't cook to save my life."

Farren crunched on a handful of sunflower seeds, slipping the shells behind the couch. He'd discovered a large bag in Keet and Tiberius' storeroom earlier that morning.

Dahlia sniffed. She rustled the book she had been immersed in as if to request silence. It was the sole piece of reading material Farren had seen on the *Wayfarer Elizabeth*: a bounty hunting log from the office. Two days had passed since the incident with Colonel Puce, and the monotonous sailing was getting to them. Dahlia dealt with boredom by reading or listening to her music box. Farren simply napped. And did his best to forget the ever-decreasing time on his watch.

They were traveling directly to Port Argun. After Dahlia faced down Keet's attackers at Lawson's Ridge and

Farren protected the ship against Colonel Puce's fliers, the two bounty hunters seemed eager to help them in any way they could.

Dahlia turned a page of the log. The sound was loud in the relative silence. Farren studied her.

"So what do you—"

"Mr. Reed," Dahlia snapped the book shut. "I've made a decision."

"Let's hear it."

"I want you to teach me to fight."

It was an odd request, coming from her. Farren ruffled his hair and picked thoughtfully at the stubble on his chin.

"I can't kill Sebastian Macall if I can't fight," she continued. "I don't even have a hope of making it past his guards. I need your help."

"I don't know, sweetheart, you did a number on that first bounty hunter. Back at the inn," Farren grinned. "He's probably still walking funny."

She smiled and threw the book at him. He ducked, spilling sunflower seed shells on his flight jacket.

"Aw, look what you did."

"Why don't you take off that ratty old thing?" Dahlia said. "Look, it has blood on it, it's torn in a thousand places... I offered to buy you a new one."

"I like this one. It keeps me warm."

She eyed the holes in his jacket again.

"You're funny, Mr. Reed."

"I try."

Dahlia rose and picked up the book, straightening pages that had been bent from its unsuccessful flight. Farren watched the sunset caress her dark skin. Part of him wished he could become that ray of light, just to touch her.

"Okay." He dropped the last of the shells behind the couch. "I'll teach you to fight."

* * *

Dahlia flatly refused to climb atop the airship despite Farren's urging. So they found themselves inside the hangar, which, now occupied by only one aircraft, would serve as a fine practice area. The smell of fire lingered. Rows of light bulbs illuminated a room composed of the same steel panels elsewhere on the *Wayfarer Elizabeth*. The aft wall was a massive hatchway for launching fliers.

"Hold your fists up like this," Farren said. He demonstrated a fighting stance. "Keep your thumb outside your fist or you'll break it. Knees bent shoulder width apart. You right- or left-handed?"

"Right."

"Ok. Then put your right leg a little behind."

"Like this?"

Dahlia stood nearby, looking awkward yet determined as she copied his pose. Her blouse and skirt clashed with the violent posture.

"Yeah. Now when you punch, get the power from your strong back foot and carry it through to your arm."

He turned away from her and struck at the air with a series of slow jabs. Dahlia observed, then tried to imitate him.

"Good," Farren said, "but more force, sweetheart. You're trying to hurt people here, remember?"

They spent the next several hours practicing progressively more involved attacks. Dahlia was a quick student and Farren an eager teacher. But he knew, somewhere in the back of his mind, that two days of training before they reached Port Argun would never be enough to help. General Macall was one of the world's deadliest swordsmen, and certainly the most bloodthirsty.

"Let's take a break," Dahlia said at last. "I'm going to the kitchen for some water."

Sweat dripped from her forehead and stained her blouse. She smiled even as she panted from exertion, fanning herself with one hand. Farren felt his heart skip a beat.

He opened the launch door once she had left. The night air felt cool in his lungs. The *Wayfarer Elizabeth* had passed over the Hattaran Mountains and, with them, the Anglian border. Farren was in his home country again.

Trees and farms dotted the landscape, interspersed with pinpricks of light from the occasional town. He wondered idly if one of the farmhouses had been his family's. Had they lived this far west? Or closer to the capital?

It was odd to be back where he had started. Only two weeks had passed since he had boarded the *Imperial Might* and cast off lines for Sainsbury. An easy operation, they'd told him. Slip in, grab Ansel Walker, and get the hell out. Then he could spend the rest of his dwindling days at home in Port Argun, pretending not to notice his watch until it ended.

"Ah, well," he murmured, "this is better."

"What's better?"

He turned and found Dahlia standing close behind, drinking from one glass of water and proffering another. He took it.

"Your fighting skills," lied Farren. "They're getting better. I was thinking you should learn to shoot too, while we're at it. That'll be more useful against Macall anyway."

"Good idea. A tesla rifle would probably be best—we can take one onto the military base, can't we?"

"No, but I know where they keep 'em once we're inside."

"Very well, then." Dahlia set her water down in a corner. "Teach me."

They unearthed a half-charged tesla rifle from the storeroom. It was an older model, without the bells and whistles Farren was used to. No stabilizers, no auto-scope, and no limited recoil. When Dahlia aimed out the open hatch and shot it the first time, the force bowled her over onto the deck.

"Stop laughing," she said in response to his guffaws. "You didn't tell me it would do that."

Farren arrested his mirth and checked her expression. Despite the firm tone, the hint of a smile crept onto her cheeks. He offered a hand to help pull her up. To his great astonishment, she accepted it. Small, soft fingers were cool in his grasp.

I can't believe it: she actually let me touch her.

When he set Dahlia back on her feet they were standing mere inches from one another. Farren's heartbeat quickened. She tilted her head back and looked at his face, bright green eyes fixed on his.

If she'd been any other woman he would have already kissed her and more. He had always prided himself on how the ladies flocked to his easygoing charm, the swashbuckling romance of his aviator's uniform. There had been so many, he had no hope of remembering them all.

But Dahlia was different. Was it the desperate circumstances they found themselves in, or was it more? The determination in her voice, the fierce streak of independence, the genuine concern when she asked how much time he had left. Or could it be that sneaking smile—like a ray of light peeking unexpected from days of clouds? She refused to pursue him, even walked away from obvious advances...until now.

"Mr. Reed…"

Was this their moment? Farren felt as if someone had imprisoned an enthusiastic drummer in his chest.

"Yes?" He bent toward her. The sweet scent of lavender invaded his senses.

"You can let me go now."

His fantasies popped in an instant.

"Oh, sorry."

His sweaty hand opened. She pulled hers back and shuffled to put some distance between them. The rifle clinked against metal deck plates.

"Would you care to show me how to avoid sprawling like a fool when I shoot this?"

Farren ran a hand through his hair in mock nonchalance. He assumed his best bored face.

"Of course."

* * *

Keet came barreling into the hangar a while later, her pink-and-blue hair in disarray. She wore a white sleeveless top and beige pants that could only be sleepwear. Farren and Dahlia glanced over from where they crouched, immersed in firing the tesla rifle through the open hangar hatch.

"Are we under attack?" Dahlia asked in alarm.

"No, but you'll be if you keep it up. What are you idiots doing shooting electricity in my ship?"

"Mr. Reed was teaching me how to—"

"No, no, no. You see this?" Keet slapped the bulkhead next to the doorway. "The engine room's through here. You mess up and hit my machines, you die."

"It'll bring down the ship?" Dahlia eased the tesla rifle to the deck, taking care not to press anything.

"No. *I'll* kill you. For waking me up."

The bounty hunter seized the weapon from Dahlia and exited the hangar, mumbling something about ungratefulness. The passageway door slammed behind her.

"Well then." Farren clapped his hands together. "I guess that's it for the evening."

"Looks like it," Dahlia said. "Would you mind if we continue tomorrow?"

"Sure, sweetheart. I've got nothing better to do."

She made for the doorway, leaving Farren to take care of the hatch and lights. But, a step away from leaving, she froze. Black hair framed her chin in a shimmering wave as she looked over her shoulder.

"Mr. Reed?"

"Yes?"

"How much time do you have left?"

Whatever he'd been expecting, it wasn't that. A 'thank you', maybe. A 'goodnight'. Or an infinitely better, yet improbable, declaration of adoration. Disappointed, Farren reached into his stained jacket pocket for his watch.

"I thought you'd have it memorized by now," he said as he opened it.

"I thought you would too."

"Eighteen days, six hours, twenty-six minutes."

Her eyes scanned his face, searching. Farren knew she was checking to see if he was all right, if he needed her to stay.

But, to his surprise, he didn't. The simple fact that she cared was enough.

Dahlia smiled. Then she turned to the doorway and, with a tiny backwards wave, left.

"Goodnight, Mr. Reed."

Chapter Twenty-nine
Madness, Murder, and a Corpse

✳

"We should have heard by now. Perhaps she escaped."

"From Puce? The man is ruthless, an excellent soldier. I can't imagine how she could have eluded him…"

Sebastian Macall paced in his office, his boots squeaking on waxed tile. He ranted to his desk, to the flag of Anglia on the wall, and to the night outside the windowpane. Hands drew furious shapes in the air. Black hair fluttered into his eyes, but he was too embroiled in the argument to brush it aside.

"He should have caught them already."

"I'm sure he has. Their radio must be broken. Yes, that's it."

A knock at the door.

"Lieutenant Warren, sir. Here to deliver a message."

"Come in." Sebastian straightened and flustered over his appearance for a few seconds. Had to look like a general, couldn't let anything fall out of place…

The man entered and closed the door on the empty hallway beyond. He stood there, fidgeting with a button on his cuff.

"Well, spit it out. Have you heard from the Colonel?"

"He…" the Lieutenant stammered. "He found Dahlia Walker, sir."

"Excellent!" An immense weight lifted from his shoulders. "See, I told you! I told you we could rely on Puce!"

The words tumbled out of Sebastian's mouth before he could stop them. He'd been talking to no one again, but now there was someone... *Idiot. You damn idiot. You're going to ruin everything.*

Luckily, Lieutenant Warren didn't seem to notice. He stared at the floor as if fascinated by it, still twirling the button.

"General Macall, sir," he took a deep breath, "Miss Walker escaped."

"What?" Sebastian forgot about his outburst. A deadly cold leached through his limbs, infecting his brain.

"She escaped, sir. Her ship bombed the *Debellatio* and knocked out the engines. The Colonel managed to radio another airship to tow it back across to our side of the border. But by the time they arrived, she was gone."

The General fell quiet for a long moment. His right arm itched. Fingernails scraped the hilt of the sword at his waist. When he spoke again, the words blossomed with wrath.

"Why didn't you tell me this sooner?"

"The radio division just heard from the Colonel a few minutes ago, sir. I came as soon as I—"

"I said: *Why didn't you tell me this sooner?*" he screeched.

Then the sword was in Sebastian's hand. Steel flashed, blood fountained, and Warren's arm thudded to the floor. The Lieutenant stared at it, uncomprehending, his mouth forming a scream.

"Silence."

The blade darted to the Lieutenant's throat before any noise could escape.

"If you make a sound I'll cut the other one off."

Warren's breath came in sharp gasps. His eyes widened, staring at the bleeding stump, then at Sebastian, then at the sword tickling his neck. But he didn't scream.

"Now you've done it," said the General. "Why did you attack him?"

"He took so long!" Macall snarled. "Think of what we could have done if we'd known about this sooner: could have sent another airship, could have caught Dahlia Walker before she escaped."

"You cut his arm off!" yelled the General.

"Sir?" Lieutenant Warren shivered violently. Sebastian ignored him.

"There's only one thing to do," said Sebastian. "You know we can't have him running around missing an arm. We can't have him talking."

As he muttered, the General's free hand slithered onto Warren's neck. The other remained steady on the sword. Was there a chain? No. The watch had to be in his pocket.

"Please, sir." The man was crying, realization sinking in. Sebastian could smell the salt from his tears. It mingled with the metallic odor of blood until he could taste it on his tongue.

A quick search of Warren's uniform pockets and the watch fell into his grasp. The General let it slide from his fingers onto the floor. It lay between their feet. Snot trickled from Warren's nose.

"Please!" he begged.

"I told you to be quiet."

One jet-black boot came down. The Lieutenant tensed, back rigid, as the innards of his watch fractured. Muscles stood out stark in his neck. His mouth gaped in silent agony. He took a last shuddering breath, then his eyes rolled back in his head.

Sebastian stepped back, allowing Warren to crumple

to the tile where he lay, facedown. The General's lips curled into a frown.

"God damn it."

"Look what you've done."

"God *damn* it!" he roared.

Fury took him. Hands quaked, then slammed the blade through the dead man's back. Slammed it again and again and again.

"See what you made me do? See?"

He hacked at the corpse.

"See?"

Blood streaked his face, spattered his uniform, stung his eyes.

"See?"

Sebastian couldn't stop until his ire subsided and he was left staring at the mess he'd created. The sword dripped. He drew himself up and straightened his clothing.

"Now you have to dispose of that."

Chapter Thirty
Farewell in Port Argun

✳

Dahlia scrubbed her hands in the sink, washed her face, changed into a clean outfit and hung her dirty clothes on hooks. She longed to take a bath in the small tub, but sleep was too tempting.

The musty bed was soft, the blankets thin yet welcoming as she fell onto them. Water dripped from a leaky tap. The engines hummed, wind whooshed on the other side of the hull. Her eyelids drooped.

"Look, sweetie! I fixed your watch."

Ansel Walker is holding it out. They stand in his workshop in the basement, or is it the sitting room?

"But Papa, it's at zero."

"Mine is too, see?" His hands are bloody, his watch a heap of shattered bits. "And your mother's. All fixed."

Sita is suddenly there too, smiling next to Ansel.

And then Dahlia is kneeling on the carpet in a pool of crimson, but it isn't her papa who lies there, it's Farren. His eyes are little watches ticking down: five, four, three…

"Don't let me die!" he screams. Then his neck cracks and he breaks apart into pieces in her arms.

Dahlia awoke covered in sweat, sprawled atop the blankets with her pulse echoing in her ears. The image of Farren screaming burned in her mind. She swallowed and rubbed her eyelids hard, focusing on the blurs of color from the pressure. The overhead light in the room was still on.

Finally, after a few minutes of breathing in the stale scent of the pillow, her body relaxed. Fingers reached under her blouse and pulled out the watch shimmering on its chain. She opened it. The pearly white face stared back at her, the thin lines of the numbers, the heavy black hands resting on zero. Always zero.

It was a long time before she slept again.

* * *

Dahlia trained with Farren the next day, and the one after that.

"Just once, you should let me win," she said after picking herself up off the floor for the hundredth time. The aviator was being gentle, but the aches in her body could only mean bruises later. Dahlia flexed her mechanical-dog-bitten arm.

"You told me to teach you to fight," said Farren. "Macall won't go easy on you."

She lunged for him, intending to catch him off guard. Farren dodged it, throwing a softball punch. Dahlia blocked it and struck back. They traded blows for a moment or two. Then Farren grabbed her healthy arm, flipped her over his shoulder, and eased her to the deck.

"I almost had you." She stood again, breathing hard.

"Almost doesn't win a war, sweetheart."

He smoothed the sleeves of his flight jacket.

"Tell me honestly: Do you think I can defeat him?" Dahlia asked, serious. She knew the answer, but she wanted to hear it out loud.

"Sure." Farren said.

"Really?"

"No. No chance."

Dahlia felt the words like a slap and twitched.

"Aww, come on," said Farren. "Don't look so down about it. Just because you can't beat him to death with your bare hands doesn't mean you can't kill him. You'll have to be more..." he combed a hand through his hair, searching for the right term, "...creative."

She flashed him what she hoped was a convincing grin. Doubt gnawed at her mind. After she'd thrown away everything, after she'd come all this way, demanded so much from Farren and Keet and Tiberius and herself, it was excruciating to think she might choke at the final stretch. Sebastian Macall had to die. She would do anything—*anything*—to make that a reality.

"Come on," she said with renewed determination. "Fight me again."

* * *

Midday hunger forced them to retreat to the kitchen. Keet was already there, devouring pieces of bread coated in butter.

"Not much left of anything," she mumbled between chews, "but we'll be in Port Argun in time for dinner. There's a fantastic restaurant there, best steak in town."

"Are you sure that's a good idea?" Dahlia said as she sat down at the table, propping a book open with one hand. "Won't the military be looking for you? They're sure to know you helped us."

Keet waved off her concerns with one buttery hand.

"Tiberius and I can handle ourselves." She licked her fingers clean. "Speaking of my darling husband—it's time for me to take over piloting for him."

Keet pushed her chair back and dumped her plate in

the sink.

"Hey, do you two mind helping Tiberius disguise the ship? We've got some fake nameplates and registration numbers in the storeroom. Can't have the *Wayfarer Elizabeth* blaring her name to the whole city."

"Sure."

"And draw up an inventory list while you're back there. I don't want to buy anything we don't need."

* * *

Port Argun was unlike anything Dahlia had ever seen. It sprawled without apparent order; a juxtaposition of glorious architecture and muddy slums, quaint churches and hulking military edifices. Other ships sailed past the *Wayfarer Elizabeth* (renamed *Bluebell* with the aid of Keet's fake plates): everything from tour skiffs to traders to black warships bristling with guns. The chaos was captivating.

Dahlia's eyes came to rest on what could only be King Alexander Bespalov's royal palace. Her gaze traced the victorious turrets and golden domes. It was enormous, squatting on a hill above the city as if to protect—or perhaps to assert dominance over—the citizens below.

But that wasn't what she wanted to see. Sebastian Macall would be in the military base. She shivered and mentally attributed the action to excitement rather than nerves.

They descended to the docks before Dahlia could pick out the base. She stepped away from the windshield.

"Prepare the docking lines, darling," Keet crowed through a speaker funnel. She lounged in the pilot's chair, guiding the airship into its berth with skill born of experience. They settled next to the metal dock.

"We're in! Secure the lines."

Keet remained at the controls long enough to ensure they were tied off, then cut the engines and stretched. She winced as the bandages tightened on her chest.

"Dahlia, I think there's a watch shop a few blocks away. I'll take you there so we can get a new thingy for Tiberius' watch."

It took Dahlia a moment to remember what she was talking about.

"Oh, that," she tugged at her hair. They had been through so much together, she had nearly forgotten the lie she'd been holding over their heads. "It turns out...I don't really need one."

Keet's eyes settled on her, calculating. "You lied."

"Yes. A little."

The aviatrix grinned.

"I would've done the same thing."

* * *

Farren helped Dahlia gather their things: the backpack, their pistols...a few odds and ends lying about the ship. They chased a mechanical spider out of the bathroom where it had been lurking under Dahlia's washcloth.

"Those things will never stop creeping me out," Farren said as it vanished around a corner. Dahlia, occupied with tying a scarf across her face, did not reply.

They rejoined Keet and Tiberius on the gangway in time to watch the hatch open. Late afternoon sunlight streamed in. The sounds and smells of the Anglian capital wafted through with it. Clamoring and shouting and the clicking of gears merged with the aromas of cooking meat and engine oil. Autumn was well under way, yet the warm air had not yet succumbed to the season.

"I guess this is it, then," Farren said. He extended a

hand to Keet. "Thank you both."

Keet shook it.

"It's been fun, Farren." She turned to Dahlia. "And you too, take care."

"It was a pleasure, Keet, Tiberius," Dahlia said. The cyborg nodded to her, his arms occupied with a body bag containing Harold Grimes.

Her green eyes locked with his yellow ones. The gaze was artificial, composed of lenses and bulbs and wires, but Dahlia understood. He had never again spoken of his revelations in the medical bay. He hadn't needed to.

"Oh, here's the list of inventory for you." Farren fished a sheet of paper from his pocket and passed it to Keet. "You're low on liquor and gelignite—we used twenty or so sticks against Puce."

"Fair enough," said the aviatrix. "Au revoir, you two."

With that, Dahlia led the way down the gangplank—a wider version of the steel plank they had used in Lawson's Ridge—and onto the dock.

As they walked off, Keet's voice carried clearly after them, "Darling, I could've sworn we had more gelignite than that."

* * *

Keet turned to her husband once Dahlia and Farren receded out of earshot.

"Thirty-thousand gilvers," she said. "We could've had new boilers, a new sofa…"

"Dahlia saved you, Keet. And Farren risked himself for the ship. We're indebted to them."

"I know, I know." She reeled up the sleeves of her green coveralls. "I was joking. Damn shame, though."

She winked and patted Tiberius' armor.

"Come on darling, let's get old Grimey to the bounty hunting office before they close."

Chapter Thirty-one
Infiltration

✳

"Mr. Reed, we have no money."

Dahlia and Farren strolled down a bustling street in Port Argun, bumping into passersby and rubbing growling stomachs. Enticing smells drifted from food carts and restaurant doors. Carriages drawn by clockwork horses clattered by on a cobblestone road beside the sidewalk. Mechanical men pulled two-wheeled rickshaws, darting between the larger vehicles with scant regard for safety or traffic laws. Bookshops filled with glorious, sweet-smelling tomes beckoned Dahlia. She took it all in. Wonder and apprehension competed for control of her expression. The occasional wanted poster trumpeted its sketch of her face, doing nothing to set her at ease. She checked the knots on her scarf.

"No money?" Farren replied as he led the way through the crowds. "We'll have to pawn something. You've gotta have things in that backpack you don't need. How about…here?"

He ducked through a door into a shop. It was dim and decked in thick tapestries that muffled the clamor outside. Shelves covered in gears, trinkets, and bits of mechanical creatures packed the space. A bell over the door tinkled. At the sound, a man sporting a pair of abnormally large auto-focusing spectacles looked up.

"Come to buy? Sell?" He hustled over to a counter in the back. "I've just got in the most fascinating clockwork monkey, it sings and—"

"Sorry, we're looking to sell," said Farren. He waved Dahlia forward and slid the backpack from her shoulders.

"Oh. Well, let's see what you've got." He wiped a string of snot from his upper lip and adjusted a knob on the spectacles.

Farren dumped the contents of the bag unceremoniously onto the counter. Metal canisters spilled out, rolling among clothing and assorted supplies.

"Hey!" Dahlia said.

Hands sifted through her belongings, holding up a shirt, a blanket, a music box. Farren watched with amusement as Dahlia stood by, fuming. He knew he would pay for his indecent treatment of her things later.

"What's in here?" The shopkeeper began undoing the drawstring on a burlap bag.

"No!" Dahlia snatched it from his hands.

The man stared at her, fingers frozen.

"That's not for sale."

He shrugged and disgorged a tendril of ooze from his nose. It hung there, quivering, as he continued his search. Canisters tinked onto the wooden floor.

"What's this?" The shopkeeper grabbed something from the pile. It was one of Keet's mechanical spiders, flailing its legs and clicking menacingly. "I've never seen one of these before!"

He poked it. A needle foot punctured his finger, yet he was unperturbed.

"That's because it's the only one," explained Farren. "It can obey commands, look after engines, even attack." He gestured at the bead of blood forming on the shopkeeper's fingertip. "Worth at least a thousand gilvers."

"A thousand—!" the man sputtered. "That's thievery!"

It took a few minutes of heated negotiation, but in the end they strolled out with eight-hundred gilvers. After a meal and checking into an inn for the night, there were still six hundred left jangling in Dahlia's handbag.

Not a bad evening, Farren thought as he sat on the edge of the mattress. He tore open a new bag of sunflower seeds and tipped a few into his mouth, relishing the familiar medley of Port Argun spices. How many times had he tasted them in this city? Catching meals between shifts, sampling cheap offerings from the street carts, or blowing his paycheck on steaks with the other airmen.

The last time he'd eaten in his hometown had been the night before boarding the *Imperial Might* for Sainsbury.

"I don't get it," his best friend, David Harper, had said at the bar while trying to put him in a headlock. "Less than a month left on your watch—I don't even know why you're going on this mission."

Farren had smiled and slipped out of the assault. He'd known why, and so had Harper, but it was the way of best friends to irritate one another. He'd gone *because* he had less than a month left. Less than a month to lie atop an airship, listen to the wind, stare at the sun, and watch the world go on below.

"Mr. Reed?" Dahlia's knock snapped him from his reverie. "May I come in?"

"Sure can, sweetheart."

She ducked inside and closed the door behind her with a click. He looked up as she cleared her throat.

"We need to plan."

"How to get you into the base," said Farren.

Dahlia slid the scarf from her face down to her neck where it wrapped like a noose. She fidgeted, pulling at her hair.

"Exactly," she said. "Into the base, and to Sebastian Macall."

Farren sighed and kicked his boots off one by one. The soles sprinkled dirt onto the wood-plank floor.

"Well, getting through security should be easy; I still have my access badge. And my face isn't on those wanted posters. It's finding the General that's going to be the tricky part."

"You can get inside, but what about me?" Dahlia pulled a chair from the corner of the room and sat. Her hands twisted in her lap.

"You…" he said, scratching his chin. "You can play a new recruit who doesn't have his badge yet. Think you can pass as a boy?"

Dahlia looked down at herself. "It's doubtful."

"Aw, come on," he chuckled. "We'll get you a really baggy uniform—either buy it or steal it. Tuck your pretty hair up in a cap; maybe find some sort of cream to lighten your skin… It's either that or jump the fence, and they have mechanical dogs watching for people to try that."

"You think I look like a boy?" Her voice was soft.

Now you've done it, thought Farren. *Now she's mad.* He backpedaled furiously, stuttering out an apology.

"No, 'course not. It was just an idea, it was—"

Farren fell silent when he realized she was laughing.

"You should have seen the look on your face!" Dahlia giggled. Her eyes twinkled.

Farren held up his hands in surrender to a prank well played. A smile pulled at the corners of his lips. This woman never ceased to catch him off guard—they had only known one another a few days, but it felt like years. Being around her seemed so natural.

"I'm sorry, Mr. Reed," she said, struggling to rein in

her mirth. "I couldn't resist."

"Apology accepted, on one condition." Farren held up a finger to illustrate his point. "Don't you think it's time you called me by my first name?"

Dahlia grinned.

"Yes, Farren. I do." She clapped her hands once. "Now. We need to plan."

* * *

Far too early the next morning, they were dragging themselves down the street on the way to the first phase of the operation: acquiring a uniform for Dahlia. They had stayed up half the previous night hashing out various versions of their plan. Farren yawned as he walked, wishing he'd thought to grab coffee at the inn before they left.

The first phase went smoothly, and an hour later, Farren stood in an alleyway using trash to cover the unconscious body of an airman. Dahlia crouched against a wall while she layered makeup over her skin to lighten it. She wore a pair of brown air force coveralls.

"Don't you think he looks a bit cold?" she said, tilting the travel mirror propped in front of her.

Farren contemplated their victim. The man had worn nothing beneath the coveralls except underwear.

"He'll survive." A few more pieces of cloth, newspaper, and vegetable peelings went onto the pile. "Come on, let's go. Ready?"

Dahlia dabbed her cheek, checked the mirror, and snapped it closed. Her complexion had reached a color partway between what it had been and that of a typical Anglian. It wasn't ideal, but it would have to do. Between that, the loose coveralls, and a cap where she had tucked her hair, Dahlia made for a passable boy.

"Ready."

Farren led her through the twists and turns of Port Argun. The streets were filled with people, noise, and the smell of cooking meat from food carts. He smiled at the familiar clamor.

"We'll go through one of the smaller gates," he said to Dahlia as they walked. "They put newbie guards on those."

She didn't reply. When Farren glanced back he saw her staring at the cobblestones, the bill of the cap shielding her eyes. It suddenly struck him that this was the first time he had seen her wear pants instead of a skirt. She brushed her ears as if wishing for hair to tug on.

* * *

Gate 12C was on the southern side of the massive military base. It consisted of little more than a glorified hole in the fence with a gate just large enough for a carriage to pass through. Three bored soldiers leaned against the wall of their guard shack, tesla rifles suspended from shoulder straps. A mechanical dog stood poised beside them.

Farren withdrew the identification badge from his pocket and handed it to the nearest soldier. The man gave it a cursory check before returning it.

"Watch?" the guard said, his hand outstretched.

"I didn't think that was part of the security procedure," said Farren. His pulse accelerated; this was bad. If they looked at Dahlia's watch…

"Been on leave, eh? New protocols—apparently there's been trouble near the border."

"What sort of trouble?" He was stalling for time. How could they get out of this? There had to be something, *anything*…

"Word on the street is Colonel Puce took the *Debellatio*

into Delmar and broke it. Idiot had to call another warship in for a tow, but they got spotted. Delmar's not happy."

"We're already at war, what more can they do?"

The guard shrugged.

"More war?"

He waggled his fingers; Farren removed the watch from his pocket and handed it over. The man looked at the name and, satisfied, gave it back.

"Have a good one."

"Thanks. Oh, by the way, I've got a new recruit here." Farren gestured toward Dahlia. She stared at the guard's chin. "I'm escorting him to get his badge."

"No problem. I just gotta see his watch."

"Right."

Dahlia's eyes darted from Farren to the guard, but she didn't reach for the watch around her neck. Farren was drawing a blank, seconds were ticking by, and now they surely suspected something… His muscles tensed. The pistol felt heavy in his belt.

"Devil's blood! Is that you, Reed?"

David Harper strode toward them from the other side of the gate, waving and grinning like a fool. "Damn, I thought you were dead!"

Farren seized the opportunity.

"Not yet, Harper!" He waved back and walked past the guard shack to meet his friend. Dahlia followed wordlessly. They might be able to escape this after all… "How've you been? Still crawling around on warships?"

"Naw, I've been promoted." Harper grabbed his hand and shook it, then went in for a headlock. Farren slipped out of it. He noticed the symbols adorning Harper's shoulders: four layered stripes. A Sergeant.

"Hey!" One of the guards jogged after Dahlia. The tesla rifle clanked against his chest. "I need to see your watch."

Farren gave Harper a look, trying to convey with his eyes that the guard could not be obeyed. And, thank God, Harper got the message.

"Oh, no," he said to the guard, "that won't be necessary. They're with me."

"But Sergeant, the policy—"

"I said it's fine. Come on, you two."

They were in.

* * *

David Harper led them around training fields and docks, barracks and repair facilities. Patrolling airships whirred low overhead. Enlisted men and officers in uniform swarmed everywhere, some of them snapping a salute to Harper as they passed.

They halted at an old, first war-era hangar. Harper cracked the door, peered inside, and motioned for them to follow. The high-ceilinged interior was dim, illuminated only by sunlight from rows of cracked windows lining the walls. Dust lay thick on the concrete. A few fliers sat derelict and crumbling at the opposite end of the large space.

Harper turned toward them and crossed his arms.

"Okay, Reed, what's going on? How are you…alive?" His voice cracked a little despite his efforts at sternness. Like everyone, Farren had lost buddies to war before. He never forgot the feeling. To believe your best friend was dead, then to have him reappear…

"Luck," said Farren, "and some help. How are you a Sergeant?"

David Harper leaned against a wall, dug a cigarette from his pocket, and lit it. Dust swirled around his boots.

"When General Macall came back alone in the flier, he

said you fell. Said you were too drunk and there was an accident. Everyone suspected. You know how it is with Macall—people have disappeared around him. So no one wanted to ask any questions, 'cept me.

"He didn't like that, but I think he didn't want another suspicious disappearance so soon after yours. So instead of making me have an accident, he made me a Sergeant. Sort of a bribe to shut me up."

Harper took a drag on the cigarette and exhaled a cloud of gray. The smoke floated through a sunbeam slanting in through the high windows, mingling with motes of dust. Dahlia coughed delicately from beside Farren.

"Now it's your turn," said Harper. "Saying you stayed alive by 'luck and help' isn't good enough. I think I deserve to know the truth."

Farren wavered. Harper was his best friend, but the man wasn't known for his skill at keeping secrets.

"It's fine, Mr. Reed," said Dahlia. Harper's eyebrows shot up toward his cap when he heard her voice. "Sergeant—Harper, was it?—already helped us once, perhaps he could do it again. We need all the help we can get."

Then, before Farren could stop her, she swept off the hat and allowed her long black hair to spill out.

"I'm Dahlia Walker."

Chapter Thirty-two
The Plan Revealed

✴

Harper stubbed out his third cigarette and studied the dwindling supply in his pocket.

"It kills me not to smoke on airships. Hydrogen leaks, you know," he said to Farren. "Unbelievable."

Dahlia had just delivered an abbreviated version of their journey and intentions. She still wasn't sure she trusted Farren's friend, but they needed allies, and he was the best they had. Sebastian Macall was the goal and anything after that—escape, for instance—was mere icing on the cake.

"So you'll help us?" she asked.

Harper scrutinized her face as he picked at a fingernail. Sunlight and dust played in the stale hangar air between them.

"You're worth thirty-thousand gilvers."

"I'm aware."

He stared at her for a moment longer, then broke into a tooth-baring smile. Relief flooded Dahlia.

"Course I'll help you! How could I turn in my buddy's lady?"

"I'm not exactly his—" Dahlia began.

"And I've got the perfect way for you to get to Macall," Harper said, ignoring her protest. "There's an officers' ball tomorrow night where he's scheduled to give a speech. You two can have my invitations. I was gonna skip it anyway."

Now that they were finished with the explanations, David Harper had dropped the seriousness and returned to his cheerful ways.

"Sounds intriguing," said Dahlia. "Do you know anything more about it?"

"Well, they're supposed to be serving dessert," Harper said.

"I'm more curious about the layout of the area, security presence, things of that nature."

"Ah," Harper replied, scratching an itch on his cheek. "It's at the Falcon Officers' Club. Security should be the same as always, and Reed knows what that's like. You've worked guard duty at these things before, haven't you?"

Farren nodded in agreement. Dahlia turned to him.

"What do you think?"

"It's better than anything we've come up with," he said.

The decision was made. Harper hurried back to his apartment and returned a few minutes later with a pair of crumpled invitations. Dahlia hid her hair back inside the cap, shook Harper's hand, and they left.

* * *

"I'll never wear pants again," Dahlia said.

She and Farren browsed the shops in downtown Port Argun, searching for clothing suitable for a ball. The daily chaos of the city was in full swing. People jostled past, swinging shopping bags or leading mechanical men who did the carrying for them. Clockwork horses clattered in the street. The sun warmed Dahlia's face where it peeked through the multicolored awnings above.

Farren chuckled at her remark. She still wore the airman's brown coveralls.

"And what's so wrong with pants, sweetheart?"

"They're uncomfortable and masculine," she said. "Well-to-do ladies should always wear skirts."

"You're not 'well-to-do' anymore," Farren said. "Look at you: only a few hundred gilvers, no job, no fam—" he thought better of it and cut the word off, but Dahlia noticed.

Her smile tripped. He hadn't meant anything by it, yet his intention did nothing to blur the memory. Ansel Walker slumped in a pool of blood on the carpet, watch shattered, eyes staring forever into death. Dahlia felt her chest tighten. She could joke all she wanted, but it wouldn't change the fact that she'd come here to commit murder.

She reached up to pull at her hair. It was tucked away in the cap and her hand found only emptiness.

"This will do," she said, gesturing at a window featuring mannequins displaying men's suits. "Here, take a hundred gilvers and find one with a decent fit."

"You're not going to help out?" said Farren. "I thought you were good at fashion."

"I'll be off picking out a dress for myself. I trust you can take care of your own clothing."

Her tone was harsher than it needed to be. Dahlia left him in the doorway and allowed the crowd to sweep her away out of sight. She felt like a pebble hurtling down a river. Uncontrolled, racing headlong for some terrible and inevitable destination.

Remember your plan.

A bell tinkled above the door of the shop she chose. The smell of leather from the goods on display overpowered her nose in a pleasant way. A shopkeeper bounded over with a polite "How may I help you?" Dahlia cleared her throat and assumed the deepest, manliest voice possible.

"I'd like to buy three belts."

* * *

Her plan was simple. She had no hope of beating Sebastian Macall with a conventional weapon. Ducking his sword, stunning him, and destroying his watch in front of a horde of ball-goers would be nearly impossible. The only option she had was one she'd hoped to avoid. But once she embraced it, it seemed the natural choice.

Belts would hold the stolen gelignite from the *Wayfarer Elizabeth* around her waist. A detonator would be in her hand. There would be an explosion. It seemed such an easy thing: to just stroll up to her enemy and plunge them both into death with the press of a button.

There was the matter of killing herself, of course. At first Dahlia had balked. But as the thought turned over and over inside her brain she came to realize it was not just the only way—it was the perfect way.

She would be free from the bullet scars and the memories of blood, free from her unresponsive watch and Farren's ever-decreasing one. Free from having to decide how to live her life now that all she'd ever known was erased.

She would meet her mother. She would see her papa again.

Dahlia's eyes burned at the thought of his smiling face.

Don't cry, she told herself as she walked down the street holding a shopping bag in one hand. *Don't cry.*

It was almost funny. After living so long without any idea of when she would die, she finally knew. Tomorrow was her day.

*   *   *

"What do you think?"

The blue satin dress stroked Dahlia's ankles as she spun to check her reflection in the mirror. It wasn't much of a mirror, only a small affair over the sink in her room at the inn. Farren stood in the doorway wearing the suit he'd picked out with his flight jacket over it.

A fashionable scooped collar trimmed with lace accentuated the neck of the dress. The sleeves were fitted; the waist and skirt fell into ruffles over her legs. Blue wasn't her best color, but with only twenty-four hours until the ball her options were limited. And the waist ruffles would conceal any bulges from her homemade bomb.

"You're beautiful, sweetheart."

The softness in Farren's voice drew her gaze to his eyes reflected in the mirror. Dahlia wasn't naïve. She'd seen the way he looked at her during their travels. At first she'd dismissed it as mere lust. But lust would not have been enough for him to shield her with his body when Harold Grimes drew his pistol. There was something more at work here, and she wasn't sure what to make of it.

"Thank you, Mr. Reed," she said stiffly.

"I thought you were going to call me Farren now."

"I thought you weren't going to call me 'sweetheart.'"

He shrugged, waving a hand to acknowledge her point.

"Now," Dahlia said, "we'll have to blend in at the ball until Sebastian Macall arrives. Have you ever danced before?"

"Does dancing in bars count? My memories of that aren't so good though."

"No. Here—I'll teach you."

Dahlia approached, took his hand, and tugged him into the open space at the center of the room. Farren did not protest.

"A basic waltz should be enough to get you through tomorrow."

Dahlia's free hand rested lightly on his shoulder. Farren looked mismatched with the flight jacket on over his suit, but she knew better than to order him to remove it. The brown leather dirtied her fingers.

"Put your right hand on my waist."

The aviator paused as if not believing his good fortune.

"Stop looking at me that way and do it," Dahlia said.

Farren obeyed. His touch was so gentle she could barely feel it.

"Like this?"

"Yes. Now, I'll lead for the time being. All you need to do is mirror my movements; at the ball you'll be expected to lead, so pay attention. Ready? And, begin."

Wooden floorboards creaked under her shoes. Farren allowed himself to be directed backward, stumbled, and came close to disaster.

"Whoa, there, sweetheart. Would ya slow down?"

He smiled as she eased into a calmer pace. Fumbling feet attacked her toes, but Dahlia bit her cheek and said nothing.

Why fight with him? she thought while they skirted the furniture. *I'll be dead tomorrow. Might as well end things on a high note.*

She squeezed her eyes shut against a sudden wave of fear. Best not to think about her plan yet, Dahlia told herself. Focus on the moment.

"Everything all right?" asked Farren.

"You're stepping on my feet."

"Sorry," he said. The apology did nothing to subdue his

widening grin as they danced. "It's the leg brace. Without it I'm not clumsy at all."

"I don't believe that for a minute," Dahlia said. Her tone carried a forced lightness that encouraged Farren. He chuckled and the hand on her waist tightened. Half of her wanted to peel his fingers off, but the other half welcomed the touch—it was almost overwhelming to be this close to someone again. When was the last time anyone had held her?

Their dance slowed, fizzled, and ceased. Dahlia's heart accelerated, and she hoped Farren didn't notice. Was it from him? Or was it the constant, incessant reminder that every beat carried her closer to death?

"Sweetheart?" Farren's breath tumbled out over the top of her head.

He embraced her.

Chapter Thirty-three
A Walk at Night

✳

She's not hitting me, Farren thought in disbelief. *And she's not crying or yelling.*

Dahlia's head folded under his stubble-coated chin; her arms partially encircled his torso. Could it be she was hugging him back? Now *this* was progress!

"You're a terrible dancer," she said. Her voice sounded muffled against his clothing.

"Are you surprised?"

"Not at all."

He reached to stroke the back of her head, hardly believing what he was doing, but Dahlia chose then to break away. She turned aside before he could see her face.

Farren felt his chest simultaneously ache with disappointment and burst with triumph. There were still a few weeks left on his watch, and after Dahlia killed General Macall tomorrow she would have no other appointments. They would spend those last weeks together.

"The dance lesson is over, Mr. Reed," Dahlia said, still facing away from him. "Go get some sleep before tomorrow."

He was taken aback.

"Don't you want to plan first? I can tell you about the security they have at these officer parties."

"Ah, yes," she said. "I forgot. Give me a minute or two to change, then we'll discuss that."

Farren had to restrain himself from leaping with joy until he was hidden behind his own door.

* * *

They reconvened later in Dahlia's room: she sitting at the desk and Farren consigned to the floor. He had tried to sit on the bed, but Dahlia had refused to allow the 'dirty old jacket' near her sleeping space. At that point he would have done anything to please her.

"Tell me about the guards," she said, "the building layout, anything that might be useful."

Farren related all he could remember from the one shift of guard duty he had served at an officers' ball. A soldier or two at the entrance, the fire exit in the rear, the stage on which General Macall would stand.

"He might have a guard on either side," Farren said, "but that's mostly for show. People know Macall can slaughter anyone who comes after him."

He crunched on sunflower seeds as Dahlia thought, tugging her hair and leaning on the edge of the desk.

"How *are* you going to take him out?" asked Farren.

"I have a plan."

When he pressed her she refused to provide further details. Normally he would have continued pestering her, but tonight he stopped rather than incense her after their recent breakthrough.

"I hope it's a good one," he said. "Macall won't go down easy. And escaping afterward might be the hardest part."

"Trust me," Dahlia said. "My plan will work."

Lips bent upward into a smile that reassured Farren's

doubts. Who was he to meddle in her plots if she had things figured out?

"Anything else you need?" he asked. "Too bad we don't have enough money left for a tesla rifle. Could steal one though."

"And where would you hide it? Under your jacket?"

Farren polished off a handful of sunflower seeds and reached into his pocket for another. A pile of shells was growing on the floor beside him under Dahlia's disapproving gaze.

Dahlia scraped back her chair, stood, and snatched up her scarf. A dim rumble of thunder issued from the night outside the windowpane.

"You get some sleep—I'm going for a little fresh air."

"I'll come along," he said. "I'm not gonna get any sleep tonight."

It was a lie—he always slept well—but there was no question of Dahlia strolling Port Argun without him. Farren pushed himself to his feet.

* * *

Lanterns on buildings and carts lit the night in pools of isolated brightness. The daytime crowds had disappeared and the nocturnal ones emerged like owls at dusk. People roamed the sidewalks. Vehicles clopped past and evening merchants hawked their wares from street stalls. A few drops of rain spit onto the cobblestones.

Steam from the food carts carried the familiar scents of Farren's home. Parsley, pepper, and thyme mingled with delicious spices he had never bothered learning the names of.

"Hey," he said, "look at this."

Dahlia was a shadow behind him. She peered past at

sheets of freshly baked muffins cooling at one stall. Farren grinned.

"Give me a few gilvers—you've gotta try these. Muffins from Port Argun are on a different level than the ones you get anywhere else."

He bought a pair of them from a plump lady behind the counter and steered Dahlia onto a nearby bench. It was the waiting area for taxi carriages, but he didn't care.

"What do you think?" Farren asked when Dahlia tore a chunk from her muffin and slipped it under the scarf into her mouth. He peeled the baking paper from his. Delicate crumbs showered the ground to mingle with spots of rain.

"It's very good," she said.

"Very good? That's all you can say for the pride of Anglia?"

Farren bit into his and was rewarded with waves of warm, cakey sweetness.

"Devil's blood, I almost forgot how incredible these things are."

Dahlia shook her head and picked at her food while Farren gulped his down.

"You're funny, Mr. Reed," Dahlia said.

A dented clockwork horse pulling a carriage clattered to a halt in front of their bench. The driver leaned out.

"Where can I take you folks?"

"Nowhere," Farren said. "We're just sitting."

The man straightened and pressed a few levers to start the horse forward again, grumbling something about freeloaders using the wrong benches.

Thunder echoed overhead. Farren glanced at Dahlia as the increasing raindrops wet his hair and darkened his clothes. She slumped forward, elbows on her knees, vacantly watching wheels and hooves go by over the street. The muffin sat half-finished on her lap. He wondered vaguely if she was going to eat the rest of it.

I should say something, he thought. She had to be apprehensive about facing General Macall tomorrow. Farren didn't blame her for it, but he'd never been good with words.

"Want something else to eat?"

He gestured at a nearby food cart overflowing with skewers of sizzling meat. They seemed sad and inadequate, glimmering there under the streetlights.

"No," she said, "thank you."

"Suit yourself."

"Mr. Reed, how much time do you have left?" Dahlia asked.

The question caught him off guard. He hadn't checked in a while, come to think of it; he'd been too swept up in Dahlia's plans. Farren dug out the grubby watch and opened it.

"Fifteen days, ten hours, sixteen minutes," he said. "How time flies."

The rain fell harder. Stall owners cursed and folded away their shelves, tossing tarps over their wares, wheeling carts into buildings or under awnings. The few brave carriages still plying the streets hurried by across wet stones. Farren almost stood to return to the inn. Almost.

Water pinged off the watch face and dripped from Farren's hair but still Dahlia sat, frowning at a puddle.

She spoke. Her words drowned in the noise of the storm.

"What?" he asked.

"How can you bear it?" Dahlia yanked the soaked scarf down to reveal her face. Her expression matched the brooding clouds above. "Knowing you'll be dead in fifteen days?"

He had been trying to forget that. A shudder started in

Farren's belly at her words. He reached into his pocket for his vodka before remembering he'd thrown it away. There was nothing left, nothing to shield him from ever-decreasing watch, nothing to dull the horrible dread.

"Answer me," said Dahlia. Her green eyes bored into his. "You'll have to answer it for yourself soon enough."

Why was she doing this to him? *She* wasn't the one dying.

Farren couldn't speak. He broke her gaze and leaned his head back to catch the rain, feeling it trickle down his chin.

"I don't know," he said finally. Water leaked onto his tongue, cold and blank and final.

"That's what I thought," Dahlia said.

Thin fingers entwined with his on the bench, his watch held between their two palms. For once, he didn't think of trying to take things further. Her hand wasn't much; it was small and cool and light. But it was enough.

They sat there in the night for a long time, hands twisted together, listening to rain wash away the stars.

Chapter Thirty-four
The 64th Annual Officer's Ball

★

"Ready, sweetheart?"

Farren knocked at the door.

"Just a minute."

Dahlia stood at her sink in the inn, wearing the pastel blue dress and burning the last of her papa's sound tapes. A small pile of ashes smoldered around the drain. She'd finished listening to them aboard the *Wayfarer Elizabeth* and, as much as she wanted to save the last records of Ansel's voice, she couldn't risk them falling into the wrong hands once she was dead. The location of the promethium would go with her.

The final tape curled and snapped like a slice of bacon in a pan. Dahlia washed its remains down the sink in an effort to erase the smells of smoke and burning chemicals. She straightened, smoothing down her hair in the mirror. Makeup lightened her skin to a color almost indistinguishable from that of a typical Anglian.

Sticks of gelignite pressed tight and bulky around her waist, hidden by the fabric ruffles. The detonator was strapped to her leg underneath the skirt. Her watch dangled on a thin gold chain between her breasts with the incriminating name out of sight.

"Come on, the ball starts in twenty minutes." Farren

banged on the door again.

"We'll rent a taxi carriage. My makeup isn't quite right."

Farren continued to complain from outside the door. Dahlia tuned him out while she unfolded a sheet of paper from her handbag: Ansel Walker's wanted poster.

The black-and-white photograph of her papa stared back at her, younger than she had known him. It must have been taken when he worked as a scientist. The top of a lab coat decorated his shoulders. Eyes twinkled above a grin. Dahlia saw him laughing too loudly, in that way he had that always made her smile. She remembered their hours spent together repairing watches at the workbench, remembered the feeling of his hugs after finishing a successful project. Remembered the brush of his lips on her forehead as she lay dying.

This is for you, Papa.

She crumpled the poster in one fist and threw it in the sink.

"I'm ready."

* * *

A bored guard gave their invitations a perfunctory glance before waving them into the base with a mass of other ball-goers. The security arrangements at the Falcon Officers' Club were similarly loose.

Dahlia and Farren waited in line on the steps of the club, shivering in the chill evening air and twitching whenever a guard happened to glance their way.

"Mr. Reed," Dahlia said, leaning close to his ear. "Will anyone here recognize you? I know your name isn't linked to your bounty, but an enthusiastic reunion could be...problematic."

Farren started to ruffle his hair, then hesitated when his hand touched the neatly combed strands.

"Maybe," he said. "Maybe not. I stayed away from officers—they tried to get me to do work."

"Somehow I'm not surprised."

She held the hem of her dress off the ground as they climbed the steps and showed their invitations.

"Go on through," the guard said.

Large double doors were held wide to admit them. Dahlia glanced skyward for the briefest of moments to look for the Pathfinder star. Her eyes found nothing but dull clouds. Then they were inside.

The Falcon Officers' Club appeared to be a newer venue, smelling of fresh paint and flooring. Round tables lined the edges of the hall. An empty dance floor gleamed in the center, and a stage rose at the far end.

Dahlia hooked her arm through Farren's, straightened her back, and swept toward a table with grace gleaned from years of upper-class living. The aviator dragged along beside her.

"We'll wait here until the dance begins," she said, and sat with a flourish.

Officers in pressed uniforms and ladies draped in sparkling gowns decorated the tables around them, filling the air with loud, happy noise. Scrambled music drifted from the orchestra warming up near the stage.

Dahlia leaned toward Farren.

"I wish you'd take off that jacket," she said. He wore the shabby flight jacket over his new suit, which rather ruined the attempt at fanciness. The thing was ripped, elbows threadbare, dark bloodstains fading yet far from inconspicuous.

"We've been through this," he said.

"I know. I'm simply saying you look like a fool."

He shrugged. "It's not gonna come off."

"Ladies and gentlemen," a voice boomed. Conversations petered out around them and all heads turned towards the stage, where a man in a medal-festooned uniform addressed the room. "Welcome to the sixty-fourth annual officers' ball. We have a very special guest today: General Sebastian Macall will be joining us for a speech later in the evening."

The announcer made some introductory remarks interspersed with weak attempts at humor. Dahlia's ears blurred the words, her mind focusing instead on the gelignite digging into her ribcage.

Macall is coming. He's close by.

Her hands clenched under the table.

"You alright?" murmured Farren.

Dahlia gave a stiff nod as the announcer concluded his speech amid a round of applause. There was a cacophony of scraping chairs as the gowns and suits paraded onto the dance floor.

Farren spat a few sunflower seed shells onto the floor, stood, and offered his hand to her in mock decorum.

"May I have this dance?"

"Fine."

The orchestra launched into a measured waltz. Dahlia allowed her arm to link with Farren's at the elbow as they sauntered to the pack of ball-goers.

They positioned themselves at the edge of the throng. Farren led the dance and his feet tangled almost immediately. Dahlia smiled, gripping his hand and shoulder to steady him while he recovered his footing. Between the flight jacket and their ungainly attempt at a waltz, they must have appeared quite ridiculous.

Somehow, two songs later, no significant dance-related disaster had transpired. Dahlia's toes stung where

Farren's shoes had crushed them, but that was the extent of the damage.

"What's this under your dress?" he asked, indicating the slight bulges around her waist.

"Corset," Dahlia replied easily. "A rather cheap one, not at all what I'm used to."

"Ah. You go to these type of things a lot?"

"Balls? Yes, many times with my papa. He taught me how to dance."

The orchestra had just begun its third number when Dahlia felt the back of her neck prickle. Her eyes darted through the faces in the room before locking with those of a middle-aged man who sported a bouquet of medals and salt-and-pepper hair. She glanced away with a sharp intake of breath.

"Mr. Reed," she said. "There's a man watching us."

Farren, who had been increasingly engaged in the waltz, leaned close to her ear without turning.

"Where is he?" Farren asked.

"Behind you. Six o' clock, I believe it's called in military terms."

The aviator continued leading the dance. The two of them rotated gradually until Dahlia's back was to their observer and Farren could catch sight of him.

"Dammit."

Farren spun so quickly that Dahlia came close to tripping. His face was ashen.

"That's Captain Raleigh," he said, "he was my commanding officer on the *Imperial Might*."

Dahlia could have smacked him. Here he was, risking exposing their identities at the most critical moment. Her revenge was mere minutes away. If Farren ruined it...

"Will he say anything to draw attention to us?" she asked.

"I don't know," Farren said. "Probably—it's not every day a dead airman turns up at an officers' ball."

Dahlia stopped dancing. Farren stumbled a little, crushed her toes with a foot, and stood still. Couples swirled past, draped in expensive fabrics.

She looked up at his face.

"Get out."

"Good idea," said Farren distractedly. "If we draw Raleigh outside we can knock him out without anyone—"

"You misunderstand me," Dahlia interrupted. Her voice was piercing ice. "I want you to get out of here, Mr. Reed. You've delivered me inside the base and fulfilled your part of our bargain. I've no more use for you."

Farren looked as if he had been punched in the gut. Confused eyes found hers and she almost looked away. It was cruel, Dahlia knew, both to him and to her. But she wouldn't allow him to bring down her chance at Sebastian Macall and, more importantly, she wouldn't allow him to see her die. Dahlia had too much pride for that.

"You're not serious, sweetheart," Farren protested, hands tightening on her waist. "I won't let Raleigh be a problem—"

"I'm completely serious," Dahlia said. Her gaze held firm. "Let me go and leave."

She pushed at his chest with one hand. His heart beat under her touch, and it almost broke her to feel the closeness of it. Music continued around them; they were an island of misery among the merriment.

"Dahlia, you don't have to do this," Farren said. "You'll be captured for sure, or killed. I can't let them do that to you, you're…you're too important to me." The aviator pulled her closer. His arms were warm around her waist, his lips mere inches from hers.

"Can…can I kiss you?" he murmured.

Dahlia almost said yes. For a moment she allowed thoughts of him to whisk her away. They could have so much, the two of them, in the few days Farren had left to live. They could escape. Sail away. Perhaps find a peaceful place to enjoy each other until his time ran out—a handful of perfect days that would end too soon. But the price for such a paradise was to abandon her papa, and that she would not do. Vengeance was within reach.

Dahlia slapped him. The sharp crack of her palm against his cheek pierced the music and drew curious faces in their direction. Farren left his head turned to one side, face red and stunned.

"How dare you. Listen to me, Farren: You're my guide, nothing more." She felt his arms fall from her. "Not a lover, not a friend. A guide. Go find somewhere to enjoy the rest of your time, away from me."

He drew back, expression a mask of hurt, staring at her as if attempting to memorize her features.

"I'm sorry, sweet—" Farren said, growing angry now. "Sorry if I gave the wrong impression. I just thought we had more."

The aviator turned and took a few steps toward the door, then looked back. Dahlia found herself longing to touch his foolish, worn jacket one more time. She'd gone overboard. But she could think of no other way to force him to leave.

"Good luck, Dahlia."

Farren walked out the door, limping slightly from the leg brace concealed under his pressed pants. Blond hair receded into the night.

Stop! Dahlia wanted to shout. *I didn't mean any of it.*

But her thoughts remained thoughts, and her mouth stayed closed. Onlookers nearby resumed their dancing with only a stray glance or two spared for the lone woman standing in their midst. Dahlia hugged herself and felt the sticks of gelignite around her waist. Farren was gone. Now it was just her, Sebastian Macall, and death.

* * *

The announcer was back on stage. He was shouting something with far too much enthusiasm. Ball-goers clapped and waiters stood at the fringes of the room ready to wheel in dishes heaped with food. Dahlia waited next to the stairs at one end of the stage. She felt detached, unreal. The metal watch was cold on her skin, and soon she would be cold with it. One hand already cradled the detonator.

"…without further ado, I would like to welcome General Sebastian Macall," said the announcer. He swept one hand back toward the stage's curtain like a magician. It parted on cue and a man strode out.

Dahlia's breathing accelerated: it was him. Obsidian hair, stark features, a pistol and sword swinging at his belt when he nodded stiffly to the crowd. Officers saluted around her. The orchestra launched into a victorious, trumpet-dominated march: Anglia's national anthem.

"Thank you," said Macall. The voice cut Dahlia to the bone.

She turned. There were no guards on the stairs, nothing between her and Sebastian Macall.

The sitting room was quiet. Dahlia coughed, rolled over onto the carpet in a pool of blood.

One foot pulled her up the first step.

A body slumped next to her wearing an ill-fitting suit. Ansel Walker's hair fell into staring eyes.

No one noticed her as she ascended farther. Everything was too bright, too loud, and too alive for a few more moments.

She looked down at the shattered remains of her papa's watch, glittering like dew.

Dahlia drew herself up onto the stage, feeling the first surprised gazes fall upon her. Sebastian Macall was beginning a speech and staring out at the audience, not paying attention. Ice grew in her veins as she watched him.

Bombs fell on the city. Heat and fire and her papa was dead. Dead. Dead. Dead.

Her fingers tightened on the detonator.

Chapter Thirty-five
The Plan Unraveled

✴

Farren drifted down the deserted steps of the Falcon Officers' Club in the cool night air. It was not quite cold enough for his breath to steam like cigarette smoke. Fingers fumbled for his watch, slipped, and dropped it into the dust where it popped open by his feet. He didn't reach for it. He didn't have the energy.

"Airman Reed? Is that you?" said a voice behind him.

Farren turned to see Captain Raleigh. His former commanding officer descended the steps with his typical assured demeanor.

"General Macall said you were killed in a fall."

"Survived it."

The Captain raised his salt-and-pepper eyebrows.

"Survived it, *sir*."

"You're the deserter, aren't you? Then that woman you were with…" His voice dropped to a growl. "She's Dahlia Walker."

A wave of exhaustion washed over Farren at the mention of her name. He was so tired of running. All he wanted was to settle down in a dingy tavern and drink until he forgot who he was. What did it matter, now that Dahlia didn't want him?

"Explain yourself," Captain Raleigh ordered. "What

are you doing here?"

"Helping Dahlia," shrugged Farren. What did it matter if he was captured? The time when he might have backed out was long past, even if he'd wanted such a thing.

"Helping her do what?" Raleigh asked. His eyes narrowed with hostility.

Helping her kill General Macall, he thought. But he remained silent, the crisp air stinging his nose. He bent, slowly, and lifted his watch out of the dust.

At any moment he expected to hear a cacophony of screams and the crackle of a tesla rifle from the ballroom. Macall would be there soon. Dahlia would stun him, smash his watch, and have her revenge. But she had no rifle…

"Answer me, Airman Reed," said the Captain.

Lungs pinched as Farren inhaled sharply with realization. Dahlia had never told him her plan because she didn't intend to come out of it alive. Keet's mention of missing gelignite, the mysterious sack Dahlia had refused to reveal at the pawn shop, her anxious questions, the bulges he'd felt under her dress…

"Devil's blood," he breathed. "She's going to blow herself up."

"What?" Raleigh asked.

But Farren was already racing past, imbued with sudden energy, the Captain forgotten. He took the stairs three at a time, slamming through the double doors past a pair of bored guards. His mind barely registered Captain Raleigh's indignant bellows.

No, no, no, no, no.

Ball-goers screamed as he shoved them aside. He sprinted through the throng toward the stage where Dahlia advanced on General Macall.

"Dahlia!" he yelled desperately.

She can't die. I won't let her die!

Farren clambered onto the stage. She saw him, her eyes went wide and she sped off toward Macall. The General unsheathed his sword as if in slow motion. The blade shimmered as it swung in an arc toward her, and Dahlia's thumb was coming down on the detonator…

Farren leapt. The leg brace seized beneath him. His tackle caught Dahlia square in the shoulders. They collapsed, tangled, onto the wooden planks and tumbled toward Macall before coming to rest in front of his black boots.

Farren ended up on top of Dahlia. He scrabbled at her hands searching for the detonator. He spotted it several feet away where it had landed.

Everything went still for an instant. He crouched there, breathing hard, waiting to feel the General's sword slice through his back. The enormity of what he had done began to sink in. He didn't care. Dahlia was alive, that was all that mattered.

She struggled underneath him and reached for the detonator. Farren pinned her arms to the ground.

"You *idiot*," she spat. "You dim-witted, maggot-brained, *shit-headed* idiot! What the hell did you do that for?"

He had never heard her swear before.

"I couldn't let you die," Farren murmured, his head drooping. "I couldn't let you kill yourself."

A blade buried itself in the wood next to his face. From somewhere in the audience people began to scream; their sounds seemed oddly muted. Farren focused on the shimmering metal weapon and the polished boots behind it.

"Miss Walker," said Sebastian Macall. "How nice to see you again."

Dahlia made a noise of frustration and fought toward the detonator, but Farren's grip was firm.

Better her captured than dead.

The General crouched, grabbed a fistful of Farren's hair, and yanked his head back. Farren winced in pain and fear. His heart felt as if it was trying to escape from his ribcage. A pulse twitched in his exposed neck.

"And you're the flier pilot from Sainsbury, aren't you? This is quite the reunion."

"Let me go, Farren!" Dahlia said, eyes full of rage. "He murdered my papa!"

"I don't think you'll be killing anyone today, Miss Walker," Sebastian said. He dropped Farren's head. Guards already sprinted through the mayhem. Officers and assorted guests streamed from the doors like insects fleeing the General's predatory gaze.

Sebastian wrenched his sword from the wood and sheathed it. Guards rushed onto the stage. Farren was wrestled to his feet, his hands twisted and cuffed with cold metal. He didn't fight; there was no purpose to it. He'd made the choice to put Dahlia's life first, and now he'd suffer the consequences.

"Take these two to the cells," said the General. "The woman is not to leave my sight; she seems to have a talent for escape."

Guards nodded. Farren allowed himself to be frogmarched across the stage, through the curtains, and away. Dahlia's frustrated screams echoed in his ears.

Chapter Thirty-six
The Torture Room

✴

Dahlia sat shackled to a metal chair by thick bands around her wrists and ankles. A brown prison jumpsuit enfolded her body. Colorful wires snaked from electrodes stuck to her skin into an electrical panel full of levers and dials. The room was windowless, white, utilitarian. Bulbs strung along the ceiling reflected from the painted cement-block walls. A single cart sat beside her. She glanced at it once, and the sight of glinting knives and needles was enough to raise acrid bile in her throat.

Sebastian Macall paced in front of her.

"I'll make it simple for you, Miss Walker," he said. "Tell me where I can find promethium and you'll be treated as an honored guest. You'll provide any clarification we need of your father's research. You'll have the best food and living arrangements, a chance to work with the top scientists on the continent...and you'll be free once we're finished. Once we've succeeded at both resurrection and time transfer."

Dahlia swallowed.

"What's promethium?" she asked. "I've never heard of—"

"Don't lie to me!" Sebastian said. "Ansel must have told you. If not you, then who?" He continued pacing and his words devolved into mutters. "He didn't write it down, the bastard. Science division went through every page of that research. He had no partner, no wife, no confidant apart from his daughter. It has to be her."

He looked up at Dahlia, who blinked in confusion. What was wrong with the man? Her papa's sound tapes had hinted at his madness, but she hadn't expected it to be so blatant.

Sebastian prowled around the room. A sword swung at his waist. He still wore the uniform from the ball that had ended in chaos several hours before.

"If you don't cooperate, I'll force the information from you," said Sebastian, stopping in mid-stride long enough to shoot her a vicious smile. "It's your choice."

Dahlia wanted to turn and check the metal implements again, but willed herself to stare at Sebastian instead. Loathing and fear distorted her mind.

What do I do? Will he keep his promise to free me if I tell him?

What did it matter? If she'd been ready to die for her revenge, a little pain would be nothing. The secret Ansel had trusted her with would follow her to her grave. It was the least she could do to torment Sebastian, and it would protect Sita from the terror of resurrection.

Dahlia sat up straighter.

"If you think I'd help you, you're seriously mistaken," she said. Her voice wavered, then strengthened. "You murdered my father. You bombed my city and took away everything I had. I came here to kill you."

Sebastian twitched as if slapped, surprise plastered across his sharp features. Dahlia felt her stomach clench as he approached.

"Your anger is unwarranted, Miss Walker," he said. "King Bespalov ordered the bombing of Sainsbury; I had nothing to do with that. And Ansel committed suicide."

"My father would never——"

"Shut your mouth and listen," said Sebastian. "Ansel did something to save you; either resurrection or time transfer, then he smashed his own watch before I could stop him. The coward couldn't stand the idea of being captured. Think of all the pain he put you through for his selfishness."

Dahlia's heart pounded in her ears. It didn't matter that her papa had killed himself—in fact, it only fed her hate. Sebastian Macall had driven him to it, and that was worse than murder.

Sebastian placed a hand on each arm of Dahlia's chair and leaned close. She struggled to twist away. The shackles prevented her from moving more than an inch or two.

"Just tell me where I can find promethium and this will all be over," he said. There was a maniacal gleam in his eyes. "You can go out and live your life again. I can give you money, protection from the Anglian government, a house, anything you want. Anything at all!"

"I don't care," Dahlia said. She held his gaze without an ounce of fear. What did she have to lose? She had already resigned herself to her fate.

Suddenly Sebastian seized her by the shoulders. He shook her, shouting,

"Don't you understand? Promethium is the only way to bring her back! Years of work tracking down that filthy traitor and for what? Nothing! Where is it? *Where is it?*"

"I don't know!" Dahlia yelled. The hands released her and Sebastian stumbled backward, sweat beading on his forehead. He squinted at her.

"Sita?"

"I'm Dahlia."

"I thought you were dead, Sita," Sebastian said, rapturous. "I missed you...you wouldn't believe..." He swallowed, blinked, and glanced around the white room. "Miss Walker?"

"You're mad," Dahlia blurted. "Sita died eighteen years ago. And listen, there's something wrong with the resurrection theories. Ansel and Sita resurrected a boy and when he came back to life he was all broken."

"They actually completed a resurrection?" Sebastian said. "Then all we need is promethium."

"I told you: it doesn't work properly. You can't resurrect Sita."

Sebastian waved her protest aside. He pulled at the edges of his uniform to straighten them, as if attempting to remove any traces of his earlier outburst. Medals clinked on his chest.

"I'll give you one more chance," he said. "Tell me where the promethium is, or I'll force it out of you."

"No. You have to listen—"

But Sebastian was already talking.

"Very well," he said.

He stepped toward a thick metal door in the wall and slid a lock bolt aside. In scampered a thin, pale man in a loose uniform who scurried to the electrical panel like a rat drawn to food. Long fingers picked at the levers with familiarity.

"Will you be watching, General?" the man asked.

Sebastian glanced from Dahlia to the cart and back, and she caught a glimpse of sorrow on his face.

"Just find out where the promethium is," he said. The door boomed behind him. Booted feet receded rapidly down the hall.

I look too much like Sita, Dahlia realized. He doesn't want to see me in pain.

The torturer shrugged and flicked the machine on.

"Guess it's just us then, little lady."

Dahlia's eyes followed his movements, watching the electrical panel flicker to life. The appearance of the torturer had plucked away her bravado in an instant. Her voice quavered.

"You're not going to use the…metal instruments?"

"Oh no. Those are for show. This thing works much better anyway," he grinned, tapping the electrical box. "Those electrodes on your skin will send all the current straight through you. More effective, and no mess afterward."

I'll be able to stand it, won't I? Hold out long enough for them to give up and execute me. I'll be dead. Sita will be safe. Papa won't be avenged, but there's nothing I can do about that.

Farren's face drifted into her mind as the torturer reached for a lever. Perhaps, with more time together, they might have had something. Things could have been so different…

Then the lever was thrown and thoughts of Farren shattered into agony.

Chapter Thirty-seven
A Trap is Sprung

✳

Sebastian Macall burst into the throne room, his steps echoing on the marble floor. Excitement erased any pretense of the formality the King preferred. Guards turned toward him.

"Your Highness," Sebastian panted as he hurried toward the robe-draped King. Alexander Bespalov blinked in irritation and adjusted his crown. "We've captured Dahlia Walker. She confessed the location of the promethium: it's in Janmasthala in a ruined city called Vatana. I've ordered the *Imperial Might* readied for an expedition."

He took a deep breath to continue, to ask permission to set sail on the airship the next day. Another formality. Courtesy dictated that such undertakings be approved by the King.

The silence following his exclamations seemed oddly pronounced.

"Your Highness?"

Bespalov cleared his throat and spoke, eyes fixed over Sebastian's shoulder on the row of guards near the doorway.

"That's good news, *General*." The title was emphasized, an admonishment against Sebastian's poor behavior. He brushed it aside. "Miss Walker in custody at last. Very good news. You've done quite a service for Anglia in finding that information."

The back of Sebastian's neck prickled and his hand twitched toward the sword at his belt. His soldier's senses tugged at him. Something was wrong.

"But I can't allow you to take the *Imperial Might*," Bespalov continued. "Our spies in Delmar have picked up increased movement at the border: troops, weapons, and airships. We believe they're preparing for an invasion."

"That won't matter if we retrieve the promethium," said Sebastian. "Don't you see? We'll be invincible once we control time technology. Stealing time from the enemy, resurrecting our people on the battlefield—what better weapon could there be?"

Bespalov inclined his head ever so slightly as Sebastian talked. The General glanced behind him on instinct and his heart leapt to his throat. The guards were raising their tesla rifles, barrels trained on his chest.

"What's the meaning of this?" Sebastian said. He drew his sword as the King thundered to his feet. Purple robes clung to him, rippling as he raised his hand.

"Sheathe your sword, Macall! You're under arrest for the murder of Lieutenant Warren. By law, you will be imprisoned, tried, and hung if you cannot prove your innocence. And I doubt you can."

Sebastian spun to face the soldiers, blade poised and with no intention of sheathing it. Wrath choked his mind, crippled his reason. He tasted salt from the sweat beading on his face.

Six men. I can kill six men.

A clink drew his attention to the tapestry-covered walls where Bespalov's mechanical guards had begun moving. Mechanicals had poor reflexes, but felt no pain, and were notoriously difficult to destroy.

"Where…" he said, "where's your proof? I didn't murder the man."

"His body was found floating in the sewers yesterday evening," replied Bespalov, "with thirty-six stab wounds and no watch. He was last seen on the way to your office, where we discovered an extensive bloodstain under the new carpet. Men have been disappearing around you for a while now, Sebastian. All we needed was proof." His eyes dropped to the floor. "Why did you do it? You were a brilliant General. Don't tell me you're working for Delmar…"

"Quiet!" Sebastian snapped. The soldiers halted just out of his reach, but the mechanical guards approached without fear. "You think this is about some idiotic war? Those men betrayed me! Warren delayed; he tried to give Dahlia Walker a chance to escape. He wanted to find her himself, that's it, and steal my promethium, steal the secrets of resurrection!"

The King slumped back into his elaborate throne.

"You're mad," he said. He waved a hand at the guards. "Take him away."

A man approached on either side of Sebastian; they reached for his arms as the others leveled their rifles. The General longed to attack. Cut off their limbs, inflict painful wounds that would incapacitate long enough for him to find and deal with their watches. But by that time a dozen lightning bolts from the mechanical guards would have rendered him helpless. There was only one option.

Sebastian leapt backward, twisted, and ducked under a barrage of tesla bolts. A moment later he yanked Bespalov to his feet. The blade rested across the King's throat, singing for blood.

"Don't shoot!" he said. He wedged the King between

himself and his aggressors. "I know where his watch is. I'll kill him."

It was a bluff—Bespalov never shared where on his person he carried his watch.

"Let His Highness go!"

"Put the sword down!"

The soldiers all yelled at once, tripping over each other's words in a rush to protect their leader. Golden mechanical guards froze on all sides. Glass eyes glinted as they watched. The King stood straight, sweating, and terrified. It didn't fit his decorous personality. Sebastian had to restrain himself from putting the monarch out of his misery.

"Put down your weapons and I'll let him live," he ordered.

The guards glanced at one another. Sebastian flitted his sword across the King's throat just enough to draw a line of blood. Bespalov gasped in fear.

"I said *put them down*."

Six rifles clattered to the floor.

"Very good," he said. His head ached; every nerve was tense and begging for him to attack. He could kill them all, but that would leave him against twenty mechanicals, and he didn't care for those odds. "Now kick them over here, put your hands behind your heads, and get out of my way."

The men obeyed. Sebastian shoved at the King's back and walked him off the throne dais. Bespalov was taller and broader than him; he had to reach up to hold the sword in position. They made their way in silence across the floor to the massive doors.

"One of you pull the door lever," Sebastian said. "The rest stay where you are."

The doors groaned open, revealing an empty corridor beyond. Sebastian spun the King to face him. He looked at him one last time: the ridiculous robes, the splendid crown now askew. How could he have followed such a man for so long?

Then he rammed the sword through Bespalov's gut. Blood fountained. Something cracked. He ran as the guards began yelling again. The King publicly claimed to have eighteen years left on his watch—the wound wouldn't kill him, yet the violence was satisfying.

King Bespalov thudded to the floor behind him, but Sebastian was already halfway down the corridor and gone.

* * *

He took a carriage to the military port. Alarms blared and soldiers rushed about in confusion, buttoning up jackets over hastily-donned shirts. One or two still wore sleepwear. Everyone knew there was an emergency; no one was quite sure what it was.

In the dark interior of the carriage, Sebastian watched the airship hulls come into view through the fog of his breath on the window. His uniform was stained with sweat that was his and blood that wasn't.

Only a few drops, not noticeable in this light.

He wiped his sword on the fabric seats and left dark streaks there like claw marks. His hand clenched on the hilt.

A man hurried by under the shadow of the *Imperial Might* floating beside the dock. Lights illuminated his face.

"Captain Raleigh," Sebastian shouted out the window. The Captain turned as he slid from the carriage. "Wait a moment."

His boots scraped the dust. The Captain saluted.

"Finish preparing the *Imperial Might* for takeoff," said Sebastian. "The King orders that we leave immediately."

"For where, sir?"

"I'll give you a heading once we're airborne," said Sebastian. "I want the ship off the ground in thirty minutes."

"Thirty minutes?" the Captain sputtered. "But the supplies...the men? I'll need four hours at least—"

Sebastian leaned forward, allowing his face to fall into and out of the strips of brightness from the dock lights. Soldiers were still running aimlessly among the alarms.

"Thirty minutes," he said, "with or without them."

Raleigh snapped a salute. "Yes, sir."

"And help me find one of your officers. I need two prisoners transferred on board."

"Yes, sir."

* * *

Sebastian reached a hand out the porthole as the airship began to rise. A few colored bits of electronics tumbled from his palm: the vital organs of the *Imperial Might's* radio assembly. There had been a general broadcast fizzling through the headset when he first approached. He listened long enough to know King Bespalov was dead.

The sword had snicked through Bespalov's watch on its way to his stomach. He was dead before the blade touched his skin. And Sebastian was the most wanted man on the continent.

"Not that it matters," he said to himself. "No radio, no communication with the outside world."

"No one can question your leadership."

"And with Ansel's research and a handful of scientists aboard, we can create a resurrection device by the time we reach Vatana."

The airship lifted faster, accelerating into the star-picked sky above Port Argun. Sebastian wavered as he struggled to replace the screws in the radio panel.

"What will you do with the crew once you have Sita back? Kill them?"

"No need. She's from Janmasthala—we'll disappear there. Build a house in the jungle, perhaps. Or at the edge of the sea."

"You've never seen the ocean."

"I will," he said, straightening and tossing the screwdriver into its bin. "I have time, and so will Sita."

Her watch hung beside his on a chain around his neck, the hands still stopped at zero. He remembered the day he had recovered it, eighteen years ago, as clearly as yesterday. The fresh grave in the forest where the traitor Ansel had buried her and her watch. The horrible, aching hollow in Sebastian's chest when he'd seen her.

His clenched his hands to stop them from shaking.

The next time I see her, she'll be alive again.

Wind from the open porthole raised chill bumps on his skin. The city lights faded, betraying none of the clamor that must be taking place below while the capital realized its King was dead. Blaring alarms lost their bite and receded into the sound of the sky passing them—or was it them passing the sky?

It occurred to him that he was leaving Port Argun for the last time. Sebastian couldn't bring himself to care. His future was ahead with Sita Senguptar, in Janmasthala.

Chapter Thirty-eight
Aboard the *Imperial Might*

✳

Farren dreamed he was flying again, and when he awoke it was true. Engines thrummed the deck plate against his cheek. He peeled free of the grimy floor, rolling over onto his back with a groan. His wrists ached. They were no longer cuffed, but the soreness remained even several hours later. Stale saliva washed over his tongue. He had spent enough time on board airships to recognize those engines: quad-propeller, with vibration reduction and turbulence compensators.

"*Imperial Might* again," he said to no one in particular. "Home sweet home."

The cell was lit by a lamp outside the door that left the corners in shadow. Bars lined three sides of his prison; the fourth was curved steel plate. *The hull.* A handful of other cells lay on each side of his, empty but for the skittering of a single rat.

Farren's watch hung on a peg under the light; standard procedure for prisoners was to keep their watch out of reach to avoid suicides. His flight jacket was next to it.

"Dahlia?" he said. His eyes roved over the adjoining cells.

The hallway door—the entrance to the brig—creaked open as if on cue. Two crewmen in air force coveralls pushed their way inside, propping up a small unconscious body between them.

"Dahlia!" Farren tried to leap up and banged his forehead into the bars. "Dammit."

Black hair curtained her face and her head lolled on the front of a brown jumpsuit. Dainty, limp hands poked above the crewmen's shoulders.

"What happened? Is she alive?" The desperation in his voice choked him.

One airman spared him a glance while the other swung open the adjoining cell door on rusty hinges. They carried her inside and laid her on a crude cot against the wall, taking more care than Farren imagined had been paid to him.

"Yeah, she's alive," the man said without further elaboration.

"What happened? They didn't...hurt her, did they?" His imagination conjured up images of Dahlia being beaten senseless by General Macall in a prison cell. Farren's stomach clenched. If they'd hurt her there would be hell to pay.

The airman shrugged and locked her cell. "Interrogation, I think. Ask her when she wakes up—doc says she'll be fine. You won't though."

He tapped Farren's hanging watch with a dirty fingernail while the other airman leaned against the bulkhead, bored.

"Fourteen days ain't much."

Farren ignored them, and the airmen exited, allowing the thick hall door to thud back into place. Their steps receded across the deck plates.

Farren slumped on the cot. It was thin, worn through in a few places, and bent disconcertingly under his weight. The stubble on his chin scratched against his folded hands as he settled down to keep watch over Dahlia. She lay facing away in the next cell. Tiny breaths rising and falling in her chest were the sole indication of life. More than once Farren felt a pang of alarm at her stillness, only to be reassured a few seconds later by another breath.

Fourteen days.

The airman had been right, it wasn't much. And now, sitting alone in the dank bowels of the *Imperial Might*, the closeness of his death was suffocating. Farren was a wide-open-skies person. Living was the wind stinging his eyes and the sun warming his hair, and kicking back after a long day in the pilot's seat. Doing whatever he wanted and damn the consequences.

He loved being alive, breathing the sweetness of it. Never looking back for an instant. The prospect of having his life torn away from him in two short weeks was impossible to manage. Spending that time lying on a stained cot listening to rats gnaw at shadowy, unseen things was even worse. Unbearable.

"Dahlia," Farren said again. She didn't move; he hadn't expected her to. Perhaps she was dreaming of somewhere different.

* * *

David Harper visited several hours later.

"I came down as soon as I heard," he said, tapping the bars of Farren's prison. "Looks like things didn't go according to plan."

Farren shrugged and put on a strained smile. "Could always be worse."

"Yeah, I guess you're right," said Harper. "How's your lady friend?"

He nodded toward Dahlia.

"The men who brought her said she'd been interrogated. Should heal up fine though. If she doesn't, I…" Farren paused.

One of Harper's eyebrows crept up toward his hair.

"She *is* your girl, isn't she?" he grinned.

"I wish," said Farren. He could have gone on, but there were more pressing issues. "Listen, Harper, you've gotta get us out. I don't know why they have us on the *Imperial Might*, but maybe when we land you could sneak the keys or something."

David Harper shifted from one foot to the other, his Sergeant's uniform rustling.

"I can try to work something out," he said, "except we're not landing for two weeks. General Macall's only—"

"Two weeks?" Farren interrupted. "Devil's blood, I'll be *dead* in two weeks!"

"I know, I know. Just listen, General Macall's only told us that we're headed to the Southern Lands. The King ordered this expedition at the last minute, but I think there's more going on."

He dropped his voice and continued, "We set sail in the middle of the night, left behind a good chunk of men and supplies because he was in such a hurry. Alarms were going off all over the base and no one knows why because our radio doesn't work. We can't contact anyone. And the General won't say exactly where we're going or why."

"He's planning something," said Farren, itching his chin. "This isn't an exploration ship, it's a warship. There's no reason for the *Imperial Might* to go to the Southern Lands."

Even as he said it, Farren suddenly knew why. But someone else spoke first.

"He's going after the promethium."

The sound of Dahlia's voice turned Farren's head

toward her like a magnet. She rolled onto her back on the cot, head tilted to watch them. There were dark circles under her eyes and when she sat up the movement was sluggish and pained. But she was alive. An immense weight lifted from Farren's shoulders.

"Don't move too much, sweetheart," he said. His boots fidgeted, wanting to carry him to the edge of their adjoining cells but unsure what her reaction would be. The memory of her slap was still fresh. "You feeling okay?"

He swallowed down the other worried questions clamoring to be asked.

"No, but I will be," Dahlia replied, brushing him off. "There are more important things. I overheard part of your conversation. Sergeant, if what you say is true and Macall is sailing for Janmasthala, there can be only one reason."

She launched into the tale she had told Farren before, when she'd made up her mind to kill Macall aboard the *Wayfarer Elizabeth*. General Macall, Ansel Walker, Sita Senguptar, and the promethium experiments that had changed everything. Dahlia paused every so often to catch her breath. The color slowly returned to her face even as her voice became hoarse from talking.

"But this is perfect!" said Harper when she finished. "You'll take Macall to the promethium, then when he resurrects Sita he'll drain his own watch to nothing. How easy does it get?"

"And where does that leave Sita?" Dahlia asked. "She can't live properly. She'd be stuck between life and death, and I'm not about to inflict that on my own mother."

"Then what's your plan?" asked Harper as he crossed his arms. "I'd like to see the General dead too, but I'm not going to risk my neck." He glanced sheepishly at Farren. "Sorry, buddy, that's the way it is."

Farren hadn't expected more from Harper. Hoped for

it, yes, but there was a limit on what a man could put on the line with such odds. It would be an immense risk.

"I don't have a plan yet," Dahlia admitted. "We can't make any sort of move until the ship lands. Until then, Sergeant, do you think you could find other airmen who might help us?"

Harper promised to look into it, but the look on his face told them it was a lost cause.

Chapter Thirty-nine
The Man in the Flight Jacket

✳

Farren slouched on his cot in the next cell, staring resolutely at Dahlia, but she refused to acknowledge him. There was no way to tell how much time had passed since she had awoken here. Hours? Days? The only way to measure the passage of time was by the periodic glasses of water and bowls of sludge-like oatmeal brought by their captors. *Three bowls*, she thought. She hadn't bothered eating it.

Dahlia shifted where she lay, curled up on the cot and listening to the thrum of the engines. Her body ached. Muscles still twitched on occasion in imitations of the excruciating electricity-induced spasms she had suffered in the torture room. She rubbed her face, allowing her fingers to comb through unwashed hair. Her palms came away smeared with the last vestiges of makeup from the ball. Dahlia wiped them on the legs of her jumpsuit.

Farren broke the silence first.

"So," he said, "how're you feeling?"

Dahlia rolled over to face the plated wall. Her ribs twinged. She ignored them.

"Oh, come on sweetheart," Farren continued, "I'm just worried. How bad did they hurt you?"

The concern in his voice twisted her stomach. He had

no business sounding like that; if it hadn't been for him, neither of them would be in this situation. If it hadn't been for him, Macall would be dead. Dahlia hugged her arms and legs tighter to herself.

"Well, if you're gonna be like that," said Farren. The legs of his cot creaked as he shifted. Dahlia could picture him leaning back in feigned nonchalance, ruffling his hair perhaps. "Looks like we're gonna be stuck together for two weeks. One of us might as well talk."

He sighed.

"You remember when we met, how you stole that horse and carriage? Drove it like a maniac." Farren gave a humorless chuckle. "Thought you were gonna kill someone. That was your first time driving one, wasn't it?"

There were a few seconds of silence. He seemed to be waiting for her to respond, but Dahlia had no intention of rising to the invitation. It wasn't stubbornness or childish indignation. She merely couldn't bring herself to care. She'd been so close—*so close*—to avenging her papa, and he'd ruined it. But next time she wouldn't let him near. When she faced Macall again there would be no one to hold her back.

Farren interrupted the quiet.

"Ah, hell with it. I know why you're mad—I stopped you from killing Macall. I effed up your revenge, got us into this mess, got you tortured..." His voice caught. "I'm sorry about what happened, sweetheart, but I'm not sorry I did it. You were gonna kill yourself and I couldn't..."

A thick, uncomfortable silence hung in the air. Farren's boots scraped dirt along the floor and he took a few steps. Dahlia could envision him standing, clutching the bars of his cell.

Why won't he leave me alone?

"Listen, Dahlia," Farren said, "you've probably known

for a while, so I'm just gonna say it. I couldn't let you die because—"

"Talk about something else," Dahlia interrupted.

"—I...what?"

"I'm not having this conversation. Talk about something else, if you must talk." She rolled over to look at him. He leaned on the bars, drawing lines in the dirt with the toe of his boot. "Tell me about your flight jacket."

His boots scraped over the metal deck, nudging dirt away to clear a small clean space. Farren spoke, never taking his eyes off it.

"It was my father's. He was a pilot in the air force." Farren blew a strand of hair from his eyes. "My family ran a farm. Well, my mother ran the farm, since he was always gone—not that he was a bad father. When he came home between deployments he'd bring me back all sorts of presents and war stories. And he'd always be wearing that jacket."

The words came slowly at first, but accelerated as he talked as if rushing to escape into the open air.

"I remember asking him—I must have been about six years old—asking him if he was scared of getting killed like the people in the stories he told me. I was pretty worried about it. He said something practical and...reassuring. But I was still worried.

"So he said, 'You see this jacket I always wear?' And I nodded," Farren inclined his head, and the blond hair fell over his eyes, "and he leaned really close and said 'It's a lucky jacket. As long as I have this, no one can hurt me.' I was little. I believed him.

"A couple years later he got called away on an emergency assignment. I don't remember what it was. A mechanical pigeon came one night, and the next morning he left. He was in a hurry I guess, because he forgot the jacket."

Farren looked at her and they locked eyes. Despite her best efforts, Dahlia felt her heart clench in anticipation of his next words.

"'Nother pigeon came after it happened. I remember my mother...well, I...his flier was shot down by Delmar over the Hattaran Mountains. That's what they said." Farren's voice was empty, devoid of grief or pain. "Went down in a fireball right onto the mountainside. My mother had unlocked my watch earlier that year and I knew I wasn't going to live...a long life... But you know that."

He wouldn't look at her. Dahlia found herself sitting up on the cot. She wished she had never asked him about the jacket—why couldn't she leave well enough alone? But now that he had started, Farren wouldn't stop talking,

"I thought...when my time ran out...I'd just fling off the jacket and that would be the end of it. Fireball. I suppose...I always saw myself dying like he did, just a hell of a lot sooner.

"But now we're stuck in here. I don't think I'm gonna see the sky again, or the sun. Probably choke on that oatmeal."

He dropped his face into his hands and turned away, but not before Dahlia saw his fingers trembling. Farren was quiet a moment, then spoke again. Softly.

"So I took the jacket and stowed away on a trader. I worked my way up, eventually became a pilot in the air force. I never took the jacket off except at night

"Look, sweetheart. I'm only telling you this because there's no point in not. I'll be dead in two weeks, and there's nothing anyone in the world can do about it."

He fell silent. This time he stayed that way.

* * *

Dahlia must have fallen asleep, because she awoke several hours later. She stretched and was pleased to find her muscles felt looser, stronger. Her body had finally shed the last vestiges of pain.

Dahlia stood, inhaled, yawned. The overlarge jumpsuit flapped about her arms and legs and folded itself around her ankles. She reached up to smooth her hair and recoiled at the mess of dirt and tangles. *What I'd give for a bath.*

Her gaze rested briefly on Farren's presumably sleeping back in the next cell. *Good.* The aviator was more likable when he was unconscious, in a state where he couldn't foil long-anticipated plans for vengeance or stumble out emotional tales. Her eyes fell on the flight jacket hanging on the wall and flinched away. She told herself she'd never liked Farren much anyway. An Anglian airman could never be her type.

Something in Dahlia's chest tightened in protest at the thoughts roving about in her head. She did her best to ignore it while she took advantage of the water and the now-cold bowl of food left on the floor. But the guilt remained.

Dahlia sat back on her heels a few minutes later, licking the last bits of gooey oatmeal from the corners of her mouth. Her body felt strong again. The next thing to do was plot her breakout and Sebastian Macall's assassination. There would be no escape from the airship—she knew that—but if she broke out of her cell she might be able to reach Macall before the Anglians found her. They would most likely kill her after she murdered their General, but that was a small matter. Dahlia had been living on borrowed time for a long while now.

Farren's cot creaked as he shifted in his sleep. Dahlia glanced up at him. His shoulders, while broad from military training, seemed small without the bulk of the flight jacket to cover them. They were shaking.

"Mr. Reed?" Dahlia spoke without thinking, and chastised herself for her concern. It was Farren's fault they had been imprisoned in the first place. If he was having a difficult time, he had only himself to blame.

He sat up and got to his feet, walking a few paces. Dahlia became suddenly conscious of her unladylike position hunched over the oatmeal bowl and straightened.

Farren silently leaned on the bars near the hall, staring at his watch on its peg. The case had been left open to reveal the time inside.

"Thirteen days," he said.

Chapter Forty
Second Chance

✳

Farren paced. Back and forth from his cell door to the far wall, hands curling and uncurling.

Dahlia watched him with concern disguised as mild interest. She devoted the majority of her attention to washing her face and hair with the cup of water left on the floor. There was only so much grime she could stand on her skin, and desperate times called for desperate measures—isn't that what they said?

Dahlia sighed and leaned to one side to allow the dirty water to drip from her hair.

"I wish you'd quit that pacing, Mr. Reed."

"Oh, come on." Farren said angrily, pointing to his watch on the wall. "At least pretend to care."

The barb hurt. She acted as if it didn't.

Farren deflated into a sitting position on the floor, batting aside a bowl of oatmeal. Dahlia's breath hitched when she saw it was untouched.

"Mr. Reed, have you been eating?"

Farren shook his head without looking at her.

Dahlia wrung her hair and shook it out, combing it with fingers that were dirtier than she would have preferred.

"You should eat something."

"Why?" The defeat in his voice was palpable. "What's the point?"

Dahlia opened her mouth to tell him that, obviously, he needed to eat to live. Then she closed it again.

He knows that.

The cell bars creaked as Farren slouched back onto them, ignoring a rust beetle crawling over the back of his hand.

"Twelve days," he rolled the phrase around in his mouth. "Can you believe that? An entire lifetime, and it's led up to...this."

He waved a hand idly at the dim gloom around them, somehow managing to capture her in it too.

The hall door opened with a dull creak. Dahlia glanced up as a guard strode in and began unlocking her cell.

"The General wants to see you," he said. Dahlia stood.

"I can't imagine what for," she said. Her heart hammered; here was the opportunity she needed to get close to Macall.

The guard grabbed her watch off the peg and pushed her ahead through the door. Dahlia spared a glance for Farren, who hunched against the bars of his cell that were shared with hers. His face was pale.

She looked away and allowed the guard to whisk her down the hall.

* * *

"Sit down, Miss Walker."

The sleek sound of Macall's voice felt like wasps buzzing inside Dahlia's skull. Her papa's killer looked on as she stumbled into the chair in front of his desk. They were in his office, somewhere along the *Imperial Might's* outer edge, with too-bright sunlight slanting in through a series of large portholes. Sebastian sat across from her. He twirled her watch in one hand, a gesture calculated to appear idle yet intimidating.

"How do you like my ship?" he asked, nodding to indicate the functionally luxurious interior of the room. Ornate shelves supported rows of books strapped into place with leather bands. Topographical charts were rolled out on neat wooden tables. The hallways outside had been simple military fare, but apparently a General afforded something higher-class.

"It's certainly nice," she responded. "Although my accommodations leave something to be desired."

She allowed her eyes to travel about the room under the pretense of admiring it. Sebastian's sword hung at his belt. The blade of a letter opener gleamed in a case on the desk. Could she kill him with that? The guard who had led her in remained outside, doubtlessly on the other side of the doorway. She would have enough time...

"Yes, well, you know," he said. "You did try to kill me. It seemed—"

"Why'd you call me here?"

Sebastian smiled, but the expression was forced.

"To see if you'd thought about sharing any more details regarding the promethium. Vatana is a big place. Searching the entire city could take weeks. I have the resurrection device your father made—all we need now is promethium."

"Are you in a hurry?" Dahlia smirked. "*I* don't care how long it takes you to find it."

Sebastian stood.

"I'm trying to resurrect your mother. I imagine you might have an interest in seeing her alive again."

"I told you: it won't work. I won't help you destroy her."

Sebastian scowled, tapping one finger on his desk as he thought.

"Something else then, perhaps? You talked about accommodations. I'm sure we could arrange something more comfortable for you and that airman. The guards tell me he hasn't been eating; I can provide something more palatable than prison fare."

While he talked, Macall turned his head to gaze through the porthole glass. The minute he stopped watching her, Dahlia stopped listening. Her eyes fixed on the letter opener.

Can I do it?

"And, if you cooperate, then we have no reason to keep you imprisoned after we have the promethium," Sebastian continued. "I'll let you go."

Yes, I can.

Macall still held her watch loosely, but Dahlia couldn't have cared less. In an instant she leapt from the chair. She seized the tiny knife.

In another instant Macall had her up against the wall by the throat. Her wrist throbbed where he gripped it. Dahlia resisted for a few moments, then allowed the blade to tumble from her numb fingers.

The door banged open against the wall. Two guards rushed in, rifles drawn and aimed.

"Freeze!"

Dahlia would have rolled her eyes if she hadn't been focused on breathing through the pressure of Sebastian's hand. *I'm not going anywhere. Idiots.* Her own lack of fear surprised her.

Sebastian didn't release her. His expression was hurt.

"Why would you do that?" he asked. Dahila's struggling breaths inhaled the air from his words and suddenly all she could think of was how disgusted she was by the warmth of it. They were breathing the same *air*.

"I was trying to help you," said Macall, pressing his fingers harder against her windpipe. Dahlia rasped and tried to bat at him with her free hand. Sebastian tilted his head as if not understanding her actions. "Just cooperate with me, Miss—"

He backed away so fast he almost fell over the desk. Dahlia sucked in an enormous breath, slumping against the wall.

"Sita?"

Then the guards hauled her out the door, pausing barely long enough to snag her watch from the floor. They were halfway down the hall when Macall shouted, "Hold on a moment!"

The men halted, one holding tight to each of her arms. Dahlia glanced over her shoulder to see Sebastian standing in the doorway of his office.

"Miss...Walker," he said with difficulty. "Do you know what the penalty is for desertion from the air force?"

"I think I can guess," she muttered.

"Death by hanging. I was going to forget about that for you, to spare your airman the pain and shame. Let his watch decide how he dies. But now," he smiled, "I think you've jogged my memory."

Her heart sank. The adrenaline faded, and hopelessness stole into her veins. Dahlia didn't resist when the guards pulled her along and out of sight.

Chapter Forty-one
Winding Down

✳

Farren wiped shaking hands on the legs of his pants, leaving streaks of sweat. He stood, paced the length of his cell, and sat again. His stomach was a hollow hole, but it was nothing next to the horrible ache in his chest. How could dread hurt so badly?

"How are you doing over there, Mr. Reed?" Dahlia asked. "You should eat something, before you make yourself sick."

He wasn't sure how long ago the guards had brought her back from Macall, or how long she had been gone. Everything blurred. Time blended into a haze of confusion throbbing through a vicious headache.

"I'm fine," he said quickly. He stood again. "Fine."

Farren repeated the word to himself as he walked a circuit of the cell, suddenly realizing how suffocating and small it was. Couldn't they build these things any bigger? It wasn't as if there were many prisoners—they didn't need the rest of the cells over there.

He wiped his hands a second time.

"What did Macall want?"

Dahlia looked over from where she sat cross-legged on her cot, her back resting against the wall.

"Nothing important," she said. "He was interested in

the promethium, of course."

"That's it?" Farren grabbed the bars of her cell. He leaned his forehead onto them and relished the touch of the cool metal on his burning skin.

"Well, I went after him again," she admitted, looking away in embarrassment, "but he's too strong."

"You tried to kill him again?" Farren said incredulously.

She nodded. "With a letter opener."

"Come on, sweetheart! Don't you have any common sense? That's goddamn dangerous!"

Dahlia sniffed and drew herself up. "Well, I'm not afraid of him."

"You mean you're an idiot. He could've killed you."

"He tried."

Farren threw up his hands, turned away, and stopped; there was nowhere to go.

* * *

Farren slept fitfully, dipping in and out of fevered dreams. Sometimes he could have sworn Dahlia was leaning over him and dabbing his forehead with a damp cloth, smoothing his hair with soft fingers. But then he would wake up—or perhaps fall asleep again?—to nothing but the sound of a watch ticking fainter and fainter. Winding down.

What if he slept away the rest of his life? He could die and never know he had. The thought, splayed against the backdrop of the constant ticking in his ears, was horrific.

There was only one time when he knew he was truly awake. He could tell by the ache of his back on the floor, and the dirt on his unwashed fingers. No dream would be that detailed. Would it?

"Mr. Reed?"

Dahlia's voice was an anchor to reality. He opened his eyes and saw her face on the other side of the bars. She held a piece of cloth in one hand. The other pressed against his cheek.

"Sweetheart, what's—"

"Shhh," she said, and the hand drew back. "You have a fever. Just rest."

The prospect of slipping back into the nightmares was the least restful thing he could think of.

"How long have we been here?" he asked.

"Sergeant Harper visited a few hours ago to check up on you. He said eleven days."

"Eleven days?" Farren sat up too swiftly and his vision swam. "But then I've only got three left!"

"And I'm sure you don't want to spend them sick like this. Lie down. Eat something."

He did, but only because Dahlia put her hand on his chest to push him down.

Three days?

He had nothing to fear anymore, nothing except the gaping black abyss waiting at the end of this inexorable journey. He was terrified. He was bold.

"Sweetheart..."

She didn't respond, preoccupied with re-wetting the damp cloth in her glass of water.

"Dahlia, listen." He reached for her hand and took it, surprised at the energy required for such a simple movement. "I love you."

Dahlia was silent. Farren scanned her face but it held only doubt. It was obvious...he should have known she didn't feel the same way. Yet he didn't regret a word. Strange, that impending death was the only thing that could give him such freedom.

"You've gotten so strong since I met you," he

continued. It half felt as if he was still dreaming, the words tumbling from his thoughts to his mouth with nothing to stop them. "But you're still so...you. Clever, brave. And stubborn." The ghost of a smile lifted his lips. "I just wish we had more time."

"Mr. Reed, I don't think I can give you a proper response..."

"I know," he said. "I don't mind. I just wanted to tell you."

It didn't hurt as much as he'd thought it would.

"Dahlia, what happened to you when the General's men shot you?"

"What do you mean?" she asked guardedly.

"You were pretty much dead, weren't you?" he said, allowing the words to cascade out. "Did it hurt? Was there a tunnel and a light? A big voice in the clouds? Was everything just...black?"

Dahlia paused a moment to slip the cloth back onto his forehead with her free hand. The other slunk gently out of his grasp.

"It was easy, Farren. Painless. Like falling asleep after being awake for too long."

But she wouldn't look at him when she said it.

"Now stop talking and rest."

"No," he said, and sat up again against the pressure of her hand. The room blurred. "There's something else I have to tell you."

"I told you, Mr. Reed, I don't have an answer——"

He shook his head. "It's not that. It's just...can you...do something for me after I die?"

"What?" she said, her voice softer.

"Promise me...you won't try to kill Macall again."

She opened her mouth to protest, but Farren held up a hand.

"Hear me out," he said. "You have time left—could be days, could be decades. Don't go throwing it away. I'm not saying Macall doesn't deserve to die. I'm saying you deserve to live. Promise me you won't go near him again once you're out of here."

Dahlia stared at the ground. "But he killed my father."

"That doesn't mean you have to let him kill you too." What meager strength he had was slipping slowly out of Farren's body; he gripped the cell bars to hold himself up. "Please, Dahlia; I don't have any time left. You do. Promise me you'll use it."

Farren summoned a wave of energy and took her hand again. It felt cool and comforting, even covered in grit.

"I promise." Her thumb drew circles on the back of his hand. "But only if you eat something."

Farren nodded and allowed himself to slump back to the deck. Nightmares raged at the edges of his consciousness, but Farren focused on the pressure of Dahlia's hand. It was an anchor against the hopeless, maddening ticking of the watch.

Damn, he thought as sleep took him. *I love that woman.*

Chapter Forty-two
Promethium

✳

Dahlia stood at the edge of her cell, watching Farren's watch tick down. Only the smallest sliver of space—barely an hour—remained between the hand and the zero mark looming ever greater in her vision. Farren's eyes were glued to it. The airman's face, which had been returning to a healthy color after his fever broke the previous day, was pallid once again.

"Should we be doing a countdown or something?" he asked with a nervous smile. He sat cross-legged on his cot, staring at the watch and ruffling his hair. "I mean, this is a pretty big event."

Dahlia pretended not to listen. Her stomach knotted and unknotted itself.

If I'm this scared, Farren must be petrified.

"So what's gonna happen? Do you think I'll just keel over right here?" He made a show of examining the dismal space around him. "Not a very fitting death for someone of my…what's the word? Caliber. Someone of my caliber."

Dahlia couldn't look at him. "They're going to hang you, Farren."

"Oh." The fake smile slid from his face. "I think I'd rather do the keel over thing. Don't you think they'll grant me a last request?"

Footfalls sounded from the hallway. A moment later the door swung open to admit Sebastian Macall, with two soldiers and Sergeant Harper trailing in his wake. The smile twisting his face was pure triumph.

"Ladies and gentlemen, welcome to Vatana."

He nodded at the two soldiers, who produced a key and set to work removing Farren from his cell. Macall leaned against the bars beside Dahlia.

"We've already been searching the city for a few hours," he said. "It's all ancient ruins, of course. Quite fascinating. You're welcome to come have a look if you want to tell me anything more about where we can find the promethium."

"I told you: no," Dahlia said.

"Suit yourself. We'll find it eventually," sneered Sebastian. He nodded toward Farren. "You're only hurting him."

In the next cell, Farren stood and allowed the soldiers to tie his hands behind his back. Panic rose in Dahlia's chest. Macall was right—it didn't matter how long it took, he would find the promethium. There was no use in letting Farren suffer simply to inconvenience the General. Her mind churned as they walked Farren out of his cell.

"The eastern edge of the city," she said breathlessly. "There's a cave—that's where my father found it."

Macall grinned. "Thank you, Miss Walker."

The soldiers began to escort Farren toward the door at the end of the hallway. He glanced back over his shoulder at her, smiled, and winked. His mouth silently formed the words 'I love you.'

"Wait!" Dahlia yelled. "Where are you going? You said you wouldn't hang him if I told you!"

"I lied."

Dahlia threw herself against the bars, fingers clawing at

Macall. She had to hurt him. Tear out an eye, rip off an ear, crush his throat in a fit of rage... The General stepped backward with easy grace. A contemptuous smile lifted the corners of his mouth.

Macall turned toward Harper, who had been observing the entire event in silence.

"Sergeant, you stay here and keep an eye on her. Miss Walker seems to be...displeased with this turn of events. I won't have her hurting herself."

Harper nodded. Satisfied, Macall gestured the soldiers out the door and followed them. When he slammed it shut, the sound echoed through Dahlia's bones like a death knell.

"You sick, slimy bastard!" she shrieked. She clutched her cell bars and shook them as hard as she could. "You lying, murdering son of a bitch! I'll kill you!"

A wordless roar tore itself from her throat. She saw her papa, lying amid the bits of his shattered watch on the sitting room floor. And she saw Farren, creaking at the end of a rope with blood dripping from his gaping mouth. It was too much. She wanted to run, to fight, to die...

No! A thought pounded through her despair. *I promised Farren I wouldn't give up! I promised him...*

Dahlia released the bars and swallowed against her own ragged breathing. Her eyes caught sight of the flight jacket still hanging on its peg outside the cell.

He needs that back.

"Sergeant," she said, turning to Harper, "I need your help."

A key jangled in his hand.

"Why do you think I came down here?" he grinned. "If you've got a plan, I've got a flier ready to go."

"Take me to it," Dahlia said as he unlocked her cell. "I'll find the promethium. I need you to search Macall's office—there should be a small copper device there. It's about the size of a fist, with two cutouts to hold watches in place. Bring it and meet me in the ruins under the airship."

"Gotcha."

* * *

Dahlia flew alone through the ruins: a vast sea of decaying buildings, crumbling walls, and plants pushing easily through cobblestone streets. The flier controls were difficult, but not completely unlike the ones for the mechanical horse she had driven in Delmar. That seemed years ago.

Her eyes settled on a patch of flowers below.

Dahlias. And the bright flowers carpeted the area around the collapsed entrance to a cave.

She allowed herself a brief smile.

This must be it. Papa was always a clever one.

Dahlia landed, leapt from the flier, and almost fell, barely managing to cling to the unlit firefly lantern in her hand. She stopped just long enough to steady herself. A glance back over her shoulder revealed the *Imperial Might* looming over the ruins of Vatana.

Long grass brushed against the knees of her prisoner's jumpsuit. The cool morning air stung her face. She rolled the overlarge sleeves of Farren's flight jacket up to her elbows in a futile effort to keep them from engulfing her hands.

Half the cave entrance had fallen in long ago, but the gaping remainder was more than large enough for her to squeeze through. Stones nipped at her hair.

It was unsettlingly dim inside. Dahlia peered into the inscrutable interior for a few moments.

Are there bears here? she wondered. *Wolves?*

She fiddled with the lantern switch, her fingers

shivering. Who cared? Right now there could be soldiers flinging a rope over a tree limb in the shadow of the *Imperial Might*. Her heart beat faster, but whether it was from fear for herself or for Farren she couldn't tell.

The firefly lantern flared to life. Dahlia glanced about, half expecting to see the maw of a predator yawning back. Her eyes came to rest on an arrow carved into the wall. It was crude, barely visible so many years after Ansel Walker had scratched it there. But it pointed unmistakably into the darkness.

"Let's do this," she murmured, and followed it.

* * *

The cave walls were damp under Dahlia's touch. Untold centuries of water dripping along rock had given birth to colonies of multicolored algae near the cave entrance, but deep inside the walls were bare.

The cave had been used as a mineshaft at some point. Portions of it had been shorn up, sculpted by human hands, and the occasional wooden support beam was still preserved. Yet much of the passageway had fallen into such disrepair that it was impossible to say whether it was natural or man-made.

Dahlia moved briskly through the darkness, holding the lantern high. Her feet slipped and scraped along stone. How long had it been? She didn't know how much time had passed underground. Her useless watch clinked in her pocket—in the pocket of Farren's flight jacket. Was he still alive?

There was no time to question her decision. When every moment mattered, hesitation would leave her with no choice at all.

Dahlia couldn't analyze her own motivations.

Everything inside her was confused, whirling around the feeling of Farren's hand in hers as she placed a cool cloth on his forehead. The vague smell of him still clinging to the leather jacket. The sight of him mouthing 'I love you' as the door slammed.

Her foot struck something and sent it skittering along the rough floor. Dahlia threw a glance at her feet out of reflex.

A skull leered back.

She clapped her hands to her mouth to stifle a shriek. The lantern clattered to the floor. It tipped sideways, the top falling open to release a few mechanical fireflies. Dahlia slapped it back on and backed away. Her terrified gasps echoed deafeningly in the otherwise silent cave.

It was the boy.

His skeleton sat propped against the cave wall, bones glowing a sickly off-white. Dahlia reeled backward. Her stomach churned and she almost vomited from the combination of surprise and disgust. The lantern flickered over a grinning skull, delicate fingers, ribs curling around insides that had long since rotted away. A cracked watch lay on a stone nearby.

She raised the lantern higher. If the boy was here, then that could only mean...

There! A cluster of crystals shimmered among the somber rock beside the skeleton. This was it, it had to be.

Promethium.

It took a minute or two for her to pry several promethium crystals from the stone with a small pocketknife she had found in the flier. In the end, Dahlia held a pair of tiny, green-tinged bits. She hoped they would be enough. There was no time to hack away more.

She tucked them into the pocket of Farren's flight jacket and took a few steps back the way she had come. The old arrows her papa had carved still marked the path out.

Dahlia turned. The boy's skeleton watched her with obsidian, hollow eyes. How horrible it must have been; trapped here for days, months, years…breathing stale air and hearing only the drip of water filtering down through layers of rock. Unable to die. Unable to live. Ansel Walker—her papa—had done this.

"I'm sorry," she whispered. Then she turned and hurried back through the cave, through the dark, to where the sky was lightening in anticipation of dawn.

* * *

Dahlia peered around the corner of a ruined wall. Chill morning air crept across her face and she shivered, grateful for the warmth of the heavy jacket around her shoulders. The *Imperial Might*'s vast shadow started a few broken cobblestones in front of her. The airship itself hung overhead: dark, hulking, ominous. But even its immense presence couldn't distract her from what was happening beneath it.

A pair of soldiers were preparing for the execution. They had chosen a cluster of trees—perhaps the remains of an ancient park, Dahlia thought—for the event. One man stood atop a tall walking platform, putting the finishing touches on a noose that swung lethargically from a branch above. The other soldier occupied himself with alternately spitting on the ground and watching his companion.

Where's Harper? Dahlia wondered. Saving Farren would be impossible without the copper device.

And even if they managed to pull off her insane plan, there was no guarantee it would be enough. Time was fickle. Her own zeroed watch was proof enough of that. She had no way of knowing how much time she had left to use, or how much she could part with.

"Dahlia."

She jumped slightly and turned to see Harper standing flat to the wall behind her. A glint of copper shone in his outstretched hand.

"Where's Farren?" Dahlia asked as she took it. The metal felt smooth, cold.

"They should be bringing him out any minute," he whispered. "You know you'll have to get closer; we can't take the watch this far from him."

"I'll move as late as I can," Dahlia said, eyeing the open space between the soldiers and where she hid. No chance of concealment out there. "You just get it to me. Can you get a tesla rifle?"

"Of course."

"Use that to distract them—if you can stun Macall, we might be able to cause enough confusion to grab Farren and slip away into the ruins."

The two of them plotted for a few more minutes before Harper left to retrieve a rifle, slinking along what was left of the walls. He reappeared a few minutes later next to a boarding platform beneath the airship. The *Imperial Might* had four platforms: two each on the starboard and port sides. They could be raised and lowered via cables linked to winches mounted in the ship's underbelly. Two currently rested on the ground.

Harper stepped onto one and fiddled with a small control panel. The platform rose. Dahlia leaned back against the wall and watched him disappear into the airship, turning the copper device over and over in her fingers. It was barely as large as her palm. Gleaming set screws stuck out each side, waiting for watches to hold.

Freedom lay just beyond the ruins of Vatana. She only needed to sneak around the wall and she could be away before they even missed her. It would be so easy... She looked across the city, past the buildings to the forested hills in the distance. A new life waited there.

Yes, Farren would die, but he would have died even if they had never met. What did she owe him? What did he really mean to her? Dahlia tugged at her hair as the smell of Farren's flight jacket washed over her again.

The copper device looked so small sitting there in her palm, but she was surprised at how heavy it was.

Chapter Forty-three
A Glorious Day to Die

✳

Farren locked eyes with Dahlia one last time before the guards hauled him from the brig. The door closed.

Farren had never fancied himself the emotional type; he took pride in being unattached to anyone or anything. Over the past few weeks Dahlia had changed that. He'd felt more since he had met her than he had for many years, and there was no shame in it. His heart seemed to expand beyond the useless organ it had been. For a while, he'd allowed himself to hope.

Now he'd lost it all. He was back at the beginning, more alone than he'd been before he knew what it was like to not be lonely.

* * *

There was a trial, if it could be called that. General Macall was the judge and jury; the only other witnesses were a token number of guards assembled in his office. He sat behind his desk eyeing Farren with a boredom that bordered on insulting.

Farren found himself staring at the letter opener on the desk. Dahlia had touched that, hadn't she? She'd been right here…he imagined the scent of lavender.

"Airman Reed, you are found guilty of desertion," Macall pronounced once he had completed the required court proceedings, "the sentence for which is death. Do you have anything further to say at this time?"

Farren shrugged and felt the ropes dig into his wrists. What *could* he say? That he didn't consider being pushed out of an airship and left behind to be an act of desertion?

"Very well," said Macall. He picked up Farren's watch from where the guards had laid it on the desk and opened it. "Sentence to be carried out in twenty-one minutes."

* * *

Farren stood shakily on a walking platform, blinking in a sunrise that seemed too bright after days of darkness. The sky was a deep ocean blue, the kind of color that preceded a beautiful dawn. The smallest breeze stirred leaves on the branches above, and somewhere a bird chirped a morning greeting. It was a glorious day to die.

A scattering of soldiers congregated under the grove of trees, watching with a mix of anticipation and morbid interest. General Macall addressed the assembled audience.

"…found guilty of desertion during wartime, the punishment for which is death."

An airman slipped the noose about his neck and began to lower the hood over his head. Farren shook him off.

"I'll do without."

"Suit yourself." The man hopped down off the walking platform, leaving Farren alone.

Macall continued, "Aviator First Class Farren Reed is sentenced to be hung by the neck until dead."

Farren suddenly became aware of how the rope itched his skin. He leaned into it for a moment, testing, feeling the suffocating pressure against his windpipe. It was utterly terrifying.

He dared to look down and wished he hadn't. The ground was there, the same as it had always been, carpeted with dry grass and scattered stones. But Farren couldn't see the ground. He saw the black abyss; the infinite, gaping maw of death opening wide to swallow him whole.

"Do you have any last words?"

Farren raised his head. His eyes roved over the chalky stone ruins of Vatana, the green hills beyond, the spilled rainbow of sunrise painted on the clouds. *Did* he have anything to say? Any closing remarks? A final few sentences to justify his existence?

He raced through his life in snapshots of memory: the mother he had left and the father he would join soon, the airmen he had served with, and the officers who had praised his piloting skills. None of it seemed fitting.

None of it, except for the one thing.

"She isn't here," he said, standing up a little straighter, "but I'll say it anyway: Dahlia, I know we didn't know each other for very long…"

The first sliver of sun peeked over the horizon.

"…and it wasn't much, what we had. But it was enough."

Farren swallowed past the pressure of the noose. His heart pumped in his chest as if trying to escape from its fate.

"That's all I've got to say."

Macall nodded. "In that case—"

"Wait—I've got something to say too."

It was Dahlia's voice. Farren found her immediately at the edge of the small crowd.

What's she doing here?

"Harper, now!" she cried.

David Harper stepped out of the audience, grabbing Farren's watch from Macall's stunned grasp, throwing it to

Dahlia... She caught it and scrambled with a glint of metal in her hand.

"How did you escape?" Macall sputtered, his eyes on Dahlia. Beside him, Harper raised a tesla rifle.

Macall's sword flashed. Electricity crackled in the air, arcing harmlessly past his face as he batted the barrel of the rifle astray with the blade. The energy scorched the grass near his feet.

Harper backpedaled, struggling to put space between himself and the General. Macall lunged forward. His blade lashed out, sharp and bright, and Harper blocked it with the rifle. He didn't notice the airman behind him until a tesla bolt caught him between the shoulder blades.

No! Farren strained at the ropes on his wrists, but they were too tight to budge. He could only watch as Harper crumpled to the ground. The rifle tumbled from his fingers.

"Stop her!" barked Macall. Two men moved in to grab each of Dahlia's arms—*Don't you touch her!* Farren thought, enraged.

"I'll deal with her when we're done here," said Macall, sheathing his sword as he recovered his composure.

Dahlia struggled against her captors, kicking and clawing at their arms. The glimmer of metal dropped into the grass just as Farren realized what it was.

They were trying to save me. The thought was comforting even in its futility. Farren wanted to say something, to tell them what it meant to him, but Macall had already turned back to address him one last time.

"Now that that's done with..."

Macall raised the control for the walking platform. He grinned. His fingers curled around a lever, pulling it as if in slow motion.

"May God have mercy on your soul."

Farren's feet slipped along the smooth surface of the

platform as it moved. He closed his eyes, allowing his boots to cling to the edge for just one moment longer.

"Dahlia..."

Then he was standing on air. The rope squeezed, pain flared, and he fell into the black abyss.

Chapter Forty-four
Au Revoir

✳

"Farren!" Dahlia screamed.

Farren swung from the tree limb, twitching and choking as he rotated slowly at the end of the rope. Dahlia's stomach wrenched. She'd been too slow...it was all for nothing... He was dying right in front of her and she could do nothing to stop it. It was incredible that one man could mean so much.

She crumpled to her knees. The soldiers restraining her didn't seem to mind: they released her and remained standing.

I'm sorry. I'm so sorry.

She felt like she was the one up there dying, not him, not her airman. Her breath came in short gasps and she bent toward the ground before she could see the life leave him. It had been only seconds, but it felt like years.

Something glittered in the dry grass: the time transfer device with both their watches secured to it. It lay right there, inches from her dripping eyes. Suddenly, hope ignited a fire in her shattered heart.

"Let this be a lesson to traitors and deserters," Macall said. "Mercy has no place in war."

Dahlia wasn't listening. Her hand leapt out and snatched the tiny bright thing, her mind barely registering the receding seconds visible on Farren's watch—*four, three, two*—no time to think, no time to reconsider... She spun the mechanism...*one*...

The rope snapped.

Farren crumpled into a limp heap on the ground in front of a startled audience. The air stilled for a moment. Dahlia couldn't breathe for fear of breaking the tenuous silence that balanced the future on the edge of a knife. Had she done it? Was he...?

The airman coughed, groaned, and rolled over.

"Farren!" she yelled.

The soldiers didn't react in time to hold her back. She bounded to her feet, stuffing the time transfer device and their watches into the pocket of the overlarge flight jacket. She sprinted through the scattered crowd, dodging the hands snatching at her. It felt like she was flying.

"Are you all right?" she asked, kneeling by Farren's side. Confused mutters filled the air behind her, but she didn't care. "How badly are you hurt?"

Her hands fluttered over him, unsure what would be most helpful. She settled for pulling the remains of the noose over his head, mussing his hair and revealing an ugly bruise on his neck. Her fingers coaxed off the bindings on his wrists. Farren still gasped for air, chest heaving, his breath coming in loud rasps. But all that mattered was that he was alive.

A hand clamped on her shoulder. Dahlia's heart sank.

"Time transfer, am I right?" Sebastian Macall said hungrily. "Give me the device."

Dahlia looked up at him, staring into eyes wide with madness.

Trapped. She had saved Farren, but for how long?

"Let us go and you can have it," Dahlia answered. "I'll even tell you where the promethium is—you'll never find it on your own."

"I doubt that, Miss Walker. Now give me the device in your pocket or I'll be forced to take it from you."

A mechanical rumble overhead echoed faintly in Dahlia's ears. No doubt the *Imperial Might*'s boarding platforms descending to bring more enemies down upon them.

She had no choice; the only option was to obey and survive for a few minutes longer. Dahlia pulled forth the device, undid the set screws securing their watches, and dropped it into Macall's eager grasp. His fingers curled around it.

"Now give me your watches."

Dahlia's mind raced, seizing ideas and discarding them. There was no way out.

Farren grabbed her arm and struggled to sit up. His mouth worked, forming words that shriveled in his crushed windpipe, but Dahlia understood enough.

Look... He pointed into the sky.

Dahlia didn't—she couldn't—not with Macall so close and their futures so hopeless. The General unsheathed the sword at his waist and let the blade drift toward Dahlia. His meaning was clear. If she didn't relinquish the watches voluntarily, she would be made to.

"Your watches, now!"

He stepped forward. Dahlia shrank back until she could feel Farren behind her. At least they were together again, for however brief a time.

Macall lunged. Dahlia squeezed her eyes closed, heart pounding, braced for the blow.

CRACK.

A rifle shot rent the air. Dahlia ducked instinctively and the bullet whizzed over her head. There was a dull thunk and a yell, a mist of blood, and when she opened her eyes Macall was falling backward.

"Did you see that, darling? What a beautiful shot!"

Keet Hawkins leaned out of the patchwork hull of the *Wayfarer Elizabeth* and waved as it soared overhead. Her pink-and-blue hair was a shock of color next to the ebony sniper rifle at her side. Dahlia had never been so happy to see someone.

"Keet!" Dahlia threw caution to the wind and hauled Farren to his feet. "Long time no see!"

The Anglian soldiers dissolved into confusion, some kneeling desperately over Macall's prone form, others sprinting toward the *Imperial Might's* boarding platforms.

"Are these men bothering you?" called the bounty hunter.

"All except that one." Dahlia smiled, pointing to Harper, who was blinking back into consciousness nearby.

Shot after shot rang out. The remaining Anglians scrambled vainly for their tesla rifles. A few managed to get off a wild bolt or two before being struck down by Keet's methodical lethality. Dahlia doubted they were dead, but she only needed incapacitation.

"Let's go!" she shouted, blinking as blood sprayed into her eyes. A soldier collapsed nearby. Dahlia grabbed his sword to fend off a man who reached for them. Keet dropped him a moment later.

Dahlia flung Farren's arm over her shoulder. Together they darted through the carnage, wincing as bullets found their marks all around them—Keet, cutting a path.

A deafening crackle interrupted the steady rhythm of shots and screams. Blue electricity leapt in a dreadful arc from the *Imperial Might's* forward guns. The *Wayfarer Elizabeth* was too close, too surprised to evade the attack. Wicked sparks spit and skittered over the hull plates. They chewed at the vulnerable mechanisms near the engines.

"Keet!" Dahlia shouted. She froze and watched, gaping, as the black airship attacked a second time. The *Wayfarer Elizabeth* shuddered.

A tesla bolt buzzed an inch from Dahlia's nose. She backpedaled, nearly fell, and turned to see a trio of men advancing on them. Her hand tightened on Farren's arm. Keet and Tiberius were too focused on the *Imperial Might* to help them now.

A fourth soldier cut off their escape route, circling wide toward the ruins. Dahlia raised the sword she had taken from the dead man.

"Grab them!" said a soldier. His tesla rifle aimed at Dahlia's chest.

She darted to the side, yanking Farren with her, trying hopelessly to dodge. But he was too close, she was too slow—

Harper's bolt caught the man in the back of the head. Electricity spread over his skin, crackling while he collapsed.

"Go!" barked Harper. He shot the man blocking their way in another fizz of sparks. "I'll catch up."

There was no time to invent a better plan. Dahlia ran. Farren's weight pulled at her. The deafening thunder of the *Imperial Might's* cannons echoed off of the ruined walls ahead, the blasts seeming to issue from every side.

She didn't pause until her feet reached the ancient cobblestone road. A glance backward revealed a turmoil of soldiers, explosions, and blue electricity where the park had once been. Somehow her eyes found Macall, sprawled unmoving beside the walking platform. He was too far to see properly, but she knew his uniform was stained with blood. A bitter smile stretched the corners of her mouth. If he wasn't dead, he was severely wounded.

He won't be following us any time soon.

She saw Harper, still trading tesla fire with the Anglian soldiers. The *Wayfarer Elizabeth* limped in a circle overhead, leaking smoke—Dahlia's stomach twisted as she imagined Keet frantically patching up the engines.

Farren seemed to sense her thoughts.

"Have...to get...away," he rasped. "Nothing we...can do."

"You're right." Dahlia tore herself away from the spectacle. She adjusted Farren's arm on her shoulder and started to drag him further into the ruins.

"I...can walk."

"Then let's go."

Dahlia dropped Farren's arm, grabbed his hand, and pulled him onward. The smell of smoke stung the air.

They stopped a few minutes later to rest inside the remains of a white stone structure that still possessed a portion of its roof. Farren leaned against a wall and slid to the floor. He massaged the bruise on his neck, breathing heavily.

"Are you all right?" Dahlia asked.

"I'll be...fine," he panted. "Just give me a sec."

Dahlia peeked out the open doorway. They had retreated a few blocks from the battle, but it was still far closer than she was comfortable with. Yells, gunfire, and the fizz of electricity echoed through the streets.

In the sky, the *Wayfarer Elizabeth* had powered up her own tesla cannons and was putting up a valiant fight. It looked like a dog nipping at an amused carriage. Dahlia couldn't hold back a surge of guilt. If she and Farren hadn't been captured by Macall in the first place, their friends wouldn't be in this dire situation.

"How's it look...out there?" asked Farren.

"They're doing wonderfully," Dahlia turned away from the door and bent down next to him. Loose stones crunched under her feet. "I think they'll have things wrapped up before too long."

She knew he doubted her, but he didn't contest the lie.

Another explosion rattled the city. She imagined the heat of flames on her face. She was back in Sainsbury, lying amid the wreck of her home and listening to that same airship rain death upon everything she'd ever known. Her mouth was suddenly dry. The smoke, the bombs...was the sky outside burned red too?

"Hey, sweetheart."

The airman touched her cheek and the memory faded. This time was different. In Sainsbury she had lost the most important person in her life, but here in Vatana he was still here beside her.

"You're okay with this," Farren said. He stroked her face with the edge of his finger as if not believing his good fortune.

"Of course I am, you fool. I don't hand out my time to just anyone."

He grinned and tapped the end of her nose. "I like this new Dahlia."

She stood in an effort to hide her smile and contemplated the top of his head.

"You seem to be feeling better," she said. "We should move on—I'd like to put a little more distance between us and the fighting."

"Too late, Miss Walker."

Chapter Forty-five
Crossing Swords

✳

Dahlia whirled. Pebbles splashed from under her feet. Farren ignored the tiny impacts and stared past her. His heart sank into his stomach.

Sebastian Macall blocked their sole escape route, slumped against the doorway with one hand clutching his sword. The other wrapped around his midsection. Blood oozed between his fingers, stained his uniform, drooled from the corner of his mouth. Sweat glued the hair to his scalp.

Farren stood slowly and laid a hand on Dahlia's shoulder, ready to fling her back if need be. No matter what sort of shape Macall's body was in, the deadliness of his sword remained the same.

"Where's the promethium?" Macall asked.

"I don't know," said Dahlia. "I used a piece my father left me. There isn't any more."

"That's a lie!"

Macall tore himself away from the wall and lifted the sword so its point wavered a centimeter in front of Dahlia's nose. Farren's eyes narrowed.

"Wait a minute." He yanked her back. "We'll show you where it's at if you let us go. Put down the sword."

Say anything. Anything to get him away from her.

"But Farren——" Dahlia began.

"I'm sorry, but helping your dead mother isn't worth getting us killed."

"He's mad! He'll kill us whether we show him or not!"

Farren ignored her. He wished she would turn toward him so he could wink.

"I'm glad you see reason," said Macall. He lowered the sword, sliding it aside so they could pass through the doorway. The expression on his face was waxen, drawn; speaking seemed to require a great effort.

Farren gave Dahlia a tiny shove from behind to urge her out the door. She shot him a glare, but allowed herself to be propelled out into the new sunshine. He followed at a slower pace, waiting for her to put enough space between them.

Farren attacked. The moment he touched the doorjamb he twisted sideways and launched his booted foot straight into Macall's jaw. The General staggered back.

The airman crouched into a fighting stance. His follow-up punch was halfway to Macall when the breath caught in his bruised throat. He choked. The power drained from his swing.

"Farren, catch!" Dahlia yanked a sword from her belt and practically threw it to him. He'd seen her grab it from a dead soldier in the park. The airman snagged it with a grin.

"Perfect."

The General caught himself with the point of his sword, planting it in the ground like an old man's walking stick. The hand grasping his abdomen fluttered up and rubbed the dirt-smeared cheek where Farren's boot had struck. His fingers painted a streak of blood. He swayed, blinking in confusion. Farren prayed for him to fall, to go down, to give up…Then Macall spoke,

"I never intended to let you live anyway, Reed."

One moment the sword was trailing forgotten by his side. The next it was whistling through the air on a collision course with Farren's chest. *Shit!*

Farren fell backwards in an undignified sort of dodge. The blade claimed a few strands of his hair.

Macall struck a second time, a third time, and Farren caught both blows with his blade. He smiled roguishly. Dahlia retreated just out of Macall's reach; far enough where Farren wouldn't have to worry about her.

"Can you beat him?" she asked.

Farren lashed out. Macall's blade blocked him with ease.

"Of course," he lied.

Macall advanced, Farren retreated. They traded blows back and forth without a hit. Feet danced among loose cobblestone—to twist an ankle here would mean death.

Farren had undergone standard military training with a sword, but never anything more intensive. What was the point? Only an idiot would use a medieval weapon over a gun. He parried another blow. If the General hadn't been wounded already, it would have been impossible for Farren to last more than a few seconds.

The swords darted between them. Parry, attack, advance, retreat. The stain on Macall's uniform was growing. Farren only needed to hold out a little longer...

But the General seemed aware of his own increasing handicap. His attacks only became more ferocious. Farren leapt backward to avoid a blow. A sting on his shoulder as the sword found its mark.

Not fast enough.

Blades whirled, glinting in the morning sun. They clashed. Instead of retreating, Macall stepped forward into the swords. A massive push threw Farren off-balance. His weight suddenly shifted to his heels. Macall rushed and

Farren blocked, but the General swatted his sword away.

He was open, defenseless.

Dammit!

The General drew back for a massive strike. Farren knew he could never have his blade up in time to block...

Then Dahlia planted her foot in Macall's side. The General stumbled, grimaced, whipped his free hand to latch onto Dahlia's ankle. He yanked her toward him and threw her to the ground. The sword came up, murderous in its intent.

"Dahlia!"

Farren attacked madly; anything to turn Macall's attention away from her. It worked too well. Another sting and the General drew a line of blood down his arm. The blades fluttered between them again, but this time Farren was the one advancing. Dahlia's boot had done its job.

Macall's sword leapt at Farren's chest and he dodged. Then he straightened, slapping the General's receding weapon into the ground on the downstroke. His fist shot into Macall's stomach. Blood splattered and he ground his knuckles into the bullet wound.

All's fair in war.

The General gasped, doubling over to clutch his midsection. Farren didn't give him time to recover. He brought his knee up into Macall's face at the same point he had kicked him earlier. The General's head snapped back. His sword smacked the ground, followed by his knees, then the palms of his hands.

Farren found himself standing, suddenly victorious, above the shaking form of his enemy. For a moment he froze in surprise. Devil's blood—he'd won! Explosions from the airship battle echoed in his ears, heralding his victory.

Then the pain returned. The wounds on his arm and

shoulder burned; his neck ached where the noose had squeezed. Breath burned in his throat and refused to fill his lungs. But he'd won.

"Are you all right?" asked Dahlia, touching his intact arm with light fingers.

"I'll live. What do ya want done with him?"

Dahlia stared down at the back of Macall's head. Farren remembered how she'd protected the bounty hunter at the inn in Delmar, how she'd shielded his watch when Farren wanted to destroy it.

She's too nice for her own good.

"Did I tell you what Tiberius said to me after he killed Harold Grimes?" Dahlia asked. Farren shook his head. "I asked him if revenge on Grimes made him feel better. He assured me it didn't."

Her voice hitched but her eyes remained dry, brimming with conviction. Sebastian Macall remained unmoving on all fours. It was so strange, so unnatural, to see the General on the ground. Dahlia continued,

"So when I say we're going to kill this man, know that we're not doing it for me. We're doing it because we have to. He's mad. It's too dangerous to let him live."

Farren smiled.

"I don't know if it's a good thing, sweetheart, but you've learned." He snuck a quick kiss onto the top of her black hair, warm in the sun.

Then he turned to the fallen General, and his voice was sharp, "You heard her. Give up your watch and we'll make it quick."

Macall groaned and eased back onto his knees. His face was drawn in pain, eyes sunken, lips pressed into a line.

"If you think…I'm going to sit here and let you—"

Farren didn't wait for him to finish. His rusty sword sliced through the General's hand and pinned it, palm-down, to the ground. He bent down and twisted the blade. His face was only inches away as Macall struggled to breathe through agonizing pain. Farren had to give the man credit: a lesser person would have been howling.

"I'm not playing," he growled, low and threatening. "If you don't give me your watch nicely in ten seconds I'm going to start cutting off limbs. And then take it anyway. You pick."

Macall spat in his face. It was a pitiful half-blood, half-saliva mess, but the point was made.

"We gotta do things the hard way," Farren sighed. He wiped the defiled cheek on his sleeve with calculated nonchalance. "Which would you rather lose first? An arm or a l—"

A piercing shriek of metal on metal. All their heads jerked to the battle in the sky a few hundred yards away. Farren's heart sank.

The *Wayfarer Elizabeth* listed to one side, leaking smoke and debris. A second metallic squeal ended in an explosion. Flames burst from the vicinity of the engine room and licked at the hull, the hydrogen tanks.

Keet and Tiberius...

He started to stand for a better look.

Macall roared. Farren saw the handful of dust fly from the General's fingers as if in slow motion. He had no time to react.

The grit tore at Farren's eyes in a flare of pain. Sharp bits of sand and rock gnawed at him, blinded him. *Shit!*

He raced to wipe it away with both hands. There was a flurry of movement in front of him, a grunt of pain. An instant too late he realized he'd let go of the sword. But when he groped for it, eyes squeezed shut, the hilt was no longer where it had been.

"I wouldn't move if I were you, Reed."

Something pricked his throat. Sebastian Macall held a sword to his neck, and Farren couldn't even open his eyes to see it.

Chapter Forty-six
The Affairs of God

✳

Sebastian made his move the moment Reed turned his attention to the sky. His good hand shot out lightning-quick, curled around a patch of dirt, and flung it into the airman's eyes. Then he grasped the hilt of the sword pinning his other arm to the ground.

There was no time to prepare. He ripped the blade out, snatched up his own fallen weapon, and pushed himself to his feet with the points of both swords. Sebastian's vision swam. The agony in his mangled gut tripled. Knives were boring through his midsection.

Dahlia Walker lunged forward. Sebastian's body brought a blade up to defend almost before he registered her movement. She stopped short of the outstretched point.

Almost simultaneously, Reed was scrabbling at the air where the rusted hilt had been. Sebastian flicked the tip of the second sword against his throat.

"I wouldn't move if I were you, Reed."

Blackness gathered at the edges of his consciousness, threatening to swallow him. He swayed.

Don't you dare! Go down now and they'll kill you.

I know! I know!

Just get the promethium.

Once he resurrected Sita she could nurse him back to

health. He had decades of time left. He would survive as long as he protected his watch. As long as these two criminals didn't succeed in murdering him.

Words forced themselves from his mouth.

"Miss Walker, the promethium." Blood trickled from Sebastian's lips, staining his uniform collar scarlet.

She hesitated briefly and Sebastian hoped he wouldn't have to deliver another ultimatum. *Give me the promethium or your airman dies...*it was all becoming so repetitive. And he was so tired.

Then Walker dug into the pocket of the jacket draped over her shoulders. She took hold of something, offering it to him.

"Let us go," she said, and opened her hand.

His heartbeat accelerated.

She held a bit of greenish-yellow crystal, perhaps the size of his smallest fingernail. A few flecks of drab rock still clung to it where it must have grown from the cave wall. All in all, it didn't look particularly impressive. Could it actually be...

"Promethium," said Walker.

Sebastian almost reached out to accept it. His mind buzzed with triumph, with possibility, with the knowledge that finally—*finally!*—the hunt was over. Only the battle instincts stopped him.

"Set it down," he said, "and back away."

Walker obeyed. She seemed to move at a snail's pace. Then she retreated and the promethium was his.

He had no time to look at it, no time to revel in the moment of victory. Sebastian slipped the crystal into his palm and held it against the hilt he still gripped. It felt strangely warm—or was that his imagination?

The swords wavered as he held them in weakening fists. Walker and Reed didn't move. They merely watched him, waiting for the moment when his strength would give out. He couldn't hold out much longer.

"Get out of here," he said. "Both of you. Our business is done."

Reed scrubbed the dust from his eyes enough to throw Walker a glance Sebastian couldn't interpret. Neither of them moved.

"Let him," said Reed. "We've done all we can." He turned back to Sebastian. "We're going now."

Sebastian waited while the two of them slowly moved off down the cobblestones, inching their way farther into the ruins. They halted fifty feet or so away. Walker helped Reed sit on the remains of a low stone wall and they directed their attention back to Sebastian.

Why wouldn't they leave? He had allowed them to live and they couldn't do him this one simple courtesy. He was a performer, standing forlorn before an eager audience while he struggled to remember his line.

"Don't concern yourself with them," he said aloud.

"They're not important."

"Not when you're so close to Sita…"

The swords clattered to the ground. His legs folded and he slumped to his knees like a marionette with its strings cut. God, he hurt. Pain blossomed in his stomach, threatening to overwhelm him. Drying blood pinched his skin.

"Just…a little longer…"

Somehow he managed to wrestle Walker's copper device from his pocket. One hand reached up and, with a quick motion, snapped the chain around his neck. A pair of watches fell into his palm. *Sebastian Macall* was etched onto one. On the other: *Sita Senguptar.*

He laid them on the ground, taking care not to scratch Sita's. The device and promethium went beside them. After decades of searching he finally had all three. It had been an immense journey, through years of loneliness and longing, and the thought of achieving what he'd chased for so long was almost too much. His impossible dream was going to be realized.

Slowly, painstakingly, Sebastian began to secure his and Sita's watches to the device. Blood made his fingers slippery.

I'm going to see her again.

Her brilliant smile, her tinkling-bell laugh...those sparkling green eyes... Days spent laughing in a café over endless cups of tea. Nights they had talked instead of sleeping, lying next to one another while the moon traced its indomitable path overhead. The moment when he had held out a diamond ring to her and tears had brimmed in her eyes. He knew she would have said yes if only they'd had more time...

Now they had all the time they could ever want. Promethium, time transfer—they could live forever if they so desired. They would be two immortals standing hand-in-hand among the vast world.

The watches had been prepared, the bit of promethium secured in place. Sebastian's breathing echoed in his ears. He teetered there, on the cusp of his dream, and all that was left was the thing itself.

Half his time in exchange for living the rest of his life with the woman he loved. It was a small price.

"Take it," Sebastian whispered.

Trembling fingers twisted the dial.

A rushing noise like the sound of heavy rain on stone, or a breeze stirring leaves. Was it real? Sebastian had no way of knowing. He squeezed his eyes closed for a moment as the bullet in his stomach gave a particularly painful stab.

When he opened them, Sita was there.

The world stood still. Sound, pain, breathing, movement…everything faded but her. She stood before him, barefoot in her favorite forest-green dress. Black hair shone in the sun. Eyes smiled down at him. Her skin was beautiful, the color of coffee with milk.

Sebastian stared up at her and found he couldn't speak. What would he say? It was all so incredible, so unbelievable, that he feared breaking the perfect silence between them. His heart could have burst from happiness. He reached out to touch her, hardly able to believe it was true.

His hand passed through her fingers.

What?

"Sebastian," she said, and the sound of her voice was a drug in his veins, "what have you done?"

His head spun. Confusion darkened his thoughts even as he tried to hold onto the dissolving joy of seeing her. But it was like trying to cup water in his hands.

"What…?" he said.

"What have you done?" Sita cried. She dropped to her knees next to him and reached for the watches he held. But she couldn't touch them.

"I brought you back," Sebastian said, numb.

"I shouldn't be here."

"Why not?" he asked. "Why can't I touch you…?"

He extended a hand and it drifted through her cheek. A tear leaked from her eye and passed through it. It was all going wrong…he didn't understand…

"You can't bring back the dead," she said softly. She pointed to his watch. "I have to go back. And now look what's happened."

His watch, which should have had years of time remaining even after giving half to her, had sunk to two years. And counting.

Sebastian's head felt fuzzy, his thoughts muddled. How had this happened? It had all failed.

"Take your watch off it!" Sita wept. She made another unsuccessful grab for it, but he couldn't feel the slightest sensation when her skin brushed his.

Sebastian took hold of the set screws clamping the watch in place. *Fourteen months, nine months...* Even if he could remove it quickly, he would have only a handful of time left. And Sita...he couldn't be with Sita... He lowered the device.

"No."

The hollowness in his own voice would have surprised him, if he had cared enough to be surprised. There was no point to any of it.

Three weeks.

"Sebastian!" she shouted.

He fixed his gaze on those beautiful green eyes. The same eyes that had captivated him and stolen his heart all those years ago. It had been worth it all simply to see her again.

One day.

Sunlight shone in her hair.

One second.

Sebastian sighed, smiled, and was gone.

Chapter Forty-seven
"It's not much…"

✳

Sita turned when they approached; she still knelt by Sebastian's body. Dahlia could feel her heart pounding against her ribcage. It was like looking into a mirror. The shape of her face, the green eyes…even the way she tugged at her hair.

"Who are you?" Sita asked.

It was hardly noticeable, but when she moved Dahlia could see through her to weeds poking through the rubble.

"It's me," she said, kneeling. "Dahlia Walker. Your daughter."

The words felt impossible as she said them. Seconds sped by, unnoticed, as the delicate moment stretched until it filled every corner of her world.

"Dahlia," Sita breathed.

Her mother reached for her, one trembling hand brushing the edge of her cheek. Dahlia closed her eyes and imagined she could feel it, imagined that they were sitting in the house in Sainsbury together with her papa. A family. Whole and complete, until her eyelids fluttered open again.

"Where's Ansel?" asked Sita.

Dahlia shook her head. Hot tears gathered at the corners of her eyes, but she couldn't tell who they were for. Her father, her mother, herself?

"He's dead," she said, and stopped herself before she could tell Sita that it had been Sebastian's fault.

It's better she doesn't know.

Sita's hands clenched in the fabric of her ethereal dress, as if she could wipe her grief away into the cloth.

"I'm sorry," said Dahlia. And she was. Sorry for everything that had happened, all the things they could have had and never would.

"No," Sita shook her head. "This is my fault. Ansel and I...we were so busy researching time, we never stopped to think if we *should.* I'm sorry I wasn't there for him. Or you."

The bright green of her eyes caught on Dahlia's again, and this time her lips lifted. The thin lines at the corners of her mouth were deeper than Dahlia's, but they traced the same paths.

"I'm so proud of you," said Sita. "You've become such a fine young woman."

Her arms wrapped around Dahlia, and even though she knew it was impossible, she pretended she could feel their warmth.

It's all worth it, she thought. *Everything I've been through is worth it for this.*

Sita pulled away after what seemed only an instant, but it was an instant that Dahlia knew would be burned into her memory as long as she lived. Questions clamored in her throat, about her mother's life, and Ansel's, and everything in between.

"I've always wondered about you," said Dahlia. "Papa told me, in a way, but still...there are so many things I want to ask."

"One question," said Sita. "There's not much time—I shouldn't be here."

Dahlia could have asked why, but that wasn't worth

the handful of moments they had.

"How could you fall in love with Sebastian?" she asked.

If she'd never fallen in love with him, he would never have been so obsessed with resurrecting her. He would never have killed Papa.

Sita tugged at her hair as the question waited between them, glancing at Sebastian's body and quickly away. Finally, she said:

"Love…is fickle. Sometimes you fall for the wrong person. That's who Sebastian was, and I took too long to realize it." She scanned Dahlia's eyes as if searching for understanding. "Your father was the right person."

Sita's gaze caught on Farren, who stood a respectful distance behind Dahlia. He was watching the *Wayfarer Elizabeth* still battling in the sky above.

"Who is that?"

Dahlia waved him forward, grinning.

"The right person."

Sita's face brightened. Farren crouched beside them and extended a hand in greeting.

"Farren Reed."

He realized his mistake instantly as Sita's fingers passed through his, and Dahlia giggled at the embarrassment coloring his cheeks.

"Sorry," he said. "I forgot. I mean, I didn't think—"

Sita joined Dahlia in laughter. Warmth filled Dahlia's chest. It was wonderful, so giddy and strange and beautiful, to be sitting there laughing with *her mother.*

But the happiness only lasted a few seconds. A thundering explosion snapped their three heads toward the sky.

Flames engulfed the *Wayfarer Elizabeth*. It swerved helplessly, struggling for control of a rudder that had been blown off. Flakes of ash floated down like snow.

"Your friends?" asked Sita. Dahlia nodded, mute.

Then the ship seemed to give up. With a final whine of the engines, it barreled forward into the side of the *Imperial Might*. An explosion scorched the air. Dahlia felt the heat on her face and closed her eyes against it.

Keet and Tiberius.

Together, the two airships plummeted to earth. There was a great screeching and crackling as they hit. A pile of flame.

"Do you think…?" she said.

"No," Farren replied. "There's no way they could have survived."

They fell silent, listening to the burning. All the happiness had evaporated. Waves of guilt washed over Dahlia: it was her fault the two bounty hunters had been there at all.

"I have to go back," Sita said quietly. She looked at Dahlia, and sadness draped itself over her face.

"Of course," said Dahlia. *I never expected her to stay.*

"I don't belong here," her mother continued. "What Sebastian did was wrong—Ansel and I learned long ago that humans are forbidden from meddling in life and death the way we did." Dahlia remembered the skeleton of the boy. "There are rules we cannot violate. There are things we cannot do."

Metal plates peeled off the *Imperial Might's* hull and collapsed, buffeting up clouds of dust.

"Dahlia, can you do it for me?" Sita asked. She pointed to the watches.

They felt heavy when Dahlia picked them up and unscrewed her mother's watch. Dread had such weight to it.

"Let me do it," said Farren from next to her, "You've been through enough."

Dahlia started to hand the watch to him, then stopped. This was her responsibility.

"No," she said.

"I'm sorry, sweetie," said Sita. Dahlia's heart lurched at the name: her papa's name for her. It stirred memories still raw in her mind.

The sitting room, the blood, the bits of Ansel's shattered watch strewn on the carpet like dew. Then Farren took her hand, and the memory faded in an instant.

"We'll see each other again," said Sita.

Dahlia smiled. "I know."

She slammed the watch against a rock as hard as she could and it splintered into a thousand pieces.

Chapter Forty-eight
"...but it's enough."

✳

"Owww!" Dahlia whined as Farren coaxed another shard of glass from her hand. "Why didn't you tell me this would happen? You've smashed watches before."

"I thought you could figure it out," grinned the airman. "Common sense. Guess you don't have any."

Dahlia would have play-hit him, if her skin hadn't been full of watch bits. She settled for sticking out her tongue in a most-unladylike fashion. It was strange, a few weeks ago she would have balked at the thought.

"Very funny, sweetheart."

He jerked out another splinter.

"Ouch!"

They sat cross-legged in the grass of the abandoned park in Vatana. The air was thick with the scent of smoke from the smoldering wrecks of the two ships. Skeletal hulls lay, sagging, like the carcasses of strange beasts.

The ground was strewn with charred bodies closer to the road. It was impossible to identify them all—most were burned beyond recognition—and they could only assume one had been David Harper.

But where they sat the grass felt clean and soft on Dahlia's skin. The sun still shone overhead. Persevering birds chirped as they hopped from one tree branch to another.

"It's not too bad, really," she said, "all things considered." The strain in her voice was obvious: they had lost three friends that day.

"No, it's not," agreed Farren.

"Well, I'm glad you two are having a good time."

They whirled.

"Keet! Tiberius! You're alive!"

The massive cyborg stood a little ways off, his wife perched on his back. Scratches and dents littered his armor. One yellow eye had gone dark, and holes were punched through the metal plates in a few places. Keet was black with soot. Cuts smeared blood onto her skin.

Dahlia and Farren gaped as Tiberius set Keet down beside them.

"I can't believe it!" said Farren, slapping the two of them on the back. The cyborg didn't even flinch. "Devil's blood—we thought you were dead!"

"Not quite," said Keet. "We managed to escape in a flier before the ship went down. Crashed the damn flier too."

She stared morosely at the smoking hulk of the *Wayfarer Elizabeth*.

"What happened to you?" she asked.

Dahlia explained while Farren continued pulling glass out of her skin ("You'll need stitches," insisted Tiberius.). When she reached the part about Sebastian's death, Keet clapped her hands.

"This is great! Don't you know what he was worth?"

"Worth?" Dahia tilted her head.

"His bounty's three-million gilvers. We're rich!"

When Dahlia still looked confused, Keet stopped grinning long enough to explain:

"He killed Bespalov before he ran off with you two.

The Anglian government put the bounty on him." She shrugged. "We followed you here. Three million's more than enough to build us a new ship!"

"We'll still need to return him to Port Argun," said Dahlia, "to collect it."

"Yeah," Keet agreed. "Should be a fun trip—you know, this is my first time in the Southern Lands. And part of that bounty belongs to you two, by the way. We wouldn't have found Macall without you."

* * *

They stayed in Vatana for a few days to recuperate and salvage what they could from the airships. Farren wanted to bury the Anglian bodies, but the sheer number made it an impossible feat.

The days were long, relaxing, and warm. Dahlia felt free for the first time. There was no revenge to be sought, no enemies to run from, no decreasing watch hanging over Farren's head... It was paradise. They even talked about the future, now that they had one.

"I'd like to get my own airship, I think," admitted Farren one day while he and Dahlia foraged in the tropical forest beyond the city. Their arms were full of bright fruit. "Travel some, do a bit of work on and off."

He looked at her doubtfully, stumbling over his words.

"I can't sail it alone. I'll need at least one other person, and I was wondering if... I mean, I don't know if you have any plans..."

Dahlia stopped him. Her eyes sparkled.

"Yes."

* * *

When it came time to set off, Dahlia was almost disappointed. She sat with her back against a tree and a rucksack next to her, and breathed in the pure wild air. Farren stood beside her. Who knew what was ahead of them? The world was starting anew, and all she needed to do was take the first step into it.

"Come on then," Keet called from the edge of the city. "We've got a long way to go." Tiberius was ahead of her, forging a path through the thick tropical forest.

"Ready?" Farren extended a hand.

Dahlia smiled, and took it.

"Let's go."

Acknowledgements

✳

More than two years have passed since I first put pen to paper (or, in this case, fingers to keyboard) and wrote the opening scene of *27 Days to Midnight*. I owe its completion to more people than I have room to thank.

Anna McCormally and Rachel Miller, for giving this book a home and for helping shape it into the best story it could be.

Mr. Risko, for teaching me to love stories.

Mike Vasich, for teaching me how to write them.

Jennifer Chang, for never forgetting to ask about the book, for your boundless enthusiasm, and for listening to me babble on about the stories in my head.

Dad, for giving me a home to write in and pages of indispensable feedback.

Mom, for your endless support and for cheering aloud when you read the end.

Matt, for being one of my first readers and the best big little brother a sister could wish for.

Steven, for the weaponry advice and your skill at naming everything from rifles to minerals.

Danny, for listening to my incessant explanations. You should read more.

Samantha Bishop, for your help with everything from my query letter to my synopsis.

Susanna Taylor, for being my oldest friend and beta reader.

Jessica Mudge, for snatching an early copy of this book away from Matt and telling me how much you loved it.

The Plymouth Coffee Bean Café and every one of its fantastic staff members, for operating the best writing nook I've found. A large portion of the work on this book was fueled by your coffee and cookies.

National Novel Writing Month and all its 2013 participants, for helping me bring *27 Days to Midnight* into the world.

Shadow and Mr. Jimbers, for being snuggly kitties on cold winter evenings.

Binders. Darn you anyway.

About the Author

Kristine Kruppa is a mechanical engineer, writer, and world traveler. Her days are spent designing cool new car parts, but her evenings are filled with writing and cats. She has traveled solo to seventeen countries on five continents. Her other hobbies include hunting for the perfect cup of coffee, exploring used book stores, and accidentally climbing mountains.

About Giant Squid Books

Giant Squid Books is a collaborative publishing community, founded by readers to support writers. We publish and distribute high-quality young adult fiction in all genres. Follow along @GiantSquidBooks or visit www.giantsquidbooks.com to learn more.

If you enjoyed **27 Days to Midnight**, *check out these other GSB titles:*

The Burned Bridges Protocol *by Abigail Borders*
How to Be Manly *by Maureen O'Leary Wanket*
The Six Days *by Anna Carolyn McCormally*